S0-ASK-446

DA
978.2
.M3
1997

Marshall, Peter H., 1946-
Celtic gold

FASKEN LEARNING RESOURCE CENTER
9000067230

67230

Celtic Gold

By the same author

William Godwin
Journey Through Tanzania
Into Cuba
Cuba Libre: Breaking the Chains?
William Blake
Journey Through Maldives
Demanding the Impossible: A History of Anarchism
Nature's Web: Rethinking our Place on Earth
Around Africa: From the Pillars of Hercules to the Strait of Gibraltar

67230

Celtic Gold

By the same author

William Godwin
Journey Through Tanzania
Into Cuba
Cuba Libre: Breaking the Chains?
William Blake
Journey Through Maldives
Demanding the Impossible: A History of Anarchism
Nature's Web: Rethinking our Place on Earth
Around Africa: From the Pillars of Hercules to the Strait of Gibraltar

67230

PETER MARSHALL

Celtic Gold
A Voyage Around Ireland

SINCLAIR-STEVENSON

First published in Great Britain in 1997
by Sinclair-Stevenson
an imprint of Reed International Books Ltd
Michelin House, 81 Fulham Road, London SW3 6RB
and Auckland, Melbourne, Singapore and Toronto

Copyright © 1997 by Peter Marshall

The right of Peter Marshall to be identified as author
of this work has been asserted by him in accordance
with the Copyright, Designs and Patents Act 1988.

A CIP catalogue record for this book
is available at the British Library
ISBN 1 85619 616 X

Typeset in 11 on 14.5 point Janson
by Falcon Oast Graphic Art
Printed and bound in Great Britain
by Mackays of Chatham PLC

For Emily and Dylan

When the wind blows and the tide runs
Down to the sea I go,
For the sea's spray and the sea's drift
Are music for me.

When the wind blows and the tide runs
Down to the sea I go,
For the shell's curve and the crab's claw
Are magic for me.

When the wind blows and the tide runs
Down to the sea I go,
For the petrel's wings and the fulmar's flight
Are joy for me.

When the wind blows and the tide runs
Down to the sea I go,
For the sail's trim and the seal's eye
Are heart and soul for me.

An té mbionn long aige, geibheann sé cóir nair éigin

He who has a boat invariably gets a breeze

Contents

List of Illustrations ix
Acknowledgements xi
Map xiv

1 Casting Off 1
2 Finding a Boat 11
3 Irish Waters 24
4 Servants of War and Love 35
5 Wind and Water 47
6 By Hook or By Crook 62
7 Old Blarney 75
8 Poetry and Prose 88
9 The Gulf Stream Coast 102
10 Islands and Bays 120
11 The Lonely Rock 135
12 Monks and Dolphins 148
13 Dingle Days 160
14 On the Edge of the World 175
15 Out West 193
16 The Mighty Shannon 204
17 Snakes in the Sea 217
18 Forts in the Mist 232
19 Islands in the Sun 247
20 The Ears of Achill 262
21 Up the Creek 278
22 The Relaunch 289
23 To Derry and Back 306
24 Rushing to Port 322
25 The North Channel 335
26 Belfast Blues 345
27 Into the Loughs 362
28 Dublin Bound 374
29 Ancient Mysteries 388
30 Over the Irish Sea 400

List of Illustrations

1 Seagull on Seagull in Baltimore Harbour
2 The ferry-boy on the say to Sherkin Island
3 Cape Clear Island, the most southerly of Ireland
4 A seal basking off Garnish Island, Glengarriff, Bantry Bay
5 The Italianate garden on Garnish Island
6 An evening sail off the Dingle Peninsula
7 Fungi, the dolphin of Dingle
8 Dunquin Harbour, the most westerly harbour in Europe
9 Fishing boat in the sound between Inishvickillane and Inishabro, the Blaskets
10 *Celtic Gold* and Charles Haughey's *Celtic Mist* off Inishvickillane
11 The author in the ruined oratory on the summitt of Mount Brandon
12 Fishing vessel at anchor off Inishboffin Island
13 Cromwell's fort on Inishboffin
14 Early morning off the Stags of Broadhaven
15 Giant's Causeway, Co. Antrim
16 A Red Admiral checks the chart off the Mountains of Mourne

Acknowledgements

First and foremost, I wish to thank my children Emily and Dylan for sharing their dad's love of the sea and for being such wonderful companions. I am, as always, deeply grateful for the warm support of my brother Michael, who offered some stern warnings, and of my mother, Vera, who followed my course throughout the voyage. My nieces, Julie and Sylvie, and their mother, Colette Dubois, all helped me along. Jenny Zobel gave me great encouragement. I much appreciated the keen interest of Emily Gwynne-Jones who read the manuscript and offered many useful suggestions. Many thanks also to Liz Ashton who made very thoughtful comments. Gillian Doyle kindly read some chapters. Without the generous help of Carol O'Brien, I may not have been able to set sail.

I would like to thank Robin Aherne, Dorothy Berry, Graham and Sheila Carroll, David Eastwood, Mary Fröhlich, Graham and Santha Hancock, Richard Haslam, Bob Hawksworth, Eddie Hawksworth, Awel Irene, Robin Kyffin, Jonathan Lumby, Livia Morrison-Lyons, Sally Millard, John and Maureen Perkins, Dafydd Philips, John Pilcher, T. E. Pritchard, John and Sarah Schlapobersky, Anna Smith, Steve Watson, Glyn Williams, and members of the Porthmadog and Trawsfynydd Sailing Club who all helped launch me in their different ways.

Without the companionship of Paul Green, Dicker Feesey, Jeremy and Jonathan Gane, Emily Gwynne-Jones, David Lea, Nicci Perkins, Jenny Zobel and my children, Emily and Dylan, the voyage would not have been so enjoyable or memorable. Many thanks, m' old shipmates.

I am indebted to Charles Harris, John Jackson and Alan Williams of Plas Menai, the National Watersports Centre in Wales, for tutoring me in the RYC Yachtmaster's Certificate, and to John Hart of Barry Island Sailing Centre for his Coastal Skipper course. Ampair generously offered me a wind generator. Ocean Safety lent me some flares and life jackets. Cathal McCosker kindly made his charts available. Paul Machell generously offered me the use of his yacht, but I was fortunate enough to find another one with a wonderful name.

During my voyage around Ireland, I met countless people who gave me a marvellous welcome and confirmed my view of the fundamental goodness of humanity. I would like to thank in particular Peter Barry; David and Mary Beechinor; Larry Butler; Seamus Byrne; Wallace Clark; Mick and Betty Cloherty; Kevin, Wendy and Natasha Donaghy; Brian Farrell; Dermot Francis; Denis Glass; John and Pat Hatchett; Charles and Conor Haughey; Naomi James; Rodney and Freya Lomax; Michael and Susan Laughnane; Eddie and Anne McCarthy; Richard Mac Cullagh; Steve Mc Menamin; Tim Magennis; Stan and Betty Miller; Con Minihane; John Moulden; Paddy Mullen; W. H. Nixon; Terri O'Neill; Anne O' Toole; Tim Severin and Don Street.

Finally, I would like to thank Christopher Sinclair-Stevenson for taking on the book and my editors Penelope Hoare and Eugenie Boyd for their excellent advice. Alison Quinn did a superb job editing the radio series. My agent Bill Hamilton has, as usual, been a great help. Fair winds to ye all!

Peter Marshall, Borth-y-Gest,
12 March 1997

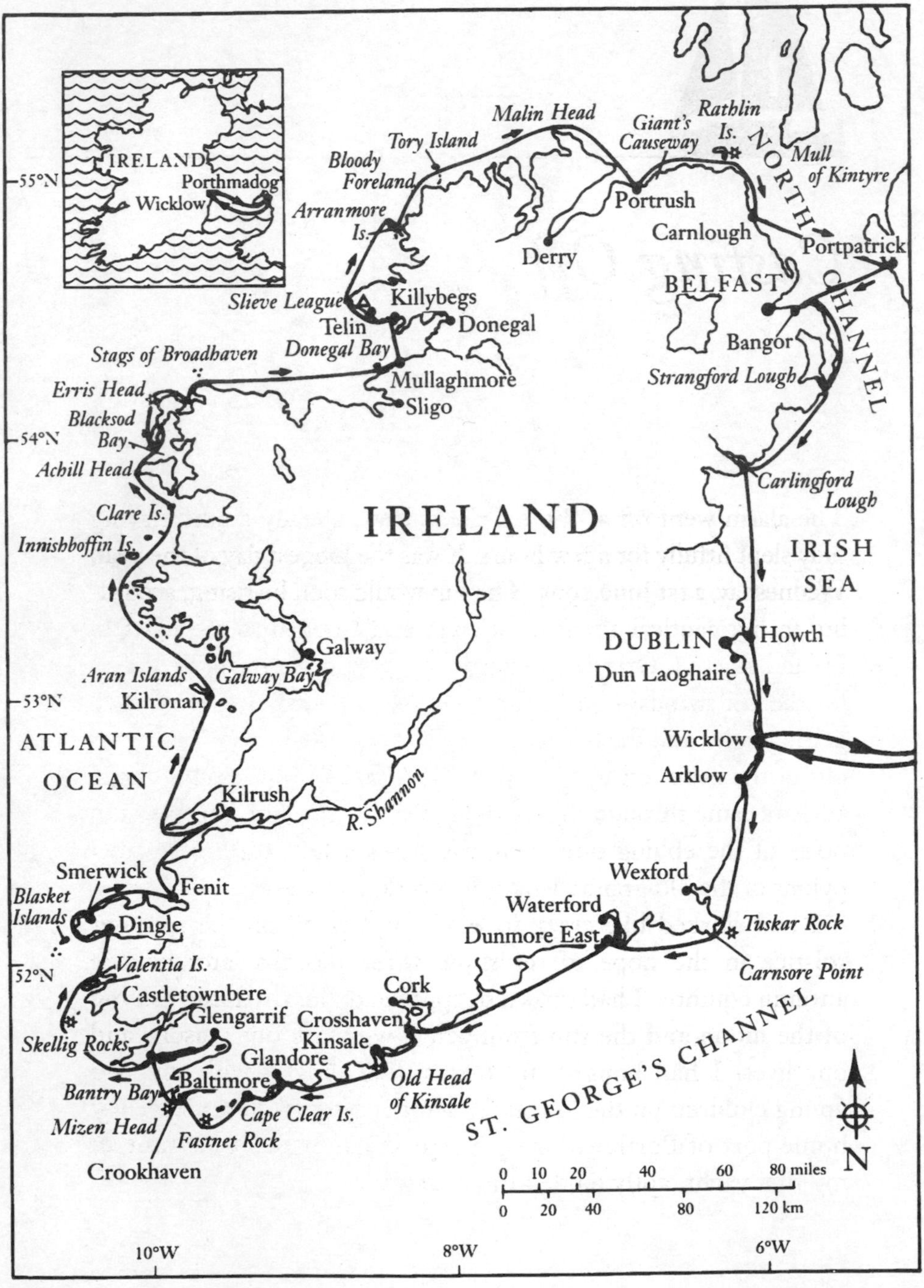
IRELAND
Porthmadog
Wicklow
55°N
54°N
53°N
52°N
10°W
8°W
6°W
IRELAND
Malin Head
Tory Island
Bloody Foreland
Arranmore Is.
Giant's Causeway
Rathlin Is.
Mull of Kintyre
NORTH CHANNEL
Portrush
Carnlough
Portpatrick
Derry
BELFAST
Bangor
Strangford Lough
Carlingford Lough
Slieve League
Killybegs
Telin
Donegal
Donegal Bay
Mullaghmore
Sligo
Stags of Broadhaven
Erris Head
Blacksod Bay
Achill Head
Clare Is.
Innishboffin Is.
IRISH SEA
DUBLIN
Howth
Dun Laoghaire
Galway
Aran Islands
Galway Bay
Kilronan
ATLANTIC OCEAN
Wicklow
Arklow
Kilrush
R. Shannon
Smerwick
Fenit
Blasket Islands
Dingle
Wexford
Waterford
Dunmore East
Tuskar Rock
Carnsore Point
Valentia Is.
Castletownbere
Glengarrif
Cork
Crosshaven
Kinsale
Skellig Rocks
Glandore
Old Head of Kinsale
Bantry Bay
Baltimore
Cape Clear Is.
Mizen Head
Fastnet Rock
Crookhaven
ST. GEORGE'S CHANNEL
0 10 20 40 60 80 miles
0 20 40 80 120 km
N

1

Casting Off

The alarm went off at three o'clock. I was already awake, having only slept fitfully for a few hours. It was the longest day of the year, Wednesday, 21st June 1995. The sun would soon be rising, according to my nautical almanac, at 0443 and I hoped to see it set in Ireland at 2144. Drizzle had been sweeping in across the Irish Sea for the last two days but it had cleared before dusk. It was already getting light, and the half moon was low in the sky. As I clambered out of the cabin on to the dew-soaked deck, the mournful cry of curlews came through the swirling mist, mixing with the gurgling noise of the ebbing tide along the sea-wracked, rotting wooden pylons of the old granite wharf. It was time to leave.

I had worked like crazy to leave for Ireland on the summer solstice in the hope of returning three months later on the autumn equinox. I had grown to appreciate the rhythmic passing of the moon and the sun from which we mark our seasons and our lives. I had bought my first sailing dinghy with my two young children on the longest day and it seemed apt to leave my home port of Porthmadog in North Wales at the same time in my first yacht, aptly named *Celtic Gold*.

I had only just made it. The stores weren't properly stowed away, the engine remained a mysterious hole (although light was beginning to be cast at its edges), and the wind generator was on the floor of the cabin.

I went through my check list: hatches and portholes closed, seacocks to the heads off, gas off, compass in its place on the port side of the cockpit. I made sure I had wet weather gear ready and had some food and drink for the day. I placed a 'grab bag' containing flares, water and the EPIRB emergency signal on the quarter berth under the VHF radio in case I had to abandon ship for the life raft. Strapping on new life jacket and harness, I felt a little apprehensive. This was the first time that I had ever skippered a yacht and I was beginning a new phase in my life.

I swallowed a seasickness pill. I carefully fixed a silver chain securing a medallion of St Christopher given to me by my son Dylan, and an ankh, the Egyptian symbol of life, from my daughter Emily. I was relying on ancient talismans as well as modern technology to see me through.

I turned on both batteries and switched on the VHF radio and Decca navigation system. As I turned the key in the ignition, the noise of the turning engine smothered the dawn chorus of sea birds and the gurgle of the ebbing tide. After a few anxious moments of straining, the engine burst into fire. The yacht shuddered, like a great creature shaking off sleep, and before long the old diesel engine settled down into a steady, reassuring rhythm.

As I cast off the moorings, the first red rays of the sun shot out behind the Moelwyn peaks and lit up the mountain of Cnicht above the Croesor valley where I had lived with my family for fourteen years. Across the swirling waters of the estuary, a sea mist hung, moving slowly like a ghostly dancer. We chugged past the crescent-shaped harbour of Borth-y-Gest: I glanced at my winter's home by the water's edge below the oak wood. In the distance was the dark grey peak of Moel-y-Gest, still part of the night world.

It was a wonderful feeling to know that the mad rush was over and at last I was underway, the boat loaded with stores, the water and fuel tanks full (with fifty litres of diesel spare), the keels well bolted below, good sails and sound rigging up above, and the right navigation equipment on board. Whatever happened now, I could survive on my own.

My voyage around Ireland had really begun eight months earlier on the day I left my home. I had lived in a beautiful house called Garth-y-Foel, the enclosure on the hill, in the mountains of Snowdonia. It was half-way between heaven and earth, land and sea, part of society yet separate from it. With its back to Cnicht, the Welsh Matterhorn, it looked south across a reclaimed estuary to the Irish Sea. The farmhouse was surrounded by ninety acres of oak woods, stone-walled fields, marshland and rocky wilderness. To the east a mountain stream cut it off from the rest of the valley and to the west stretched miles of trackless bogs and ridges where only hardy sheep wandered and buzzards soared.

I had lived there for fourteen years, starting my career as a writer and raising my children. Every day I walked with them along the river to the village school, a mile away through oak woods, over stone walls and along the trout stream which became a torrent after rain. It was a magical place to bring up children, with rolling fields sheltered by beech, ash and oak, with secret places for dens and bubbling streams to dam. If *tylwyth teg* – Welsh fairies – were ever to be seen it would be on the sloping field in front of the house on a warm summer's evening.

Like any remote cottage, it did have its drawbacks. My partner grew tired of the life at the end of a muddy track in the Welsh hills. Tensions grew and eventually after my return from a long voyage around Africa, I realised that things would never be the same. Two years later, we decided to separate and I closed the gate leading to Garth-y-Foel for the last time. I decided to go on a sea journey to clear my head and to come to terms with the changes in my life. My voyage had begun.

But why a voyage around Ireland? It had long beckoned me. I often looked out of my study towards the Irish Sea and wondered about the land beyond the horizon, the most westerly in Europe, swirling in mist and rain for much of the year. I had only visited it for a two-week walking tour on the west coast in winter and a couple of day trips to Dublin. Its mysteries beguiled me. There was the mystery of its earliest inhabitants who built great forts and megaliths revealing an advanced knowledge of the heavens; the mystery of the Celts who had swept across the island and left their language, their intertwined designs, their legends and myths and their love of nature and violence; the mystery of Celtic Christianity which became the light of the western world during the Dark Ages; the mystery of a country divided by tribal loyalties and religions; and the mystery of a society which had absorbed waves of conquerors – Danes, Normans, and English – to create a paradoxical people who were both lyrical and harsh, violent and sentimental, generous and unforgiving.

Although I had never lived in Ireland, I was well aware that Irish blood flowed in my veins. My grandmother on my father's side came from Limerick, but since my father left me before I was two I never got to know her before she died. As for my father, I had only seen him half a dozen times in my adult life. When I contacted him in Barbados, where he continued his career as a successful racehorse trainer, he told me he knew nothing of his mother's relations in Ireland. The only anecdote I know about her was that after my father had run away to sea at 15 and returned two years later from Australia, he found her bending over the stove at their home in West Sussex. He slapped her on the bottom and said 'It's me!' She beamed and said: 'What will you have for breakfast?'

I only learned about my Irish great great grandfather on my mother's side from my great aunt just before she died at 92. He had never been mentioned by my grandmother and remained a skeleton in the family cupboard. His name was Charlie Cullen and he came from Wicklow. He was one of twenty-two children born into a two-bedroomed house. As soon as they were old enough they were turfed out to fend for themselves. After trying to find work in Dublin, when he was 14 he caught a ferry to London where he lodged with a Welsh family who owned a pub. At 16 he married their daughter who was two years older. He worked as a carpenter, but fell on hard times and once had to work away from home for seven years on a castle in order to support his family. He had five children and died at 96. The family was upwardly mobile, for his grandson George Bull became a Tory mayor of Islington and drank himself to death at the age of 68. There used to be a drawing of the self-important dignitary in all his regalia on the sideboard in my grandparents' house where I grew up with my mother and brother. But I never knew that his grandfather had been an impoverished Irish emigrant.

The greatest mystery of all was neither Ireland nor my forebears but the sea itself: that great symbol of eternity and the fleeting moment, of purity and cruelty, forever changing yet always the same; that living, pulsating presence which creates and claims so many lives.

I had grown up a stone's throw from the sea in Bognor Regis, Sussex, on the south coast of England. One of my earliest memories is of the sea crashing over the promenade, clawing back the shingle in the undertow. At the age of 10, I had with my brother an old clinker boat, which had a plaque on it that said that it had participated in the evacuation of Dunkerque. Every fine day of the summer holidays we would spend fishing out in the bay, under the watchful eye of the fishermen who still made their lobster pots from the willows which grew around their tarred huts.

After leaving boarding school, I decided to follow my brother to sea. My uncle wanted me to take up a profession, but I could not face the stifling provincial life around me. My brother's tales of the Far East and Australia were too exciting and alluring. So at 18, I joined the P & O Shipping Company as a purser cadet, too old to become a navigating officer and too literary to be an engineer. I did not enjoy the work but it enabled me to sail around the world and cross the Pacific three times. I resigned to take up a teaching job in West Africa before returning to pursue my studies at university but I never lost my contact with the sea. I periodically sailed with my brother in his yachts in the North Sea, along the Channel, and once across the Atlantic Ocean.

All my life I have loved the sea and one of the main reasons for living in North Wales was to be near it. As a writer, I had sailed in a dhow from near the Mozambique border to Mafia island near Zanzibar and down through the Maldives archipelago in the Indian Ocean. I had travelled in all manner of boats – trawlers, container ships, coasters, cargo ships, yachts and dhows – during my circumnavigation of Africa. But the closest I got to sailing my own boat was with my children in Tremadog Bay. I shall never forget the joy when, after camping in the mountains to celebrate the rising of the sun on the summer solstice, we decided to abandon our tight budget and to march down to the harbour to buy our first dinghy. It was a home-made wooden boat built like a Heron with cut-down sails. Some of the happiest days of my life were getting up early in the summer with my children and sailing across the estuary to have a second breakfast at Porthmeirion, an Italianate village set in wild woodlands on a small peninsula. But for all my love of the sea and experience of sailing, I had never mastered the art of navigation nor been able to skipper my own yacht.

Like many Celtic adventurers before me, I had been settled in my life in North Wales, only to hear an inner voice calling me from the ease and comfort of the hearth to take a voyage to a foreign land across the sea. My voyage around Africa had ended in confusion; perhaps this one around Ireland would be a holistic and healing experience.

I had come back from my seven-month voyage around Africa realising just how important my partner, my family and my home were to me. But within a few days of my return, I found that my partner was living in a completely different world. It took two painful years before I made any sense of it. It's a strange world: I had to travel 18,000 miles around a continent to appreciate fully what I already had, only to lose it in the process.

I left my old home in the autumn. I went to visit my neighbours and to say farewell with a sprig of bay leaf and a blackcurrant cutting from my abandoned garden. There was a strange symmetry; I was leaving exactly fourteen years after my arrival – to the very week. I was once told that it takes seven years to prepare a garden and seven years to get it right. I had got it right but it would be for others to enjoy the fruit.

I was most concerned about my children. My 16-year-old daughter Emily had already decided to live at a friend's house during the week in a nearby town to do her A-levels and she would come and see me at the weekend. My 12-year-old son Dylan would live with me for half the week.

I only took our old sheepdog Cai, our fish tank of three fish, my curious library and a few personal belongings. Our horse Black Jack was farmed out to some friends. Our 20-year-old cat Lucy was left buried under a beech tree amongst the daffodils. The few pieces of furniture I gave to friends and neighbours to use. I left my old motorbike covered in dust in the barn amongst broken bales of hay. I had been secure and rooted in this place where my children had grown up. Now I was going to live the life of a wanderer without a home. The thought of getting a boat and sailing around Ireland kept me sane. It was the only decent prospect on the horizon.

I was very fortunate to find a house to rent in Borth-y-Gest near my sailing club in Porthmadog. It was owned by the aunt of a friend of my daughter's. The house was called Tan-y-Bryn, 'Under the Hill', and was next to a defunct hotel appropriately called Min-y-Mor, 'The Water's Edge'. It was a hundred yards from the silted, crescent-shaped harbour formed by two bold headlands. From my study window I could see the sea come in and out across the mud and sand flats and watch the moored boats turning in the tide. Just outside the harbour the waters of two great rivers met and then flowed through an estuary full of sea birds out into the Irish Sea. It was a perfect place to recover and to prepare for my forthcoming voyage.

Before the First World War, Borth-y-Gest and neighbouring Porthmadog had been bustling harbours, building and repairing wooden sailing ships which took slate from the North Wales quarries to Europe and carried phosphates from the West Indies all over the world. Ships of up to 300 tons had been designed, built and sailed by local men. Until recently in the old garden sheds of the neat terraced houses could be found the rusting carving tools of the dead shipwrights. Taking my old dog for a walk on a stormy night, I often thought of one of the young pilots who had been drowned whilst guiding a ship called the *Wave of Life* through the narrow channel of the outer bar. A great wave had capsized his small open boat as he had held up a light and his body was washed up in the harbour close to his home.

But the days when the dockers and shipwrights cried, sang and cursed in Welsh had long gone. Borth-y-Gest had become a picturesque seaside village, with pretty villas painted in pastel shades. Many English newcomers had second homes or had retired there. Pleasure boats and yachts had replaced the working schooners.

For months, I went for walks along the coastal path from my house in Borth-y-Gest to a headland overlooking Garreg Goch, the 'Red Rock', and looked out towards the waves which crashed on the sand bar in the wide estuary. The distant rumble of the surf mingled with the screech of the seagulls and the sucking and slurping of the tide at my feet. I had on several occasions ventured out with the children in my small dinghy on a calm summer's day beyond the bar into the open sea. It seemed like going to the edge of the world. 'Soon, in the spring,' I would say to myself on the windswept headland, 'you will be heading out beyond that bar and into the dark sea and there will be no return.' The prospect filled me with excitement and apprehension in equal measure.

It was not easy living on my own in Borth-y-Gest, especially as I had never done so except for short periods earlier in my life. In the weeks and months which followed my move, I felt both upset and relieved; upset that the family had been broken up but relieved that the everyday tension had gone. I often felt homeless, familyless, alone. Friends and my mother and brother did their best to reassure me that I was still connected with others.

Travelling a thousand miles, I told myself, the essential still remains in place. If I could develop my inner strength, if I could rest in the whole, there would be no end to the wonders of change. But in order to undertake the voyage and to meet the challenge, my first task was to find myself a boat.

One sunny day in early spring, I wrote in a notebook: 'I'm fed up going around being solemn and sad. I will not sink gently into that dark night of the soul. I will cast aside the dead weight of gravity. I have the children to care for, friends to see, books to write, the mountains, the trees, the stars to enjoy, and there, always renewing itself, always pulsating with life, the sea, the sea. Above all, I have a boat to find and a voyage to undertake!'

2

Finding a Boat

If I wanted to get away by the spring, there was a lot to do. The first thing I did was to enrol on the Royal Yachting Association yachtmaster's theory course at Plas Menai, the National Watersport Centre in Wales. Throughout the winter, through snow, hail and steady rain, I attended. Armed with navigation tables, protractor and dividers, I began to understand the arcane mysteries of charts, tides, pilotage, meteorology, safety at sea, emergencies and passage planning. What had seemed for years part of the occult, soon became clear as a wonderful blend of art and science, poetry and philosophy. I acquired the knowledge and skill to work out a course to steer and to mark an estimated position on a chart, taking into consideration the influence of the tides, the magnetic variation of the compass, the deviation of a boat's magnetic field, and the leeway caused by the wind. I was well aware that at sea it would be very different from plotting a course on a rock steady table in a warm brightly lit room. I often wondered how I would manage on a pitching boat at night in the Atlantic off the west coast of Ireland, feeling exhausted, cold, lonely, and frightened, with waves crashing over the boat and the wind howling in the rigging.

I loved learning about navigation because it brought me closer to the great and permanent forces of nature: the influence of the moon on the tides, the play of the sun on air, the effect of wind on water.

I also found studying charts and working out positions, using simple geometry, the brass dividers and protractor, remarkably calming. I felt like a careful artisan plying his trade. There was no controversy involved, no moral dilemmas, no emotional pull. It could, in practice, be a question of life or death, of safe passage or shipwreck, but on the desk of my study it involved simple calculations and critical judgment. It was strangely therapeutic.

In order to apply my navigation, I decided to do a practical coastal skipper course at a sailing school run by John Hart on Barry Island, South Wales. We set sail in a twenty-eight-foot Morgan-Giles and criss-crossed the Bristol Channel in light winds and warm spring sunshine. John was a former pilot and coxswain of the local lifeboat. We spent a beautiful starry night in a hole in Porloch Weir surrounded by steep wooded hills. Another night was spent in a marina in Cardiff where they were building a new controversial barrage which would ruin the wildlife of the mud flats. Sailing along the Bristol Channel, I was disgusted by the untreated sewage floating in its murky waters, despite the sun glittering on its surface. John was philosophical, having lived with it all his life.

At the end of a five-day course, John signed my log book and I asked him to tell me truthfully whether he thought my intended voyage around Ireland was crazy.

'If properly prepared, I don't think what you're doing is irresponsible. It all depends on the boat. You'll need a good boat; a good boat will look after you. You also need to know your limitations.'

'Will it be dangerous?'

'You haven't got to be a Shackleton, but it's a serious voyage. If you're not prepared to face bad weather, don't go. Most insurance companies consider the west coast of Ireland to be as great a risk as the Atlantic. But it's a marvellous thing to do!'

Before I left, he observed: 'The danger of sailing is often exaggerated. Three million people take to the sea around Britain each year but only about a dozen people die as yachtsmen. More people drown getting from the shore to their yachts in dinghies than out at sea. I know someone who did a two-week course and then went off round the world with his wife and came back ten years later.'

I returned to North Wales with a Royal Yachting Association shore-based yachtmaster's theory certificate and a few days' experience of cruising. I'd also been on a VHF radio course.

I was now reasonably prepared in theory but I still did not have a boat. I often read the Irish saying I had pinned above my desk in my study: '*An té mbionn long aige, geibheann sé cóir nair éigin.* He who has a boat invariably gets a breeze.' What happens, a sneaking inner voice said, if you can't get a boat in the first place?

At the London Boat Show I had met an Irish charterer who said he was confident he could get a boat under me by applying for a grant. Would a Beneteau 351 do? 'If I were a betting man, Peter,' he said, 'I'd put a few bob on it.' I was and I did, but in April, a month before my proposed date of departure, he told me that he would be unable to help. I fell back on my second plan – a friend of my brother's had bought a new yacht and said I could use his old Kingfisher. I went up to Maryport in Cumbria to see it, and arranged for a survey, but it failed. More expense, more wasted time. The situation was becoming serious. If I was not careful, I would miss the season.

I scanned the yachting magazines to no avail. I went to local boatyards in North Wales and visited several yachts but they were either too expensive or not good enough. A card caught my attention in the marina in Pwllheli advertising a twenty-six-foot sloop, £8,000. Perhaps this is what I had been looking for. I was shown round by a friend of the owner. It was neat and snug. I sat at the table; yes, I could live in this and do my navigation and brew up and write my journal. Having been disappointed in Maryport, I insisted on a survey.

I contacted Robin Kyffin of Gwynedd Marine Boatyard in Porthmadog. He was an ex-Royal Navy engineer, ex-whelk fisherman, and a large, bluff, humorous man who often wore no socks. He was the official pilot for Porthmadog although he had only brought in one boat in two years.

I met him at Pwllheli, in the boatyard. He was armed with a great spanner and small screwdriver. He stood inside the cabin as if meditating. 'I'm just getting the feel of her,' he explained. He went about his task systematically and in silence, first bashing the bilge keels with his spanner. One sounded distinctly hollow. 'That's no good, the weights have become unattached.' He then lay on his back under the keel, and scraped off some of the immaculate blue anti-foul paint. 'My fear is that you'll never sell it. It could be on the market for years.'

Then a devilish grin came to his face: 'The juice! The juice! The poxy juice!' Sure enough, his screwdriver pierced blisters of evil-smelling liquid, produced by the break-down of the fibre-glass. It was a common problem in elderly fibre-glassed hulls. 'Osmosis! She's riddled with osmosis!' he exclaimed. 'There's no point continuing.' He threw his spanner back into the boot of his old car and sped away to another survey. I was left standing in the cold windswept yard, a thick drizzle sweeping across the grey waters of the harbour and my mind, without a permanent home and without a boat.

The time came in early June when I had to move out of my winter let in Borth-y-Gest. I spent a week emptying the house with the help of friends and went to live in a loft of my friend David Lea, an architect who lived on a smallholding in the hills. I scattered my worldly possessions to half a dozen houses, mostly boxes of books with a few sticks of furniture and gardening tools. As I hauled and shoved and lifted, I reminded myself that a man is free to the degree he can leave his possessions. I just kept my books on navigation, books on Ireland and Chuang Tzu and Lao Tzu, my beloved philosophers of Taoism.

It was the local chandler David Eastwood who first told me about her. She was a Westerly Centaur, a twenty-eight-foot sloop laying in Porthmadog harbour, only a few hundred yards from where I had lived during the winter. You can travel the world looking for something only to find it on your doorstep. Her name, *Celtic Gold*, could not have been more appropriate for a summer voyage around Ireland, and I liked the idea that she was a Centaur, half horse and half human, perfect for riding the waves.

I went to see her alongside the old slate wharf at low tide. She had a white hull, light-blue deck and royal-blue spray cover. Best of all for a single-handed yachtsman, she had a self-furling jib and in-mast reefing which meant that I could reef the fore-sail and mainsail by pulling on ropes in the cockpit without having to go out on the deck. She also had an automatic helm, an electric arm which could be attached to the tiller to hold a particular course; it would enable me to work around the boat or go down below to calculate my position or have a brew-up.

Down below there was a main cabin with two windows on either side. The galley on the starboard side consisted of a small sink and two gas rings. Opposite there was a table with two rows of seats either side: it was the ideal size for a folded chart and dropped down to form a double bed. At either side of the hatch there were dark recesses which led under the cockpit to form two 'quarter berths'. The forecabin was separated from the main cabin by a door which gave way to a small lavatory on the port side – the 'heads' – and a 'wet locker' on the starboard side for heavy-weather gear. The forecabin had two small portholes on either side and a double bunk shaped like a triangle which pointed to the anchor locker in the bows. You could clamber through a small hatch on to the foredeck in front of the mast.

It had some useful navigational aids. There was an old VHF radio, but good enough to keep in touch with coastguards, coastal radio stations and other ships. A mechanical 'log', driven by a small impeller projecting from the hull, recorded the distance covered and gave the speed in knots (nautical miles an hour); it replaced the real wooden log which used to be thrown over the stern to see how fast knots made in a line ran out. In place of the time-honoured lead and line, a new echo-sounder measured how long it takes for an ultrasonic pulse to be reflected from the seabed, thereby measuring the depth of water in metres rather than the traditional fathoms.

It boasted a Decca navigation system which picks up radio signals from coastal transmitters and works out the ship's position on a grid which is displayed as latitude and longitude. There was also a fancy collection of sailing instruments in the cockpit showing the direction and strength of the wind, the angle of running (with the wind behind the sails) or sailing close-hauled (when tacking into the wind), and the difference made in speed by trimming the sails.

The owner, John Pilcher, had recently bought a larger yacht and was eager to sell. He was an engineer in the oil industry. His son showed me around the boat. I implicitly trusted their assurances that the engine, a twenty-four-horse power Volvo MD2B was in good condition. The oil and fuel filters had been changed and new piston rings fitted. I had done some car repairs as a student, but I had never handled a diesel engine before: when we opened the cover to the engine in the cockpit it was like looking into a black hole. I knew that I would need a reliable engine, especially on the west coast of Ireland which was exposed to the full force of the high Atlantic swell.

Would I ever understand how the diesel engine worked? I took careful notes of the owner's basic instructions and hoped for the best. When I turned the key for the first time the engine turned over for a while and then burst into action, pumping out a mixture of water and gases from the stern exhaust pipe. I was elated. My dream of finding a yacht and undertaking my wonder voyage around Ireland at last seemed to be turning into reality.

Robin Kyffin assured me that he knew *Celtic Gold* well and she was in good condition. There was no osmosis problem and she had been well looked after. I started to draw up lists of extra equipment I would need, and then my luck turned again.

The owner's son rang me up with some worrying news. They had just gone out for a sail and noticed some water weeping in where the metal keels were bolted on to the fibre-glass hull. They would contact the boatyard about it. Robin's verdict was severe: the yacht would have to be hoisted out on the hard and the keels unbolted and reset.

Every day I travelled down from my friend's house in the hills and worked on the boat. I began to build up the necessary extra equipment. I hired an EPIRB, an Emergency Position Indicating Radio Beacon which transmits on aeronautical and marine band frequencies and helps the rescue services home in on you. I was lent some flares: orange smokes, red hand flares, and parachute rockets which are visible for twenty-eight miles on a clear night. I was offered an Ampair wind generator. I ordered life jackets and heavy weather gear.

I also bought a GPS, a Global Positioning System, as a back-up to my traditional methods of navigation. Developed by the American military who still control its use, this navigational aid is based on twenty-one satellites orbiting the earth. A hand-held receiver selects signals from three of the best satellites in order to calculate a three-dimensional fix. It has a phenomenal accuracy to within a metre twenty-four hours a day, in all weathers, anywhere in the world. It can even give the navigator's altitude. The only drawback was that it could be scrambled by the US military in times of conflict. It could also break down or be dropped overboard. It was no replacement for traditional methods of navigation, only a useful means of confirming them.

From my local chandlers, I bought a new VHF radio, a hand-held compass, self-focusing binoculars, 260 feet of extra warp for my two Danford anchors, a fog horn, and miscellaneous screws, bolts and shackles. I hired a four-man life raft which came in an orange rubber bag and which I hoped that I would never open. I ordered the minimum number of charts, from Imray and the Admiralty. I quickly realised the truth of the saying that sailing is like standing in a shower tearing up twenty-pound notes. I wouldn't have minded so much if it had been for the fun of conceptual art but I was paying cash now to avoid having to pay with my life later.

At last the work on the keels was completed and I went down with Robin to check the boat. The keels had been well embedded with some wonder adhesive and firmly bolted on. The cabin stank of fibre-glass resin. All was as it should be. And then, just as we were leaving, Robin's eye caught a slight stain at the bottom of an outer shroud which held the mast up. He got out a penknife and poked about the thin strands of curled wire; one came away.

'It's rotten!' he said. 'That's a major setback. I can't let you go off like that. If one's gone, then all the others could go. You'll have to change all the rigging . . .'

I couldn't believe it. It was now mid June. How on earth would I get away? There seemed no end to my bad luck. I told myself stoically that without problems, there can be no personal growth; without contradictions, there is no progression; without obstacles life would be like a stream without rocks and bends, as flat and uninteresting as a straight line.

But you can never know what is good or bad luck in the long run. What appear at first to be stumbling blocks often turn into stepping stones. The owner agreed again to pay for the new rigging as well as for repairing the keels. In the week that followed, by dismantling and resetting the rigging, I got to know how it worked and became familiar with the boat. I pored over the instruction books for the engine and the sailing manual for the yacht. It was a crash course indeed. With help from members of my sailing club, what would normally have taken months of preparation was squeezed into a few weeks. I woke up every day with a huge list of things to get through which included many which I had not got through the day before.

My good fortune at this time was Nicci. She was staying for a while on her parents' yacht, having a year off and wondering what to do with her life. She was a graduate of marine biology and an advanced underwater diver. She started helping me with the rigging and before long it was agreed that she would come with me to Ireland for a week or so. Effervescent, sunny, full of good humour, a competent sailor and a lover of the sea, I could not have imagined a better sailing companion.

Nicci and her mother helped me repaint the anti-fouling on the hull. At last it was time to hoist *Celtic Gold* back into the water, the bilge keels solid and bright blue, the mast held by shining new wire rigging. I half expected her to sink but she bobbed merrily on the incoming tide. The engine fired when I started it and I carefully took her from the boatyard downstream and moored alongside the old slate wharf of the sailing club. It was the first time I had held her tiller and it felt very strange and exhilarating. I came alongside the wharf without mishap, reversing the engine to bring myself to a gentle halt against the tide.

In the days that followed, I sorted out the stores and the last pieces of equipment: batteries, coils of rope, fenders, spare blocks and so on. I got waterproof plastic boxes for the dry stores. I made sure that I had two good anchors and plenty of chain and warps, for I would have to rely almost entirely on natural anchorages on the west coast of Ireland. I had a large bag of brown rice and many cartons of soya milk: if I was going to be demasted out in the Atlantic, I would at least have enough food to keep me going for a while. The only red ensign available to fly from my backstay was huge, and I bought a small Welsh flag with its red dragon and an Irish one with its green, white and orange bands to fly from the cross trees of the mast. Nicci's family gave me a Tilly lamp, made in Northern Ireland, to light me in my darkness and to keep me warm. Everybody warned me that I would probably be cold, wet and miserable during my voyage.

Before I left, I had only one sail in *Celtic Gold* for a couple of hours in the bay with my son Dylan and his mother Jenny; it was quite rough and they both felt ill. It was the first time that I had handled the yacht and I sailed in a figure of eight to get used to the sails; she responded well though it was very different from sailing a day dinghy. It was poignant to think that we had separated as a family and that I was heading overseas for the summer. I hoped they would both be well during my absence. When I looked out of the bay into the grey, choppy Irish Sea, I felt a tightening of the stomach to think that I would be leaving for a voyage of no return in a few days.

Dylan was critical to the end, upbraiding me for not getting a boat earlier. He could not see the point of sailing around Ireland.

I tried to explain to him that I wanted to learn how to skipper a yacht and was intrigued by the mysteries of Ireland. He was a tall 13-year-old at the time and beginning to shape his own identity and make up his own mind. He was also probably worried about me. When I was circumnavigating Africa a couple of years earlier, some boys in his primary school had told him: 'Your dad's going to die at sea and he'll never come back!' Apart from anything else, when he stayed with his mother, he had a spectacular view of the sea from her house perched high on an escarpment; it made the yachts sailing in the bay look like fragile specks in the vast expanse of sea and sky.

I said good-bye to my daughter Emily. She was full of enthusiasm for the project. She wanted to join me for a while in August. She was keen to get to know Ireland; she had been going out with a student from Dublin for a while and had heard about the great open air music concerts in the country.

When I went to visit my brother Michael in Portpatrick in south west Scotland, he was not at all reassuring, and warned me of the dangers I would face. But when I had my last conversation with him, he had mellowed a little. 'I thought you were nuts when you first told me about your voyage. You've no experience of skippering a yacht, let alone sailing single-handed. You can meet waves as big as cathedrals off the west coast of Ireland. I still think you're making a mistake by not getting to know your boat better before leaving.'

'Well, don't worry,' I said, trying to convince myself as much as him. 'I'm going to be very cautious and I'll turn back if necessary. I'm not going to be driven by a deadline.'

'OK,' my brother replied. 'I can see you've got a seaworthy boat, now I can go away to the Caribbean more relaxed. But remember what I said, listen to the weather forecasts religiously and if you're caught out in a gale head out to sea. There's nothing worse than being swept on to a lee shore. The biggest worry will be seasickness which makes you disorientated; you won't be able to go down below to do the navigation.'

His last words were: 'Take lots of seasick pills with you!'

Mine were: 'I'll see you in Portpatrick in the autumn.'

Then a sad thing happened. I received a letter from a friend, Sally Millard, with some family contacts in Ireland. Her mother was from near Letterkenny in Donegal. 'She can't promise how much hospitality you might get,' Sally wrote, 'but she feels sure that at least you'll get cups of tea and hellos. It is all a bit Irish, but that's normal in all senses.' She ended the letter with: 'I wish you a very good trip full of adventures and no storms at sea and all the best of luck.'

A week later, she was dead. In her late thirties and an experienced traveller, she had been hoping to study architecture in India and Africa. Just as I was about to set sail, I heard that she had had a car accident whilst travelling from North Wales with her 11-year-old niece. The child survived but Sally was killed. I took with me her letter which she had carried around with her for several weeks; it still felt warm.

I rang my 78-year-old mother who was living in Paignton, Devon, to say good-bye. My father had been a Spitfire pilot during the war and had been shot down several times; she knew what it was like to wait for bad news. She had received many last-minute telephone calls from me over the years just before setting off on a long journey: around the world in the Merchant Navy, teaching in Africa as a young man, and in more recent years, sailing down the Indian Ocean and circumnavigating Africa. She was as encouraging and concerned as ever, and tried to hide her anxiety.

'If you're in trouble, do you have a signal to give out?'

'Yes, don't worry, I'll be fine.'

'It's really a great adventure. You'll look after yourself, won't you, Peter!'

'I will. I'll have some good summer weather.'

'Your luck's changing. You'll be all right, Peter, I know you will. I'll be thinking of you. Let me know where you are in Ireland so I can follow you on a map.'

Before she put the phone down, she joked: 'If you can't be good, be careful!'

I had a strange premonition all would be well. When I had first moved down from my old home to my winter let by the sea, I had seen a heron stand motionless at the water's edge. During a last supper with friends in a remote cottage in the mountains, just before my departure, the setting sun created a rainbow across the valley: a heron flew through the halo and out towards the Irish Sea.

Another bird proved a good omen. On my first walk at Borth-y-Gest along the coastal path overlooking the estuary, I came across a robin sitting on a wire fence amongst the blackthorn bushes. It did not fly away at my approach. It puffed up its red feathers and wiped its beak on the wire. I went up to it without hesitation and it let me stroke its chest. I stayed with it for about ten minutes. I never saw it again. Six months later as I moored *Celtic Gold* alongside the wharf for the first time, a robin jumped on to the warp and then flew on to the guard rail. It puffed up its red feathers and wiped its beak on the wire. It marked my transition from the mountains to the shore, and from the shore to the sea.

3

Irish Waters

When I cast off the moorings at four on the longest day, and steered *Celtic Gold* out towards the bar of the estuary, it was with a huge sense of relief. Seeing the sun rise behind the pointed peak of Cnicht, I thought of my former home in the valley nestling below it. The memory of those happy years bringing up my children there would always remain with me, but I would not be lost in the mist of regret and what could have been. And as I passed the crescent harbour of Borth-y-Gest on an ebbing tide, I looked at my temporary winter home and was grateful for its shelter in difficult times. Now I was starting a new chapter and had the most challenging adventure of my life ahead.

I had roughly planned out the voyage around Ireland. I had taken with me the minimum number of charts, a *Nautical Almanac* and the Irish Cruising Club's *Directions* for the south and west coasts and the north and east coasts. It seems that most British yachtsmen sail around Ireland clockwise; while most Irish yachtsmen sail around anti-clockwise. According to the Irish Cruising Club, analyses of fair wind records coast by coast for June and July show only a three per cent variation so this must say something about the different attitudes of British and Irish yachtsmen!

Although I had circumnavigated Africa anti-clockwise following the route of Vasco da Gama, it seemed instinctively right to sail around Ireland in a clockwise direction. Perhaps I should say that I was sailing in a 'deasil' direction, Gaelic for clockwise and not in a 'widdershins' direction, old English for anti-clockwise, words evolved before the inventions of clocks to describe an object turning against the sun. Either way there was something very special about a circumnavigation: I would never have to retrace my steps and each day would bring something new and exciting.

There was one definite advantage travelling in a deasil direction. It would be easier to beat into the wind along the east coast where there is less swell than on the west. A large swell and awful sea, I read in the *Directions*, can persist long after its cause has ceased, shaking any wind out of the sails and creating miserable conditions. A storm in the Caribbean can create rollers which travel three thousand miles to crash on the western shores of Ireland. Indeed, Ireland stands out in the Atlantic like a great natural breakwater for the British Isles, taking the full brunt of the sea. A great swell can roll in on the west coast, however calm the local weather, for weeks on end.

I had already missed the best sailing month of June, when the gales are fewest and the days are long. In July, I could expect two Force 7 gales, and more in August and September. Although generally there is good warning, I would have to watch the sky and barometer as sometimes the warning comes after the gale. At least I should be spared the worst danger: persistent fog is rare.

I had decided to make my first landfall in Ireland at Wicklow. It seemed an obvious place: it was the nearest town to my home port and Porthmadog and Wicklow Yacht Clubs were twinned across the Irish Sea. It had the added attraction of being the birthplace of my great great grandfather. The night before my departure, I therefore made a careful passage plan. I estimated the distance to be seventy nautical miles, which would take me about seventeen hours, all the hours of daylight on the longest day of the year. The tides up and down the Irish Sea would roughly cancel each other out. Since high water at Porthmadog was at 0345, I would have the ebbing tide behind me until I reached the notorious Bardsey Sound, at the most westerly point of North Wales, twenty-five miles away. If I got into trouble, I could head for one of the ports along the Lleyn Peninsula.

The weather report at 1900 hours on the previous night had been good: a weak cold front had passed over and a high was on its way. Patchy sea fog overnight would clear to give good visibility. Winds would be light north westerlies, Force 2–3.

It always takes longer than you think to get away, and I slipped my moorings at 0400. The tide had just turned. I steered along the buoyed fairway past Garreg Goch, where the depth suddenly changed from five to fourteen metres, and kept to the channel scoured out by the combined forces of the Rivers Glaslyn and Dwyryd. There was no solitary figure where I had stood countless times on the headland and pondered my fate during those difficult winter months. Although the reddish golden rays of the rising sun lit up the mountain peaks of Snowdonia behind me, I entered a swirling bank of mist. I slowed down and tried to hop from one buoy to another. At times, we were completely lost in sea fog. Nicci kept a constant lookout.

Suddenly, some muffled shouts came across the grey waters. Was it the voices of the drowned pilots? The mist lifted for a moment and I could just make out a yacht which had gone aground on the side of the channel. It had left a quarter of an hour before me, owned by an RYA instructor with four of his recent graduates on board. I slowed down and offered to give them a tow off; I decided it would be best to keep in the channel and they could row across in a dinghy with a warp. Just in time, for the tide was on the ebb, the burly men managed to rock their yacht free from the clutches of the sucking sand.

We continued gingerly to hop from one buoy to another, turning the corner of the dog's leg through the narrow gap in the bar where the sea was dark and confused with unknown tidal eddies. Here the full force of the gushing waters of the Glaslyn and Dwyryd punched through the tumbling sands which constantly tried to block the estuary. The waves were more steep-sided and close; in the distance, I could hear the ominous rumble of waves crashing on the shore.

There was a local tradition that seamen from Porthmadog and Borth-y-Gest would throw their religious cloaks of puritanical restraint on the old black buoy here and enter the joyous spirit of a voyage to foreign lands. Once through the bar on their way to South America, they would say, 'That's the worst part of the journey over.'

At the bar I deliberately threw overboard my cloak of gloom which had been wrapped around me for the last few years. A great weight lifted off my shoulders, and I breathed in the deliciously cool and salty air. Like the Swahili sailors of East Africa who took off their shoes before stepping on to a boat, I would not let the trouble of the land come with me on the sea.

As if in sympathy, the mist lifted with the rising sun, its red rays turning a bright yellow. I could make out in the morning haze the Lleyn Peninsula in the distance beyond Tremadog Bay. We crossed the imaginary line between Harlech and Criccieth castles, one built by the English, the other by the Welsh. It felt marvellous, the wind in my hair, the throbbing boat beneath my feet, the mast towering above. And all around the immense space of blue sky and sea, dwarfing the green-brown headlands and rugged mountains of Snowdonia. I felt calm and steady and couldn't believe that I was on my way.

I took a fix with my hand-held compass and went below to work out our position. I could see to the south on the chart the long finger of Sarn Badrig, a ridge which dries at low water, known as St Patrick's Causeway in English since according to legend the saint used it to cross the Irish Sea. I felt much safer in *Celtic Gold*. Trusting in modern technology as much as God, I called Holyhead coastguard – the first time for real – for a radio check. The coastguard replied that we were 'loud and clear'. I informed him of my ETA in Wicklow of 2100 hours.

The sun soon burnt out what remained of the mist and the sea turned a deep aquamarine. There was a slight swell. The wind picked up by eight o'clock to a pleasant north westerly breeze, about Force 3, and I hoisted the main and the jib and turned off the engine. It was the first time that I had used my navigation skills in a real situation so I systematically took fixes every hour as long as land was visible.

I also made up the log book every hour, entering the time, distance covered, course steered, estimated leeway, wind direction and speed, barometer reading, and visibility – a habit I tried to keep up throughout my voyage. With the boat beginning to pitch and roll in rising waves, I stayed down below as little as possible and kept my remarks in the log to a minimum: the state of the sea, the setting of the sails, the use of the engine, or the alteration of the course. I had not had the time to work out how to use the GPS so I used the Decca, which picked up enough signals in the Irish Sea, to confirm my position.

By mid morning we passed St Tudwal's Island, with its mournful bell warning of danger, and then sailed close by Twyn Cilan point to avoid the treacherous bay of Hell's Mouth (Porth Neigel) on my starboard side and the sinister overfalls and races of Devil's Ridge on my port. By mid morning a fine breeze took us through Bardsey Sound, an hour before the turning of the tide. I had escaped the worst of the notorious tidal races which can run up to six knots.

I had always dreamed of sailing through Bardsey Sound, ever since my daughter, at the age of nine, had spent several days on the last farm of Bardsey Island, or Ynys Enlli, to give it its Welsh name. She had described to me her wonder at the sudden return at dusk of thousands of Manx sheerwaters to their screaming young, their wide wings caught in the loom of the lighthouse. She had also come across a cave full of seals. Like all wild islands in the West, Bardsey had attracted the early Celtic Christians: twenty thousand 'saints' (are there that many in the wide world?) are said to be buried under the rough turf of the island.

With a stiff north, north westerly breeze, I managed to scrape through the sound which cut it off from the Lleyn Peninsula just before the slack, narrowly avoiding the boiling rocks on the island's easterly shore. I then swung west and set sail for Ireland, tingling with exhilaration and joy. I had come through my first major test and the open sea was before me.

I only saw a few cargo ships in mid channel of the Irish Sea but none came too close and I did not have to take any action to avoid them. Half-way across, I set a new course for Wicklow and then worked out a new one every time I halved the distance to my destination. The wind swung from the north west to north, so we sailed on a beam reach in a pleasant Force 3 breeze. The sea was quite choppy in mid channel but eased off as we approached the Irish coast.

It was a delight to work on the Admiralty charts of Cardigan Bay and then of the Irish Sea, with its yellow shading for land, green for the foreshore, blue for shallows, and white for the deep. The old charts were black and white and were often elaborately engraved. I had come across some beautiful ones whilst my daughter and friends cleared out the cellar of the manor house of the architect Clough Williams-Ellis, creator of Porthmeirion, for her thirteenth birthday party. One was 'A New Chart of the West Coast of Ireland drawn from the latest survey for William Heather. 1818'. As I carefully unfolded it, small pieces of rotten and mouse-eaten paper fell away, but there were marvellous engravings of the western coast of Ireland, especially from Dingle Bay to the Great Blasket, the most westerly point of Europe. Another chart was of the Solent, dated 1770.

I thought of the old charts again during the 1994 Christmas dinner at the Geographical Club in London. I had just delivered a lecture to the Royal Geographical Society about my travels around Africa. As guest of honour, I was seated near Rear Admiral Hill who had recently written the official history of the British Royal Navy. I told him about the charts I had discovered and he urged me to contact the curator at the Hydrographic Office of the British Admiralty in Taunton, Somerset.

When I visited him, the curator, Ken Atherton, expressed a keen interest. He explained that the British Admiralty had only begun producing charts in 1795. Before that date, they were drawn up by private individuals; Captain Cook, for instance, drew up a chart of the Pacific after his voyage. It was the war with revolutionary France which spurred the Admiralty on.

'At the Battle of Quiberon Bay with the French in 1792,' the curator told me, 'the British captains used eight different charts and all of them were wrong! We only won the day by following the movement of the French ships. It was estimated at the time that eight out of ten ships were lost through bad navigation! The captains had to buy their own charts in a coffee house or tavern. In order to get some reliable charts, the Hydrographic Office of the British Admiralty was set up in 1795.'

During my navigation studies, it had also become clear to me that charts, like maps, reflect how people see and think about the world. The early Chinese, who under Admiral Cheng Ho escorted some Swahili sailors back to East Africa after they brought over a giraffe in a dhow as a gift to the emperor, had charts which ran from east to west. The medieval Arab maps placed Ireland closer to the Iberian peninsula than the rest of the British Isles: it was closer in their minds. Modern European charts were not developed until, in the eighteenth century, John Harrison invented the chronometer to work out longitude as well as latitude. It was then possible to impose a grid on the earth's surface in which one could fix one's exact position. It was part of the wider attempt of the Scientific Revolution to conquer and control nature to benefit humanity.

Charts were also developed by imperial powers for trade, plunder and war. Those great European rivals, the French and the English, entered a long dispute over the positioning of the zero longitude meridian on the world's charts. The French wanted Paris and the English wanted London; in the end the English won out, and now, as every school child knows, the zero meridian runs through the Observatory at Greenwich. My children, with countless others, had straddled the zero meridian at Greenwich, with one foot in the Western hemisphere of the earth and the other in the Eastern hemisphere.

Charts have never offered an exact description of the sea and its bottom. The problem all cartographers have struggled with is how to represent the curved surface of the earth on a flat piece of paper. In the most common Mercator projection, which most people in my generation used at school, the scale expands and the land mass becomes increasingly distorted the further one goes away from the equator. As a result, Greenland seems huge and is quite out of proportion. This distortion has important implications for mariners. The rhumb line – a straight line drawn on a chart between two places – is not the shortest route. Because of the curvature of the earth's surface a curved line known as the Great Circle Route is the shortest and is followed by ocean-going vessels to save fuel.

The hydrographers are constantly trying to make their charts more accurate but they are well aware that they are approximations. One should not confuse the chart with the territory. Many are based on old surveys. When I sailed through the Maldives archipelago in the Indian Ocean, I noticed that the charts being used were still based on lead and line soundings made by young lieutenants of the Indian Royal Navy in the 1820s. They rightly warned navigators to proceed with extreme caution. It had proved impossible to record the exact number of islands in the atolls. Islands not only come and go but it is not always clear what constitutes an island: when does a sand bar at low tide become an island? Again, the modern charts of Western Ireland are still mainly based on the soundings given in my old nineteenth-century charts of the region.

Charts are constantly being updated and corrected. The Admiralty issues weekly notices to mariners detailing corrections to all charts worldwide. There are even chart agents to correct your own charts for you. But not everything can be recorded: the shifting shoals and bars at the entrance of a large estuary constantly change. Satellite navigation has shown up even greater inaccuracies; for instance, my chart for the Irish Sea needed correcting by 0.01 minutes southward and 0.07 minutes eastwards. For my purposes, I could ignore such details. A yachtsman should be prepared for a degree of inaccuracy of up to ten per cent in his calculations because of such variables beyond his control as the state of the sea, weather, leeway and so on.

I made good use of my Admiralty chart of the Irish Sea during the crossing for it was the first time I had ever used one for real. I was pleased to pick up, as planned, the Codling Racon Buoy about nineteen miles off Wicklow at tea time – my calculation of the tides and my navigation had been correct. But the coast was lost in haze, and soon all we could hear of the buoy was its mournful horn every twenty seconds. The tide was beginning to run south now and I made allowances for it as I steered towards Wicklow, avoiding the string of banks, shoals and overfalls which run down the east coast of Ireland in this region. Nicci had installed herself on the foredeck in the warm late-afternoon sun, and since the wind had dropped I was motoring. I asked her to look out for a southerly cardinal buoy which marked the southern limit of the India bank; she spotted one in the haze but said it was a northerly one (its top two triangles facing north rather than south). I assumed that I had overcalculated the strength of the tide and was further north than expected. I headed south only to pick up another northerly buoy. By this time I could make out the coastline and the old lighthouse on Wicklow Head, and I quickly realised that I had come too far south to the north of Arklow Bank. One of the cardinal rules of navigation is to arrive up tide of your destination and I was now down tide.

We must have mistaken the northerly buoy we had been looking for for a southerly buoy, something easily done in the thick haze after a long voyage. With the tide running south, we had to struggle against the current along the coast to reach Wicklow. By this time, I was beginning to feel exhausted. The weeks of preparation were beginning to take their toll. It was a great relief to leave Wicklow Head behind me and keep clear of the rocky coastline and eventually swing into Wicklow Harbour at 2100 hours. The Celtic golden sun was setting behind the Wicklow mountains and there was traditional music and dancing on the quay in the warm evening air. I slowly turned around the wide harbour and decided to moor alongside a raft of yachts on the east pier. Along the sea wall, there were some colourful murals of ships, painted I was later told by the local postman. Families strolled along the pier, their faces red from the sun.

After spending sixteen and a half hours at sea and sailing seventy-six nautical miles, I had at last arrived at the birthplace of my great great grandfather. The berthmaster, with tousled red hair and freckles, came over and said with a smile: 'Welcome to Ireland!' I had no change for the harbour fees. 'Pay me when you can!'

It was my first voyage as a skipper and I had proved to myself I could manage. I also found that I had loved every moment of it, despite the fatigue and apprehension. I felt a bit dizzy and had a sore throat but I had managed to keep a clear head (despite the seasickness pills) and a steady hand. I might have overdone the navigation but it was best to veer on the side of safety. I contacted Wicklow Radio to confirm my arrival and they said they would relay the message to Holyhead coastguard. I had arrived.

4

Servants of War and Love

The port of Wicklow is very much a working port, accessible twenty-four hours a day, with a large new quay on the west side. Stacks of timber and colourful steel containers fill the dockside. In the summer it is also a busy port for yachts, the main harbour south of Dublin Bay on the east coast of Ireland. I went to the local Yacht Club. Yachts were coming over from the twinned club in Porthmadog the following day in an annual race. I learned from the secretary that every other year the Round Ireland Race also starts and finishes in Wicklow. It takes the professional racing yachtsmen about three and a half days to complete the circumnavigation. I was planning to follow the relaxed and leisurely way and take thirty times as long!

My first Guinness, cool, thick and white-headed, in the nearest pub, at the end of the inner harbour – the Bridge Hotel – went straight to my head. I rolled from side to side, listening to Irish traditional music. The place was packed with men and women sweating in their smart clothes, their faces red with alcohol, music and the day's burning sun. It was good to escape into the cool evening air and look at the reflection of the moon in the dark tidal waters of the river below a fine stone bridge.

The next day I walked into Wicklow and discovered a pleasant market town. The shops were all brightly coloured, their doors painted with primary reds, blues and greens. Traditional butchers with bloody carcasses of beef hanging in their windows vied with smart coffee shops offering wholefoods. One shop had a small mangy dog on a couch in its shabby window: it was 'Sharpe's Dog Sanctuary'.

As I went along the street, an old lady sitting in the sun on a bench smiled and said: 'Tis a wonderful day, thank God!' It was indeed, and the temperature soon climbed into the eighties. Browsing in a bookshop, I came across a little volume of Irish proverbs. Two seemed particularly apt: 'There's no need to fear the wind if your haystacks are tied down' and 'You'll never plough a field by turning it over in your mind.'

I decided that a new life deserved a new haircut. A black-and-white striped barber's pole at the end of a small dingy arcade (up for sale) pointed me in the right direction. Inside a small, dark room, there were two old men. I was beckoned into an empty chair by one of them. I was a million miles away from a unisex salon.

Ensconced in an old barber's chair, my neck pinched by a tight apron, I glanced at my face in the mirror: clean-shaven, grey-blue eyes, a slightly twisted nose (broken at boarding school), well-shaped ears (I liked to think), and wavy salt and pepper hair going thin on top. Not bad for forty-eight, I thought; at least you have some laughing lines at the side of your mouth and crow's feet at the corners of your eyes.

'Are you visiting Wicklow?' came the thick Irish accent through the clip-clip of the scissors.

'Yes. I arrived last night.'

'How did you come here?'

'By boat, from Wales.'

'How long did it take you?'

'Seventeen hours.'

Silence, except for the coughing of the old man in the neighbouring chair and the clip, clip, clip of the scissors.

'I see Major has just stepped down. It doesn't surprise me. The pound's weaker than the punt now,' he said proudly.

I was already well aware of that. With the exchange rate and higher cost of living, everything seemed about twenty per cent more expensive in Ireland than in Britain.

'While you're here, you ought to visit Glendalough,' he chatted on. 'It's a beautiful place. I was there yesterday with my wife. I was thinking about it this morning. I didn't want to come into work.'

'What about my wispy bits on top?' I said. 'They always get blown by the wind. Should I have them cut short?'

'No,' he replied firmly. 'I wouldn't do that. I'll just trim them a little. The problem will be solved when you go completely bald. No, for the time being I would keep them.'

He grew serious and kept silent for the rest of the session. It enabled me to overhear the conversation of the old man next to me, a man called Charlie who had a slight shake in his head. He was having what my children would call a very 'radical' haircut, a serious short back and sides.

'I worked in the forestry for twenty-four years,' he told his barber, not waiting for a reply. 'I was earning £4 a week. When I went to England I was paid £6 14s. I couldn't believe it. I thought there had been some mistake.' As if worried that he might be stopped in mid flow, he went on: 'Religion's on the way out. Women are not the same. There's no house wrens anymore . . .'

My hair cut had come to an end. My grey curls were on the floor, mixing with whiter, straighter hair. In a hand mirror, the barber revealed a severe chisel cut at the back of my head with a new white line above my tanned neck. I paid my money and gave a tip and left Charlie rambling on about the general decline of the Western world.

In the evening, I went south for a walk along the sea cliffs towards Wicklow Head. I passed the remaining fragments of the Black Castle which had been built in the twelfth century by Norman invaders from Wales, a reminder of the former close links between the two countries. Six centuries earlier St Patrick had come from Wales, and St David from Ireland. Until recently the Irish Sea had been a thoroughfare, not a boundary. My own crossing by sail in a day underlined the closeness between the two countries. The Vikings too had swept down the channel and many of the towns along the east coast of Ireland, including Dublin, Wexford and Waterford, had first been Viking settlements. The name Wicklow came from 'Vykinglo', a Viking word for look out or signal point.

Clear of the town and a golf course, the winding coastal path passed along steep cliffs and small sheltered coves where a few lads swam. In one a handsome black youth was kissing his girl friend. The sea shimmered silver as the hazy sun fell towards the purple hills. At the side of a small promontory, I came upon a small cave which had some of the most beautiful stones I had ever seen. I chose two for my children and some for my friends.

It was the day after Midsummer's Day. A small green tent was pitched on the rocky promontory facing east. It had a perfect view of the sea on three sides and of the daily trajectory of the sun across the sky. I thought of the Irish hermit who had written, over a thousand years ago:

> As I look out from my cave, I can see the wide ocean,
> stretching west, north and south to the ends of the earth.
>
> I watch sea-birds swoop, and I hear them shriek;
> and in my mind I can see the ocean depths teeming with fish.

> The earth is both majestic and playful, both solemn and joyful; in all this it reflects the One who made it.

There was a high anti-cyclone over Ireland and it was very hot. The winds too were quite strong – north easterly, Force 4 to 5 – so I took my barber's advice and decided to head inland to Glendalough. I took a minibus from the Bridge Hotel and we were soon climbing the hills along winding roads with high hedges. I suddenly realised that after the months of gloom and tension, I was happy and foot loose. I had all the time in the world to stand and stare. I would live in the present and not worry about past difficulties or the uncertain future. I sat back in the bumping bus and admired the shining coats of the fat cows in the lush green sunlit fields.

The driver of the minibus was a talkative man; he liked to keep his passengers in the picture. We swept through the imposing gates of an estate and drove along a tree-lined avenue to a solid Georgian building.

'This is Avondale House,' the driver announced proudly. 'It was here the national patriot Charles Stewart Parnell lived.' An old man got off the bus with his shopping.

'I believe he got into trouble with a woman,' I said to the driver.

'Where's the bloke who didn't get into trouble with a woman!' he replied.

Parnell was in fact the son of a Protestant landowner in Wicklow who had helped form the Land League in 1879. It developed the strategy of 'boycotting' agents and landlords who refused to lower rents (Charles Boycott was one of the first to experience such ostracism). Parnell went on to support Home Rule for Ireland in the British parliament, with Gladstone as an ally, but both were defeated. When the news of his affair with Kitty O'Shea was made public in 1890 Parnell's party split and he lost his seat. He died a broken man a year later.

Leaving Avondale House behind us in its leafy stillness, we made a detour into the market village of Rathdrum which was undergoing a transformation. All the shops and pubs in the high street were being repainted in bright primary colours and the overhead telephone lines and TV aerials were being taken down. It looked delightful.

'They're making an American film about Michael Collins,' the driver declared. 'He was an IRA leader. He was a schoolboy down in the west of Ireland.'

Michael Collins was another central figure in the Irish struggle for independence. It was Collins who went to London with a delegation and signed the Anglo–Irish Treaty with the British government in 1921 which gained Ireland its independence but which enabled the six counties of Ulster in the north to remain part of the United Kingdom. It also recognised the British king as head of the Irish Free State. Collins knew the risks: 'I have signed my death warrant,' he declared. It also proved to be the death warrant of thousands of others.

Back in Dublin, the new president, Eamon de Valera, was incensed. The pro-Treaty faction won the first general election in 1922 but the bitter dispute, mainly about the oath of allegiance to the British Crown, soon broke into open civil war. Collins was ambushed and shot. De Valera went on to form the new party Fianna Fail (Soldiers of Destiny) and win the next general election. He eventually drew up a new constitution in 1937 which claimed sovereignty over the six counties in the north, and of course the troubles have rumbled on ever since.

Several films were being made in Ireland at the time, according to the papers; even the great bulk of the Godfather was a recluse in some remote country hotel doing a shoot. Ireland is a tax haven for film makers as well as authors. It is also very contradictory. Because of its strict laws of censorship, inspired by the Catholic Church, many films made in Ireland in the sixties were not allowed to be shown in the country. In more recent times, the law has been eased, but Madonna's steamy workout on *Sex* was still banned – after all the imported copies had sold out.

As we wound our way up along the narrow, winding roads towards the Wicklow Mountains, we almost ended up in a ditch, trying to avoid a speeding juggernaut and a crawling horse-drawn gypsy wagon. The bus driver's mind was on weightier matters: he was discussing atheism and Darwin's theory of evolution with a young Dutchman.

'I have an open mind,' he declared, keeping his eyes off the road.

There were only a few foreigners on the bus and an old thin woman with heavy bags of shopping.

'I'm going the long way,' the bus driver told her, without asking her permission. 'I'm taking them up to see a bit of the military road. There's a lovely view up there.'

It was good to be in a country where spontaneity occasionally overcame the rigidity of timetables, although someone waiting at a pick-up point might have different ideas.

'Why is it called the military road?' I asked.

'Because it was built by the British during the Occupation. It goes all the way to Dublin. It was built after the '98 uprising against the British; they wanted to reach the rebel strongholds in the mountains. Michael Dwyer was one of the leaders.'

When we got to a junction at Drumgaroff, he said: 'You can still see some of the old British barracks over there.' I noticed some crumbling brown walls overgrown by grass and brambles.

I assumed he was referring to the 1798 Rising inspired by the United Irishmen who in turn had been inspired by the American War of Independence and the French Revolution. In another ironic twist of Irish history, the republican United Irishmen had originally been founded by Belfast Protestants. Three years after the Rising, Britain imposed the Act of Union which abolished the independent Irish parliament. It was strange to see these momentous events remembered by a friendly and accommodating bus driver who nevertheless described the British presence in Ireland as if it had been the German occupation of France. Feeling ran deep and long.

My barber had been right. Glendalough – the 'Glen of the Two Lakes' – was in a beautiful valley high up in the Wicklow Mountains. It had been carved out by glaciers from a great granite spine beyond which stretched the limestone central plain of Ireland. The sides of the lower lake were thickly wooded while the upper lake was fed by a mountain torrent and had steep rocky sides.

I stopped by a winding stream at the bottom of the valley to admire a tall, pencil-shaped tower which dominated the ruins of a monastery and cathedral. The impressive round tower had served as a bell tower as well as a place of refuge. I imagined the monks running to the tower at the sight of the wild Vikings with their axes, with their manuscripts and grain, pulling up the trap door, and trembling and praying until the pagan marauders had pillaged their beautifully made stone houses and carefully tended gardens.

Founded by St Kevin in the sixth century, the community grew into a great monastic city. Its light of Christian scholarship spread across Europe during the Dark Ages and helped earn Ireland its reputation as a land of scholars and saints. It remained a great centre of learning until Viking raids in the twelfth century brought it into decline; English forces then destroyed it once and for all at the end of the fourteenth century.

Kevin, the son of a local chieftain, first came to live here as a hermit in the early sixth century. He felt closer to God in the wilderness and lived in a hut near the upper lake in the valley. Other seekers joined him and built a stone monastery further down. They all shared the belief of the desert fathers that God dwelt in wild places and that the face of the Creator could be traced in the animals, birds and plants of the Creation.

I was far from alone in the glen that hot, sunny day. There were many like my Wicklow barber who came for a little peace and quiet in the countryside. But there were others who came from all over the world to Glendalough as pilgrims on their own path to resurrection: for them, it was a holy place, a great spiritual centre. As I bathed my feet in the cool upper lake, my head reflected in its still, clear waters, I realised that I too was a pilgrim of sorts; my outward journey around Ireland was part of an inward journey, seeking a way to feel at home.

I climbed through the great towering trees to Kevin's Cell, a ruined beehive hut built on a rocky spur over the lake. Many delightful stories have gathered around his name, stories which show a great love of wild creatures. One day, it is said, as he prayed with outstretched hands, a blackbird landed on one of his palms. It built a nest and laid an egg. Kevin remained motionless and kept vigil until the egg was hatched and the fledgling flew away. I can imagine him so lost in contemplation that the world faded around him.

But there is a darker, less attractive side to St Kevin. He was a handsome man: Kevin or Coemhgein means 'Fair begotten'. One day a beautiful young woman fell in love with him. Although he scourged her with stinging nettles, she visited him one moonlit night whilst he was asleep in a small cave hewn in the rock face above the upper lake. As she tried to make advances, Kevin spurned her angrily and with a mighty kick hurled her to the dark waters of the lake below where she drowned.

*

Back in Wicklow the next day, I came across by chance a very different community of monks and nuns who were continuing the tradition of Celtic Christianity. I needed some brackets made up to attach the stays of my wind generator and strolled along the wharf of the inner harbour in search of a workshop. I met an old fisherman and asked if he knew any welders. He immediately pointed to an alley between two warehouses and told me to go to the top of the hill where I would see a blue door with the words S.O.L. on it.

'They're a group of monks and nuns in blue robes,' he said. 'They call themselves the Servants of Love. People say they have sex together; all I know is that they do some very good welding. They give us fishermen a good deal.'

I went up the hill and knocked on the door. It was opened by a handsome middle-aged man with long hair and a beard in a light-blue cassock. A group of laughing nuns and monks, their Volkswagen bus full of sailing gear, came out of the courtyard.

'They're off sailing, are they?' I observed.

'Yes. We've always liked boats and the sea.'

I explained my problem and I followed the calm and thoughtful man into his workshop. It was dark and crowded with tools and old benches but all was neatly organised. He took a long time silently looking for the right stainless steel and nuts and bolts and asked me to come back the following day.

When I returned, he invited me into their refectory which was clean, neat and simple. The community seemed to be living in an old factory or garage. I was offered some herb tea and bread and butter and honey by a nun. The relationships between the two seemed natural and relaxed. The atmosphere reminded me of a community in the country I had once helped set up in my early thirties. Although we did not have a common spiritual goal, we had tried, like the Servants of Love, to live a new way of life close to the earth and to share our goods and skills.

The monk's name was Seamus Byrne. He explained to me that they had only moved to Wicklow recently and were committed to serving seafaring communities. They had lived before in Roundstone on the west coast of Ireland, developing computer systems for the fishermen and mending their boats. I asked him about the studio.

'It's a recording studio. We record music and make our own cassettes.'

He showed me the wide variety they produced, most with a New Age tinge. He was a composer and film maker as well as a welder. He gave me a copy of a cassette called 'The Healer', which mixed natural sounds of the sea with haunting melodies.

I asked him about the relationship between the nuns and monks in the community.

'We believe that it's possible to have relationships between each other; we become better people and our work improves when our lives are based on love.'

'Does that mean you are not celibate?'

'No, we are celibate. But we can love each other in the way St Francis loved St Claire, like brothers and sisters.'

I felt I was in the calm presence of a man who knew his vocation and whose earthly struggles were largely over. In the weeks that followed, I often played his music when I worked out my navigation on *Celtic Gold* and found it both soothing and inspiring. The ancient voice of Celtic Christianity came through the modern idiom as the song of the sea waves and birds mingled with the fluting aspirations of the soul.

The brackets he made for the wind generator were also very carefully shaped. I liked the way the Servants of Love were concerned with practical, aesthetic *and* spiritual matters. On my yacht, it was my intention to ensure that the mechanical systems of the engine were kept in good order along with the rigging and the sails. While appreciating the beauty of the billowing canvas or the merry cut of the hull through the water, I wanted to know that the pistons down below were freely turning and the oil and fuel were flowing smoothly. I wanted to feel good about cleaning out the bilges and heads in the dank darkness as well as coiling ropes and washing down the decks in the sunshine.

I carried one souvenir from Wicklow which I could well have done without. Returning from an evening walk, I clambered over a raft of yachts to reach *Celtic Gold* only to see a middle-aged man staring glumly at the side of his yacht and mine which were bouncing together in the swell. I quickly saw the cause of his dismay. Despite the fenders holding our two boats apart, a large chunk of my rubbing strake and a smaller piece of his had been broken off. The broken ends of the teak told a tale of great force.

My neighbour, who came from South Wales, was deeply apologetic: 'I can't believe it. A large coaster came in a couple of hours ago and went straight aground on the sand opposite. He immediately went full astern and sent a great wave across the harbour. When it reached us, it rocked the boats so much that the fenders were forced out and you can see the result for yourself.'

He offered to repair the damage for me, although it was not his fault. I explained that I was planning to leave the next morning. I had been held up in Wicklow for three days because of the wind, and it now looked as if it would slacken.

'I'm terribly sorry,' he repeated. 'It's the first time this has happened to me in the thirty-five years I've had my yacht!'

'It's the first time it's happened to me,' I replied, 'and I've only had mine for three and a half days!'

5

Wind and Water

The wind had been blowing hard for four days since my arrival in Ireland, but it eased off in the morning of 26th June to a north easterly, Force 4 or 5.

I decided to leave Wicklow for Arklow which was only thirteen nautical miles away, and with an average of four knots the voyage should not take more than four hours. I did not like the look of the sea, though, from the east pier of Wicklow: large white horses were sweeping in and crashing with great plumes of spray on the rocky sea defences.

I had managed to put up my large wind generator, with its foot bolted to the transom, its head attached by an arm to the backstay of the mast, and its sides held by brackets made by the Servants of Love. It looked like a great star in the stern. I was now independent in energy as well as in housing and transport; almost, but not quite, as free as the wind. I still needed the mainland for food, fresh water and diesel.

We set sail after lunch in warm sunshine under blue skies. The breaking green sea looked ominous as we left the safety of the harbour and *Celtic Gold* began to pitch and roll in the white-capped waves. Travelling south, I kept clear of Wicklow Head with its old lighthouse and sailed close to the shore inside the Arklow Bank, in order to avoid its turbulent and treacherous overfalls. We passed a string of fine sandy beaches along the flat and featureless coastline. The wind steadily increased in strength and I reefed the main and jib sails. *Celtic Gold* was plunging and rearing, but she sailed well with the wind on her port quarter. With a strong tide running with us and mounting seas, I was worried that she might get the better of me. At times we seemed to surf down the green waves, the whole boat humming. I hadn't taken a seasickness pill on this short passage but because of the high sea running, I felt a little queasy so I tried to keep up on deck as much as possible.

At tea time, I searched the hazy coastline with my binoculars for the factory with its tall chimney which was meant to be close to the north pier of Arklow's harbour entrance. The sun beat down on my head and for a moment I felt as if I was off the west coast of Africa, surveying thatched huts amongst mangrove trees.

As we approached Arklow, Nicci shouted something which I did not catch in the wind but she was pointing straight ahead. About twenty metres away lying crosswise directly in front of the bow of the yacht was a great silver lump of metal attached to a long black shape half-submerged in the dark-green water. I swung the tiller hard to starboard and none too early; we just missed the object by a whisker. If I had hit it, it could well have been the end of the boat, the end of the voyage, and possibly the end of me.

Rushing by in the green choppy water I realised that it was a huge telegraph pole, with a metal cross tree waving drunkenly in the air, which had become entangled in some lobster pots. Wicklow Radio Station had been issuing 'Securité' messages about it all day, but had given its position way to the north. I took a fix with the GPS and contacted the station on our VHF to give its new position. I could not believe how lucky we had been to miss it. Then it occurred to me it was incredibly unlucky that we should have been nearly mowed down by the only recorded navigational hazard in the vast expanse of the Irish Sea.

'It doesn't surprise me,' said Nicci, the marine biologist. 'It's the sea saying, here, here, here!'

Soon after, I spotted the factory chimney I had been looking for but for the life of me I could not make out the narrow entrance of the harbour. The coast seemed to fade into a hazy brown. I sailed towards the factory, the sea turning sandier and sandier and the waves becoming more close and steep-sided. Not far away they were curling and breaking on the sandy shore. This was a classic case of 'long-shore drift', the waves breaking at an angle on the shore and then picking up the sediment in their backwash to deposit it further along the beach.

Still a few hundred yards off the shore, I put on the echo sounder as a precaution. I was horrified for a second time that afternoon. It registered only 1.5 metres, and in the trough of the next wave, just 1.2 metres! The draught of *Celtic Gold* was only one metre; it was a miracle we hadn't already touched the ground. The chart had shown a gradually slanting seabed, but I had not expected such shallows at that state of the tide. Just in time, I swung the yacht round, worried that we might be washed ashore abeam to the waves. Reluctantly at first, *Celtic Gold* gradually turned and headed out to deeper and safer water.

I had read with some trepidation that there was a narrow entrance to Arklow, and that the entrance was unsafe in strong north east onshore winds when the waves break on the bar and there is a nasty sea at the entrance. It should be attempted only 'with care and in full control' when the winds were Force 5 or more. The phrase 'in full control' worried me. It had been comparatively calm crossing the Irish Sea and I had never before experienced seas like this in my own boat. I did not feel in full control, but tried to hide the fact from Nicci who appeared as nonchalant as ever. I asked if she felt frightened of the sea. She said: 'I don't fear the sea, but I fear the wind.' It was already a Force 5. I wrote in the log book in capital letters: 'HIGH WAVES SURGING AT NARROW ENTRANCE. ARKLOW.'

I made allowance for the ebb tide and then, with my hand firmly on the tiller I aimed midway between the piers. Large, steep-sided, breaking waves surged through the narrow gap. I said to myself it's now or never. At that point a lifeboat came careering around the bend in the river, smashing into the waves at the entrance. I let it pass and then summoned up my courage once more, knowing that the lifeboat would not be around if I needed it in the next few minutes.

I entered under power at a good rate of four knots, riding the waves which lifted *Celtic Gold* high out of the water only to drop her into the troubled sea. The piers blanketed the wind but the ebbing tide set south east across the entrance and pushed the boat towards the south pier. I did my best to counter the movement on the tiller but its dark, slimy metal sides seemed dangerously near. At last I slewed around a sharp bend and suddenly the sea lost its fury, the waves crashing into the north wharf only sending ripples up the river. We were safe. I eased off the engine and slowly chugged up the channel of the River Avoca. Despite the difficulties, it was only half past five. With the stiff north easterly winds on our quarter, it had only taken us three and a half hours to sail from Wicklow to Arklow.

Arklow had busy commercial quays. I passed the entrance to a sheltered dock full of trawlers on my port side. Near the dock, a red car screeched to a halt. A large man leapt out and waved me to go further upstream. He jumped back into his car and sped off towards the stone bridge which spanned the river in the distance. He reappeared on the other side and started shouting. I slowed down the engine, and tried to make out what he was saying. He was gesticulating wildly. Had I made some dreadful mistake? Eventually I gathered he wanted us to moor alongside a small pontoon by a large spiral-shaped building.

Having gone alongside and secured the warps, I climbed up the bank to meet the man who had helped me in. Sweating profusely in the bone-dry heat, he was the harbourmaster. He pointed out the closed yacht club nearby and said we could get a key to have a shower. I needed one after all the excitement.

I went back to *Celtic Gold* to check the moorings. Suddenly a great whirring noise and a strong wind descended from the heavens and I looked up to see a huge helicopter blocking out the sun. It swooped low over us and landed thirty yards away by the side of the spiral building, sending up a great cloud of dust and small stones which descended on the boat like a sand storm before I could close any hatches. It took weeks to get the grit out of all the nooks and crannies of the yacht.

A customs officer in a crisp white shirt and black tie turned up. On seeing Nicci in shorts in the cockpit, he said automatically: 'Is the skipper on board?' Despite all-women Irish yacht racing teams, people still assume that the skipper of a yacht is always a man. I hadn't reported to the customs or the police (the Gardia) on my first landfall in Ireland, but the formalities were straightforward and I merely had to sign a declaration which said I had no drugs on board.

Away from the fresh sea breeze, it felt like Africa again. Although only the end of June, it was so hot that the grass on the verges was turning brown and the wild flowers growing in the crevices of the stone river bank were parched dry. I walked over the stone bridge into town. The tyres of the cars were sticking to the melting tarmac as they moved slowly up the narrow winding high street. At eight o'clock that evening, the temperature in the cabin of *Celtic Gold* reached 34 degrees. On the news I heard that it was expected that the record of 35 degrees made in 1885 would be broken on the east coast of Ireland on the following day.

This was a summer that everybody would remember. I had been warned that I would be cold, wet and miserable, but here I was hot, dry and happy. As the sun began to set in the late evening, I went for a walk along the Avoca river, and appreciated the cool greenness of its tree-lined banks and its still brown waters above the weir by the old stone bridge. Swallows swooped down for insects, and a lonely heron took off into the setting sun which was red and round in the heat haze. A couple of cold pints of stout in the cool dark interior of a waterside pub rounded off the day.

Two days later the strong dry winds began to ease. On 29th June I decided to head for Waterford around the most south easterly point of Ireland through St George's Channel. The sea might be called Irish, but the charts insisted that this short stretch of water between south west Wales and south east Ireland was to be named after the patron saint of England. It was the same on my early nineteenth-century charts.

I had intended to visit Wexford, a Viking settlement founded on the banks of the broad estuary of the River Slaney, set amongst the flat lands of south east Ireland. The Viking name of Waesfjord means 'harbour of mud flats' or 'sandy harbour'. It was both, with an intricate network of sand banks in the estuary.

Wexford was only one of a string of Viking settlements along the east coast which became the first cities of Ireland. By 823, the Vikings had circumnavigated the country and settled soon afterwards. Although often depicted as fierce pagan marauders, they integrated with the local population. They not only gave the country its first minted coin, but with their longboats they started a clinker tradition of building boats along the east coast.

I was advised against visiting Wexford by a Dutchman living on board his yacht moored opposite the yacht club in Arklow. Twenty orange buoys had been put out in the summer to mark the channel between the sand banks in the estuary, but some of them had recently been stolen. What could you do with an orange buoy, I wondered. The *Nautical Almanac* also warned sternly against attempting to enter the estuary in strong easterly winds. I therefore decided to give Wexford a miss and sail straight to Dunmore East at the mouth of the River Suir which led to Waterford. The ferry port of Rosslare, which linked southern Ireland with South Wales could be a secondary port if I got into trouble.

It was going to be a long voyage. We had a choice of two routes. One was to avoid the natural hazards and pass outside Tuskar Rock but it would mean going near the busy Separation Zone, a kind of motorway of the seas, used by ocean-going vessels passing through St George's Channel to or from the main ports of Ireland, England and Scotland. The other alternative was to risk the inner passage between Tuskar Rock and Carnsore Point with its fast running currents, treacherous rocks and notorious Saltee islands. I chose the latter: the weather forecast was good – light winds and good visibility – and I calculated that if we left at dawn we would get the benefit of a three-knot tide to carry us through.

We got up at five on a glorious summer's morning and left by six thirty. The sea was calm and it soon turned a sparkling blue in the rising sun. We left the dirty sandy waters of Arklow and headed out to sea, passing outside the sand banks which made Wexford so difficult to approach. The names of the buoys – Blackwater and Lucifer – reflected the dangers, real and imagined, of the area. We tried to turn off the engine several times and sail with the full genoa and mainsail, but the light winds forced us to motorsail much of the way. When the engine was switched off, a beautiful calmness befell us, made all the more peaceful by the gentle ripple of the blue water alongside the yacht's graceful hull.

Most of the morning, we made a good five knots through the water, but a contrary tide of two knots reduced us to three over the ground. The heat had created a haze along the coast, but offshore the sun continued to sparkle on the dark-blue sea. Sitting in shorts, the warm breeze playing around my head, the boat sailing well, the navigation sound, I thought contentedly, 'there's nowhere else on earth I would like to be at this very moment.'

By noon, I could make out Tuskar Rock, a great jagged pinnacle topped by a white lighthouse. Set in the silver sea, shimmering in a heat haze, it appeared like a fairy castle. I had a great urge to land and talk to its enchanted keepers but I did not go too close because I was fearful of their spell. Apart from the tide setting on to the rock, there was probably an eddy running back towards it on either side. By mid afternoon we had slowed down to three knots, but we had two knots of tide with us.

These were some of the most dangerous waters around Ireland. The *Directions* of the Irish Cruising Club pilot warned that they should be avoided in bad weather as the tide runs strong right across the entrance to St George's Channel so it can be very rough even right out to sea. There are many rocks and shoals up to seven miles offshore. In recent years many yachts have been lost in the area.

The chart showed several wrecks below Carnsore Point, the most south easterly point of Ireland. It had first appeared on a map drawn by the Egyptian Ptolemy in the second century AD, thanks to the intrepid Phoenician explorers who had reached this part of the world seven centuries earlier. I felt privileged to be able to sail this ancient waterway in my own yacht. I kept well clear of the Saltee islands, made from some of the oldest rocks in Europe, which were nicknamed the 'graveyard of a thousand ships'. I had no intention of adding to their number.

The colour of the sea began to alter from browny green to greeny blue; we were passing out of the Irish Sea into the Gulf Stream and the farthest reaches of the Atlantic Ocean. Having turned Carnsore Point, the coastline too was no longer flat and featureless but became increasingly steep and rocky, with bold, jagged headlands. I began to see those birds associated with the wild coastlines of southern and western Ireland which were to become my constant and beloved companions throughout my voyage: the great soaring gannets stretching their yellow-brown necks and black-tipped wings, a flash of white as they dived from a great height straight into the sea; the bluish black cormorants, their long thin necks suddenly appearing above the water before they disappeared like seals; the convivial groups of black-backed guillemots with their white bodies bobbing up and down in the swell; the elegant kittiwakes, flying low in lines across the waves, flipping the black tips of their grey wings.

I threw the remains of my lunch to some guillemots, who, mistaking us for one of the many trawlers in the area, had been hoping for fish guts. These auks, with their cousins the razorbill, have been seen diving as deep as three hundred feet, the maximum for unaided divers (including humans) of the upper air before their lungs collapse with the pressure. Soon after, a lone dolphin joined us; he showed his sleek, rounded back with its sturdy fin a few times, and then lost interest and disappeared into the deep.

The water grew confused here, a sign of unseen overfalls created by fast currents encountering underwater cliffs or falling over shelves of rock. It is easy to forget that the sea bed can be as rugged and broken as the adjoining cliffs and hills along the shore. The waves were moving about as if they had nowhere to go, the crests and troughs irregular and coming in different directions, rather like water slopping about in a bowl. It was bizarre and unnerving turbulence, but it did not last for long.

Whereas the sail from Porthmadog across the Irish Sea to Wicklow had been serious and tense, the one from Wicklow to Arklow, short and hectic, this one was proving to be better than I could have imagined. It was perfect cruising: I felt relaxed and confident and bouts of excitement were followed by calm stillness and profound satisfaction. I shut my eyes to dancing stars of gold, only to open them to a vista of sparkling sea, arching blue sky, and billowing canvas.

During my winter studies, I had learned that wind passing over water in different strengths creates all the variations in the states of the sea. In the early nineteenth century, Admiral Francis Beaufort of the British Royal Navy had devised a scale from 0 to 12 to describe the strength of the winds. It was originally defined in terms of the amount of sail a square-rigged frigate could carry. The Beaufort scale has now been adopted throughout the world, and describes wind speeds and the sea state which might be expected to accompany them. It ranges from Force 0 where all is calm and the sea is like a mirror; to a Force 5 when a fresh breeze blows and moderate waves with many white horses and spray appear; to a Force 8 Gale when crests break off the moderately high waves in 'spindrift' (what a lovely word!) and foam is blown in well-marked streaks. In a Force 10 Storm, the very high waves have long overhanging crests, foam is blown in dense white streaks, and the tumbling of the sea is very heavy; in a Force 12 Hurricane, the air is filled with foam and spray and the sea is completely white.

And where does the wind come from? From the effect of the sun. When the sun heats the earth, the hot air rises and is replaced by cold air. The spin of the earth disturbs this air movement and forms winds. The uneven heating of the world causes bands of different pressures and winds. The British Isles are situated between bands of high pressure to the south and low pressure to the north; on the boundary of the cold air masses of the polar regions and the warm air of the Tropics. They are constantly shifting and interacting; hence the unpredictability of the weather and its unending popularity as a topic of daily conversation.

When warm and cold air masses meet they form an eddy which swirls anti-clockwise into a low pressure system – a depression or low. An anti-cyclone or high pressure system on the other hand swirls in a clockwise direction. Having experienced the unreliability of British weather for nearly half a century, I was not surprised to learn that the British Isles lies in a region of 'disturbed westerlies', constantly threatened by dry cold weather from the north east, dry tropical weather from the south east, warm tropical weather from the south west, and wet polar weather from the north west.

Although it is impossible to predict the onset of a low and it can travel at speeds of sixty knots or more, it does follow certain broad patterns. It is normally associated with a warm front followed by a cold front, which forms an occluded front if the latter catches up with the former. Clouds build up, air pressure falls, and it begins to rain. The wind increases and changes direction for a while:

> When the wind shifts against the sun
> Trust it not for back 'twill run.

As the warm front passes, any rain decreases and the wind becomes squally. The pressure falls again near the following cold front and then suddenly rises. The sky clears with gusty winds:

> When rise commences after low,
> Squalls expect and then clear blow.

Beautiful Latin words describe the types of cloud to be expected: high wispy *cirrus*, great blossoming, piled-up, white *cumulus*, dark layers of *nimbostratus*. For millions of years humans must have observed the weather, the constantly changing skies, the waxing and waning of the moon, the passing of the seasons. Sailors were probably the first to understand the patterns behind the sudden changes in the weather and make short-term predictions. They knew that a halo around the sun or the moon meant the coming of bad weather. If they looked up at the sky to see wisps of cloud (mare's tails) thickening into mottled cloud (mackerel sky) they knew that it would be followed by freshening winds and rising seas:

> Mackerel sky and mares' tails,
> Make tall ships carry small sails.

The captains of the tall ships would also set sail in the summer on a clear night, because they could expect a land breeze to take them out to sea; during the afternoon, a sea breeze would probably set them on to the shore.

I liked the way the weather obstinately escaped our attempts to predict it. There might be a hurricane season, but no one can say when one will suddenly develop. A storm might be threatening, but why does it suddenly peter out? Even the flapping of a butterfly's wings can influence the weather. With so many natural variables at work, I suspect meteorology will for ever remain an inexact science.

I also loved the cryptic poetry of the shipping forecasts and the reports from the coastal stations, with their information about the expected weather, the direction and strength of the wind, visibility, air pressure and rainfall. Even the names of the coastal stations, such as Tiree, Royal Sovereign, Valentia and Ronaldsway, had an exotic and enticing air about them. The voices of the BBC were distant, clipped, and reassuring, but the Irish coastguards sounded much more warm and human, often shuffling their papers and having to repeat phrases they tripped over. The litany of regions echoed in my head: Irish Sea, Lundy, Fastnet, Shannon, Rockall, Malin . . .

Nicci explained how it is the wind on the water which creates waves. At first the wind causes stress on the water which creates a wrinkle which then becomes a tiny capillary wave. These gradually combine and build up across the ocean, eventually forming the huge rollers which crash on the exposed coasts of Ireland. From a tiny wrinkle to a tidal wave, the process is the same. And the huge amount of energy, built up over thousands of miles, suddenly disappears as the wave crashes on the shore.

Yet however large the waves and turbulent the sea on the surface, deep down all would be still and calm, apart from the slow movement of the great currents of water circulating in the oceans. It seemed a good symbol of the collected and centred person: while all around might be rush and confusion, he would remain calm deep within himself.

But it was the power of the wind that most impressed Nicci. 'A sailor plays with fire,' she said. 'The wind is unstoppable energy on a global scale.'

'At least we can learn how to channel it to our advantage,' I observed. 'But why does a yacht have a maximum speed? I've noticed that however strong the wind *Celtic Gold* won't sail much more than six and a half knots.'

'You can only go through water up to a certain speed because of the resistance. You can't plane in a yacht like *Celtic Gold*. You can only lean and bow to the overwhelming force of the wind. And what's harnessing it are the sails which are attached to the mast and the rigging – which can easily break! When the sheets are like piano strings,' she went on, 'and the whole boat sings, I often think that only a bolt holds it up!'

Not something to dwell on, I thought, especially on my own.

Whenever I looked at the tightly stretched main and jib, I would think how lucky I was to have replaced the rigging and checked the mast before I left. If I hadn't, the rotten strands of wire could have slowly unravelled until, with a sudden squall, they would have parted and the mast and sails would have tumbled down in frenzied chaos.

'What draws you to sailing?' I asked Nicci.

'Freedom,' came her unequivocal reply. 'You can sail anywhere where there's water. From here you could sail to the Mediterranean, to South Georgia, to the Arctic Circle. And the sea is still untamed!'

That's what appealed to me about the sea. Humans had cast their shadow across the land, had reshaped its rivers, transformed its soil, covered it with concrete but they would never be able to transform the sea. Their boats floated on its surface, nets dragged up its creatures, rivers polluted its waters, waste fell to its bed, but it always escaped them. They did not know its depths; they could not predict its moods. Making up seven tenths of the earth's surface, the sea was the last great wilderness on earth and would always remain so. Its size was unimaginable, its depths could not be fathomed.

But we could learn how to live well on the land from sailing on the sea. To sail involves an understanding of the course, currents and patterns of moving water. The ancient Taoists understood that the nature of water can teach us many things. The highest good is like water. It nourishes everything without striving. The fluidity of water is not the result of any effort on the part of the water, but its natural condition. Nothing in the world is weaker than water but nothing is better at overcoming the hard: it divides at the headland but eventually wears it down.

I had come to realise that to be well on the sea, I should accommodate myself to the sea, and not the sea to me. A good sailor is oblivious to the danger of the water around him; if he falls into it, it is like falling out of a chair. The best way to keep afloat is to not struggle and be ready to sink.

To me sailing is the ultimate ecological parable. By trial and error thousands of years ago, sailors discovered how to channel the wind for their own purposes, momentarily harnessing its energy, only to let it go without harm. A sailing boat leaves nothing behind except a wake which is soon absorbed in the great ocean of being. The slight disturbance in water and wind disappears like a tiny ripple fading on the surface of a pond.

As I watched, mesmerised by the white foam and little waves disappearing behind us, I thought that if we could only follow on land the example of sailing, and channel the forces of nature without harm and leave nothing in our wake, the world and its creatures would be far better off.

A sudden lurch of the boat brought me back to my senses; it was time to check our position and work out a new course to steer if we were to make land before nightfall.

6

By Hook or By Crook

I was now sailing due west into the setting sun and towards the great Atlantic Ocean. The rising swell was a reminder of the vast movements of water I would have to negotiate in the coming months on the exposed west coasts of Ireland. I set a straight course for Hook Head, making allowances for the two-knot tide which was setting me down south west. I kept well clear of the Saltees by sailing around the Coningberg light vessel, a red ship permanently at anchor and covered with the white droppings of squawking seagulls who squabbled for room on its iron decks. It was by now seven o'clock in the evening and, having been up since four, I was beginning to feel the strain of the day. A cool easterly breeze brought a chill and I went down below and put on warm clothing.

I was determined to make it to Dunmore East that evening 'by hook or by crook'. I did not particularly like the associations with Cromwell who coined the phrase when he declared that he would take Waterford whether he landed at Hook or at Crooke, two settlements on the opposite banks of the wide Suir estuary.

The Hook Head lighthouse, a massive white tower with two black bands, is situated at the end of a long finger of land. It is reputed to be the oldest lighthouse on Europe, some say in the world. From around the fifth century, monks used to light a beacon on the headland for mariners, a generous gesture fully exploited by the Vikings who arrived in the ninth century and made their way up the River Suir to settle at Waterford.

The present lighthouse is on the site of the earlier beacon built by the Anglo-Normans who came from south Wales in the twelfth century. Landing in Baginburn, Raymond Le Gros and his men defeated 3,000 Irish-Norse soldiers from Waterford in 1170, even though they were outnumbered seven to one. The axes and linen of the local forces were no match for the spears, iron helmets and chain mail of the invaders. It was a key moment in Irish history: 'At the creek of Baginburn,' the verse goes, 'Ireland was lost and won.' Strongbow landed with more troops soon after and their united forces marched on Waterford. He sealed his victory by marrying Eva, the daughter of the defeated king of Leinster, Dermot MacMurrough. Thus began 800 years of foreign rule in Ireland.

I cleared Hook Head by a little more than a mile and joined a number of trawlers who were crossing the estuary and heading for Dunmore East. I had to get out of the way of a very large tanker, high out of the water; it knew its right of way in the restricted fairway and was not going to worry about gnats and beetles. The harbour of Dunmore East was packed with trawlers, so I decided to moor amongst the yachts of the local club to the north east, under dark red sandstone cliffs. Kittiwakes, fat on the fishermen's offal, struggled and fought to keep their place on the overcrowded ledges.

We picked up a mooring at ten o'clock, the last golden red rays of the sun spreading out behind the dark cliffs of the mainland and shining warmly on the stone harbour and its handsome

Doric lighthouse. It had been a fifteen-hour day, sixty-two miles of glorious cruising on one of the hottest days on record. The sea was dead calm, the tide slack, and *Celtic Gold* hardly moved at its mooring. It was the first time that I hadn't taken shelter in a harbour and it felt good to be washed by the clean waters of the open sea. Only the noise of the gulls disturbed the peace, although they too fell silent as night fell and the moon spread its silver threads across the wide estuary.

The next morning, we slipped our moorings at eight o'clock and headed upstream towards Waterford. We tacked up the wide estuary in north westerly winds towards Duncannon Fort, positioned perfectly to blast any intruder out of the water. The estuary then narrowed and we motored along the buoyed channel, slowing down to avoid the Ballyhack car ferry, the ebbing pea-green water forming little eddies and torrents. But they did not check our passage upstream. In the distance, palls of brown smoke spread out across the blue sky from two tall chimneys. The hay had already been cut in the small stone-walled fields which sloped down to the green wooded river banks. I could not have been happier, in good company sailing up a river on a hot, still summer's day, the systems of the yacht going smoothly and the voyage gradually beginning to unfurl.

At noon we turned a bend and reached the junction of the River Barrow which was spanned by a great railway swing bridge. At its side rose the two tall chimneys, polluting the heavens with waste from an oil-fired power station. We dropped anchor on the opposite side of the river, by a cluster of cottages and a small jetty called Cheek Point. Nearby there were some large salmon traps made from wicker, but they had been abandoned a few years earlier because a new stone breakwater to keep the main channel deep had silted up their approaches.

I rowed ashore in the sweltering heat in our rubber dinghy. From an old pub I tried to contact John Seymour, the writer on self-sufficiency, who had made his home near New Ross on the banks of the River Barrow. I liked his earthy wisdom tinged with spirituality: the earth worm, he considered, was the most important creature in the world for it was primarily responsible for the fertility of the soil on which all life on land depended. He had invited me to visit him, with careful instructions on how to arrange the opening of the railway bridge and how to navigate the waters to his riverside dwelling. Knowing what sailors need, he held out the enticing prospect of 'plenty of booze and grub and HOT WATER!' He had dreamed of sailing around the country in his own Galway Hooker, but he had been forced to sell it. He told me that it was the main regret of his long life. Unfortunately, there was no reply from his house and I missed the opportunity of sailing up the river and seeing him.

Gasping with thirst in the heat, I had a cool Guinness seated on an old stone wall by the water's edge at Cheek Point. A middle-aged couple of city dwellers out for the day were discussing the exceptional weather.

'What is it with the weather?' the man asked, drawing deep on his pint of stout. 'Is it global warming, the ozone layer, the government or God?'

'I've no idea,' said the woman. 'On Inishbofin Island, they've been praying for three days and now they've had a massive storm. Who's responsible for that?'

'Well, I think all of us could take a lesson from the weather. It pays no attention to criticism.' He fell silent, musing into his empty glass. He then added, no doubt inspired by the chimneys on the other side of the river: 'Well, there's no need to worry. If the Gaia idea is true, then we can pollute the earth as much as we like and it will always recover.'

I wanted to point out that there is a limit to Gaia's ability to heal herself but it was too hot to argue.

In the late afternoon, while I was having a cup of tea on board *Celtic Gold*, half a dozen young lads swam over. I could see through the porthole that their necks and arms were burnt by the sun, while their lithe bodies were white as chalk. I heard one of them exclaim: 'There's pussy on board!' Another said: 'Let's board her like pirates!' I could see Nicci getting anxious.

I went up on deck, and, pretending not to have heard anything, asked if they could tell me whether there were any buses from Cheek Point to Waterford. They replied politely that there was only one in the early morning and evening.

'Where are you from?' a tousled youngster asked.

I said I came from Wales, pointing at the Welsh dragon flying on the port cross tree of the mast with the Irish tricolour on the other side. When I added that I was trying to circumnavigate Ireland, they all seemed impressed. They gave me the benefit of the doubt: maybe I was a fellow Celt, despite my posh English accent! They wished me well and waved to Nicci.

They returned to larking about, diving down for handfuls of slimy mud which they threw at each other; when some splashed on the white hull of the yacht, they apologised. I was tempted to join them in the water: the glorious heat, the clear blue skies, the waving green of the trees, all urged me to jump in. But I didn't fancy the look of the mud. I would wait and bathe in the limpid waters of the Atlantic.

Whenever we had landed in our previous ports, I had noticed young men would come and chat to Nicci. I could see why: it was hot, she was in shorts and T-shirt and she looked very good. She rejected their advances with tolerant good humour. I asked whether she minded being harassed.

'All the men look at you in Ireland,' she confessed, 'as you walk down the street, even the old men. In England, they still do it but they don't do it so obviously. They're much more jolly here when they try to pick you up. Rather than saying "What's your name?" like an Englishman, they say, "Can I have your autograph, love?"'

The following morning, 1st July, we weighed anchor at Cheek Point and headed upstream to Waterford. With the last stroke of the lavatory in the heads, a little fish appeared in the pan only to be sucked down into the nether regions, poor thing. After passing the large Little Island with its silted backwaters, the river narrowed to about 100 metres although it was still sufficiently deep to allow ocean-going ships to reach the city. My echo sounder registered twenty metres in the middle of the channel.

By now the tide had turned, so we had to struggle against the ebb. The factory chimneys and cranes rising above the trees and fields announced Waterford around a bend in the river. Following the *Directions* of the Irish Cruising Club, I made for a pontoon on the south side above Adelphi Quay, opposite a solid round tour built by Raymond Le Gros, the Norman conqueror of Waterford. It looked like a fat stone barrel.

There was already a yacht moored along the old pontoon, an elegant white boat about thirty foot long with a couple of middle-aged men on board. Its name was *Mustard Seed*. A large white flag with a maple leaf fluttered from the stern. I hovered almost motionless, motoring against the current, and asked permission to come alongside. A man in long shorts replied with a Canadian accent: 'Sure, you're welcome. Throw me your warps.'

I came in gently alongside and when we had made fast, he observed: 'That was some very good manoeuvring. I'm impressed.'

I thought of my sailing instructor and my unfocused steering in the Bristol Channel in the spring and glowed.

'I'll leave the warps,' he said. 'A captain should always play with his own ropes.'

There was a whole art and science of warps, I was learning, which involved judging the rise and fall of the tide, the pressure on fenders against another boat or a wharf, and the direction and rate of the current under the boat. Bow and stern warps were fairly straightforward, but their combination with 'springs' (ropes running fore and aft) required frequent adjustment and special understanding.

Two women turned up with some hand-blown Waterford crystal and we were introduced to Stan and Betty Miller, who owned *Mustard Seed*, and their friends John and Pat Hatchett who had joined them for a while from Vancouver. They were planning to circumnavigate Ireland like me but they had started off from Milford Haven in South Wales. For the past seven years, they had been living on their yacht and only went home for three months in the winter to Vancouver where their children lived and where Stan would give classes in electrical navigation. He and Betty had sailed *Mustard Seed* from Canada down the west coast of America through the Panama Canal and up to Newfoundland before crossing the Atlantic. They had come from the Mediterranean through the canals of France.

'We're just a couple of boat bums,' he said, laughing contentedly.

Their yacht was cosy and snug and extremely well organised. Everything was carefully stowed away; after seven years, they knew the best place for every object. They had a marvellous stove which ran on a gallon of diesel a day and which provided hot water, cooking and all the heat they needed. 'When it's twenty below, you need something like that,' commented Stan. Crystals were hanging from the windows. 'My wife's psychic,' he observed without further explanation. He gave me the impression of a very practical man who understood machines well but who also knew the poetry of sailing and understood the spirituality of the sea.

Stan had been a telephone engineer but had developed cancer and had been told that he had only six months to live. When straight medicine had failed, he turned to faith healing and it had worked. He and Betty were determined to do exactly what they wanted with the life left to them. Sailing was first on the agenda. They would carry on, leaving the boat wherever they reached in the autumn, at least until the year 2000. It was Scandinavia next year, and maybe the Mediterranean the year after. They had honed their needs to a minimum and were completely independent and self-sufficient. They had even sold their house back in Canada. They and their friends were on their way out, so we said good-bye, hoping to meet up with them again during the voyage.

The deep River Suir had enabled Waterford to become Ireland's second city in the Middle Ages and its chief port for European trade. It remains an important commercial port, with a new container terminal connected by a railway just downstream. On the quay opposite us were great blocks of peat wrapped in plastic waiting to be exported to the gardens of the world. The ancient peat bogs were fast disappearing in Ireland. For centuries they had provided the country's principal fuel, once back-breakingly dug out with a deep and narrow spade, but now scooped up by great machines.

The city of Waterford spreads out from the old Anglo-Norman town. I strolled through its narrow alleys, tripping on its cobbles. I passed by the ruins of a French church, built in the thirteenth century by Franciscan monks. There is also an eighteenth-century cathedral which has a carving of an earlier Lord Mayor of Waterford which depicts worms and frogs crawling out of his decomposing body. I would definitely prefer to be buried at sea full fathom five and be eaten by fishes.

It was Saturday morning, I wanted to find an engineering

works to buy a thermostat, but everywhere was closed. I asked a young man mending a lawn mower in a small workshop down an alley where I could get one.

'Sorry,' was his reply. 'Waterford's a lazy town. You couldn't buy a car on Saturday even if you wanted to.'

I wandered too into a 'heritage centre' in a former church which had an exhibition of Viking life in Waterford. The Viking settlers had lived in small houses made from post and wattle like weaved baskets with thatched roofs. They made most of their small everyday objects from the shed antlers of red deer. Shards of pottery from south west France reflected the ease of transport in those days between Ireland and the Atlantic seaboard of Europe. The Vikings had been badly misrepresented by legend. They were not tall warriors but fairly small. Nor were they bloodthirsty wanderers; they settled in villages along the east coast of Ireland where they grew oats and barley as well as looking after livestock.

That evening I enjoyed Irish music in one of Waterford's oldest pubs. It advertised 'Ballads & Craic' at its door. I asked the barman under an old ship's lantern whether he would take English money.

'We take anything here, your fist or your arm!' was his reply. I half expected some redcoats to burst in and round up some tars who had jumped ship.

The band of five greybeards with guitars, accordions and drums, played some lyrical and stirring traditional ballads. On one occasion a beautiful young woman with red hair got up to sing a haunting love song which brought a crescendo of maudlin applause. An old man also leapt up and asked a young girl to dance and they performed an amazingly intricate jig to the clapping and cheers of the bystanders. It was indeed a fine example of Irish *craic*, that word which cannot be translated but which has something to do with humour, warmth, good conversation, music, booze and conviviality, spiced with a little devilment and ribaldry.

Towards the end of the evening, when the air was thick with smoke and laughter, they played some old rebel songs. Outside the pub were green Sinn Fein posters declaring 'No to Peace Talks'. The session ended with everyone standing for the Irish National Anthem.

I left the city of Waterford with the important knowledge that the first frog in Ireland was released there, that the man who chose the Irish national flag was born in the city, that it was the only place in Europe where the Roman and Protestant cathedrals were designed and built by the same man, and that the first steamship – the *Zenobia* – to round the Cape of Good Hope was built there.

When I left Waterford on 1st July, the weather had broken. There was a cool, swirling mist along the river at first and as the day wore on it became increasingly cloudy. Thunder rumbled in the distance.

I had a slight worry. The yacht's log did not work at first, and it only cleared after I had revved up the engine. No doubt the river current had wrapped some weed around its little propellor that struck out of the hull – even a barnacle has been known to stop a log. But it was essential for navigation: without a log, it would be extremely difficult to estimate distances covered and therefore to plot my position on the chart with accuracy.

After Duncannon Fort, the estuary broadened out towards the sea. With the wind behind us, we sailed goose-winged, the jib out on the opposite side of the mainsail. Because the wind was gusty, I fixed a pole to hold the jib out from the mast and a preventer to stop the mainsail from gybing. If your head is in the way, a swinging boom can knock you out or worse. Just before I had left my home port, I had seen a yachtsman go away in an ambulance with blood pouring out of his ear after being hit by a swinging boom.

It was Saturday and several small fishing boats were heading out to sea, keeping clear of the main channel which was being used by a new blue container ship and a rusty old red coaster. It was good to see one small boat full of waving and laughing women and children, out for a pleasant cruise despite the worsening weather. Salmon, heading upstream to spawn, leapt out of the dark green water. The cruisers were out again from the club at Dunmore East and racing around buoys in the estuary.

I moored in the same place as before outside the harbour under the red cliff of the kittiwakes. It was another calm evening and we settled down to a pleasant supper. I was glancing at the Hook Head lighthouse in the distant haze, when, suddenly, through the porthole the great black bow of a trawler appeared. It was very close. I rushed up on deck to see it drifting without an engine on the tide, straight for us and another moored yacht. There was an old man on the bridge shouting at a boy on the rusty deck, who then leant over the side with an oily rubber tyre attached to the end of some filthy rope. It was all they had to lessen the impact of the inevitable collision. It would have been a slight blow to the thick-plated hull of the trawler but to a yacht it spelt disaster.

I pulled up the duckboards in the cockpit, pressed the cold start on the engine, and turned the ignition key. By this time, the trawler was almost upon us. Nicci rushed up forward and was desperately trying to undo the bowline which attached us to a mooring line. The engine burst into action just as she threw the mooring line and buoy overboard with a splash. As *Celtic Gold* moved forward, I could see out of the corner of my eye the trawler scrape past the bows of a neighbouring yacht. An eddy of the tide had just saved it. But it still had a couple of yachts to smash through before being swept on to the dark brown cliffs. I was clear but I stayed nearby in case I could help the trawler men and lessen the carnage. Sweat was dripping from the brow of the frantic skipper.

Finally, the trawler shuddered and the engine started, belching out a black cloud of exhaust. The skipper swung his wheel to starboard and headed out to sea. He returned and steered straight for the moored yachts. What was wrong with these people? This time the boy was joined by another man and they had a huge lump of concrete at the end of a chain and some stout ropes. Under steam, they gingerly went between the moored yachts and in the only spot available dropped the lump of concrete to its unknown destination in the murky depths. They had laid out another yacht mooring. I looked on with frank amazement at the ability of the skipper to manoeuvre his great vessel of rusty steel in such a small place. One mistake could have resulted in thousands of pounds' worth of damage. I've seen yachts going in amongst trawlers, but never the other way round.

They were good men, the trawler men of Dunmore East, at least the ones I met that night were. I went to the local yacht club and burst in on the presentation of a cup to the winner of the race earlier in the day. I asked at the bar where I could find some diesel since I wanted to leave for Cork at first light the next day. I was told to be quiet until the end of the speech.

There was a great controversy going on between the commodore's husband (yes, the commodore was a woman) and one of the committee who both claimed victory in the race and were arguing over the rules. The full committee had retired and awarded the prize to the member. The club was in an uproar; passions at the bar were excited and the only conversation was about the minutiae of the case. Different camps tried to win me to their cause, but all I wanted was some diesel. I was eventually directed to a large man with a beard who said he couldn't help me until ten o'clock when the trawlers came in for fuel.

I waited on the quay with my can, surveying the rusty trawlers, their lights ablaze, making ready to leave. A strong, bronzed man in oily overalls grappled with a huge snake of a pipe and filled his trawler with diesel. The man with the beard from the yacht club then turned up and made out an invoice for 2,000 litres.

'It's not a very good evening; they usually take three or four thousand litres. And how many would you like?'

'Twenty-five, please,' I said boldly, holding up my plastic can in the orange arc lights of the dock.

The trawler skipper returned for his invoice and saw me waiting. He took my can and filled it up with the foaming green fuel, and then carefully wiped it down with a rag.

'There you are, that should see you through,' he said, smiling, his steady blue eyes looking straight into mine.

It was not his job. He had important work to do, a large humming trawler and half a dozen men waiting to go prawning off the Saltees that night, but he was prepared to take time to help a stranger. Who said fishermen hate yachtsmen? It might be true elsewhere, but not yet in this part of Ireland.

7

Old Blarney

I woke up early on 2nd July to find the sky a dark grey. The forecast was not very good, either. With a weak front over the north coast of Ireland, the wind had backed from the north east to the north west and was expected to blow fresh to strong. Rain, drizzle and mist would be widespread at first.

My intention was to head straight to Cork, one of the safest harbours in the world. The passage should be straightforward, due south west, with no obvious navigational dangers. Apart from adverse weather, I only had to contend with a one-knot tide either way. There were harbours in Dungarven, Youghal and Ballycotton which could provide shelter in an emergency. The distance was about sixty miles and I estimated it would take about twelve hours.

We set off soon after eight o'clock in the morning, leaving the squabbling kittiwakes, the friendly trawlermen and the traumatised yachtsmen of Dunmore East behind us. The wind was a fresh north westerly, about Force 4, so I was able to switch off the engine as soon as we cleared the harbour entrance. There would be no need to tack as the wind was on our starboard beam.

An hour later we had passed the tidal rips sweeping across the estuary of the River Suir and were heading due south west with a reefed main and jib. The sky was still cloudy and the sea had turned greeny grey. Whereas we had been in Greece, with sparkling blue waters, and even in Africa for a while, with the great heat, we were now definitely back in Ireland.

By mid morning, the wind had picked up to a Force 6, and we rolled and pitched through seven-foot breaking waves, the spray flying from their foaming tops. *Celtic Gold* took it in her stride although I felt a little queasy. The sight of hundreds of guillemots, black-backed and -headed, bobbing up and down on the water like rafts of ducks, made me forget my discomfort. Some of them dived at our approach, while others took flight with very fast wing beats, revealing their white undersides.

Bending over the side of the cockpit to loosen the rope of the self-furling jib, my blue cap was suddenly blown off into the sea. I decided there and then that it would make a good opportunity to practise a man-overboard drill. I immediately set *Celtic Gold* on a beam reach and counted ten seconds. I then turned her to windward and sailed back on a beam reach with the wind on the other side. After ten more seconds, I spotted the cap just breaking the surface. I steered *Celtic Gold* into the wind, the sails flapping wildly, so that we could come gently alongside the drowning hat. It was a good manoeuvre; if it had been a body we would have been able to recover it. But when we were only two yards away the cap sank and slowly disappeared beneath the waves.

I imagined the cap gently swaying to and fro as it headed down into the increasing dark to the bottom of the ocean, almost 180 feet below, and consoled myself with the African saying that if you lose your hat at sea it will bring you a year's good luck. The Victorians believed that bodies and boats sank until a certain depth where they then gently moved forever in limbo. The deep still remains mysterious and awesome, a solemn place of darkness and stillness, a symbol of the unconscious where monsters lurk and unspeakable horrors dwell. Indeed, the phrase Davy Jones' Locker does not refer to a Welshman but probably derived from the phrase 'Devil Jonah'. Jonah, as the Bible has it, was thrown overboard by his shipmates as a human sacrifice during a storm in an attempt to appease God. Jonah's locker proved to be the stomach of a whale.

Although I had not taken any seasick pills, a strange drowsy melancholy befell me as I thought of my cap and dwelt on these matters of the deep. I had experienced a similar melancholy almost every day whilst crossing the Atlantic in my brother's yacht. Perhaps it was a sense of being literally 'at sea', away from any recognisable bearings and any firm points in one's life. The sea has a remarkable ability to swallow and erase the past and all its landmarks; like a ship's wake, it absorbs all and leaves nothing behind. It can appear a live and pulsating being and then become a reminder of the nothingness from which being emerges and returns. I went down below to make a brew up. A cup of tea and a biscuit soon pulled me out of my reverie.

We passed a series of bold brown headlands during the day which offered good landmarks to take bearings from with my hand-held compass: Brazen Head, Mine Head, Ram Head. The rocky Capel Island off Knockadoon Head and the larger Ballycotton Island were also useful features. Passing around Pollock Buoy with its mournful bell, I managed to make out the white lighthouse on the low lying Roche's Point at the entrance to Cork harbour. All day it had been grey and dreary, with squalls of rain blowing in from the north west, a day to suit my mood. But just as we were sailing into the mouth of Cork Harbour, golden rays of the setting sun suddenly lit up its headlands. It was a glorious welcome after twelve hours of hard sailing and choppy seas.

Entering Cork Harbour I couldn't escape the burden of history. Two sinister forts on either side guarded its entrance which then opened into one of the world's largest natural deep-water harbours made from a drowned river valley. I could make out the Gothic spire of St Colman's cathedral above the docks of Cobh on Green Island. In its heyday up to 300 tall ships would be at anchor in the waters off Cobh, formerly Queenstown. It was once Ireland's main port for transatlantic liners: *Sirius*, the first European steamship to cross the Atlantic, left in 1838 and it was the last port of call of the *Titanic*.

Cobh (pronounced Cove) was also Ireland's principal port of emigration. From 1848 to 1950 over 2.5 million out of the country's six million emigrants passed through the port. I imagined them glancing back at Roche's Point, the final landmark of their native land which they had been forced to leave out of grinding poverty in order to start afresh in the New World. I thought of the young men and women who saw the flashing light of the lighthouse fade, thinking of their sweethearts whom they would probably never see again. I pictured whole families huddled together in rags guarding their small bundles of possessions, feeling the sickening disorientation of the sea which they had never seen before and would probably hope never to see again.

The forts at the entrance of Cork Harbour had long been abandoned, but their military significance had not been lost. Daubed on Fort Meagher on the western promontory was the slogan in large white letters: 'RELEASE IRISH POWS'. Just after the fort, I turned hard to port and headed up the Owenboy River to Crosshaven, the site of Royal Cork Yacht Club. It claimed to be the oldest yacht club in the world and had just celebrated its 275th anniversary.

It was a pukka marina, strange after the working ports of Wicklow, Arklow, Waterford and Dunmore East. Two earnest and obliging young men in a club boat came out to lead me to a pontoon and told me where I could find the bar, restaurant and office. After securing the moorings, I had a marvellous hot shower and then wandered around the club which had only a few visitors that night.

The club itself had been founded by British naval officers in Queenstown in 1720 as the Water Club of the Harbour of Cork with a maximum membership of twenty-five. On the wall of the bar was a list of the original rules, which included the important resolutions 'that no Admiral presume to bring more than two dozen of wine to his treat' and that 'such members of the Club, or others, as shall talk of sailing after dinner be fined a bumper'.

Glancing through the Visitors' Book, I was delighted to come across an entry in Portuguese from the captain of the *Boa Esperanza* (Good Hope). She was a replica of the caravel sailed by Bartholomew Dias, the first European to find a passage around the Cape of Good Hope five centuries earlier. I had started my voyage around Africa three years earlier in her, sailing out of the River Tagus in Lisbon into the Atlantic Ocean before she left for the Tall Ships Race.

The captain had written in Portuguese the saying attributed to Socrates: 'There are three types of men – live men, dead men, and men of the sea.' Presumably, old Socrates thought they were of an indeterminate type, half alive and half dead, neither at home on water nor on land, for ever condemned to move across the waters. If that was so, I was pleased to be in their company. It gave life an edge and put the puny ambitions of landlubbers into perspective.

I went ashore and explored the nearby village of Crosshaven, a popular seaside resort for Cork residents, which nestled under a wooded hill around a bend in the river. It was a quiet little village with one grand Georgian house and a fine Gothic church designed by Edward Pugin. Walking along the riverbank road from the yacht club, I was amazed by the number and proximity of pubs: in a hundred yards or so, there were three adjoining each other, and a couple more with a shop or two separating them.

On my way back to the yacht, I stopped to look, on hands and knees, at the shining swathes of brown kelp streaming in the tide from the pontoon, with beautiful red sea anemones and dark-blue mussels attached to it. Two little fish darted amongst the weed in the clear water. I would have loved to have joined them, returning to the sea from where I came.

The following day I caught a bus into Cork, passing along the River Owenboy and then winding through small villages set amongst rolling limestone hills until we reached Ireland's third and the Republic's second largest city. Corcaigh, the Irish name for Cork, means marsh, and the city was built on islands of silt and sand on marshy ground which was flooded regularly by the River Lee. Its main streets had once been riverways. It was strange to walk along the arched Grand Parade and curving Patrick Street and to think that sailing ships once glided where motor cars and lorries now jostled. There were even bollards on the pavements where they would have moored until the river channels were covered over two hundred years ago.

Despite its fine setting, the place had an air of having seen better days. The old buildings were in need of repair. Once salmon leapt in the clear, bubbling waters of the two channels of the river but now they were a milky lime green and smelt bad in the hot sun. What could have given sparkle to the city appeared like a diseased artery. Below the many bridges of the city, I could make out large ocean-going ships unloading their cargo.

After buying some large fenders from the chandlery near the bus station, I went for a walk along St Patrick Street and cut down a narrow alley to the Oyster Tavern. Built in 1792, it was reputed to be the oldest tavern in Ireland. It was empty:

Wimbledon was on the television and Ella Fitzgerald sang the blues. I turned up the Grand Parade, with its monument to Irish patriots and then over a little bridge to St Finbar's Gothic-style cathedral. On the opposite side of the river stood the shining steel of Murphy's Brewery, nicely juxtaposing the two religions of Ireland: the bar and the altar. As a sign of the times, the brewery of Cork's famous stout had been taken over by Heineken.

It was a muggy day and the fumes of the traffic clogged my nostrils. Oh where were the fresh salty air and cool breezes of the sea? I crossed the River Lee and climbed the hill to Cork's most famous landmark, the tall square tower of St Ann's in Shandon, an eighteenth-century Anglican church topped by an eleven-foot metal salmon which acts as a wind vane. I noticed that the south and west sides of the tower were made from grey limestone and the other two sides from red limestone; hence the Cork saying: 'Partly coloured like the people, red and white is Shandon steeple.'

The bells of Shandon ring out every quarter of an hour across the city and remind the good citizens of Cork of the necessity for enterprise and punctuality. Some laggards prefer to take their time from the clock on each of its walls: it is known as the 'four-faced liar' since east and west faces tell slightly different times. I did not envy the lot of the local residents who were the victims of the tyranny of amateur bell ringing: anyone could climb the tower and ring its bells for a small fee. I tried 'Waltzing Mathilda' and gave up in sympathy for the damned who were forced to hear the racket. In the belfry, I read the inscriptions engraved on the huge bronze bells: 'Prosperity to all our benefactors 1750' and 'Peace and Good Neighbours'. The constant ringing of the bells hardly created the former or encouraged the latter.

Another inscription on the clock of Shandon steeple read:

'Passenger, measure your time, for time is the measure of your being'. I gave a sigh of relief that I had escaped the tyranny of the clock for a while, and measured my time by larger natural movements, by the state of the tide, the position of the moon, and the passing of the sun through the heavens.

I could not leave the Cork area without a visit to Blarney Castle. The Irish, of course, are famous for their Blarney, for their gift of the gab, their flattering talk, their ability to wax eloquently and wittily about all manner of subjects. If they did exaggerate and embellish in their story-telling, it was in the name of the truth of fiction rather than any intended dishonesty.

I caught a bus in Cork and was jolted for almost an hour over hill and dale until we reached the twee village of Blarney, north of the city. It was late afternoon and the grounds of the castle were closed but I managed to blarney my way in. I wandered through the grounds, admiring the great trees, and climbed the spiralling stairway up the massive square keep. There was a fine view from the low parapets of the ruined tower over wooded hills. A few rooks jumped into the air at my approach only to land a little further away.

I came across several different versions of the Blarney story that afternoon but then where are you going to get some Blarney if not in Blarney itself? The two most plausible seemed to be a political and a romantic version. One refers to a dispute between the Lord of Blarney and Queen Elizabeth about democracy and the ownership of property. Elizabeth's deputy, Carew, was sent to get Blarney to renounce the traditional custom by which the clans elected their chief and to accept the tenure of his lands from the English Crown. The sword of the Leviathan was dangled over his head, but the wily chieftain stalled Carew day by day 'with fair words and soft speech'. Eventually an exasperated Elizabeth recalled Carew and exclaimed: 'This is all Blarney: what he says he never means.' In this version, Blarney means pleasant bluster which is intended to deceive, a skill cultivated to this day by most politicians and diplomats.

The other version holds that the poor Lord of Blarney was infatuated by a beautiful young girl who rejected his advances. As the lovesick lord was pacing his castle walls in despair, a fairy appeared in the mist and said that if he kissed a particular stone in the ramparts he would gain the powers of eloquence and win his love. He did and she succumbed.

The Blarney Stone itself was lodged low in the parapet. It had been worn smooth by countless kisses, from all the varied lips of diverse humanity. No one seemed to worry about transferring dreadful diseases. In order to kiss the Blarney Stone you have to lie on your back and arch your neck and head backwards. Two iron bars embedded in the tower wall offer hand grips, while a few bars across the void prevent you from falling eighty feet to your death on the rocks below. My heart fell there even if I held my body back. As I gingerly kissed the stone, I felt a strange tingle. After struggling to defy gravity and to become *homo erectus* again, a great compulsion came over me to laugh and – yes, I'm afraid – to talk.

Back at Crosshaven I spoke to a member of the committee of the Royal Cork Yacht Club. He had no problem with the monarchist associations of its name in a staunch republic: 'The name's just stuck; no one takes any notice of it.' Discussing my voyage, he urged me to visit Kinsale, Cape Clear Island and Dingle – 'a smashing place to victual'.

'After that,' he warned, 'you're pretty much on your own out there. There are no coastguards and not even the lighthouses are manned these days. You must watch the weather all the time. Don't go near the Shannon as it will take you a day in and out. There're not many ports of refuge. The Admiralty charts are very old and the marked rocks are not always in the same place. The prevailing wind is westerly. You can expect to be storm-bound for a few days every three weeks. If the weather's good, just keep going. If it hacks up nasty, you've got 3,000 miles of sea coming at you. If you're caught out, stay out!'

It didn't sound at all promising. I was already late in the season and had only just begun my voyage. I further read in the *Nautical Almanac* that from mid-summer the sea off the west coast of Ireland 'breaks dangerously on shoals with quite substantial depths . . . a stout yacht and good crew are required. Even in mid-summer a yacht may meet at least one gale in a two-week cruise.'

I wasn't at all sure whether I could meet the requirement in terms of yacht or crew. Indeed, for much of it, I would be on my own. The almanac further warned that there were few lights on the west coast and inshore navigation was not wise after dark. A good watch should be kept for drift nets off the coast, and for lobster pots in inshore waters. Stores, fuel and water were not readily available.

I had been warned. To increase my anxiety, I heard on the radio that a Welsh couple in their home-made boat had been rescued off nearby Ballycotton. They had tried to keep afloat by bailing and pumping the bilges for a couple of days but in the end had had to send out a May Day. The life boat picked them up just in time as their boat sank. But I was still determined to go on, to go west, to sail beyond the sunset, towards the dwelling of the western stars.

The night before I left Cork Harbour, I sailed up the Owenboy River about a mile from the Royal Cork to Drake's Pool. It was a wide pool in a bed in the river with mature oak and Scot's pine trees coming down the steep banks to the water's edge. I had never seen so many herons along the banks revealed by the ebbing tide. They remained motionless amongst the mud, rocks and bladder wrack. We dropped anchor and gently swayed on the ebbing tide, little eddies and wayward currents disturbing the flat surface of the grey-green waters.

There was a fine wooden schooner anchored nearby, a ghost ship without sails. It reminded me of the story behind the pool's name. Sir Francis Drake is said to have been chased with a small squadron of five ships into Cork Harbour by a superior Spanish fleet. A pilot with local knowledge instructed his men to punt their ships up the river at high tide to the pool where they would lay hidden amongst the trees on all sides. Dumbfounded and vexed, the Spaniards departed in search of easier prey.

After dusk, I lit an old paraffin storm lantern, rusty with sea air, and tied it to the forestay as an anchor light. I sat for a long time on the dewy deck in the cool air looking up at the bright stars. I could easily make out the star-studded belt of Orion and followed the trajectory of the Plough pointing to the North Star. Owls hooted in the dark woods. The gentle splash of salmon making their way upstream came across the swirling mist. It was very quiet and still, the opposite of being at sea, and I soaked up the calm tranquillity.

I reluctantly weighed anchor early next morning, said farewell to Drake's Pool and chugged along the river towards the wide expanse of Cork Harbour. We passed under the forts and then headed south west out to sea, leaving Roche's Point on our port side. It was good to feel the swell of the sea again and to smell the salty air as we swept over the waves with a steady Force 3 easterly breeze behind us. We were goose-winged and fancy-free. As the morning wore on, it grew increasingly hazy, but we safely cleared Daunt Rock and its buoy by midday and picked up the Little Sovereign and Big Sovereign Islands off Oyster Haven before tea time. I could just make out the famous landmark of the Old Head of Kinsale on the horizon.

It was a quiet, steady sail, and I began to think about the deep. A hundred and forty miles off the coast of Ireland, the continental shelf drops off 4,000 metres to the seabed. If the theory of continental drift is correct, then the continents are not only drifting apart but the seabed itself is constantly changing, especially where the tectonic plates separate or push against each other. There are some places on the earth, such as the Java trench, which is deeper than Everest is high, while not far below the summit of Everest there are rocks embedded with sea shell fossils.

It had long been thought that little life can exist below 150 metres because the lack of light makes the photosynthesis of plants difficult. That is true for ordinary plants which rely on oxygen and sunlight. But huge plant-like beings have been found around 'black smokers', vents at volcanic sites at the bottom of the ocean where no life was thought to dwell. Huge crabs, oysters and giant tube worms and other creatures have also been seen, living off bacteria which use sulphur from the vents for their metabolism instead of oxygen.

Ever since I had read Jules Verne's *Twenty Thousand Leagues under the Sea* as a boy I had been fascinated by the thought of monsters of the deep. He was right about giant squid: huge specimens have occasionally surfaced, and fragments of even bigger ones have been found bobbing on the sea. Sucker marks on dead whales also suggest that Titanic battles have occurred in the middle deeps with squid of a size imagined only in nightmares but never yet seen by the human eye.

In mid afternoon, as we approached the estuary of the River Bandon which lead to Kinsale, I saw scores of Mirror dinghies sailing in the shimmering silver sea. I sailed past a large fort on my starboard side and then turned to port around a bend in the river and made for the crowded harbour of Kinsale below a hill. There were many French yachts which had come over from Brittany and English yachts which had sailed from the Channel via the Scilly Isles. I was in the sailing centre of the south west coast of Ireland.

Amongst all the modern luxury yachts, I was delighted to see the black bulbous hull and long bowsprit of a Galway Hooker. Moored to the harbour wall, she was about forty feet long and lay deep in the water. Two women were sunbathing on the deck. Galway Hookers had once been the main working boats of the west coast, carrying potatoes, peat, stores and cattle between the islands and the mainland. It was now a classic wooden boat, admired as much for its elegant shape as for its seaworthiness.

Nicci left me in Kinsale. She had come for a week and stayed longer than two. I saw her off early in the morning on a coach to Dublin. Her last words were: '*Celtic Gold* will look after you, if you treat her kindly.' I hoped she was right. The further west I went, the harder it would become.

I missed Nicci's warm presence and sense of fun, but soon settled down on my own. I could see why some men like to live alone on their boats. Masters of a tiny kingdom, they have total control. When all around them is changing and confused, on sea or on land, they have one fixed and reliable point: their boat. Boats are not messy like human relations. At the same time, there is something very reassuring and satisfying to be warm in a bunk in a sound yacht securely at anchor, like a foetus in the warm waters of its mother. A cabin even resembles a womb; it is no coincidence that sailors should refer to a boat as 'she'. A good boat will look after you like a good mother.

I was enjoying being on my own in my own space for a while. I had no wish to be anywhere else in the world. I felt fit and well. The skin of my palms was toughening up and the muscles in my shoulders and arms were hardening. With my needs reduced to a minimum and a comfortable home and reliable means of transport, I was independent and self-reliant. I could come and go as I pleased. I had time to stop and stare. I could wish for nothing more.

8

Poetry and Prose

During my first night in Kinsale Harbour I was woken up by a clap of thunder and the sound of hail hammering on the cabin roof. Lightning lit up the river and surrounding hills. The south easterly wind was strong and gusty and *Celtic Gold* tugged at her moorings. The next morning was what the Irish call a 'dirty day' – wet, humid and close. Since it looked as if I would be weather-bound for several days, I shifted my moorings from the harbour over to the other side of the river, to the new marina under the ruins of an old British fort.

Kinsale was packed with holiday makers – Americans, Dutch, French, English and Japanese all jostled with the Irish in its narrow streets. I quickly realised why. Virtually every other building of the old seaport was a pub or a restaurant. I was in the 'gourmet capital' of Ireland.

I met Peter Barry, a spry Cork Irishman with an impeccable English accent, who lived in a small white cottage next to his Spaniard Tavern overlooking the harbour. He had a mongrel dog called Scrawny whom he had found starving on Cork railway station and a quote from Antoine de Saint-Exupéry on his wall: 'It is only with the heart that one can see rightly.'

Peter claimed to have started the gastronomic trend in Kinsale by opening the first restaurant. Now there was a Good Food Circle of restaurants which attracted connoisseurs of food and drink from all over the world. Even fish, long despised by the Irish as a food of penance on a Friday, was being served.

'Thirty years ago,' he told me, 'the town was poverty-stricken, with one in three houses derelict. The garrison was closed and fishing had collapsed; people were leaving the place and boarding up their houses. Now its bursting at the seams. It's not a question of spotting the visitor, but spot the native. In the winter, there are 2,000 people living here; in the summer, 5,000.'

Peter had interests in sailing as well as food, the two main attractions of Kinsale. He helped organise the Le Figaro Yacht Race which was held every year in early August between France, Ireland and Spain. The course was from Arcachon to Kinsale, round the Fastnet and then via La Rochelle to Gijon and then back to Brest. It reinforced the close historical maritime links between the three countries.

He was also a local historian. Some of the most crucial events in Irish history had taken place in Kinsale. Founded by the Anglo Normans, it became, in the Middle Ages, one of the most important harbours in Europe, with substantial trade in wine and salt. When the two seventeenth-century forts were built by the British on either side of the river, it developed into an important naval base and garrison town.

'Because the barracks were for single men,' Peter said, 'There was a saying: "Are you married or do you live in Kinsale?"'

The most important event in its history, and one of the most important in Irish history, was the battle of Kinsale in 1601. During the rebellion led by Hugh O'Neill and Hugh O'Donnell in the North, the Spanish Crown, at war with Britain, sent a fleet under the command of Don Juan D'Aguila with 4,000 troops to support their cause. The Irish chiefs wanted a landing north of the Shannon, but the Spanish, remembering perhaps the fate of the Armada along the exposed west coast, chose Kinsale instead. They were soon besieged by Lord Mountjoy, the Lord Deputy of Ireland, who had declared 'The coming of the Spaniards will be the War of England made in Ireland.'

O'Donnell and O'Neill then brought 12,000 of their men from the North in a gruelling forced march and arrived to confront 3,000 English troops on Christmas Eve. Outmanoeuvred, the Irish and Spanish were roundly defeated in a few hours; O'Donnell and O'Neill went into exile and the Spanish surrendered. The flight of the Earls saw the passing of the old Gaelic feudal order; henceforth, the English and their language were to reign supreme until Irish independence. Their departure allowed the Crown to go ahead with the policy of 'loyal settlement' in the Ulster Plantation by the English and Scots, thereby sowing the seeds of the future troubles.

Kinsale was caught up in another historic event which was to have long-lasting repercussions. After being deposed, the Catholic monarch James II went to France and then landed at Kinsale with an army and marched to Dublin. His forces were defeated by the Protestant William of Orange and his mercenaries at the Battle of the Boyne in 1689. It marked the end of the old Norman and Celtic aristocracy and the doom of Gaelic culture in Ireland and heralded the Protestant and Anglican ascendancy for another century and a half.

As the urbane and whimsical Peter Barry observed, I was in Kinsale during 'a very sticky week'. By a great coincidence it was 12th July, the day the Protestants in Northern Ireland celebrated the Battle of the Boyne and the defeat of the Catholic forces. The Orange Order had been having its parades and bonfires, marching with their drums and pipes as they had done for 180 years through the Catholic area of Belfast. These marches, the

Protestant leader Ian Paisley asserted, were 'a matter of life and death, freedom and slavery' but they ensured that sectarian strife would continue in a divided Ireland.

On Peter's suggestion, I visited the twelfth-century Norman St Multose Church. It too had witnessed another momentous event which was to shape Irish and British history. It was here that Prince Rupert proclaimed Charles II King of England, when news of Cromwell's execution of King Charles I in London reached Kinsale. Charles' fleet was at anchor in the harbour at the time. This provocative act only encouraged Cromwell to come to Ireland in 1649 and defeat without mercy the royalist forces which consisted of the majority of the Catholics and the Ulster settlers. Under Cromwell's notorious Act of Settlement, Clare and Connacht, west of the Shannon, were left to the Irish gentry while the remaining twenty-six counties were confiscated for the English

The existing church was built by the Normans in 1190 on the site of a sixth-century church, one of the earliest in Europe, at a time when Christianity was only just beginning to make inroads against paganism and the Druidic religion. The influence of the earlier beliefs lives on in folk superstition, in the practice, for instance, of tying rags to bushes near holy wells or in the Sheela-na-Gigs, grotesque figures exposing their exaggerated female genitalia which were carved in medieval churches. Hidden in a dusty room near the belfry, facing the wall, I came across a worn white stone of great antiquity with a primitive outline of a figure which looked like an alien. It was dark in the church and the warden was impatient to leave. I asked him why the mysterious figure was hidden away. 'There are old laws,' he replied, 'which say it's illegal to have pagan statues in church; they've never been repealed.'

The Protestant church was now Church of Ireland, in the same tradition as the Anglican church. As he turned the great key in the door, I asked the warden why he had to lock up.

'Vandals,' he declared. 'They throw stones at the stain-glassed windows. It's the drugs, I blame. Kids can't do anything nowadays without these ecstasy tablets. They come in on the yachts. They're dropped off in lobster pots and the fishermen go out and collect them.'

Before I left the churchyard, I visited the graves of three passengers from the ill-fated liner *Lusitania*. Kinsale was formerly a port-of-call from New York to Liverpool. It was off the Old Head of Kinsale that she was torpedoed by a German submarine in 1915 whilst heading for Liverpool. Out of 1,959 passengers, 1,195 drowned. The exact cause of the disaster is still a mystery. The Germans claimed that she was carrying arms as well as passengers; there was certainly a major explosion on board. Her loss precipitated the entry of the USA into the First World War.

The wind continued to blow hard and gusty so I stayed on in the shelter of the marina in Kinsale. A partner of the marina's owner was Michael Loughnane, the managing director of the charterers Sail Ireland which was based below the concrete and glass block of the Trident Hotel by the harbour. A former rugby coach, Michael seemed to know everybody in Kinsale. He introduced me to Conor Haughey, the son of the former taoiseach or prime minister of Ireland, Charles Haughey, who had sailed in on board *Celtic Mist*, a fine motor-sailer somewhat larger and newer than *Celtic Gold*. Conor was of solid build, in his thirties, with short auburn hair. He was an engineer by profession but seemed to spend most of the summer on his luxury yacht with his mates. During a lunchtime session with his wife and some friends in the Trident, he told me that he had sailed three and a half times around Ireland. I asked him what he meant by the half.

'We hit a rock called Ireland – just below the Mizen Head lighthouse to be precise.'

'Did you lose your boat?'

'Yes, she sank but we managed to row away in a dinghy with a bottle of brandy.'

I later learned that his father had been with them at the time, in 1986, returning from a poetry book launch. The Baltimore life boat came to their rescue. It was flat calm. The former prime minister had a lot of explaining to do that day to the press.

Like most Irishmen – and unlike me – Conor sailed around Ireland anti-clockwise – widdershins. I asked him why.

'Well, we like to get round the north as quickly as possible, get it out of the way. Psychologically, it's then down hill. It gets better all the time!'

Given the South's relationship with the North I could see why. He gave me a detailed account of places to visit and people to meet on the west coast, particularly recommending the islands of Inishbofin, Clair and Caher – 'a very mystical place'.

Conor was continuing his voyage the next day. As he left he said: 'If you're in Dingle early in August, call us up on the radio on board *Celtic Mist*. My family will be on Inishvickillane, an island in the Blaskets. Maybe you'll be able to come over and visit us. It's a beautiful place, the most westerly inhabited island in Europe. We've tried to introduce hares, deer and sea eagles on the island.'

'I didn't know you had sea eagles in this part of the world.'

'They used to be along the whole of the western seaboard. Unfortunately, ours were bred in captivity, and the male flew off. We shall have to breed some on the island, and then they might stay.'

Another sailor preparing for a voyage in Kinsale was Tim Severin, the writer and traveller. He had made Cork his base for the last twenty-five years and from there had organised his journeys on horseback or in ancient sailing craft. After sailing in the wake of Ulysses and Sinbad, he had won the hearts of the

Irish in 1976 by building a hide-covered currach with which he re-enacted St Brendan's legendary voyage across the Atlantic. With four others – including Conor Haughey's brother – he had sailed to Newfoundland via the Faroes, Iceland and the coasts of Greenland and Labrador, showing that the Irish could have reached the New World 800 years before Columbus.

Severin invited me to join him in his house near Courtmacsherry, about twenty-five miles west of Kinsale. I drove along the coast road, up and down hill and dale and through the high flowering hedgerows, skirting the wide Courtmacsherry Bay. I stopped in one cove and saw the great Atlantic rollers crashing on to the sand and wondered whether I would be able to face them again on my own in a few days. I eventually found Severin's home down a leafy lane in a courtyard surrounded by old stone buildings. They were part of an old mill house which he had converted into fishing lodges.

Severin's carefully restored stone house was as immaculate as the man himself. He was trim, formal, courteous, neatly dressed and short-haired; very much the English gentleman. He introduced me to a slender, thoughtful woman with long blonde hair in her early forties called Naomi whose accent betrayed slight traces from down under. Separated from his wife and living alone, Severin took pride in always cooking for himself, serving the locally caught sole for dinner. Like many sailors and travellers who spend much of their time in chaos and confusion, it seemed as if he wanted to make his own living space as settled and ordered as possible. He enjoyed the antics of his dog and cat as they played around the sparsely furnished sitting room under drawings inspired by his various voyages.

His first book had been about his journey in the steps of Marco Polo and when he turned from horse-riding to wave-riding, he had little experience of the sea. 'I've only owned one boat, a Volk boat,' he admitted. I knew them well; elegant and very seaworthy wooden vessels, but so small that you couldn't stand up in them.

Severin had given a talk a couple of months earlier than me at the Royal Geographical Society about his most recent voyage across the Pacific. He had intended to show that the Chinese could have reached America. His bamboo raft, made in Vietnam, sank, but he was close enough to demonstrate his point.

He took a very practical approach in his historical recreations and would not be lost on the wilder shores of speculation: 'I like to test any hypothesis. I always like to consider the consensus of scholars and check the evidence to see whether a particular journey was in the realm of possibility. There's a great need for careful research. I was interested to find that after all the talk about corn circles they were found to be a hoax.'

He planned his voyages meticulously, raising funds from commercial sponsors as well as rich sultans. 'I've never failed to get a project off the ground,' he declared proudly.

I asked him whether he saw sailing as a co-operative enterprise as I did. He had a very different attitude: 'At sea, I'm definitely in charge, very much the captain on board.' He also had a firm preference for professional seamen. 'Whenever I've sailed with intellectuals, there have been problems. I now always take blue-water sailors with me. The simpler, the better. They just get on with the job without raising objections. They're just interested in survival.'

One person who always accompanied him was a fisherman from the Faroes whom he felt he could completely rely on. As one travel writer and sailor to another, I was keen to find out what motivated him. I was still trying to understand why I should put myself on the edge.

'Are you driven like St Brendan to look for the Isle of the Blessed?'

'No, I'm not driven, I'm not looking for a Promised Land. I

do it just for the enjoyment.'

'What has a lifetime of travelling taught you?'

'Always have an alternative,' was his unequivocal reply. 'I've learned never to get in a position where you can do only one thing!'

That was not only one of the first lessons of navigation but exceptionally sound advice for life.

We had a different attitude to the sea though. It might be indifferent to humans, but I had never found the sea cruel. So far in my voyage it had seemed, if anything, like a living, benign presence, inspiring me with awe and reverence; it was certainly not a malign force.

Severin, on the other hand, maintained: 'The sea is always hostile in North West Europe. St Brendan, who was influenced by the Desert Fathers, went to sea in search of the wilderness. The sea is the desert. A Mongolian who lived in the desert flew in here once and I took him to the shore and showed him the sea for the first time. He said it was like the desert. He understood; he knew what I meant.'

For me the wilderness is not hostile, something to be fought or checked; indeed, the wilder the sea, the closer I felt to the real. Teeming with animal and plant life below and above the surface, feeding birds and humans, the sea seemed the very opposite of a desert. Indeed, far from being a biological desert, the deep sea may rival tropical rain forest in species diversity. It not only had an extra billion years of evolution, but contains possibly up to 100 million different species.

What was Severin planning next? 'Something in the Far East; I don't want to go into it at this stage.'

And how did he get on with his neighbours? 'The Irish are very outward-going and tolerant of eccentrics. There are quite a few New Age travellers who have settled in the area and they get on fine. The Irish seem less tolerant of their own itinerants though. Still it's very safe round here; there's no need to lock your car.'

During the dinner, Tim did most of the talking but it soon became apparent that Naomi was also a sailor and writer in her own right. She told me that she was originally from New Zealand but after a spell in France had settled in Crosshaven with her daughter for the last couple of years. She seemed particularly interested in my writing on ecological thinking and the way I had set off to go round Ireland with no experience of skippering a yacht. She was also interested in alternative medicine; she had been suffering from headaches but a practitioner of Chinese medicine in Kinsale had managed to unblock the flow of energy.

We got round to discussing why people go off on crazy and dangerous journeys.

'That was the subject of my third book,' she said. 'It's usually because people are psychologically driven to prove something.'

She knew all about racing and blue water sailing and had been in the Round British Isles and Ireland Race. While we were discussing the merits of cruising versus sailing, I suddenly realised that my dinner companion was none other than Naomi James, the first woman to circumnavigate the world single-handed. A New Zealand sheep-farmer's daughter, she had set off in 1978 in a fifty-three-foot masthead cutter at the age of twenty-eight with less than two years' sailing experience and that mainly as a cook.

She had been a complete novice in navigation. For a while she could not understand why her estimated positions seemed more accurate closer to the equator than further away, until she realised that she had been measuring off her distances from the bottom of the chart – along the latitude scale – rather than from the longitude scale on the side of the chart. It would be difficult to make a more elementary mistake. She also applied magnetic variation the wrong way in calculating her courses to steer. Yet despite her inexperience, she had managed to overcome her fear, to survive a capsizing in a storm and to complete her circumnavigation in a record of 273 days. She only called in for a few days in Port Stanley in the Falkland Islands and Cape Town for emergency repairs. She returned and sailed up the River Dart in Devon, a changed woman, immeasurably enriched by her experience, confident in the possibility of fulfilment.

She had just married Rob James, the racing yachtsman, and on her return became involved in the most competitive and high-powered aspects of the sport. One day, while returning from a practice sail in a swift trimaran, Rob had fallen overboard and drowned. How the accident happened remains a deep mystery. The yacht was moving too swiftly to save him. Naomi was pregnant at the time.

Naomi confessed that for the last five years she had given up sailing. I asked her why. 'I've nothing else to prove,' was her reply.

Tim seemed content to enjoy life as best he could, creating an armour of order around himself, whereas I sensed Naomi was still searching for something. She had suffered greatly and come through and knew what she did not want. She was no longer driven by an inner compulsion but beginning to determine her own life. I hoped she would find it. I left them in the early hours of the morning as they walked under the full moon down a leafy lane by the slow moving salmon river.

That night, back in Kinsale, the wind roared down the Brandon river, and I woke up several times trying to stop the halyards from slapping on the mast of *Celtic Gold*. The warps tugged at the pontoons of the marina, and the water slapped against the hull. The agitated wind generator whirled and whirled until I threw a rope over it. With a deep depression over the eastern Atlantic, the weather was still overcast and blustery. The wind, a southerly Force 5 to 6, was too strong for me to nose out of the shelter of the river, so I decided to use the time to do some engine maintenance. The thermometer gauge had packed up and the fan belt was slipping. I also needed to buy some large wire cutters in case the mast gave way in a gale and I had to cut it away from the rigging.

I was pleased next morning to see *Mustard Seed* had made it to Kinsale. Stan came over and helped me test the thermostat, enjoying boiling it in a bowl of water heated on his Vancouver stove. I warmed to his attitude to the engine.

'You must treat it like a good friend; one day your life might depend on it.' Seeing me struggling in the black hole of the engine, trying to mend a leaking fuel tank, he insisted reassuringly: 'If someone put it in there, Peter, you can get it out.'

His motto was 'Eternal vigilance is the price of freedom'. It was very apt when applied to maintaining the systems of a yacht. An engine works best when well looked after; when it is allowed to realise its essential function. And while an engine is a human creation it is still made from natural products and part of nature. The Buddha is to be found in a piston as well as in a water-lily.

Before I left Kinsale, I was invited to a party at the Trident Hotel to celebrate the twenty-fifth wedding anniversary of the owners of the marina where I was moored. It was secretly organised by their children and the whole family clan turned up from all over Ireland.

To begin with, the conversation was polite and restrained over pints of the dark stuff. The charterer Michael Loughnane told me an anecdote about the writer Brendan Behan, the drunken Borstal Boy and self-confessed Irish Rebel, whom he had seen thrown out of a restaurant by three waiters in Dublin when he was a boy. Behan had been invited to Oxford to debate the differences between poetry and prose. His opponent talked learnedly for two hours. Behan got up and declaimed a solid Irish stanza:

> There was a young man from Ringsend
> Who worked for farrier Pollocks.
> He went for a walk along Sandymount Strand,
> And the water came up to his ankles.

'That's prose. If the tide had been in, it would have been poetry!'

I got talking about divorce with Michael's wife Susan: 'Women don't divorce in Ireland. They just separate. There's a referendum coming up which will be a close thing. The women in the country don't want it. The farmers don't want it because they're worried about property rights. But most people in the cities are in favour of it. It's the Church which is opposed to it. Without divorce, people are forced to live in sin if they want a new partner.'

Whilst standing at the bar, a young Irish woman called Sinead told me a story about Fionn Mac Cumhail, one of the most celebrated heroes in Irish myth. The tales about his exploits probably inspired many of the Arthurian legends. It was strange to be transported back to Druidic times amongst the bright lights and hubbub of the bar.

'We call him Fionn Mac Cumhail, but he's got a great name in English – Finn Mac Cool! Well, when he was a boy he was taught by the druid Finegas. The old man caught the Salmon of Knowledge and gave it to him to cook. Finn burnt his finger but when he sucked his blister he acquired knowledge. After many adventures a princess took him to Tír na Nóg, the 'Land of the Young'. When his son Oisín was wounded in battle Fionn came back into this world to take him to the Tír na Nóg. He rode on horseback because he wasn't allowed to set foot on land. But when he bent over to take Oisín on to his horse, the weight of his son was so great that he pulled him to the ground. Fionn gained all his years back, aged and died!'

A couple turned up, Des and Sally, who soon got the place rollicking. He bashed away at an upright piano stripped for action, while she sang robust Irish songs and wistful blues *à la* Bessie Smith. As the evening wore on and midnight passed, the songs got more and more risqué, the singing more raucous and the dancing wilder. A song about Alice, who had an affair with a man next door, had the good citizens of Kinsale standing up and shouting out the refrain in merry unison: 'Alice, Alice, who the fuck is Alice?' I decided it was time to leave. It was four o'clock in the morning. Another good craic, but one I paid for the next day.

9

The Gulf Stream Coast

I had been in Kinsale WOW – waiting on weather – for nine days and was keen to get going. I had been in Ireland for nearly a month and had completed less than a quarter of my voyage. The fine weather had turned changeable and with a deepening low to the west of Ireland, the country was swept by fresh south westerly winds with spells of heavy thundery rain and drizzle. It was warm and humid, the type of weather, as the Irish Meteorological Service put it, which was conducive to the spread of potato blight. A hundred and fifty years earlier, the first signs of the potato crop turning to rotten pulp were being found – the beginning of the Great Famine.

The forecast for the next few days was for more wet weather, with winds increasing from fresh to strong and gusty. I therefore decided to leave Kinsale on 17th July even though it would mean beating into a heavy sea. This was going to be my first single-handed voyage, and I was eager to see how I would stand up to the strains and challenges of difficult weather. I had got to know *Celtic Gold* well and had confidence in her seaworthiness. Light had even begun to shine in the engine room as well as at the masthead. During the next couple of weeks along the Gulf Stream Coast lay some of the best cruising grounds in Europe, with bold headlands, deeply indented bays and remote and mysterious islands.

I got up from my bunk and went out on deck early on the 17th to feel a blustery wind from the south west sweeping over the hills. The sky was overcast and white horses rolled in along the Bandon river. The only cheerful object around was the wind generator which whirled away to its spindle's content. I slipped my moorings from the marina at ten thirty and motored down the river towards the Old Head of Kinsale. I had decided to head for Glandore, an inlet which provided good shelter at all times. It was approximately thirty-two miles away: at an average of four knots, it should take me eight hours to reach it. On the way, there was a possible refuge in Courtmacsherry Bay although its dangerous rocks and shallows made it far from ideal.

For most of the day the one-knot tide would be in my favour but since the westerly wind would be against the tide, I could expect short, steep waves. I set my course to clear the overfalls round the Old Head of Kinsale by a couple of miles. As soon as I cleared the lee of the peninsula of the Old Head, I felt the full strength of a Force 4 westerly wind and had to reef both the mainsail and the jib. Since I now had to set a west south west course, I was obliged to tack around the headland. It was no joke. I soon realised that the wind was setting me dangerously close to the overfalls. *Celtic Gold* was bouncing like a cork in the steep-sided, breaking waves. I had almost no control on the tiller and was unable to swing the bows round in order to tack.

As the waves swept me sideways, closer and closer to the headland, I decided to try and start the engine and motor sail. If the engine failed, my only course would have been to turn tail and head back to Kinsale with a quartering wind. It was already two thirty in the afternoon; I had been at sea for four hours and had made little headway. After straining for some time, the engine eventually started, and I slowly increased the revolutions as it warmed up. With the additional thrust, *Celtic Gold* slowly responded to the tiller and I headed into the raging sea. I was now in the Gulf Stream and taking the full impact of the Atlantic swell.

It was not easy. The tide was now against a Force 5 westerly and I had to head straight into it. The sea was choppy and lumpy and the breaking waves crashed over the bows of *Celtic Gold* as she smashed into them, angry green water swilling down the decks and back to the cockpit. I ducked behind the spray hood. Putting the tiller on autohelm for five minutes, I went down below to get my lunch of soda bread and cheese and a cup of tea only to find water leaking through the side windows and dropping on to the chart. The cabin was in a mess with stowed gear having broken loose. I cleared up as best I could, but staying below just made me feel queasy. The autohelm was struggling with the buffeting the boat was receiving from the combined force of the waves and wind so I quickly took over. So much was going on that I didn't have a chance to consider at the time whether I was frightened or not. I was determined to pull through and tried to conserve my energies.

By tea time I had just pulled abeam of the Seven Heads with its old lighthouse about two miles off. I still had almost twenty miles to go to Glandore with no port of refuge in between and less than six hours of light left. At my present rate I was only making three knots and soon the tide would turn against me. Time was running out and in the forefront of my mind was the warning in the *Cruising Directions* that there are no leading lights in Glandore and that it should not be approached at night.

Seven Heads was aptly named and it was confusing to work out which headland related to the ones on the chart. I skirted Clonakilty Bay, but by five o'clock I was still only half way to

Glandore. I began to have serious doubts about making it by dusk. The high swell with its breaking waves seemed increasingly threatening. *Celtic Gold* went down into deep troughs and was unable to pick up her bows in time and crashed through the oncoming crests. As I approached Galley Head, my speed over the ground was reduced to about two knots and I had to take the sea and the wind on the nose. I seemed to be getting into a situation without an alternative except to go out to sea for the night. There was no port of refuge except Glandore. I began to appreciate Severin's talk of the hostility of the sea, but I still felt it to be indifferent rather than cruel.

I saw no boats out that day except a fishing boat off the Old Head of Kinsale and a well-reefed yacht running downwind like a rocket close to Seven Heads. It was reassuring to hear some fishermen talking to each other in their soft Cork accents over the VHF which I left on at all times at sea. In the early evening, the weather became more squally and the cloud broke up a little. At last, at eight o'clock, I rounded Galley Head. With the benefit of the wind on the port bow and the tide now running with me, I stopped the engine and hoisted the sails for Glandore. But where was it? Try as I might, I could not make out the narrow entrance amongst the small islands and rocks. 'Great care needed approaching at night,' was the refrain at the back of my brain; it was getting darker by the minute. What if the engine failed? The setting sun suddenly disappeared behind a dark bank of billowing cloud and all the features of the coastline faded into a common gloom.

I went below and made myself some hot chocolate and a couple of slices of soda bread. I carefully worked out a course and kept to it although it seemed to be taking me closer and closer to disaster. I told myself that if I could not find the entrance I would head out to sea for the night and heave to, although I was already feeling very tired after a long and hard day's sailing.

The entrance to Glandore is particularly difficult because on the west side there are two islands called Adam and Eve and on the east side several submerged rocks ominously called The Dangers. The local advice is to avoid Adam and to hug Eve, advice which had universal appeal, at least for a man. Just as I was about to abandon all hope, a miracle happened. For about five minutes, the dark bank of cloud ahead of me separated and a glorious shaft of golden light broke through and lit up an island where Adam Island should have been. I adjusted my course and soon was able to distinguish it from Rabbit Island further up the coast. Then, at last, the entrance to the inlet came into view. I followed local knowledge and gave a wide berth to Adam with its jagged rocks and steered close to diminutive Eve. It was a wonderful feeling to have a respite from the lumpy, steep-sided waves which had battered and tossed me all day. I then made out in the twilight the perches on my starboard side marking The Dangers and slowly nudged myself forward in the rapidly disappearing light. I eventually dropped anchor at ten thirty in the dark near a French and a British yacht, a cable south west of Glandore pier.

I had arrived safely. It had been my first single-handed sail in very difficult conditions. I had come through and was quietly pleased rather than elated. To my pleasant surprise, I had a call on the VHF from Stan on *Mustard Seed* who had left Kinsale before me and had seen me come in. He said he had been held up in the creek for five days because of the prevailing south westerlies: 'We've been here so long that John is thinking of seeking election as president!' He was surprised that I should have attempted the leg from Kinsale in such conditions, especially on my own.

I could see the lights and hear the warm laughter from a pub about half a mile away; after the wildness of the sea, they were very reassuring and enticing. I wanted to go ashore and celebrate but I felt too tired to pump up the rubber dinghy. With the release of the tension, I was ravenous and I dined in the dark in the cockpit on a large plate of noodles, cheese, carrot, tomato followed by an apple, yoghourt, and a pint of soya milk. The simple fare felt like a feast.

After hanging up my anchor light from the forestay, I tumbled into my bunk and fell asleep immediately. But it was not for long. The westerly wind was still blowing hard down from the hills. I woke up with a start to find *Celtic Gold* pitching and snatching at its single anchor like an angry horse. I was not in deep water and had let out all the chain but I was worried that I would drag the anchor and be swept on to the rocky shore only a cable away. I got out of the hatch several times during that night to check my position against the corner of a church and the chimney of a house. There was a constant racket, the halyards knocking against the mast, the waves slapping on the hull, and contents of the cabin banging and groaning. Rain swept across the choppy water in the creek. When I got up soon after dawn, I found the windows were still leaking and everywhere was damp. I made myself some porridge and hot tea and consoled myself with the thought that the Vikings survived in open boats.

The weather forecast for the next few days was for persistent rain from the south west so I decided to explore Glandore and its environs. I pumped up the dinghy, rowed ashore and with difficulty pulled it up the slipway above the tide line in Glandore harbour. A cluster of houses huddled around the harbour and stretched along the cliff road. It was pouring with rain so I kept my yellow oilskins on. I decided to go and visit the Dromberg Stone Circle.

It was about four miles away. I trudged up the hill out of town and past hilly fields of rough pasture grazed by fat cows hunched in the rain. After a new and ostentatious Catholic church set in a sterile lawn, I turned down a lovely lane, its luxuriant borders overgrown with young hazel and ash trees interwoven with red and purple fuchsias, flowering blackberries, and spiralling honeysuckle. Despite the rain, the mild climate enabled violets and anemones to grow even in winter. I left my dripping, entangled lane to follow a grassy track which took me to the stone circle.

It had a very dramatic setting. The circle was on a wide shoulder with a high green hill to the north and a series of hills undulating south towards the sea. Heavy drizzle from the south west swept across the ancient stones, running down their grey, craggy sides amongst the yellow and brown lichens. I was alone and cut off from the rest of the world by the mist. As I entered the circle of stones, I felt I was treading on hallowed ground.

I walked slowly round and weaved amongst the stones. I touched their cold, wet roughness. I knew science would describe them as a chance collection of atoms, but I could not help feeling a kind of vibrating energy emanating from them. Perhaps it was my imagination, lost as I was in Celtic mist in a place where unknown rituals and ceremonies had taken place; perhaps I was succumbing to a millennarian longing for contact with lost civilisations; perhaps there really were some invisible forces at work. I had become, during my weeks of navigation, very aware of my position on earth and the direction of the North Pole. Yet when I took out a small hand-held compass in the middle of the circle, I found that its needle swung round indecisively and failed to point to magnetic north.

It seemed that the measurements of the circle were based on the 'megalithic yard' which measures 2.72 feet. I paced the diameter and found that it was about ten megalithic yards. Originally there must have been seventeen stones in the circle which varied in size and shape. Two appeared to be male and female symbols. I noticed that on the west side was a horizontal stone faced by two stones on the east which were larger than the others in the ring. The builders were clearly aware of the alignment of the sun and its diurnal and annual passage through the heavens, for the axis of these two stones with the recumbent one opposite was aligned to the mid-winter sunset. In addition, cup marks were visible on a large lying stone to the south west as well as on one of the tall portal stones to the north east.

I tried to imagine how the site on the wooded hill by the sea must have appeared to the Middle Stone Age hunters who first penetrated the dense woodland of ancient Ireland from the north west of Britain, probably crossing over a land bridge from Scotland 12,000 years ago which disappeared when the sea rose at the end of the last Ice Age. The megaliths themselves were left by New Stone Age people who came later from Europe about 5,000 years ago and who farmed the land and who dwelt in wattle and daub houses with thatched roofs. They probably did not live to more than thirty years old. I pictured them wrapped in skins gathering with their shaman around the stone circle in the pouring rain on the winter solstice. On that dire day, when the sun had reached its lowest ebb of the year, they no doubt prayed for its return to northern climes to bring new life to the plants and animals and light to their long darkness. If the sun should shine that day as it set in the west and align with their circle, it would have been a time of great celebration.

Later generations clearly felt the spiritual energy of the stone circle at Dromberg on the hill looking south over the sea. When the Celts arrived about a hundred years before the birth of Christ, they no doubt took over the circle for their own rituals; it was still known locally as the Druid's Ring. I found this ancient site far more spiritual a centre than the new church on the hill I had seen on my way over. I was intrigued by its mysteries. Why should those Stone Age people have built these circles and raised massive columns which still have such aesthetic and spiritual power? Was it to focus the earth's energies, to align with underground water courses, to link heaven and earth? Did it stand as a symbol of harmony, both for the local community and the widening circles of life which embraced the cosmos itself? Did it generate a subtle energy which ensured the fertility of the soil and the health of the tribe? Was it even an observatory capable of predicting complex astronomical phenomena, including lunar eclipses?

What is certain is that although the creators of the megalithic monuments were simple farmers, they had great architectural skills and were highly sophisticated astronomers. The site at Dromberg is only one of over 1,200 Megalithic sites in Ireland. They could be linked with each other, for many form straight lines – leys – over hundreds of miles across the countryside. Whatever their exact relationship and meaning, they reflect a huge investment of energy by a scattered farming community who did not possess the wheel or the horse. Even more fascinating, there are common elements in the megaliths – dolmens, menhirs and passage graves – built all along the Atlantic seaboard from Morocco to Scotland which suggest that the builders shared a common seaborne culture, a culture which was seriously fragmented in later centuries. It was indeed an Atlantean culture created by seafarers who travelled in wooden ocean-going boats. Certainly at that time, over 5,000 years ago, it would have been safer and easier to travel by sea than through the dense forests which were inhabited by wild animals and marauding bands.

On my return to Glandore, I stopped to have some tea in Casey's Bar on the outskirts of the village which overlooked the inlet. Its Gaelic name was Cuan Dor, 'Harbour of Oak', and oak trees still grew on the surrounding hills. In the drizzle-filled bay, I could just make out *Celtic Gold* swaying at anchor and the hazy outlines of Adam and Eve, a mile apart, for ever separated by dark grey waters.

Alone in the polished snugness of Casey's Bar which was almost four centuries old, I chatted to grey-haired Mrs Casey who was the fourth-generation owner. She was concerned that she might be the last: one of her sons was out fishing with the trawlers with 'the Brandon boys', while the other was only too ready to take off in a visiting yacht 'at the drop of a hat'. Her dead husband had clearly been a local character, for a poem on the wall by a visiting bard celebrated his powers of story-telling – 'a gift of whose worth he was sure'. His widow clearly disapproved of the literary company her husband kept in his drinking days; she turned very cagey when I said I was a writer.

I went outside to make a telephone call to my son Dylan and friends back in Wales. Luxuriant ivy had virtually covered the telephone box and was beginning to invade the interior. As I was dialling, a young woman appeared with a baby in a buggy and waited patiently in the pouring rain. I suggested she went before me as I was well protected in my oilskins. When she had finished, she asked: 'Did you come here by boat?'

'Yes, my yacht's down in the creek.'

'I've done some sailing myself. You must be in need of a hot shower. If you want one I'm staying in the cottage down there.' She pointed down towards the harbour.

'That's very kind of you. I've got a few telephone calls to make and I'll decide afterwards.'

Given the fact that I was a complete stranger, I thought that it was a very brave and generous offer from a young woman with a baby. I was cold and truly in need of a shower, so after my calls I went down the steps to her house. She provided me with a clean, thick towel, soap and shampoo. I had a gloriously hot shower.

Her name was Mary Beechinor. Over tea, I learned that she was on holiday from Cork and that her husband would be joining her later. He worked in the computer industry – Cork has become a European centre of micro-electronics – and she worked as a physiotherapist. With her nine-month-old baby crawling on the carpet, she told me how she had done postgraduate studies in Belfast. She had had no trouble there as a Catholic staying with a Protestant girl friend, although she admitted she would not like to make her home up north. She and her husband had sailed with friends up the west coast of Ireland as far as Inishbofin Island and had enjoyed every minute of it, especially the hot showers they had managed to grab on the way.

When her husband David turned up, he was equally hospitable and insisted that I stay for dinner. He first took me through several villages in search of some two-stroke fuel for my Seagull outboard engine until we found a petrol station open. Although a Catholic himself, he recognised that the close links between the Catholic Church and the Irish State was a real problem for northern Protestants, especially in their opposition in the past to contraception, abortion and divorce. Only recently were contraceptives freely on sale, while abortion was not available and divorce due for a referendum. But he insisted that the Protestants were not discriminated against in the South. Indeed, they generally had a good reputation: 'Many people think the Church of Ireland people are more honest because they keep their word!'

After my hot shower, dinner and wine, I returned to my yacht, my whole body firing as well as my Seagull engine with its stomach filled with two-stroke and petrol. I had enjoyed the comfort and order of their house, but I was pleased to be back on my cosy, floating home. I lit the Tilly lamp and pondered on human generosity. I had experienced once again old-fashioned Irish hospitality from a couple working in the most advanced fields of technology. It was good to know that in this troubled world there were still Good Samaritans ready to help and trust passing wayfarers in the pouring rain.

The next day I made enquiries about a former resident of Glandore. In the early nineteenth century, it had been the home of William Thompson, author of *An Inquiry into the Principles of the Distribution of Wealth* (1824). He had developed a scheme of 'voluntary equality of wealth' and had looked forward to a time when the growth of reason would encourage all to contribute to the general good and to live in a society without government, private property, marriage and the family. But he was not one to rest in theory. After inheriting land to the north of Glandore, he formed a co-operative community in which his tenants shared any profits. Not surprisingly, Thompson's neighbouring landowners were alarmed by his utopian scheme since it might put ideas into the heads of their own tenants. And he was unable to win over the citizens of Glandore: they considered this atheist, humanist and rationalist to be a 'mystic' because of his eccentric ideals.

I was interested in Thompson not only because I had earlier in my life helped set up a rural community in which we shared our skills and goods but also because I had written a book about his intellectual guide, William Godwin, the father of philosophical anarchism. It was through Thompson that Godwin's vision of a free, classless and stateless society reached Marx, who mentioned the great Irish socialist in *Das Kapital*. Yet Thompson's kind of libertarian socialism was very different from the socialism which came to dominate the Irish working class movement, and he would have found the notion of the Irish Free State, founded after independence, as a contradiction in terms: no State can be free. No one in Glandore, sadly, had heard of him.

Until the rise of holiday making, the people of Glandore had relied on fishing. It was also the first harbour in Ireland to host an annual regatta (beginning in 1830) and it still continued the tradition. In the Glandore Inn, I noticed behind the bar a photograph of an old yacht called *Iolair* with the inscription that it had taken part in the Fastnet Race in 1975 on its seventieth birthday and that it would be back to participate in the race on its ninetieth. I thought no more of it until I saw a very similar yacht moored alongside Glandore pier. I spoke to a long-haired, bearded young American who emerged from a hatch and said that they had just sailed over from the Caribbean via the Azores. They had come to take part in the Fastnet which was to start in a couple of weeks. The yacht's name was the *Iolair*. It had two headsails like a cutter and a mizzen sail like a ketch. I would find the owner, Don Street, in a cottage up the hill, opposite the fishermen's chandlery.

I had vaguely heard of him. I knocked on his door and a sparse, wiry American in his late fifties invited me in in a croaky voice. He said it was his wife's house who came from West Cork.

'I live on my boat now; it's my home. My base is in the Caribbean. I used to have a house in Grenada until the Yanks blew it up when they retook the island from the Cubans.'

He was very proud of the fact that his yacht had no auxiliary: 'Some years ago, I threw my engine overboard. It was one of the best decisions of my life. I built myself a fine chart table in its place and since then I've written seven books and over a hundred and sixty articles on it.'

He seemed a man who knew his own mind and was not shy about his achievements. He told me that he had recently sailed to Brittany and back in a Dragon, two hundred miles in an open boat. He had offered a trophy for the oldest boat to take part in the Fastnet and seemed poised to win it himself. He also claimed to have written the first guide to the Caribbean. 'Everyone keeps taking from it; it's annoying but they tell me plagiarism is a form of compliment.' That's how I knew his name. My brother had also written a cruising guide to the Caribbean – one that I knew for a fact had been his own work! – and had once mentioned him.

Before I left Don Street in his wife's parlour, I asked him what sailing had taught him. 'Self-reliance and independence,' was his reply. 'Never rely on anyone except yourself.'

*

I spent two restless nights off Glandore, the boat crashing and banging and swinging in the unpleasant swell. Several times a night, I clambered through the fore hatch from my bunk to check the anchor. On the third day, the weather was still drizzly and windy, so I decided to shift moorings further up the creek off the little harbour of Union Hall. I only just managed to pull up the anchor on my own from the thick mud. As I motored across the creek, the head of a large seal with long whiskers and doleful eyes surfaced at my side and gave me a penetrating glance. I kept well clear of the fairway along which trawlers passed day and night. They would go out for more than a hundred miles, competing with Spaniards in the rich fishing grounds of the so-called Irish Box. Here was the new money which took the sons of publicans from behind the bar and out to sea. Union Hall, once a sleeping fishing village, was now the fourth largest fishing port in Ireland.

The old Irish name for the village was Brean Traigh, which means 'Foul Strand'. There was certainly some evil-smelling mud at the end of the creek but it probably earned its name from the time when warriors killed in battle were placed on the strand at the ebbing tide to be borne away for burial at sea. I would not mind going that way, although I would prefer to be reduced to ashes first.

The village, like its neighbour over the water, had sheltered another Irish radical in the previous century. Jonathan Swift came to stay in 1723 at Rock Cottage to get over the death of his friend Vanessa and wrote the poem 'Carberiae Rupes'. Born and educated in Dublin, the Protestant dean had won the love of his countrymen by his support for Irish independence. His most bitter satire had been *A Modest Proposal for Preventing the Children of the Poor People of Ireland from being a Burden to their Parents or County; and for making them beneficial to the Publick*. Turning the tables on those economists who argued that people are the real wealth of a nation, he suggested that the poor should devote themselves to rearing their children to be killed and sold for meat. In this outrageous essay on cannibalism, he even gave mouth-watering recipes. Although a Tory dean, he was in many ways a philosophical anarchist like William Thompson. This tendency comes through strongly in the last part of *Gulliver's Travels* (1726) where he contrasted the voluntary commonwealth of the Houyhnhnms – benevolent, sincere and rational horses – with the grasping, egoistic, deceiving and violent Yahoos who are all too human.

There was another ironic link with Union Hall. It had been the express purpose of Swift's *Drapiers Letters* to incite his fellow countrymen against a new coinage because it was introduced without the consent of the Irish parliament. The village of Union Hall had earned its unfortunate modern name to commemorate the abolition of that very parliament and the Act of Union of Great Britain and Ireland in 1801 which created the United Kingdom 'for ever'.

I walked from the new wharf at the harbour into the small village of Union Hall a mile away, past a collapsed house and up the curving main street with its four pubs. The first one, called The Boatman's Inn, was owned by a middle-aged Englishman, John Barclay, who had blown in from Liverpool via the Middle East and had married a young Cork girl called Jane. With his long grey wavy hair and moustache, he looked like a lean cross between a policeman and an ageing hippy.

He was under no illusion that he would be accepted by the local close-knit fishing community. The Irish owner of a neighbouring pub, he told me, had been there for twenty-nine years but she was still considered a 'blow in'. Nor did he expect to make his fame and fortune in the quiet backwater: 'Ireland's one of the greatest countries to live in – the way of life is much more relaxed – but it's hard to make a living here. Ireland has the highest cost of living in Europe after Sweden. A lot of people in the village have to do two or three jobs to make ends meet.'

It was true that the Irish economy was doing well, especially compared to the UK, its main trading partner. Ireland had the largest trade surplus as a percentage of GDP in the developed world and one of the highest growth rates coupled with low inflation: 'We're no longer a potato republic. It's a small country with a population of only three and a half million but the economy's so strong now that in a few years the EEC will turn the tap off. The only real problem is the high rate of unemployment; it's still about twenty per cent of the workforce and the young are not so keen on emigrating any more. Still, we'll muddle through. We'll sort out the lads in Brussels.'

But he was not impressed by the bureaucracy in the system which he claimed hampered entrepreneurs: 'My father had a business importing clothes in Wicklow but the customs made him fill twenty-three documents every time a shipment came in. In the end he had to stop because of all the red tape.'

My naturalised Irishman behind the bar was so keen to correct any possible misconceptions about his adopted countrymen: 'There's no class system here like in England. It's based on money. One generation can be working with their hands and the next generation's huntin' and dinin' with the highest in the land.'

And what of the Irish character?

'The general view that the Irish are cheerful, fun-loving and straight is true enough but they're not a nation of boozers. I wish they were! According to a recent survey, only a third of the Irish drink; a third are social drinkers; and a third are teetotallers. But I suppose the drinkers make up for the rest of them!'

We certainly did some drinking that night. Some English people came in from a yacht from Southampton sporting the blue ensign (the owner had been in the RAF) and the parlour filled up with locals young and old. It was a special occasion. A young musician, muscular with red curly hair, was going off to Germany in search of fame and fortune the next day. It would be the first time that he had ever left home. The curtains closed, the singing and drinking went on to the early hours. The old ballads of loss and departure that night were more poignant than ever.

It was lovely 'seagulling' back to *Celtic Gold* in the rubber dinghy. The drizzle and mist had at last lifted and the stars shone brightly in the dark sky. After all the troubles and worries I had left behind me, I felt at rest, centred and calm. I had a beautiful, deep sleep and woke up to see blue sky and sunlight dancing on the water. The yacht had swung on its anchor to face the north west during the night which meant that the wind was perfect to continue my voyage. I felt the exhilaration of the wild rover again.

I had already made a passage plan for the next leg. I intended to make for Baltimore, a large natural harbour, approachable in any weather, which was protected by Sherkin Island and Cape Clear from the swell of the Atlantic and the Gulf Stream. I was impatient to get going: *Mustard Seed* had already left and I had been holed up in Glandore creek for almost a week. Baltimore was only fifteen miles away, about four hours, and I decided to leave after lunch to make the best of the tides.

It was the first fine day for a couple of weeks and fluffy white clouds scudded across the blue skies in a Force 3 north westerly breeze. Perfect. The boat had become damp in the warm humidity and it was lovely to have a drying wind flowing through it, clearing the moist cobwebs of my mind as well as the mould spores of the cabin. I had a good lunch of soup and soda bread and cheese and stowed all the gear carefully. I deflated the rubber dinghy and lashed it to the coach roof.

I was all set at one o'clock to leave and confidently turned the key in the ignition. Nothing happened. I tried again. Nothing. I felt a hot flush across my temples and a terrible sinking feeling in my stomach. I couldn't face spending more time in Glandore and Union Hall, unlashing and pumping up the dinghy again and going in search of an engineer. I had already had trouble with a leaking fuel tank – a drip fell from the sump every two seconds which worked out about a pint of diesel every twelve hours – and I had been unable to find anyone to help me.

'Please God,' I implored under my breath, praying to a personal deity in whom in theory I did not believe. I tried a third time. Nothing happened. 'Damn it!' Invoking the Devil whose existence I also denied. I sat in the cockpit in despair.

'Well, the engine is my friend and I must find out what ails it.'

Flat batteries, was my first thought, as the engine did not turn. But on reflection I found that difficult to believe because the wind generator had been whirring away faithfully and I couldn't have used up all the electricity with the cabin lights. I went through the main connections from the battery to the ignition switch and to the starter motor. I turned the switch for a fourth time. Still no joy.

I tried to remain patient and rational. 'I will start the motor with the handle.' I got out the instruction book and went through the various stages, tying one of the piston levers to a piece of twine so that I could pull it down with my teeth once the engine was turning. I got the starting handle out and tried to swing the heavy fly wheel with all my might, but as soon as I pulled down, the piston lever lost its momentum and ground to a halt. I simply did not have enough strength to keep it going. The more I tried, the more tired I became. I eventually gave up.

What to do next? I would give the ignition one more try before going ashore to look for help. I turned the key: to my utter astonishment the engine turned and burst into fire. Thank God – perhaps He existed after all!

But then another thought struck me: 'What if the engine stops and fails to start at sea? Will I have to enter Baltimore Harbour and anchor under sail and single-handed?'

10

Islands and Bays

After hugging Eve and avoiding Adam for the last time, I hoisted the sails in the north westerly breeze and steered south west to Baltimore. It was a beautiful stretch of coastline with small pasture fields, some the better for bracken and gorse, subdivided by ancient stone walls. I had to keep clear of a string of small islands and submerged rocks. I enjoyed the challenge of sailing solo again and found I could manage easily on my own, especially with the help of the in-mast reefing and self-furling jib.

After passing by the enticing inlet of Castletownshend, I had an exhilarating sail through the sound between Toe Head and the Stags. The Stags were aptly named, a cluster of jagged rocks rising out of the long swell; they looked like a great black ship ploughing through the steep waves, sending spray and foam in all directions. They had taken the toll of many an unwary vessel, the most recent and spectacular being the *Kowloon Bridge* which went down nearby in 1987. Since she was carrying 2,000 tons of crude oil as well as iron ore, the sinking caused a major ecological disaster.

There was a confused sea in the sound. It was clearly a good fishing ground, for several small fishing boats had their nets out and I had to dodge and weave between the lobster pots. I found that a north westerly stream was setting me dangerously close towards the Stags so I had to tack sharply away.

During the previous night a cold front had passed over Ireland. The wind grew increasingly blustery during the day and the sea became choppier and more lumpy, but I enjoyed every minute of the invigorating sail. I felt confident in myself and the yacht. I had not taken any seasickness pills and did not feel the need for them. The only drawback was the noise of the engine which I kept going in neutral just in case it failed to start again.

Having passed the land-locked sea of Lough Hyne and skirted Kedge Island, the two large white beacons on the high cliffs which marked the entrance to Baltimore Harbour came into view. The harbour itself was formed by several islands – part of the Carbery hundred – and surrounded by low-lying hills. As I was tacking towards the narrow entrance between the two beacons, I suddenly heard out of the blue on the VHF a call for *Celtic Gold*. It was a woman's voice, with a Canadian accent: '*Celtic Gold*. This is *Mustard Seed*. Would you like to come to dinner? Over.'

It was Betty. How on earth did she know I was there? I had not told them that I would be leaving Glandore that morning and they could not yet see me.

'*Mustard Seed*. This is *Celtic Gold*. Yes, I would like to come to dinner. But how did you know that I was coming into Baltimore? Over.'

'*Celtic Gold*. This is *Mustard Seed*. I just had a sudden feeling that you were nearby. Over.'

I could see why Stan called her psychic.

Although the engine was still going, I wanted to see if I could come in under sail. Once through the entrance, it was difficult to make headway against the gusty wind from the west north west and I made slow progress along the buoyed channel. I eventually dropped anchor north west of the new pier in open water.

It was a difficult manoeuvre amongst the other yachts. After playing out the full chain in the shallow water I quickly realised that I had drifted back too close to some of them. I pulled the anchor up and tried again. It was better this time, but, still worried that I might drag the anchor, I decided to put out a kedge. Three times I tried to row out against the wind in the rubber dinghy piled high with the extra anchor attached to three metres of heavy chain and sixty metres of nylon cable. Three times I was driven back. I eventually got the Seagull outboard going and laid it, but not without getting wet from the spray.

It was a lovely feeling to sit down at last in the cockpit with a hot cup of tea and know that I was safe. I watched a seagull land on the fuel tank of the Seagull, totally unperturbed by the rocking and bobbing of the rubber dinghy. I would like to be like that. I threw it some biscuits which it gobbled up greedily and thanked me by shitting on the tank.

Later that evening, I had a relaxing meal on board *Mustard Seed* with Stan and Betty and their friends John and Pat. John told the story of a gent in a thick coat who asked a street urchin the way to the post office. He added, pulling up his warm collar: 'If you say your prayers, boy, you'll find your way to heaven.'

The boy replied: 'How do you know the way to heaven when you don't even know the way to the post office?'

Stan had more or less forsaken the land for the sea. He hardly ever left his boat. During the ten days they had been holed up in Glandore because of the weather, he had only gone ashore once and then with great reluctance. He told me that although he had been a telephone engineer for most of his life, he had always wanted to go to sea. His grandfather had been a captain on one of the last of the tall ships ('it had a lot of string') and his father had been a chief engineer in the Merchant Navy. I left the cosy snug of *Mustard Seed* with some of Betty's peanut cookies in my pocket, still warm from their wonder stove, and turned in for an early night.

I spent most of the next day with my head upside down in the well of the cockpit trying to extract the old fuel tank which was leaking more than ever. I had filled her up just before leaving Kinsale so I had a major job emptying her first by using a small cut plastic container. With the blood pulsating in my temples, I tried to remind myself that the bilges were as important as the sails.

Stan rowed over with a multimeter during the morning. I liked the way he always took his shoes off before coming down the hatchway into the cabin, like a Muslim entering a mosque. The batteries seemed fine and we checked the electrical contacts. But as soon as I turned on the ignition, the solenoid on the starter motor clicked and nothing happened. Stan suggested that it could be dirty brushes in the starter motor; he would help me clean them when we got to Dingle.

While I was working on the tank, a tough-looking character rowed over in an old clinker boat and demanded £6.00. I asked him what for.

'Harbour dues. I'm the harbourmaster.'

'That's a lot,' I said, thinking that I wouldn't be able to stay very long. 'It was only four pounds a night in Wicklow.'

'Well,' he said, 'in Baltimore it's six pounds.'

'How long can I stay for that?'

'A year.'

Baltimore was now a peaceful holiday resort and a convenient haven for visiting yachtsmen, but it had once been a centre for piracy and smuggling.

Along the remote headlands, I had seen several ruined castles which were part of a string of castles along the coast built by the O'Driscoll clan who had held sway for more than a thousand square miles between the Kenmare and Bandon rivers of south west Ireland. With their chief source of revenue from plundering ships and extracting harbour dues, they built the castles to defend themselves. The needed to: in 1537 Baltimore was sacked by the men of Waterford in revenge for the seizure of a Waterford ship.

The most notorious chief of the clan was Sir Fineen O'Driscoll who seized Spanish ships which ventured along the coast in the early seventeenth century on behalf of the English. Unlike Blarney, he readily handed over his clan lands to the English Crown to obtain Elizabeth's approval. He further angered his countrymen by leasing out Baltimore to English Protestant settlers from the south west of England.

The settlers must have rued the day they ever landed on these shores. On 20th June 1631 two large ships landed in Baltimore on a still summer's night, guided in by a local man from Dungarven. They had come from Algiers in North Africa, sailing through the Strait of Gibraltar and then steering due north across the Bay of Biscay to the southern shores of Ireland. Roughly awakened from their slumber, the good citizens of Baltimore were confronted with their worst nightmare. On their doorstep, they saw a fierce black intruder:

> And meet upon the threshold stone the gleaming sabre's fall
> And o'er each black and bearded face the white or crimson shawl,
> The yell of 'Allah!' breaks above the prayer, and shriek, and roar –
> Oh! Blessed God! The Algerine is Lord of Baltimore.

So wrote Thomas Davis in 1844, an Irish Protestant nationalist. The pirates from the Barbary Coast killed two people and shipped the entire populace of 163 souls – men, women and children – back with them to North Africa where they were sold as labourers and concubines. Only one man escaped and made it back to his native land to tell the tale. The pilot from Dungarven, who possibly resented the English settlers, was hanged by the Crown.

The sack of Baltimore was not an isolated case: Algerian ships once sailed as far north as Iceland and returned with 300 captives. It shows again the close maritime links between North Africa and Ireland since Phoenician times. Nevertheless, the Barbary pirates were no worse than the French, Spanish and English, who all engaged in privateering, and considered the merchant vessels of other nations to be fair game.

Apart from having a long tradition of piracy and boat building, Baltimore had given its name to the city in Maryland, USA. I learned in the Bushe's Bar overlooking the harbour that the link was reaffirmed by the arrival of the 129-foot schooner *Pride of Baltimore* in 1985. With his eye on the Irish vote, President George Bush also claimed that his ancestors came from Baltimore, but sceptical locals in Bushe's Bar chuckled in their pints at the thought.

The next day was Sunday and I decided to visit Sherkin Island for the day. I caught a ferry across the harbour from Baltimore's old stone pier. While I was waiting, kids dived into the clear water, splashing each other, shouting, 'You bastard!' and loving every minute of it. It was a blustery day, with dark-grey clouds sweeping in from the Atlantic.

It was so obvious who were the islanders and who were the visitors. The visitors wore shorts and short-sleeved shirts and sandals; they had tanned, oiled faces. The islanders were dressed in their Sunday best, the men uncomfortable in dark suits and black leather boots, the women in sober clothes and scarves. Once on board the old ferry, the tourists looked beyond the natives, their soft hands with gold rings grabbing the rough gunwales. Some stood in suede shoes on the hard wooden seats. A suave middle-aged man travelling with a well-dressed Dubliner discussed in Italian on his portable phone the merits of Sherkin Island as a film set. He had to shout above the noise of the engine and the sea; he could have telephoned in peace on the island, but he knew what sounded dramatic and adventurous to his boss.

The island men sat silently and stiffly, their boots tucked under them. As we hit the waves beyond the stone pier, they were out of the wind, wisely; they half smiled, serenely. The visitors, the full spray hitting their red faces and black cameras, ran for cover.

We landed below a ruined abbey, built by Franciscan monks in the fifteenth century. It had been a centre of Latin learning until it was burned down by a band of Waterford men. I made my way to a remote strand on the Atlantic side of the island. There were a few scattered cottages along the winding track which ran through a copse of elm and sycamores and then passed bare, stone-walled, hilly fields. I came across a small school overlooking a creek and a little library for the resident population of ninety. After the stench of the diesel on board, the moist earth smelt sweet, strangely familiar, like a lost memory slowly re-emerging. It was strange too to have flies buzzing around my head and to see butterflies flit over the long grass of the verges. The fragrance of honeysuckle and mowed hay carried on the wind which tossed the heads of the red and purple fuchsias in the hedgerows. An old jalopy, its one wing dented badly, narrowly missed me as it lurched into a pothole. No MOTs here. I met one or two people on the road who simply said 'Hello, there' and smiled.

The sea was always around the corner, and I was never more than fifteen minutes from the shore. I managed to find the beach I was looking for – Silver Strand, a secluded cove between two rugged headlands resolutely facing the Atlantic. I sat on a large ancient tree trunk, whitened by salt, which had been washed ashore by the winter storms. In the distance, I could make out Cape Clear Island rising high out of the grey, wind-tossed sea. I noticed that there was none of the plastic jetsam to be found on the shores of England and Wales, only pieces of well-weathered wood, dried seaweed, and a few nylon strands of fishing net. Looking more closely at the fine silver sand which poured between my fingers, I realised that the grains were not grey but made of tiny pieces of blue, yellow and white stone.

The water was as limpid as I had ever seen in the Indian Ocean or in the Caribbean. From behind a dark, wrack-weeded rock two little girls emerged and went down to the sea with their buckets and spades. They were the only signs of a human presence. Leaving their buckets at the edge, they rushed squealing into the water, skipping and playing amongst the waves that curled, rolled over and spent their force in a mass of boiling spray on the silvery strand.

On my return to the ferry landing, I climbed a hill to the Jolly Roger tavern overlooking the sparkling bay of Baltimore Harbour. Below, by the shore, were the collapsed walls of Dun na Long, the 'Fort of the Ships', another O'Driscoll castle. The bar was packed with islanders and visitors. A young Welsh woman with her fiddle joined the battered guitarist and jovial accordion player who were all the better for drink. An old man at the bar, no doubt settled there since his return from the mainland church, was slumped in his tight Sunday suit and polished boots. Red-faced and weatherbeaten, he was undoubtedly a fisherman-farmer like most of the islanders. After a particularly moving ballad in Gaelic, he tried to wipe away the tears from his red eyes; he forgot that he wore thick black-rimmed glasses and knocked them off. A young woman came up and gave him a hug.

On the ferry back to Baltimore, a young man suddenly got up

on his own and danced with his hands straight down his sides in traditional Irish fashion. The sea was his music, the wind his song. The last golden rays of the setting sun lit up his smiling face. It had been another good day.

Having run out of money, I caught a bus the following morning to Skibbereen where the English Protestant settlers had moved after the raid by Barbary pirates. It was a bustling and picturesque market town stretching along a high street which led to a square. It had a fine statue dedicated to the rebels of 1798 called the 'Maid of Erin', a sturdy woman with her left arm across her ample breasts and her right hand on a harp at her side. Half a century later, the town had been badly hit by the potato blight and the Great Famine which followed. The actions of the English landlords and wealthy Irish farmers who continued to export grain at the time had not been forgotten. A well-known song of a poor farmer who managed to emigrate with his two-year-old son ends with the stanza:

O, father dear! The day is near
When in answer to the call,
Each Irish man and woman
  will rally one and all;
I'll be the man to lead the van
  beneath the flag of green,
When loud and high we raise the cry:
  'Revenge for Skibbereen!'

Skibbereen was now fast becoming the cosmic centre for New Age 'blow-ins': many Dutch, Germans and English had settled in the area. In the local wholefood shop, where I stocked up on victuals, I read signs on the notice board offering services to heal and expand the body, mind and spirit: reflexology, Tarot reading, shiatsu, astrology, massage and movement therapy, spiritual healing, as well as a 'Ballroom of Romance'. There was also an intriguing guide to the Sheela-na-Gigs of Ireland, those crudely carved images of women exposing their inflated genitalia found in obscure places in medieval churches. Some say they date back to pagan times and the worship of Mother Earth; others that they reflect male fear of being absorbed and engulfed by the female; others again that they are a Christian warning of the destructive temptation of women.

I fancied they contained elements of all three, but I was informed by the guide that they represented 'one of our most important connections with the Ancient Goddesses of the pre-historic era forming a bridge between us and the long-forgotten time when the Goddess was revered as the natural, most obvious symbol of All Life. In losing the *sheela-na-gigs* from our churches, we lost the feminine aspect of religious belief and their removal from places of worship is illustrative of the loss of the 'women's church' and the place of women within Christianity. *Sheela-na-gigs* were an expression of our essential connection to the Mother, the Goddess of the Land, and the essence of women's place in religion and society.'

Up the road from the wholefood shop, strong female warriors were running the oldest pub in Skibbereen, the Wine Vaults, (established 1854), in New Age fashion. The owner, Lynne Deakin, with flowing robes, red hair, blue eyes and a ring through her nose, had blown in from Sheffield, where she had been a probation officer. She had bought up the derelict pub, cleaned out the cobwebs and empty bottles, and now served a fine pint of stout with vegetarian food. It had become a centre for traditional music. I supped with a couple of old locals at the bar, who seemed to enjoy the homespun and caring atmosphere.

Back on board *Celtic Gold*, I was still having trouble with my fuel tank. Having at last extracted it from the black hole of the hold, I rowed it ashore in my rubber dinghy to get it repaired. The tank was heavy and difficult to manoeuvre and I lugged it up to a yard on the quayside in Baltimore. Having no joy in the boatyards on the quay, I rowed it to a huge boatyard half a mile away at the end of a creek. At first sight it seemed completely derelict but around the hull of an old wooden fishing boat, there were a couple of people moving. The boss, Con Minihane, was a tall man of few words. He was busy but after much pleading on my part – I would be stuck otherwise and my grand venture would grind to a halt – he agreed to try and weld the tank.

At the turn of the century, Baltimore had been the largest fishing port in Ireland with about eighty vessels registered locally. Before the US fishing market collapsed in the 1920s, it was said you could walk from Baltimore pier to Sherkin Island across their decks. It had also been a great boat building centre. The old Baltimore boatyard had built in 1923 the *Saoirse* in which Cruise O'Brien sailed around the world and as late as 1975 had launched the *Emer Marie*, the largest wooden fishing vessel built in Ireland. But it had gone bust and had remained derelict until Con Minihane had taken it over.

Minihane took me to show me the burnt-out metal hull of a yacht in the dim interior of the boatshed and asked me whether I thought it was worth repairing. It did not look like it.

'It was owned by a Swiss man who said he was going around the world,' he explained. 'The yacht caught fire in the harbour. The owner got £75,000 insurance money and sold the hulk to me. The funny thing is that he came ashore dressed in a suit and carrying a suitcase when it caught fire!'

After leaving the fuel tank at the boatyard, I caught a ferry to Cape Clear Island, the most southerly in Ireland, rising about twenty miles out in the Atlantic. The new fast ferry was called the *Naomh Chiaran* after St Kieran who was born on the island. The ferry was the islanders' lifeline, bringing in summer visitors and everything they needed and taking out their rubbish and exports of fish and pottery. We sped through the narrow sound between the jagged shores of Sherkin and Spanish Islands out into the long Atlantic swell, pitching and rolling in the fresh balmy breeze. The next inlet was scattered with islands exposed to the prevailing south westerlies and had the marvellous name of Roaring Water Bay. It was a beautiful sunny day, with a few white puffs of clouds high in the light blue sky. I could have been in the Aegean.

We passed the infamous Gascanane Rock which lies between Cape Clear Island and Sherkin Island and is often submerged in the strong tidal currents and swell. Tradition has it that each new visitor to Cape Clear should compose a verse or poem to appease the rock; if not the sea will become treacherous on his return. I came up with:

Great Gascanane
Swirling in the Gulf Stream
Guard your secrets
And stay gloriously green.

Cape Clear Island rose out of the sparkling sea, a large rounded dome. I could just make out some windmills on its bald summit. Its steep slopes were divided by small stone-walled fields, many overgrown with bracken, and scattered with isolated white homesteads. The fields had been created by the islanders, who cleared the stones and made the walls as they went along, carrying up seaweed and sand on their backs and by donkey to improve the fertility of the rocky soil. They had become almost entirely dependent on the potato crop: when the harvest failed during the Great Famine the population was decimated. I could still just make out the remains of the potato ridges high up the slopes. The old marks remain but not the hands that made them.

There was a narrow entrance between the steep rock cliff and pointed rocks into the small harbour. Young boys dived from the stone quay into the crystal clear water, the sun's rays reflected by the white sandy bottom. Great waves of shining dark brown kelp attached to rocks swayed and danced in the gentle swell. I looked out for the otters, which islanders call water dogs, but they were too wary that day.

I asked an old islander on the quay the time of the last ferry. 'Nine o'clock tomorrow morning,' he replied. My heart sank but then I noticed a twinkle in his grey eyes. He was joking.

The signs along the island's narrow tracks were only in Irish. I was in a Gaeltacht area, one of the few remaining Irish-speaking pockets in the republic. A crowd of youngsters from Dublin with their backpacks had got off the ferry to enjoy a spell of freedom from home and their first contact with their ancient linguistic roots on this remote island out in the Atlantic.

By the harbour there were the ruins of an old church named after St Kieran dating from the twelfth century. I took the very steep climb out of the harbour through abandoned fields overgrown with brambles, gorse and bracken, to the spot where St Kieran was born in 352. At the age of thirty, he went to Rome for twenty years to learn about the new religion and then returned in 402 to preach the gospel to the islanders, long before the arrival of St Patrick. In Cornwall, St Kieran is known as Piran. He is also celebrated in Brittany on his feast day of March 5th.

Piran took Christianity to Cornwall, a two-day sail away via the Scilly Isles. Like so many early Celtic Christians, he had a great love of wild creatures. There is a delightful story that on his arrival in Cornwall he sat under a tree where a boar was lying. Sensing his love, the wild boar began tearing branches and grass with his teeth and built Piran a simple shelter. They were soon joined by other animals of the forest: a fox, a badger, a wolf and a doe. Thus the first animal monastery was founded.

The Irish summer school pupils and day trippers brought by

the ferry had helped check the continual emigration of the islanders. But the most far-seeing innovation in recent times had been the development of an island co-operative. It drew on the islanders' age-old tradition of mutual aid and had developed a direct and participatory form of democracy, with all the 200 islanders deciding on the important issues. It had even pioneered a wind energy system, the first of its kind in Ireland.

I walked across the island – about three miles long and a mile wide – in search of Megalithic sites – dolmens (boulders on stone pillars), ogham stones (stones inscribed with the early Irish ogham script) and standing stones. On the eastern end were the Gallan Stones which were meant to represent three warriors who had been petrified by a spell, although only two stones were now standing. On my way to the old lighthouse, I also passed the site of the famous Cape Clear Stone, some 4,500 years old, with its beautifully carved spiral designs, zig zags, and snake lines. The designs probably represent maps of the heavens. I looked for but did not come across any of the several underground tunnels or souterrains said to be on the island. Perhaps it was just as well; I liked the idea that there were still hidden mysteries, as mysterious as the weird spirals on the ancient rocks.

I then made my way to Lough Errol in the south west of the island. I skirted the lake and walked across fields to the edge of the high rocky cliff, the most southerly point of Ireland. About four miles away in the west, I could make out the infamous Fastnet, an isolated black rock surmounted with a grey lighthouse which rose like an arthritic finger out of the surging Atlantic swell. The very name of the Fastnet filled mariners with fear. My own stomach tightened at the thought that I would be rounding it in a few days' time. Beyond, in the blue haze, I could just see Mizen Peak which rose behind Mizen Head, the most south westerly point of Ireland.

*

Before I left Baltimore, Paul Green joined me. I had got to know him during the navigation course held on dark winter nights in North Wales. We had a common interest in East Africa. He had worked in Zanzibar and its neighbouring island Pemba in the Indian Ocean as a surveyor, correcting the old colonial maps which he had found to be surprisingly accurate. He was an experienced dinghy sailor, with an excellent grasp of the theory of navigation, but like me had had little opportunity to practise it. Our abilities would be well tested in the next leg of the voyage.

I picked up a specially-made fuel tank from the boatyard and spent a difficult morning putting it back into place. Testing the engine, I found again the electrics would not work: we traced the fault this time, to a bad connection to the starter motor. The whole system would have to be overhauled. It was not very reassuring to know that I could not rely on the engine as I headed westwards to the exposed coasts of Ireland and the full force of the Atlantic. Having experienced his fair share of breakdowns in the African bush, Paul sagely observed that when you solve one set of problems, another one always comes along.

I had now been in Baltimore for a week and was anxious to get going. The weather was far from ideal but there was no forecast of a break. It was already the end of July and according to past analyses of the weather it could only get worse. I could expect more rainfall, stronger winds, and an increased risk of gales. And I still had the most dangerous part of my voyage to complete in the remotest and wildest part of Ireland.

11

The Lonely Rock

It was now 26th July and I'd been at sea for over five weeks. Cloud was building up and blowing in from the east and the hazy visibility was moderate to poor. As soon as we passed through the narrow entrance of Baltimore harbour with its white beacons on the cliffs, we experienced a strong swell with very high waves and deep troughs. The easterly wind gusted up to twenty-two knots, a Force 6, on our port quarter. *Celtic Gold* began to roll sickeningly and I soon felt queasy. After clearing Cape Clear Island, a strong tidal stream set us towards the Fastnet and I had to keep adjusting my course accordingly in order to round it safely.

The Fastnet lived up to its Irish name, Carraig Aonar, the 'Lonely Rock'. It was, as I had seen from the cliffs of Cape Clear, a jagged finger which rose eighty-five feet out of the grey waters and pointed accusingly to the dark-grey heavens. A giant was said to have picked it up from Mount Gabriel and hurled it far out into the angry sea. For centuries, its visibility was a good indication of the weather for local fishermen. Many a ship came to grief on its serrated sides before the first lighthouse of cast iron was built there in 1854. Even that could not withstand the force of the winter storms. After a fierce Atlantic storm had taken away part of the rock, grey granite blocks were shipped in from Cornwall to build a new lighthouse which took ten years to complete, in 1906. The foreman in charge sometimes stayed on the rock for a year at a time; what could have been his thoughts and feelings while he surveyed his bleak watery kingdom?

Although the Fastnet became a shining beacon for many in their darkness and fear, for countless thousands it had tragic associations. As a natural landmark for ships on the transatlantic routes, it became known as the teardrop of Ireland: it was the last sight of their homeland for emigrants on their way to a new life in America. And in recent times, it has given its name to the gruelling race which took so many lives in the storm of 1974. The very word Fastnet sends a tingle down the spines of most yachtsmen.

It was with all these thoughts in mind that I sailed around the lighthouse. It was an awesome sight: I could see the waves surging and crashing on the island, only to withdraw with white water pouring off the black rocks. It was the most southerly point in Ireland, and I kept clear of the traffic separation zone for the transatlantic ships by sailing close inshore to it.

After the Fastnet, I set course for my next port of call, Crookhaven, which was seven miles away just tucked in from Mizen Head. The wind was beginning to ease, but running with it still caused *Celtic Gold* to wallow uncomfortably. Wind was now against tide which made the high swell worse. It was therefore a pleasure to see the solid white lighthouse on Rock Island at the entrance to the inlet of Crookhaven. The sky had cleared by now and we ran in on our jib until we were abreast of the village. It was a lovely anchorage, accessible by day or night. To the north of the inlet there was a steep cliff of granite and the signs of an old quarry; on the southern village side, the rough terrain was flatter, with coarse grass, flaming yellow gorse, and bright green lichens on the scattered grey rocks.

After dropping anchor, we went ashore to a pub where we met Jim who played an accordion. In the summer, he lived on his motor-sailer *Quest* moored in the inlet with his daughter who worked in a local garlic butter factory.

'What's a man from Tipperary doing with a boat?' he joked rhetorically and then answered his own question. Although he came from the landlocked town in the middle of Ireland, his great grandfather had been in the British Navy and had ended up as a coastguard in nearby Schull. After a severe car accident, Jim had been drawn to the sea, although he knew little about sailing. He had chosen Crookhaven as his base because of fond memories of holidaying there as a boy with his father. Becoming depressed, he had overeaten, but now proudly boasted that a high protein diet had enabled him to lose five stone in six months.

Winking at me, he accompanied some holiday makers from Dublin who sang sugary English and American pop songs while he clearly preferred to sing traditional Irish ballads. I suspected they cared little for local sensibilities, like the Frenchwoman who had blown up a famed landmark on her property – a watch tower built in Napoleonic times – simply because it was in her way. The Dublin crowd became increasingly raucous and boorish. When it came to singing 'My Old Man's a Dustman', Jim packed away his accordion and we went back to his yacht for a drink before turning in.

He read all the yachting press although admitted that he had difficulty in understanding the principles of navigation. He was a careful observer of local weather and warned me that the westerlies funnelled down the inlet and could create problems. During the notorious gale which caused such havoc in the Fastnet race, a local fisherman had, on his own initiative, shifted all the moored yachts over to the shelter of the quarry pier in the lee of Granny Island. He rang up the owners to let them know, but one ungrateful woman insisted that he return her yacht to its mooring. As expected, it was swept away and wrecked on the shores of Cape Clear Island. Was this another canny insurance claim, like the one of the Swiss round-the-world-yachtsman in Baltimore, I wondered.

We set off next morning to sail around Mizen Head to Castletown Bearhaven. The forecast was not good. A frontal trough was coming in from the Atlantic bringing thundery showers. We left our snug anchorage at eleven o'clock under a cloudy sky which threatened rain. I gave Mizen Head a two-mile berth and made sure that the tidal streams, which could run up to four knots during springs, were in our favour. It soon began to rain and visibility grew poor. We lost sight of Mizen Head, the most south westerly point of mainland Ireland, where Haughey's *Celtic Mist* had once come a cropper on a calm, clear day.

Despite the weather, I felt relaxed and *Celtic Gold* sailed well in the south easterly breeze on a moderate swell. The grey-green sea looked mysterious and I liked the feeling of being cut off from the rest of the world in the heavy rain, neither seeing nor being seen. Twice we heard the engines of boats in the distance, one for quite a long time, but they eventually faded away. We were left to our splendid isolation from the rest of humanity. The area was renowned for its seabirds and it was a delight to see the gannets swooping by in a line and groups of kittiwakes bobbing on the surface of the sea. Little black storm petrels skimmed the waves like swallows. As if to confirm that all was well, two dolphins joined us for a while after lunch.

The rain ceased in the early afternoon, long enough for us to get a fix from the low-lying Mizen Head, identifiable by Mizen Peak a mile to the north east, and Three Castle Head further west. Neither was very spectacular, although the cliffs between them were rugged, steep and uninviting. We set a course northwards across Dunmanus Bay and Bantry Bay towards Bere Island. Drizzle descended and the wind from the south east picked up to a Force 4. At least it was behind us and we did not have the prevailing south westerlies to beat against. In the thick mist and drizzle, visibility grew very poor, and all around was grey. The sea was grey, the sky was grey, the very world was grey. It was beginning to feel eerie.

I went down to put on the kettle and check the chart for our entrance to Castletown Bearhaven by Bere Island when I heard Paul shout insistently: 'Peter, you'd better come up on deck!'

I couldn't believe my eyes. The thick mist had suddenly lifted and there straight ahead towering over us was a great black cliff face. Perched incongruously high up on the rocky cliff was a white lighthouse; it looked as if it had been left high and dry by a sudden and drastic drop in the sea level.

I had not expected to make landfall for at least half an hour. I quickly hove to by backing the jib, and, with the mainsail flapping wildly, went down below to check our position. I told Paul not to take his eyes off the lighthouse and to take a bearing off it. It soon became clear that the lighthouse on the rock could only be the one on Ardnakinne Point on Bere Island at the entrance to Castletown Bearhaven. We were exactly on course but we had underestimated the effect of the tides in our calculations. We had been incredibly lucky. If the mist had not lifted at that moment we could have merrily sailed right into the cliff. Equally, if we had not made landfall at the foot of the lighthouse, it would have been difficult to work out exactly where we were. The incident underlined the need for a constant lookout, especially in poor visibility. After sailing up the Piper Sound, I appreciated the full import of Paul's observation that a pilot's definition of a good landing is 'one you will awake from'.

Bere Island seemed large and bare. I later met an islander who recalled that when he was a boy in the fifties there was no electricity and little to buy. People lived off a few acres of land and fishing. 'We were happy,' he recalled, 'and there was a strong sense of community. We did not go without. In the evenings we would entertain each other with stories. It's not the same any more. Young people of my generation left and now foreigners are buying up the old cottages for holiday homes. There's no more water in the wells.'

It is the same story in the remote islands all over Europe: the drift to the cities of the young and the seasonal take-over of the traditional dwellings by the urban rich. As a result, the local economy is undermined and a traditional way of life and culture is being slowly strangulated.

I thought of the anonymous poem of the *Old Woman of Bere*

The sea crawls from the shore
Leaving there
The despicable weed,
A corpse's hair.
In me,
The desolate withdrawing sea . . .

And still the sea
Rears and plunges into me
Shoving, rolling through my head
Images of the drifting dead.

The Berehaven Sound between Bere Island and the mainland provided excellent shelter. It was the second-largest natural harbour in the world. The British Navy maintained a base there until 1938 and Churchill is said to have considered at one time swopping the six counties of Ulster for a permanent naval base in order to protect the south west Atlantic approaches to the British Isles.

Castletown Bearhaven on the chart, or Castletownbere as it is locally known, is not a very inviting place. The tide does not flush out its waters which are oily and dark brown. It is the largest whitefish fishing port in Ireland with over eighty trawlers. The tell-tale smell could not be avoided and when the wind was blowing in the wrong direction, the smell of the fish meal factory was almost unbearable.

It poured with rain all next day and a thick mist hung over the port. Apart from wandering around the windy and wet streets of the grey town and watching the trawlermen on the quayside unload their catch, there was little else to do. The men wore yellow oilskins and cowboy boots. I assumed there were not many visiting English yachtsmen to annoy them. We were a different breed: the trawlermen went to sea to earn a livelihood and often hated the sea, while yachtsmen spent a great deal of money sailing and loved it.

Shrouded in fog and drizzle, I thought how similar Castletownbere was to any other trawler port in Britain: there were the same busy quays, the same opportunist gulls, the same dull food in the cafés. The difference was that the pubs were cosier and the people seemed warmer. And of course there was the inevitable monument in the main square to local Irish rebels; this time a battalion of the IRA.

Paul and I spent a morning squeezing ourselves into the transom locker of *Celtic Gold* in order to fix the exhaust. It was dirty, back-breaking work. I was becoming a spelaeologist as well as a yachtsman and engineer. But at least it meant that I had become familiar with every nook and cranny of the yacht. At one moment, as I was stuck with my head and shoulders inside the locker, the blood rushing to my brain, I wondered why the hell I got myself into these crazy predicaments. But the next minute I was brewing a cup of hot tea in the cosy cabin and knew why.

I regretted the fact that I was unable to tour the archaeological sites on the barren and desolate Beara peninsula, since it is dotted with stone circles, gallans (pillarstones) and wedge tombs. It also had the largest ogham stone in Ireland, an upright stone inscribed in the lines and notches of early Irish ogham script, probably commemorating the name of an individual or recent ancestors. According to the *Leabhar Gabhála* ('Book of Invasions', the national epic of Ireland), the first invaders of the country were the sons of Mil who journeyed from Egypt and landed in the far west of the peninsula about 4,000 years ago. Before they could set foot on the shore, their bard Amairgen had to chant the land into existence:

I am wind on sea
I am ocean wave
I am roar of sea
I am bull of seven fights
I am hawk on cliff
I am dewdrop
I am fairest of flowers
I am boar of boldness
I am salmon in pool
I am lake on plain
I am word of skill . . .

The poem superbly demonstrated the intertwined relationship between humans and the natural world amongst the Celts. It also expressed their wish to go out of themselves and take on the shape of other animals and birds, to imagine what it must be like to be a force of nature.

We set off from Castletownbere at midday on 28th July. I was pleased to leave the smell of the fish and to be clear of the dank fog. It was difficult to wash from our hands the stink of the anaerobic mud which came up with the anchor – all life had been killed off in the harbour. Its oily, rotten smell lingered in the chain locker for days despite several washing downs with clean water.

Our destination was Glengariff at the head of Bantry Bay. We sailed out the same way we had come in and turned east after Ardnakinne Point. The cloud hung low, and there were occasionally showers, but it gradually brightened as the day wore on. The swell eased and the calm waters of the bay became a beautiful dark green. The Miskish Mountains to the north were lost in cloud, as were the hills on the southern side. But there was a fine south westerly breeze behind us and we sailed goose-winged in hazy sun. Bantry Bay was a magnificent inlet, twenty-six miles long, seven miles wide. It was accessible to the largest ocean-going vessels.

The weather had been very different two hundred years earlier when Theobold Wolfe Tone arrived on board a ship of a great French armada. Revolutionary France was at war with England at the time. Wolfe Tone and the United Irishmen seized the opportunity to invite the French to invade Ireland and to help them expel the British, in order to create an independent republic. So in the winter of 1796, forty-three French warships sailed from Brest carrying some 15,000 hardened republican troops, the vanguard of the greatest revolutionary army the world had ever seen. Their intention was to sail up with the prevailing south westerly winds and to land at the head of Bantry Bay. They had not counted on the winter gales. Although the prevailing winds are from the south west, by a quirk of fate which changed British history a furious storm blew in from the east along Bantry Bay. One by one the French fleet was forced to cut its cables and to retreat into the open sea. Wolfe Tone, in a French uniform on board the *Indomptable*, wrote that he had been so close to landing that he could have tossed a ship's biscuit to the shore. Weather had saved England from the French as it had saved them earlier from the Spanish Armada.

By contrast, it could not have been a more pleasant cruise on board *Celtic Gold* that summer's afternoon at the end of July. We passed through the green waters on a gentle swell, and as if by a miracle the clouds broke above us and we sailed up a narrow band of sunshine towards the old oil terminals of Whiddy Island. We then steered west towards Glengariff. The creek was scattered with islands and surrounded by wooded hills and cloud-capped rocky peaks. Gnarled Scots pines grew amongst the boulders around the still, dark-brown waters of the natural harbour. It felt like entering a Japanese Zen garden, a place for quiet contemplation.

It was an idyllic anchorage in perfect shelter. In such beautiful surroundings the Irish Cruising Club was born, when nineteen yachtsmen aboard five cruising yachts happened to meet up here on 13th July 1929. More than sixty years later, I was one of their beneficiaries. Without their sailing directions, I would have been hard-pressed to circumnavigate Ireland.

We anchored amongst half a dozen visiting yachts at the head of the creek in the lee of Garnish Island, opposite the grand Eccles Hotel. We went ashore in the dinghy and for the first time since my departure from Wales I had a long and gloriously hot bath in one of the hotel's rooms. In its heyday, the hotel had been the haunt of Queen Victoria, Thackeray, George Bernard Shaw, Yeats and Synge. But tastes had changed: the 250-year-old hotel had been forced to close for a time and much of its furniture sold off. The new owner, a man who had made his money in the building trade in Britain, reminisced, starry-eyed with a sprinkling of 'By Jesuses', how in the eighties yuppies had flown in and spent almost a thousand pounds a night, ordering more than a dozen bottles of champagne at a go. Times were leaner now and he had to rely on the coach trade and the odd visiting cruise ship.

Sheltered by mountains, washed by the warm waters of the

Gulf Stream, sprinkled by heavy rainfall, the climate was almost sub tropical. Rare rhododendrons and azaleas flourished amongst the luxuriant mosses, ferns and trees. In the rear garden of the Eccles Hotel grew the oldest eucalyptus tree in the British Isles. The mean temperature was higher than that of the French Riviera. During my stay, the evenings were warm and humid and the exotic fragrance of the flowers and shrubs made me think of the East African coast.

Not far from the hotel were the Glengariff Woods where oceanic Sessile oaks grew with some birch and rowan on the old red sandstone rock of West Cork. It was one of the few ancient woodlands left in Ireland which had, at one time, been widely covered in trees. From 1200 onwards deforestation gathered pace to allow for all-year-round grazing. But in the seventeenth century, the process accelerated alarmingly to supply wood for ship-building, house-building, barrel-making, iron smelting, glass making and leather tanning (which took large quantities of oak bark). With their woods gone as a source of fuel, the Irish people had to turn to the bogs for peat. The British authorities were not displeased, as the woods had always offered a place of refuge for rebels and outlaws.

The forest, like the sea, has always meant wilderness and freedom. In Celtic times, the woods in Ireland were considered common land, a gift of nature for all alike to use. They had a ritual value too. The Irish have never lost the Celtic love of trees, growing ash around holy wells and yew in sacred places and sanctuaries. Until quite recently country folk would hang branches of rowan over doors and in byres to keep away witches and fairies who might spoil the milk or raise a fire.

I was drawn to times and places which are neither this nor that: dawn and twilight, sea shore and river ford, sea mists and mountain clouds. It is part of the folk wisdom of Ireland that in such places the supernatural enters this world, and poetry and wisdom are revealed. I found such a place in Garnish Island. We rowed gently over from *Celtic Gold* in the dinghy early on a Sunday morning, pausing to watch the fat seals, many with their young, basking on the wrack-strewn boulders at low tide.Only if we came very close would they reluctantly roll over and slip into the brown peaty waters. I wondered how they could see their prey in the murky deep.

The island had long been a barren place of gorse, heather, rough grazing and bog. A Martello tower from Napoleonic times was a reminder of the French threat. After the First World War, it began to blossom when the owner Annan Bryce, a former British MP, commissioned the architect Harold Peto to design a mansion and garden in the grand Italian style. The mansion ended up as a cottage but the garden grew to become one of the best in Ireland.

We landed by the fine stone quay that early Sunday morning and had the island to ourselves. The heady smell of pine trees, azaleas and hibiscus wafted on the air. I made my way through the luxuriant growth of ornamental trees and shrubs. All was fresh after an early morning shower and the flowers were beginning to release their fragrance in the warm sun's rays.

I emerged from thick undergrowth onto a broad expanse of lawn. At its far end stood a handsome *casita* with graceful wings and colonnades made from imported sandstone. It was a delightful tea house, where Bernard Shaw, bushy-eyebrowed and white-bearded, wrote his play *St Joan* in 1923. I could understand why he should have chosen the site, for it is a writer's paradise: perfect peace combined with superb views to renew the spirits during a hard day's work.

The *casita* formed part of the Italian garden, with its carefully placed flights of steps and terraces. Its centre was a rectangular pool with red water lilies which reflected the sky. Its position led the eye from the stillness of civilised order to a wild panorama of rugged mountains and billowing clouds. It reminded me of a

Japanese print by a Zen master. I sat for some time meditating in front of a 300-year-old Bonsai Larix tree, growing in an original Roman marble urn, wishing to liberate its roots so it could grow like the rugged Scots pines amongst the boulders by the sea shore. I spent some of the calmest moments of my voyage on the island.

Before leaving, I talked to Maggie O'Sullivan. A woman in her eighties, she still lived on the island and had only recently stopped rowing over every Sunday to go to mass and to get her week's shopping. She recalled the 'grand old days' – the colonial days – when the owners for whom she had worked as a housekeeper had entertained senior officers of the Royal Navy when their ships anchored offshore. She also remembered the visits of the writers A.E. (George William Russell) and George Bernard Shaw whom she thought 'a very polite gentleman'.

On our last night in Glengariff, Paul and I walked from the harbour along the wide road bordered by fine-cut stone walls into town. The pubs there were overflowing into the streets with holiday makers, Guinness, music and craic. It was after midnight before we made our way back. A balmy breeze brought the smell of the damp earth and musky fragrance of azaleas. Midges buzzed around our ears and distant owls hooted in the woods. The stars shone brightly, vibrating pins in the great black dome of the sky. From a well-lit bedroom in a dark, stone house set back in spacious gardens, some young girls wolf-whistled, waved and giggled at us as we went by, two middle-aged men with daughters of their own.

When we got back to the dinghy in front of the Eccles Hotel we found that the tide had gone out; there was a long stretch of soft mud between us and the water's edge. We carried the dinghy round the corner to the old stone jetty and quietly rowed back to *Celtic Gold*. The dark silhouette of the yacht moved gently in the still waters. All was calm. It had been another deeply satisfying day.

12

Monks and Dolphins

After taking on board stores and water in our dinghy, we left Glengariff at tea time on 30th July. I was reluctant to leave this beautiful haven amongst the woods and mountains, but as always the lure of the sea beckoned me. The early morning mist had been burnt off by the sun and an onshore south westerly sea breeze meant we had to tack up the bay. It was humid and sunny. Fluffy white clouds enhanced the dark-blue of the skies and the purple of the mountain slopes.

The main event of the afternoon for me was the loss of a brown woollen sock which was blown overboard whilst drying. It had been knitted by my mother who had made them for me ever since I was a boy; at boarding school, their texture and form had always been deeply reassuring. Shop socks, however well made, were never the same. They did not have the imprint of her deft fingers, warm touch and love. I pictured the sock gently falling down to the bottom of the sea and then being rolled and tumbled by underwater currents until it was tossed on some deserted strand. Perhaps its wool would end up in a bird's nest.

We motored steadily up the sound between Bere Island and

the mainland into the setting sun, unable to tack in the close waters. By seven o'clock, the silver light of the low sun bounced off the sparkling water and made it difficult to see. In the distance, I made out a number of posts sticking up out of the silver water in mid channel with the binoculars, which I thought were the poles of buoys marking lobster pots. I could not understand why they should have been placed right in the middle of the channel and it was not clear on which side I should pass them. The light dazzled my eyes. Only when we were almost upon them did I realise that the poles were made of metal; they did not mark lobster pots, but were the mast tops of a submerged wreck. I swung to starboard and then made out an easterly cardinal buoy. The mast tops were unlit, and I could easily have hit them if I had passed by a few hours later, after dusk.

There was no mention of the wreck on the new chart nor in any of the sailing guides. I later learned that it was the wreck of a merchant vessel which had caught fire eight years earlier. The Irish Navy had offered to tow it out to sea but because there was a dispute about the insurance payment it was eventually scuppered in mid channel off Bearhaven, where it will no doubt remain for a long time, a hazard to shipping and a major blot on the world's second largest natural harbour.

Rounding Bere Island, I did not make for the smell and refuge of Castletownbere but crossed Piper Sound for the shelter of Dunboy Bay. It was a tight anchorage. To avoid a submerged rock half a cable from the shore I had to keep the front door of the ruined Dunboy House at the end of the little bay to the left of a small tree. It was still light at a quarter to ten when we dropped the anchor in this delightful haven. A mare came down with her foal to graze on the rough grass on the rocky ledge at the water's edge: its whinny mingling with the raucous cry of the crows settling for the night on the embattlements of a ruined castle hidden amongst trees and thick undergrowth. A few sheep bleated and scrambled over collapsed stone walls. It was magical to hear these familiar earth sounds so close in a boat whilst gently swaying at anchor.

It could not have been more peaceful that summer's evening but the place had seen much bloodshed. For three centuries Dunboy Castle had been the stronghold of the O'Sullivans of Bere until it was destroyed in 1602 by Sir George Carew, President of Munster, with cannon and 4,000 men, after the Battle of Kinsale. Its defenders made an heroic last stand after the Irish leaders O'Neill and O'Donnell had been routed and escaped back to the North and overseas.

The roofless Dunboy House at the head of the bay, now a useful feature for passing yachtsmen, had once been the seat of the wealthy Puxley family, whose fortunes inspired Daphne du Maurier's novel *Hungry Hill*. It was known locally as Puxley Castle. Built in the nineteenth century, its former grandeur reflected the wealth generated by the copper mines on their estate. Having exhausted the local workforce with low wages, unhealthy conditions and unremitting toil, the family imported Cornish miners to dig the ore which happened to be on their land. The house was burned down during the War of Independence and the last copper mine closed in 1962.

The setting sun erased the memory of those past struggles and I slept well at the quiet anchorage. We got up at six next morning to another calm day. It was mild and dry with a weak cold front stationary over the west coast of Ireland. The best we could hope for was some onshore sea-breezes to develop during the day.

We reluctantly weighed anchor at seven o'clock and headed out to sea for a long day's sail. It was our intention to sail around the Skelligs and make for Valentia Harbour some forty-five miles away. I had started the voyage by estimating our average speed to be four knots but experience had taught me that I should not count on more than three knots, in order to veer on the side of safety. It should take us about fifteen hours to Valentia; ETA 2200 hours. It would be almost dark by then.

The sea was calm all morning with a slight swell in the lee of Beara Peninsula. A few local fishermen in their colourful wooden boats waved as we went by. Some gannets flying westwards turned their heads slightly and eyed us for a brief moment before journeying on. We too sailed west on a light easterly breeze. By mid morning we were off Dursey Island where 300 people had sought refuge during the siege of Duboy Castle but had been caught by the English troops and thrown into the sea.

I took a fix from the three rocks strung out at the end of the Beara Peninsula called The Bull, The Cow and The Calf, their shape and size reflecting their names. As soon as we had passed them, we hit a big Atlantic swell. Because the winds remained light, our sails flapped and the yacht rolled in the troughs between the long waves. Fortunately we had a two-knot tide under us and made reasonable headway. Who said there was no free lunch in nature?

I wrote in my notebook that morning as we headed towards the Skelligs: 'I can't think of anywhere in the world I would rather be.' I had long looked forward to seeing the three Skelligs, especially the Great Skellig or Skellig Michael, so called because of a legendary appearance of St Michael on the island. It was one with St Michael's Mount in Cornwall and Mont St Michel in Brittany. Local legend also has it that from this rock St Patrick drove all the venomous serpents and evil things of Ireland into the Western Sea, although some escaped back to the mainland to work their mischief as evil spirits.

The rock is also said to be the burial place of Ir, son of Mil, the leader of the first settlers from Egypt via Spain. One day he rowed so hard in his boat, that the effort killed him. Its name comes from the Irish *sceilig*, which means a splinter of stone, and probably has a common root with Scilly.

Skellig Michael is seven miles off Bolus Head. Approaching it from the south, it first appeared like a triangular rock rising straight out of the sea which on the chart was seventy-five metres deep on its western side. As we came closer, I could just see the remains of an early Christian settlement below its 700-foot high summit. It had lasted from the seventh to the twelfth century. The steep stone steps leading up from the sea passed along a dip in the central ridge to the settlement with its stone beehive huts. They had survived the winter storms for 1,400 years as well as the ravages of Viking raids. I could also make out the path to the lighthouse at its southern end, cut out of the solid rock. Below its steep dark cliff the sea surged around the Washerwoman Rock, creating a foaming surf ready to suck down anything which was foolhardy enough to approach.

I tried to imagine what it must have been like in those damp stone dwellings at the summit of the rock, cut off for months from the mainland, lost in the sea fog, buffeted by fierce winds, living on fish, birds and their eggs and mouldy wheat. The hermits deliberately chose this wildest of places to be nearer God and away from the greed, deceit and hypocrisy of their fellow humans. Influenced by the desert fathers whose Coptic Christianity they had inherited from Egypt and Libya, they searched for God in the solitary wilderness, in the elemental and permanent forms of nature. They would have known the way of the grey seals, dolphins and porpoises which would play in the turbulent waters, and would have watched the killer whales, minke whales and sixty-foot fin whales which arose from the deep.

I tried to work out why the Skelligs were so impressive and then it dawned on me that they formed three pyramids. They rise out of the sea like archetypes rising from the unconscious in the creative imagination. They belong to the dream world rather than to the everyday. They are symbols of the sublime, something grand and terrifying in nature which inspires awe and which reminds us of our all-too-human frailty.

I sailed as close to Skellig Michael as I thought wise in the great swell which crashed on its cliffs and threw spumes of spray high into the air. I could not believe my eyes when I saw a small sailing boat going right into the surf at the bottom of the black towering cliffs, like a white seabird glorying in the force of the elements. I thought it was out of control, and was concerned that I might have to go to its assistance, when it suddenly turned at the last moment, like a surf rider on the crest of a tidal wave. It did this several times and turned away at the very last second before disaster struck.

We left it to its mad frolic and rounded the northern headland to Blind Man's Cove, the best landing place. The Irish Cruising Club warned that landing was no longer permitted on the island but we came across some fishing boats which rushed in with the swell, dropped a few passengers off on an old stone quay, and then retreated in reverse as fast as possible. It was done with great skill and daring. I had wanted to land myself and to climb to the oratory but the swell was far too great that day for a yacht: the sea surged in and out of the narrow cove, rising and falling several metres at a time. *Celtic Gold* would have been smashed to smithereens.

All around us were groups of gannets flying in low towards the Little Skellig, a smaller and more jagged rock to the north. Its peaks were covered in the white of countless tons of guano. More than 20,000 pairs of gannets breed there each spring in serried ranks on every ledge and in every nook. I noticed that the gannets were gliding in downwind from the west like we were, drawn - as we were repelled – by the tremendous stench of their accumulated droppings. It made it difficult to breathe deeply. We went in close enough to see the caves, spires, pinnacles and arches of the rugged cliffs and to marvel at the second largest gannetry in Irish and British waters. I thought it strange that no gannets should nest on Skellig Michael where puffins and kittiwakes bred. Perhaps the human presence or some ancient spell had frightened them off.

The acrid stench was too great to linger long and, besides, the afternoon was drawing on. We set a course for Valentia Island, keeping Lemon Rock, the smallest of the Skelligs, and Puffin Island on our starboard side. We were off Bray Head by five o'clock, a bold, high headland on the south west of Valentia. We motored in the light breeze and high swell along its west coastline, passing a high slate cliff. The seam, now exhausted, had supplied slates for the roofs of Charing Cross Railway Station in London as well as the railway station in San Salvador. Above Reenadolaun Point, I made out the white buildings and tall mast of Valentia Radio Station. Its name had taken on mythic proportions in my imagination when listening carefully to the weather forecasts. Valentia Island had another place in radio history: it was the site of the first transatlantic telegraph cable, linking, in 1858, New York with the local town of Cahirciveen.

We anchored in the sandy bay at the south east end of Beginish Island opposite Knightstown on Valentia Island. I was very tempted to go for a swim but it was already after seven. During supper, we watched a farmer and his boy unloading plastic bags of fertiliser on to the stony beach from his bright-red clinker boat. Throughout the night we could hear the roar of surf crashing on the other side of the island in the still air. Only a thin strip of land protected us from the full fetch of the Atlantic. After the excitement and weariness of a long passage, secure in our quiet anchorage, I slept a deep and dreamless sleep.

I woke up next morning, Tuesday 1st August, to find warm sunshine burning off the dew on the deck. There was not a cloud in the sky. During breakfast, an old man in his graceful black currach rowed uptide to lay out a net supported by orange corks and two black flags on a pole at each end.

When I shouted to ask him what it was for, he replied, 'Bass' and added: ''tis a grand day, thank God!'

Soon after, a bronzed and muscular young man rowed ashore in a black currach with a beautiful woman with long blonde hair flowing in the warm gentle breeze. She wore a long pink dress which she gathered up to step ashore. They laid out a rug on the deserted beach and went for a swim in the cool, clear water. As we made to leave, the lovers went off hand in hand over the small stone-walled fields towards the crashing surf on the Atlantic side of the narrow island.

We weighed anchor after lunch and, at low tide, made a tricky passage amongst the rocks in a minimum of two metres, through Lough Kay to the east of Beginish Island. Coming out into the clear water, we sailed past the bold outcrop of Doulus Head and set a course across Dingle Bay to Dingle town on the Dingle Peninsula. The very name evoked merriment for me, and reminded me of a light-hearted jig.

We beat and dingle-dangled across the bay in beautiful sunny weather under blue skies. During the afternoon, the warm breeze from the north east dropped, but after a lull it suddenly picked up and veered north. *Celtic Gold* surged merrily forward. Sitting in the cockpit in shorts and a short-sleeved shirt, surrounded by a calm sea and dramatic mountains, I thought: 'This is the life of Riley if there ever was one!'

As we approached the entrance to Dingle Harbour around six in the evening on a high tide, I suddenly saw a large creature in the water heading straight for us. It was none other than Fungi, the dolphin which had put Dingle on the map and which attracted thousands of visitors every year. At that hour, there were only a few lingering on the shore nearby.

Fungi began to play and leap around *Celtic Gold*. I asked Paul to heave to and I dived into the sea from the bows. Fungi's great grey body surfaced and then dived in the green water. He swam around and around me, coming closer all the time. I put on my mask and fins so I could have a better look underwater. At one moment, I saw his great fin gliding fast towards me and I dived. It was very frightening. His huge body with small eyes and bottled nose came straight at me; for a flash, I saw him as a shark coming to devour me. I didn't think he could see me in the murky green and I was ready to jump out of the way. I had swum with sharks off the coral reefs in the Maldives in the Indian Ocean, and I tried to reassure myself that this was only a friendly dolphin. At the last moment, with a flick of his tail, his great shining grey body skimmed passed me. I could have touched his powerful flanks. I came up gasping for breath, triumphant. I had swum with Fungi.

After a while, he seemed to lose interest and he swam off towards the harbour. We followed him discreetly. It was by now eight o'clock. Then we witnessed something truly magical. By a red buoy in the narrow dredged channel, he suddenly leapt out of the water and twisted in mid air, coming down on his back to create a great splash and turmoil of spray. He did it several times in the golden rays of the setting sun. It was almost as if he were performing to the sun to make sure it would return with life-giving light and warmth the next day. We could not have had a better welcome to Dingle.

I had already made my acquaintance with Fungi a couple of years earlier. I had visited Dingle with a friend during an icy spell in February. We had walked along the deserted headland in a cold wind at dusk and waited on a small stone jetty in the hope of getting a sighting. I waited half an hour, getting colder all the time. Eventually, a wave of the incoming tide splashed over the jetty, soaking my legs with icy water. I said to myself that I would wait three more minutes and then go. I started counting. At the end of the last minute, I suddenly saw in the distance the unmistakable shape of a dolphin leaping in a perfect curve across the last silver rays of the sun. I thought I might have imagined it; I told my friend; but no, there he was again leaping out of the water, this time almost in slow motion, heading out to the dark sea. We waited longer but he never reappeared. We pulled up the collars of our coats and headed back to the roaring fire of a pub in town.

I was told that evening that many years ago Fungi had come to stay at the entrance to the harbour with his mate, but she had died and her body had been washed up on the beach near where I had waited to see him. He never left the place after that. Sometimes in past summers he would go out and play with schools of visiting dolphins for several days but he would always return to lead his solitary life at the same spot.

Fungi had become big business for the small town. Many fishermen had abandoned fishing and enticed visitors to come out in their boats at the harbour entrance by offering five punt if they did not get a sight of the dolphin. Every day half a dozen large boats and many surf boards and canoes cruised around and chased him, but he did not seem to mind. Even jet skis were harrowing him now with their high-pitched sounds which were known to disorientate dolphins.

I took seriously the accounts of Fungi's healing powers. The very experience of being immersed in cold water near a great mammal has its beneficial effect, providing shock and balm to an urban soul. But beyond that there is undoubtedly a strange affinity between humans and dolphins and whales. They are all warm-blooded mammals with large brains. Indeed, whales even have larger brains than humans in ratio to their size.

I have always been deeply moved by the presence of whales and dolphins. When I crossed the Atlantic in my brother's yacht, I would often hear from my bunk, through the thin aluminium hull, the sound of the dolphins whistling and singing. At night, during my watch, they would join us and trace magical abstract patterns in the water by disturbing the phosphorent plankton.

We are not only wiping out dolphins and whales, but we are also bewildering them with our noise. We ignore their music of the deep as we ignore the music of the spheres.

Dingle marina is little more than a string of pontoons behind a protective stone arm. When I arrived, I was delighted to see Stan standing on an outer pontoon, waiting to catch my warps. As soon as I had made fast, I went over to *Mustard Seed* to tell them about my exciting encounter with Fungi after a lovely day's sail. I felt high as a kite. It had been a magical dingle-dangle day, for sure. 'You must calm down,' Betty said with an indulgent smile. 'You won't get around Ireland if you carry on like that!'

I said good-bye to Paul in Dingle. He had been an excellent sailing companion, relishing the navigation, keen to discuss and practise the finer points of sailing. He was a practical man with a surveyor's sense of precision and accuracy. He had remained steady in moments of crisis, such as our unexpected approach to Bere Island in the mist, and enjoyed the challenge of sailing in difficult waters around the Fastnet and the Skelligs. We generally shared watches but on a few occasions it had been good to let him take over so I could have a rest in my bunk, knowing that *Celtic Gold* was in reliable and knowledgeable hands.

Arriving in Dingle marked the end of the second leg in my journey after my first landfall in Wicklow. I was now about a third of my way around Ireland. Everyday I was discovering different aspects of sailing and myself. Ireland was more than living up to my expectations. I had never imagined anything as spectacular and beautiful as the indented coastline of Cork and Kerry, where red sandstone had crumbled into a series of rough ridges and broad valleys flooded by the sea. I felt centred and relaxed, involved in a challenging and thrilling adventure which was testing my mental and physical skills to the utmost. I had well and truly left my cloak of gloom at the sand bar off Porthmadog.

13

Dingle Days

The very next morning after my arrival in Dingle I set off to climb Mount Brandon, the second highest mountain in Ireland, which rose over 3,000 feet straight out of the Atlantic Ocean. There were no buses, so I walked up the hill out of town and turned north along a long straight road towards Brandon Creek on the other side of the Dingle Peninsula. It was so hot that the tar on the roads was melting. On either side abandoned fields were turning to brush with long grass and reeds waving in the warm breeze. Many were divided by tall lines of bright red and purple fuchsias which flourished in the mild, damp, frost-free climate.

Along the sides of the road, the tangled hedgerows were entwined with honeysuckle, yellow ragwort, more fuchsias, and ripening blackberries. Little green finches chirped and flittered, nervous and hyperactive. Peacock butterflies slowly opened and closed their red wings painted with blue eyes, winking alluringly at the sun. I thought of Albert Schweitzer who said one should not wantonly destroy a wild flower but picked a sprig of honeysuckle all the same to take back to the boat.

After about an hour of steady walking along the long road, an old dusty car stopped and a bearded, middle-aged man offered me a lift. He had large strong hands on the wheel. His name was Eddie Hutchinson. By an extraordinary coincidence, he was the last currach builder on the peninsula and had helped build Tim Severin's boat which had left Brandon Creek to sail to Newfoundland in the wake of the saint. I had seen some of his handiwork on the quay in Dingle – elegant, light-weight currachs with high bows made from black tarred canvas stretched over a light frame. These buoyant fifteen-foot canoes made for three rowers used to be the only means of transport to the Blaskets. They could carry a bull across the sound as well as thousands of mackerel. The ancient craft of fashioning them would not die on the peninsula for Eddie's two sons worked with him and he had taken on a German girl as an apprentice.

He dropped me off at Kilmakedar Church by a rough track which led up the sloping west flank of Mount Brandon. I took the longer track, known as the Saint's Road rather than the Military Road; it seemed more in keeping with my pilgrimage to pay homage to the great sailor-saint after whom the mountain was named.

In the foothills, I passed a beautiful young woman with red hair and freckles bathing her chalky white feet in a stream by a bridge. ''Tis hot, 'tis hot for sure,' she said, smiling contentedly. She had just come off the mountain. It was a long slog up, first along a rocky track and then across boggy, coarse pasture. It was still wet underfoot despite the heat. I stopped by a cairn and had a delicious lunch of fresh soda bread, cheese, two oranges and some cool gulps of spring water. Nearby perched on a rough stone wall was a ram's skull with two great curling horns, a reminder of what happens to us all. In the far distance, I could just see and hear a shepherd calling and whistling to his dog, who chased sheep among the ancient ruins of some beehive huts.

Humans had lived on the peninsula for at least 6,000 years but the vast slopes of the mountain were empty now except for a few sheep and ravens.

I slogged on along the side of a ruined stone wall which was being reclaimed by the bog. I found it strangely hard going that sweltering day. Perhaps it was because I was dehydrated after using up all my water in the heat, or because I had not used my leg muscles after being so long at sea. Or perhaps it was simply my age and blood pressure. Whatever the reason, I felt exhausted and dizzy. But I strode on, only pausing to catch my breath after reaching a cairn on the skyline. I told myself that a pilgrimage should be arduous: the deeper the suffering, the greater the reward. But then it occurred to me that the effects of the climb might take me nearer to my maker than I had anticipated . . .

Even at the foot of the last ascent towards the rounded summit of Brandon my watch said that it was 80 degrees Fahrenheit. I looked out at the end of the peninsula towards the Blasket islands which stretched out into the silver sea. Beyond them, far out in the Atlantic Ocean, I thought for a moment I caught a glimpse of the Island of Promise, the island that Brendan and his seafaring monks were searching for. But perhaps it was the heat, a trick of the light or a spark of my imagination . . .

As always, the last part of the climb to the summit was the hardest. Soon my heart was pounding, my breath was short, and my temples throbbed. The path seemed to wind endlessly around the summit through rocky crags. Quite accidentally I discovered a little spring under one large rock. Tucked away in the dark shade were a couple of small bottles full of deliciously cold water. I drank both of them and replenished them for the next pilgrim. It was a holy well, providentially flowing close to the summit.

Not long afterwards I came out on to a plateau with a wide

track which sparkled miraculously in the sun, as if countless gems had been strewn on the roof of Ireland. On closer inspection, I found that the mirror of heaven was made up of tiny pieces of quartz crystals. But the bejewelled path did not lead to a temple of great beauty. A crude, rusty cross made from scaffolding and bent by the winter's storms was stuck in the ruins of the oratory. Next to it was the rough concrete pyramid of a trig point. A cold wind suddenly blew and some clouds rolled in, swirling around the summit and obscuring the valleys and sea below. I lay down in a ditch amongst the stones of the ruined oratory which was like a coffin. I was content with the cold earth and the rough stones against my back. Thousands make the pilgrimage to the summit on 28th June, St Brendan's Day, to hear a sermon on the mount, but I preferred the solitude of the whistling wind and the company of ravens.

I thought of St Brendan. It is said that he came to the summit of the mountain with fourteen monks to prepare himself spiritually and physically for his voyage to the Island of Promise in the Western Sea. They prayed and fasted for forty days, taking food only every third day. When they descended the mountain they went to a nearby creek – Brandon's Creek – and built themselves a currach from a wood frame covered with ox hides tanned with oak bark and smeared with grease at the seams. After making a small mast and simple sail, they loaded enough food for forty days. When they grew tired of rowing, Brendan said: 'Have no fear, brothers, for God is our captain and our pilot; so take in the oars, and set sail, letting him blow us where he wills.'

The Latin version of Brendan's voyage circulated throughout Europe. It relates how they reached the Faroe islands where the birds accompanied their songs, encountered a towering column which shone like silver, yet was clear like glass and was as hard as marble (an iceberg?), held mass on an island which turned out to be a whale's back, came across an island covered with slag which vomited flames (Iceland?) and landed in a country (Newfoundland?) where an old hermit lived off a fish laid every day at his feet by a seal.

At last they reached the Island of Promise and met a young hermit who knew their names and said: 'Welcome. You have at last reached the land you have been seeking all these years. The Lord Jesus did not allow you to find it immediately, because first he wanted to show you the wonders of the ocean.' They returned to the Dingle Peninsula with their currach filled with precious stones. Brendan had found what he had been looking for. Soon after his return, he put his affairs in order, said farewell to his brethren, lay down in his cell, and set off on the final voyage across the ocean of eternity.

On the windy summit, I recalled parts of Brendan's prayer on the mountain, a prayer which had moved me so much during my own difficult preparations which now seemed in another life:

> Shall I abandon, O King of Mysteries, the soft comforts of home?
> Shall I turn my back on my native land, and my face towards the sea?
> Shall I take my tiny boat across the wide, sparkling ocean?
> O King of the Glorious Heaven, shall I go of my own choice upon the sea?
> O Christ, will you help me on the wild waves?

While meditating on these matters, I suddenly heard some children's voices: one red-faced boy in shorts with his shirt flying in the wind turned up and then another. We said hello and I remarked that it was as hot as Africa on the way up. The first boy with ginger hair agreed and said that he lived in Dar es Salaam in Tanzania where his father – who now appeared – was an engineer. By another extraordinary coincidence, one of his teachers was a good friend of mine with whom I had stayed during my circumnavigation of Africa and who had recently visited me in Wales. It is, as they say, a small world, especially on mountain peaks.

Dingle is a town of pubs, forty-six to be precise. Not only do shops have a bar, but at the cobbler's, grocer's or ironmonger's, you can have a tipple. Many offer live traditional music. My favourite was An Droichead Beag by the small bridge in the High Street. Every night local musicians played on the accordion, fiddle, flute and bodhrain and sang wistful or stirring ballads. In the old days, the musicians would have played and danced at the crossroads after a gruelling day's work – helped by potcheen – but now they were in the dark interiors of the pubs.

Despite the pressure of the visitors, the stout was good in Dingle and carefully served. The more I drank during my voyage, the more I appreciated the art and science of supping it. In a pub by the harbour, I had a near perfect pint of Guinness (true perfection only exists in the mind). The barman first poured half a pint and then let it rest, the countless tiny bubbles in the creamy liquid slowly making their way to the top to create a white head on a black body. After about five minutes, he filled the glass up, wiping off the excess with a knife. Even then he did not serve it immediately but let it stand and compose itself. I noticed that at the end he moved the pint around to catch a few last drops of beer. When he placed it in front of me, I realised that he had made a beautiful outline of a shamrock on the white head. It slowly disappeared, father, son and the holy ghost fading together into eternity. The long wait only enhanced the final satisfaction. It was now time to drink the pint. I took a long and slow draught, the cool, bitter liquid passing through the thick creamy head. When I put it down I had foam sticking to my upper lip. It was not my last pint: one for thirst, one for replenishment, and one for pleasure.

When I finally refused another pint, the barman insisted:

'Someone has got to do the drinking to keep the country going!' I said that a few pints were enough for me. He replied: 'The lads have that just to warm up before even coming to Dingle!'

I always tried not to have too much before returning to *Celtic Gold*, aware that more drownings occur between land and yacht than out at sea. As the Irish saying goes: a man takes a drink; the drink takes a drink; the drink takes the man.

Apart from the pubs, I enjoyed taking tea in An Cafe Liteartha which was down a little side street in the centre of town. It was the best bookshop in Dingle, stuffed with works on local history and writing in Irish. In the back tea room, earnest young men discussed art and literature, New Age women flowed in to have tea and sympathy, and well-heeled Dubliners came in search of their Gaelic roots. Copies of the day's Irish newspapers were for all to read. Amongst the works of local artists on the walls, there was a copy of the poster addressed 'To the People of Ireland' and signed by 'The Provisional Government of the Irish Republic'. The political sympathies were clear.

The bookshop contained the wonderful books written by the Blasket islanders, such as Peig Sayers' *An Old Woman's Reflections*, Maurice O'Sullivan's *Twenty Years A-Growing*, and Tómas O'Crohan's *The Islandman*. Over the years, the Irish-speaking islanders had been encouraged by visiting scholars to write down their life stories. The result was a remarkable flowering of peasant literature and fascinating accounts of a community on the edge of the world which was close to the land, to the sea and to each other.

With the increasing pressure of population on the mainland during the nineteenth century, the Blasket islands were inhabitated once again. Unlike the Aran islands, they had peat for fuel, soil for potatoes, as well as rich fishing grounds. The settlers built themselves long single-storeyed houses, with the west or hearth gable bedded into the hill slope. They thatched them with rushes until they found that tarred felt was easier and more lasting. Everything was done by trial and error for there were no experts.

Their whole life depended on the sea. After the seizure of their wooden boats in the 1880s for the non payment of rent, the islanders bought in currachs from the mainland. About fifteen foot long, they had the advantage of being easily carried and 'walked' up the beach; upturned on three men's shoulders they looked like strange caterpillars crawling from the deep. The currachs enabled them to harvest the sea: fishing, sealing, lobster-potting, egg-hunting. They provided the link with the mainland where they ventured for the key events in their life – baptisms, weddings and funerals (no islander was buried in the shallow soil of the Blaskets). And they were used for wild expeditions to Dingle for shopping, boozing and fairs. For good reason, each currach had a bottle of holy water in its upturned prow. The islanders feared and respected the sea, with its sudden changes of mood, its cold, back-breaking currents, and its monsters of the deep – sharks and whales – which could easily surface and sink an unwary currach at night.

Certain experiences stand out for me in the simple and lyrical accounts of island life: Tómas O'Crohan going by currach to Dingle as a boy to buy his first pair of boots and nearly being pulled overboard after catching a huge conger eel; Maurice O'Sullivan smelling the foul breath and looking into the blue gullet of a whale so big that it could have swallowed three currachs; Peig Sayers trying to reshape the rock-smashed skull of her youngest son after he fell over a cliff so that the mourners would not be horrified at the wake.

But what struck me most about their stories was the bright spirit of a people who eked out an uncertain living from a stony land and treacherous sea, cut off for months on end from the rest of the world. Without shops or trades or electricity, these hardy fisher-farmers developed all the skills necessary for survival. They had no doctor, no teacher, no priest. They only had their toil, courage, solidarity and simple faith in God to support them. It was a desperate life on the edge of violent death and hunger; they lost their children to accidents, disease, to the sea. In the face of the unrelenting storms of fate, they developed a profound sense of stoical resignation. Tómas O'Crohan, who saw one son fall from a cliff to his death and another drown whilst trying to save a visitor, spoke for his fellow islanders when he said: 'We must endure it and be content.'

Yet for all the harshness, isolation and poverty of their lives, the Blasket islanders had a rich social and imaginative life. They spent their lives helping and consoling each other. Whenever they met to talk, they would call it a 'parliament'. The islands might have been lonely out in the Atlantic, the last remnants of Europe, but not the inhabitants.

The island community was gradually bled by disease, poverty, and above all by the emigration of the young. The final indignity was a visit by two priests who came to the Great Blasket in 1936 and left written rules for visitors:

> No mixed bathing allowed.
> White Strand alone for women to bathe and bask.
> No dancing in any house, day or night.
> No-one out later than 10.30.
> No boy or girl to walk with any visitors.

Two sign posts were erected on different beaches, one for 'Men' and the other for 'Women'. Fortunately, the islanders ignored these killjoys: for generations, they had swum together on the beautiful white beach below the village, danced and sang to the fiddle into the early hours, and welcomed visitors into their hearths and hearts. But they could not withstand the attraction of America. After the young had emigrated, the last islanders left the Blaskets in 1953 to scatter to their graves on the mainland. Europe will never see their like again and all that remains are their ruined houses and field patterns on the islands and their stories in the bookshops.

Whilst I was in Dingle, David Lea joined me, my old and close friend from North Wales. As an architect, he stands in the organic tradition of modern architecture and was partly inspired by the imaginative creations of Frank Lloyd Wright, as well as by the deceptive simplicity of traditional Japanese buildings. His designs are invariably elegant, light and airy, subtle symphonies of wood and stone and glass; they seek an austere poverty of means and a harmonious unity with nature. He is eager to design buildings which enhance the landscape, use local materials and are constructed and maintained with the minimum of energy. He is not only the nephew of Commander 'Bill' King, the round-the-world yachtsman, but as a young man sailed across the Atlantic himself.

He was an ideal companion to join me on a visit to the Gallarus Oratory, reputed to be 1,300 years old and the best preserved Celtic building in Europe. It is the only remaining corbel-built oratory on a rectangular plan in perfect condition. We took the same long road which I had taken to the slopes of Mount Brandon and had the same sweltering weather. There was a lovely stone path to the oratory with high hedges of flowering red and purple fuchsias on either side. The building, which looks like an upturned boat, is orientated on an east–west axis, with its back to a sloping hill and its front looking over a hill which runs gently down towards the wide open expanse of Smerwick harbour. It is about eight yards long and nearly two yards wide. It has a window in the east gable, and a doorway about six feet high at its west end. The low double lintel would have forced the monks to bend their knees on entering. The corbelled building is entirely constructed from carefully chosen gritstones, each stone smaller than the one beneath it until they finally meet to form the roof. After so many centuries, no stone is loose and it is completely dry inside: the inclination of the joints of the stonework directs the rain to the outside. It is a simple but stunning building on a carefully chosen site, standing on a slight terrace within a walled enclosure. Near the oratory is a tombstone with ogham script carved on it.

After slowly encircling the building and taking sketches from different angles, David felt the stones in the walls and was impressed by their solidity. Having built dry stone walls with his own hands in Wales, he recognised the work of master craftsmen. After some time, he gave his verdict: 'It's a wonderfully archaic building, amazingly well-preserved. The doorway is beautifully done.' He particularly liked the setting, although, like me, was disturbed that a hut from the heritage department obscured the magnificent view towards the setting sun over the wide expanse of Smerwick harbour.

On our way out, David observed: 'It's a pity we haven't built you a house yet.'

'Yes. I would like a house which could be a home for my children and which could be a fulcrum on which I could raise the world!'

'I was reading Kahlil Gibran's *The Prophet* the other day and thought of you. He said that the lust for comfort murders the passion of the soul and then walks grinning in the funeral.'

'I'm all for simplicity, but that sounds a bit extreme!'

'You'll like this. Your house, he said, shall not be an anchor but a mast. It shall not be a glistening film that covers a wound, but an eyelid that covers the eye.'

Yes, an eye which could see the way to heaven from the threshold, a mast with which to sail to the farthest shores of the mind.

*

Back at the marina in Dingle, I learned from Stan and Betty in *Mustard Seed* that they had decided to head up the west coast of Ireland as quickly as possible to spend some time with friends in Lough Foyle. Before they left, Stan told me a moving story, especially coming from such a practical man.

Their itinerant life at sea for the last seven years had begun after Stan had been told that he only had six months to live with cancer. When all orthodox medicine had failed, he had turned to alternative ways of healing: 'I was told about the power of visualisation, the power of visualising yourself getting better. You can imagine, Peter, at that stage I was prepared to try anything. One of my best friends was a helicopter pilot; I worked with him once in the far north. Well, every night I used to wake up at two o'clock and was unable to get back to sleep. I decided to try and visualise my friend flying in his helicopter through my eye and down through my body to where the cancer was in my side. I visualised him hacking away at the cancer, filling up the helicopter and then travelling back up and out through my eye to dump it. This went on all night until about six o'clock in the morning when I usually fell asleep. After a while I felt a warm feeling in my side where my friend was working away. About three months before I was meant to die, they operated on me and took out the cancer which was as long as my forearm. They couldn't believe it when they found all the cancer cells were dead. My friend had done the trick. I was cured. That was seven years ago and, touch wood, I'm still OK!'

Stan warned me not to dally too long on the west coast. He brought out his Admiralty Pilot chart on the likely occurrence of gales: in August they were twice as likely as in July, and three or four times more likely in September. 'If you get caught out in one, stay out to sea,' was his advice. 'The coast is too rocky to attempt finding a refuge.'

Before I said farewell, Betty gave me a necklace with three beads, two amber ones on each side of a dark blue stone cut at many angles. Stan had tied the thong on which they dangled. 'We came across the beads on the deserted shore of an old Indian settlement in a creek in north west Canada,' Betty explained. 'We only just managed to get *Mustard Seed* up there. They would have been used as trading beads. The blue bead is probably from Russia. They'll protect you and bring you luck.'

She gave me a piece of paper with a drawing of a soaring seagull over the quote from Matthew 17, 20: 'If ye have faith as a grain of mustard seed . . . nothing shall be impossible unto you.' So that was the origin of the name of their graceful yacht. Their address card had a picture of a sailing boat and the phrase: 'Friends in Sailing'. They were indeed. I never saw them again, but their faith and friendliness and good advice stayed with me for the rest of the voyage.

Walking down the gangway to the pontoons of the marina, I was surprised to see a thin white kayak, little more than a quill, with a white carnation tucked under a rope. A notice said it was being used for a solo circumnavigation of Ireland. Before my departure Cathal McCosker, a schoolmaster at Eton, had contacted me. He had the previous year broken the kayak record by circumnavigating Ireland with a friend in sixty-seven days. They had slept on land each night. Their worst problem had been diarrhoea and being stung by jellyfish. Cathal returned having lost two stone of weight. He had lent me some of his large-scale, salt-encrusted charts and maps.

The owner of the kayak in Dingle turned out to be Nigel Smith. He had set off in Northern Ireland at the same time as me but was going round much faster. He told me he could average four knots in a Force 5 wind. The carnation was from his Scottish girl friend for whom he had just broken off his voyage because of a crisis. He was not a large man and had thin delicate wrists. His greatest problem was the pain in his wrists caused by the constant paddling. Knowing what it could be like in five-metre swell, I deeply admired his courage and resolve whilst battling through the waves and wind on his own in his tiny vessel.

I could have stayed in Dingle for the rest of the summer, even for the rest of my life, but I had not forgotten Conor Haughey's invitation to visit Inishvickillane in the Blasket islands. I contacted the harbourmaster, Commander Brian Farell, who confirmed that the Haughey family were in residence on the island and Conor would be passing through Dingle in *Celtic Mist* on his way to join them. I arranged to call him on the VHF.

The harbourmaster invited me to his home. His wife Elizabeth not only repaired the seam on the leech of my jib sail which had been catching on the cross trees of the mast but offered me some superb carrot cake. We sat in the garden watching the red orb of an African sun descend over the bay.

Despite the jolly atmosphere of Dingle Harbour, tragedy was always lurking just below the surface. The harbourmaster told me the tale of a fisherman who had given up fishing to take the visitors to see Fungi. His wife had died of cancer and he was left with two children to look after on his own. One evening after tidying up, he had fallen between his boat and the pier. No one heard his cries and he drowned. His young children were now orphans.

Our conversation inevitably turned to the number one attraction of Dingle, Fungi. I described how he had leaped out of the water for us on our arrival.

'You were lucky to see him do that. He's getting old now and doesn't jump like he used to.'

'Doesn't he ever get fed up with all the boats after him?'

'They chase him every day in the summer and he's got many

scars on his back where he's been hit. But he still puts up with it; otherwise he wouldn't stay around.'

'Do you think he really does have healing powers?'

'Some people go way over the top about him. We've had film crews coming here from all over the world filming him. If you ask me, he's no different from a dog chasing cars!'

We decided to set sail on the Saturday, 5th August in mid afternoon for Ventry Harbour which was only nine miles away along the Dingle Peninsula. It was yet another lovely day, the skies deep blue, the sea deep blue, and the hull of *Celtic Gold* a sparkling white. The breeze was variable, enough to fill the sails and bear us westwards towards our haven for the night.

At the entrance to the shallow harbour of Dingle we saw Fungi being harried again by a cluster of vessels – fishing boats, jet skis and canoes. They had been there all day, driving him round and round in circles. I had been told during my stay that he had once given an underwater diver a pollock. But he was no longer so active or benevolent. As he leaped half way out of the water, showing the scars on his shining grey back, it suddenly occurred to me that he was not playing any more, but desperate. Having lost his link with his fellow species, unable to lead a natural life, addicted to the constant attention, perhaps he was a soul in torment, longing to leave but unable to do so, a prisoner of his dead love.

14

On the Edge of the World

I had always been drawn to the Blaskets. The first time I saw them was from the old road which climbed between the pointed peak of Croaghmartin and the long body of Mount Eagle. There below me, in the shimmering light beyond a turbulent stretch of water, rose the Great Blasket. It was flanked by a ragged group of islands which stretched out into the wild Atlantic Ocean.

The Blaskets are the most westerly islands in Europe, on the edge of the world. They form a jagged breakwater for the mountains of the Dingle Peninsula. The name of the islands in Irish is An Blascaod Mor which probably comes from the Norse word *brasker*, meaning a 'sharp reef of rock'. On the earliest charts the name of the Great Blasket was marked Brasker. In winter, when the terrible south westerly gales blow in day after day, the islands are often cut off for months on end. The black-tarred currachs in the tiny harbour of Dunquin at the bottom of a steep cliff on the mainland are then turned over on their backs like seals and firmly lashed down amongst the lobster pots.

We could not have had a better day to visit the islands. We got up at six o'clock to a glorious morning in Ventry Bay. The red orb of the sun rose over the sea and there was not a cloud in the sky. A high was still over Northern Ireland and we could expect variable winds and fair visibility. The outlook was good.

Ventry is a broad bay with an entrance nearly a mile wide. Oyster-catchers shrilled along its long white strand and took off, veering strong and direct as a single creature across the bay. It was 6th August 1995, the fiftieth anniversary of the dropping of the atomic bomb on Hiroshima. I remembered the occasion ten years earlier when David and I had launched little paper boats with candles on a river in Wales to commemorate the dead.

I had read so many accounts of the dangers of the waters around the Blaskets with their strong tides and overfalls that I carefully calculated the tidal streams to get their maximum benefit. The *Cruising Directions* warned that because of their exposed position and lack of safe anchorages they are rarely visited by yachtsmen; in bad weather, their appearance could be 'utterly forbidding'.

We weighed anchor soon after seven. The water was so clear that we could see the anchor creating a cloud of white sand two metres below as it broke from the seabed. After rounding the point of the wide open bay, we steered south west towards the funnel formed by Inishvickillane and its neighbour Inishabro. The savage rocky coastline took my breath away. The sea swirled around the jagged stacks of Slea Head. Although there was only a gentle swell we could still hear the waves pounding the rocks. Great swirling banks of thick sea mist rolled through the Sound and threatened to engulf us. For a while we were lost in it, and old fears of the Blasket waters rose in me again. The mist came and went, but eventually the strength of the rising sun dispelled it and we could see the Blaskets stretched out in the sparkling blue sea.

Out in deep water three miles off the mainland, we kept the submerged bank with its overfalls of turbulent water on our port side and passed on our starboard the narrow rounded back of the Great Blasket. Three miles long and a mile wide, its steep cliffs and grassy dome were lit up by the bright morning sun. Some white foam floated on the swirling water. It was warm and the gentle breeze brought the refreshing smell of salt and seaweed.

It took us a little over three hours to sail the eleven miles from Ventry to Inishvickillane. On the way David read out some reflections from the old Blasket islander Peig Sayers on the trials of old age: 'My sorrow, isn't it many a twist life does! Isn't Youth fine! – but alas! she cannot be held always! She slips away as the water slips away from the sand on the shore. A person falls into age unknown to himself. I think there are no two jewels more valuable than Youth and Health.'

Having almost reached half a century, I found that each age brought its own pleasures and rewards. I was happy to have left the uncertainties and vicissitudes of youth. But then I still had my health and I had never suffered like the Blasket folk.

Since there is always a two-knot tidal stream running west in the funnel between Inishvickillane and Inishabro, I kept close to the Inishvickillane which rose sheer out of the sea. Conor Haughey had suggested mooring alongside *Celtic Mist* and we found her nestling under a steep cliff on the north east side of the island. The south west and the south east sides were foul with stacks, rocks and breakers for at least five cables. A low bank of sea mist descended, sending a chill through the body, as we approached the island, but the sun soon broke through and it rolled out to sea.

As planned, I called the Haugheys up on the VHF radio. The skipper of *Celtic Mist* answered and said he would meet us on the landing stage near the anchorage. After mooring *Celtic Gold*, with its British red ensign fluttering in the breeze, astern of *Celtic Mist* with its large Irish tricolour, we pumped up the dinghy and rowed ashore. A large seal suddenly popped its head out of the water and looked at me steadily with its large doleful eyes. Maurice O'Sullivan mentioned in his book *Twenty Years A-Growing* how one man landed in Bird Cove on the south side of Inishvickillane and saw a young seal and went after it with his stick. A cow-seal leapt straight at him, snarling, and said: 'If you are in luck you will leave this cove in haste, for be it known to you that you will not easily kill my little son.' The man, trembling hand and foot, called for his companion to back their currach away as quick as he could. From then on, he never saw a day's health. The seals were no longer hunted as they used to be, so I hoped they were more forgiving now.

On the little concrete landing spot the skipper of *Celtic Mist* and a security man met us. David joked that it seemed like some James Bond movie, arriving at this private island bristling with antennae in the middle of the Atlantic. Despite the calm, the sea surged in and out of the little cove, so we had to jump up quickly to stop the dinghy from being damaged on the barnacles. We hauled it out and tied it down.

We then walked up the steep steps to an eight-wheeled vehicle. We all clambered in and it bumped us up an extremely steep grass slope to the centre of the island, bursting a tyre on a rock on the way. After we had passed an old hut, a new stone house came into view further up the hill. It had been built by the Haugheys as their summer residence. I regretted the fact that we had not been able to walk, looking for the rock pipits and storm petrels and enjoying the view. The island was only about a mile long and half a mile wide.

Charles Haughey was waiting for us at the side of his house. He was wearing shorts. He walked over to us, barefoot on the springy turf, a shortish portly figure with a puckish smile, white thinning hair, and a strong nose. He welcomed us warmly to his Celtic fiefdom. 'Marshall and Lee,' he joked. 'You sound like two confederate generals about to take over the island!'

He introduced us to his wife Maureen, the daughter of another former Taoiseach of Ireland, Sean Lemass. She was brown as a berry in her white dress, reading a romantic novel on the terrace. Conor was there and his sister Emer came out of the house to say hello. Conor's wife, whom I had met in Kinsale, was resting inside. There were no other humans on the island except the two men who had met us and had now disappeared.

I knew little about the man who had governed Ireland for nearly a decade during the Thatcher years, except that he was reputed to be a wily and colourful character. I had been told by someone not of his political persuasion that he was an amiable rogue, very calculating, as sharp as a knife, and full of devilment. He was known as 'The Boss' to his entourage and as 'C.J.' to his friends.

He had come to power in 1969 as minister of finance, been arrested and freed in 1970, elected Taoiseach in 1979, lost the election in 1989 and finally resigned as leader of his party in 1992 in a haze of accusations of financial impropriety. He had misused his position, it was alleged, to help his family and friends; there was, among other deals, a spot of bother about his son Ciaran's business Celtic Helicopters. He had been replaced by Albert Reynolds who had made his fortune in bathrooms and pet food.

I later learned that he came from the staunchest tradition of Irish nationalism and republicanism. His party Fianna Fail, Warriors of Destiny, took their name from the Fianna, a legendary band of warriors who guarded the High King of Ireland from around 300 BC who may have been the model of King Arthur's Knights of the Round Table. The party had been called the state's vicar on earth. It exerted tribal loyalties and generally defended conservative Catholic values, although Haughey himself supported demands for the referendum on abortion and divorce. It saw itself as the guardian of the spirit of the nation, maintaining the tradition of the Celts and Gaels. It had been in power for most of the history of the Irish State.

As with the other main party, Fianna Fail descended from Sinn Fein of the first Dáil (parliament) of 1919. Led by de Valera, Fianna Fail regarded the treaty of 1921 made by Michael Collins with the British government as a betrayal. The treaty won independence, but gave away the six counties of Ulster. Haughey's father had been a leader of the IRA in the North at the time of the civil war which followed the founding of the Irish Free State. Before entering politics, Haughey had been an accountant and not a rich man. In power, he had proclaimed a new economic order and insisted on the government tightening its belt. Cutting the health budget helped lose the 1989 election. Yet he retired one of the richest men in Ireland, unrepentant. In his grand house outside Dublin, he was said to collect portraits of himself, kind and unkind.

Haughey's main claim to fame was having started the peace process with Thatcher in 1980, the first meeting between British and Irish prime ministers in Dublin since the Treaty. It seems that he gave a silver Georgian tea pot to Thatcher, a gift which many I met seemed to remember and resent, as if he had given away the nation's silver. Their meeting, however, produced a joint communiqué which spoke of the unique relationship between the two countries and of 'possible new institutional structures'. While Thatcher seems to have been confused at the time, Haughey was clear, like his father and his wife's father, about his long term aim: to secure the final withdrawal of the British military and political presence from Ireland, an Ireland reunited in peace. Not surprisingly Paisley's answer, as it had always been, was no surrender.

For some reason, Thatcher's name came up during my visit and Haughey spoke warmly of her: 'She was a woman who knew her own mind and could take risks.' He went on to praise her policy of decentralisation. Perhaps he was thinking of her desire 'to roll back the frontiers of the State'.

David protested: 'I don't think she could be praised for that. She destroyed the power of the local councils in Britain and abolished the Greater London Council. At the same time, she strengthened the coercive power of the State . . .'

Haughey refused to be drawn. 'It's too nice a day to talk politics,' he declared with a knowing smile.

He was right of course. Who wanted to talk politics on a magical island out in the sparkling Atlantic on a glorious summer's day?

But I had to ask him about the peace process in North Ireland. His daughter Emer interrupted and said enthusiastically, 'The ceasefire's got to hold. Everybody wants peace now. They've got used to it. There's no going back.'

I turned to Haughey again, and I noticed that his eyes had become hooded like an eagle's. 'I'm not so sure . . .' He knew the bloody history of his country in the twentieth century and the complex blend of powerful forces and deep currents at work. He would not be drawn any further.

Although I had no faith in governments and politicians, I could not help warming to Haughey. Perhaps I was in danger of becoming another victim of his Celtic charm. I had come ready to sup with a long spoon but quickly threw it away. He was entirely without ceremony, and we sat down around a sandstone table on the terrace – made from great flagstones quarried from the cliffs of Mohar – and drank French white wine in the sun. Conor drank continental lager – not a very good advert, as his father joked, for Irish beer.

At one stage, Haughey brought out a small camera – given to him as a present, he said – and asked permission to take a photograph. My immediate thought was that it was for security reasons, but was I being too suspicious? 'C.J. calls a spade a spade; he's very down to earth; he's very easy to get on with,' I had been told in Dingle. It seemed to be the case. But while he was relaxed and hospitable, it was difficult to read what was going on behind his still face and watchful, hooded eyes. He was not a man to be duped.

Haughey clearly loved the island which he had bought twenty years earlier. He had built a solid house of local stone, shipping in materials by boat and helicopter. It was situated in an open rocky place known as the Hollow of the Eagles, looking south towards the Atlantic. It appeared plain from the outside, but inside it had medieval pretensions. The phrase which sprang to my mind was Celtic baronial. A large fireplace with great candles on the mantelpiece took pride of place. The solid chairs were covered with sheepskins. There was a large collection of old bottles on the massive wooden tables. In the bathroom, the shower was made from slate-slabs shipped over from Valentia. I mentioned the roofs of the railway stations in London and El Salvador. 'The mine could reopen,' Haughey said. 'But it's a very Irish situation. The farmer who owns the land won't sell. It could involve a lot of litigation!'

There were some large telescopes by the wide windows and a great brass telephone, the hot line to the world. The only pictures on the walls were portraits of the men who had built the house. 'They put a lot into it and ought to be appreciated,' Haughey observed, much to David's approval.

Haughey was clearly interested in the history and ecology of the island. He read in a deep, sonorous voice a passage from an old copy of *I Know an Island* by R. M. Lockley who had visited Inishvickillane before the Second World War in search of Leech's storm petrel. 'He didn't find one, but they're breeding here now.'

As we sat on the patio in the sun, our bare feet on the warm slabs, he pointed out something brown moving amongst the bracken on the hill which led up to the highest part of the island. It was a stag with magnificent antlers. 'We've introduced a herd of red deer here. It's the only herd of native Irish red deer apart from one in Killarney. They've settled and are breeding well. We've got fifty deer and two stags. We'll have to cull one of them. Deer are only healthy with one male stag. Animals are territorial, aren't they? Soon we will be able to take some back to the mainland and start a new herd.'

Conor had told me that they had also introduced hares and sea eagles onto the island, which, with red deer, were the Celtic symbols of Ireland. There had been a pair of eagles, but one had died and the other flew off. Sea eagles had been common all down the west coast of Ireland but were now virtually extinct. They would try again to reintroduce them. I could not imagine what the long-term ecological effects would be of introducing these new species, but in the past islanders had kept sheep, cows and goats. They, and the wind, had made sure there were no trees, except the willows down by the old hut grown for weaving lobster pots.

Haughey did not seem too concerned about global warming, despite his interest in alternative technology for his island domain. 'It would be a good thing for Ireland,' he declared.

'What about future generations?' I suggested.

'What have they done for us?' was his reply.

Haughey told us how in the First World War young men from the Great Blasket had taken refuge on the Inish to avoid military service. 'There was one young man who galloped on a horse off a cliff into the sea rather than be taken by the soldiers.'

He also recounted how in the Second World War, on 28th November 1940, a German bomber had crashed into the sea in the sound between the two islands after a strut had broken. They had come from Brest in France and were searching for convoys. The five crew members made it in two rubber dinghies to the pebble beach on the east side of the island. 'To get some food, some of them rounded up the sheep and chased them across here,' he pointed to the flat area in front of the house. 'One of them shot the sheep with a machine gun!'

After a few days, realising that they might spend the winter on the inhospitable island, the Germans had paddled across the Black Sound to Ceanh Dubh on the western end of the Great Blasket. Two of them then climbed the steep Hawk's Cliff and walked until they came across the village on the other side. They were eventually picked up by the Irish navy and spent the rest of the war in an internment camp. 'Not long ago when I went to Germany we had a reunion with the men,' Haughey said.

I raised the delicate matter of his own shipwreck in *Celtic Mist*. 'We were returning from launching a book of poetry. We'd had a few drinks. When we hit the rock, we got into the life raft. Fortunately it was very calm. We spent several hours in the dinghy, just steadying it in the water. We were fine; we had a bottle of brandy with us. I had a lot of explaining to do though to the press the next day!'

I remarked how the Irish did not seemed impressed by anybody. I had noticed that people would come down to look at *Celtic Mist*, but not be overawed by its owners. 'You're right,' said Maureen. 'When Teddy Kennedy came here and went to the Dingle Races – they're flapper races without any rules – nobody paid him any attention. They were too interested in the horses!'

'It's a wild place,' Haughey added. 'Once the stewards were called to settle a dispute. They called the Gardai. They then all adjourned to Murphy's pub and that was the end of that.'

It was not only German pilots who had been living on the island of Inishvickillane. Local legend had it that it was 'black with fairies'. It didn't surprise me. If the two worlds ever came together, it would be on this remote island in the Atlantic. I mentioned the story I had come across in *The Western Island* by

Robert Flower, of how a man who lived on the island sat alone one night in his house 'soothing his loneliness' by playing the fiddle. As he played, he heard another music outside in the air: 'It passed away to the cliffs and returned again, and so backwards and forwards again and again, a wandering air wailing in repeated phrases, till at last it had become familiar in his mind.' The man played, note by note, the lamenting voices as they passed above him until he knew it by heart. In time, the tune, known as *port na bpucai* ('the fairy music'), was passed down through his family and had become one of the most popular in the Dingle Peninsula.

Haughey put a different gloss on it: 'Not long ago a researcher came here with recording equipment and recorded the sounds of the hump-backed whales which pass through the sound between Inis and Inishabro. When he compared them with the "fairy music", he found that they were exactly the same.'

Unlike the *tylwyth teg* in Wales, the Irish fairies can be nasty as well as mischievous. Blasket legend has it that when St Patrick came to banish the venomous serpents and evil things out of Ireland into the Western Sea some of them escaped his sweep. And when St Michael and his host cast Lucifer and his rebellious angels down to Hell, some did not reach the gates of Hell before they were closed. Finding no home with the good or evil angels, they became the fairies, who continue to play tricks on humans.

'Why don't you show them the chapel?' Haughey said to his son.

He chose to stay in the sun with his bottle of cool white wine and his wife sunbathing next to him. We made our way across rough pasture dotted with yellow ragwort, collapsed stone walls, briars and low bracken, towards a ruin half way up the side of the hill. As we approached we disturbed the great stag which raised its magnificent head above the stone wall. It scrambled up to the higher rocks and then looked down upon us, keeping its distance.

Amongst the bracken, I could make out the collapsed walls of a small rectangular building, about six feet long and four feet wide. It had a doorway four foot by two: the monks would have had to bend their backs in order to enter it, at once teaching them humility and keeping out the wild winter winds. There were some graves nearby, where holy men were buried. Many of the stones of the chapel had been plundered to make the nearby walls for the fields, but the ones which remained were extremely well put together, without mortar or lime. The islanders, until recently, had continued the tradition, exemplifying the old proverb used by the Blasket man Tómas O'Crohan: 'All things in the world are growing better except poetry and the craft of stone working.'

Conor pointed out a simple Celtic cross leaning against a wall. 'It's a replica. We've sent the original to a museum on the mainland.' There was also a stone with some rough scratches – lines and notches – carved on the stone. It was an example of ogham script, usually used to commemorate the names of recent ancestors. Here many more recent visitors had cut their names into the stones.

We continued our ascent of the island summit which was crowned by a five-watt wind generator.The former prime minister of Ireland was experimenting with wind power, while the present Irish government was letting the well-organised system on Cape Clear Island fall into disuse. At its base were the tortured blades and head of another wind generator. 'It was brought down during a winter storm,' Conor the engineer explained. It was difficult to imagine the force that could twist such metal like a child twists plasticine. 'We're self-sufficient in energy here on the island. We pump up water from the sea for the pool and pumps bring freshwater to the house from the well above the old house,' he explained.

At the summit, more than 400 feet above sea level, a great slab of stone reached for the sky. Ravens took off at my approach. From here I had a magical view all around the Blasket islands. To the south east were the almost submerged Great Foze rocks which were such a hazard to shipping, and to the north east was the Inishtearaght lighthouse which did its best to keep it at bay. Completed in 1870, after five years of rock blasting, it stood two hundred and fifty metres above the waves, the most westerly lighthouse in Europe. It had only recently been automated.

To the north from my vantage point, I could see Inishabro just across the sound. A long way north east was Inishtookert, its serrated back looking like the comb of a cock. To the east rose the dome of the Great Blasket itself. But, most impressive of all, way east in the distant blue haze, I could just make out the black pyramid of the Skellig Michael, and its white sister off the mountains of the Ring of Kerry.

As I stood marvelling at these islands in the shimmering sea, the stag which had been watching us, disappeared around a crag. I left David and Conor chatting about alternative energy and pursued the fabled creature. Each time I approached, it moved on, leisurely, not afraid, but always keeping its distance. Its brown eyes looked at me without fear. Perhaps it was leading me to a magic place. I began to sweat in the hot sun as I scrambled over the warm rocks. Then the stag disappeared below a low ridge. When I reached it, I could not believe my eyes. Below me, on a grassy headland, was a large herd of red deer, moving as one across the bright swathes of green grass. Behind them a great jagged stack rose sheer out of the sea, the swell crashing on to its black rocks and sending up white spume even on this calmest of days.

Alone now, I suddenly felt the remoteness and loneliness of the island, with its whining gulls and screeching ravens and ceaseless murmur of sea and wind. Sitting on the edge of the cliff, lost in reverie, watching the guillemots, razor-bills, and kittiwakes diving for fish, I suddenly had a sense of my own insignificance, a tiny figure under the arching sky on this dot in the huge expanse of water.

When I returned to the house, I found David and Conor already there. It was now mid afternoon. It was hot and we had drunk a lot of wine. Haughey suggested a swim and we all strolled barefoot across the rough pasture amongst the low bracken to his pool under a great outcrop of rock. On our way over we passed a flat round area of grass – the helipad.

'You know, they wanted to build it in concrete, but I insisted we kept it as grass. It wouldn't have looked right.'

I commented on the amount of ragwort which was growing everywhere. It was a beautiful plant with its yellow flowers but it was poisonous to horses and sheep. 'Yes, it's a nuisance,' he said. 'When Mitterrand flew in here a few years ago, his pilots really liked it. They had never seen it before!'

I explained that I had no swimming costume or towel. No problem. I went in my underpants. The water was deliciously cool in the hot sun. 'Mind the lobsters!' Haughey joked. Sure enough, in the shady corners of the deep end there were a few dark green monsters with large claws. 'They're for the evening meal!' I kept my distance, not wanting to be their meal in the meantime. Afterwards, we dried ourselves amongst the warm rocks.

David and I had decided that we would not stay for dinner as we wanted to continue our sail to Smerwick harbour that night. After some sandwiches, Haughey accompanied us, still barefoot but now with a shirt draped over his red shoulders, back to the landing spot. We walked along the whole length of the island. On the way, we came across the two men driving the jeep. The security man was standing up, his hand on the windscreen. 'Here comes Rommel!' Haughey joked. They swept by.

We stopped half-way down the island at the small low stone

hut, now with a new roof, which had been the dwelling of the former inhabitants. It was of the utmost simplicity, bare and functional. Its two rooms were divided by a stone wall. The walls were still whitened with lime and the floor was of beaten earth. The crickets, the heart beat of an islander's home, had long fallen silent in the blackened fireplace where they used to live. Outside, I could see the outlines of an old garden where cabbages and onions had once grown. Old lazy beds for potatoes stretched up towards the summit of the island. At one time, islanders had kept cows, asses, sheep and goats and had grown fields full of oats, wheat and potatoes. It was said that the soil was so rich and sheltered that they could grow tobacco.

Although there were no official records, the Blaskets had been inhabited for at least two hundred years. There were signs of other ruined houses nearby and in its heyday as many as five or six families lived on the island, planting crops, herding sheep and cows and fishing. They would eat gulls' eggs and hunt the rabbits which had their burrows on the ledges of the cliffs. They worried about the weather and the harvest from land and sea but they never had to worry about taxes, rents or rates.

In the nineteenth century, Inishvickillane supported a family of about seven. They told a visitor in 1856 that one stormy season their fire went out and, not having the means of relighting it, were reduced almost to starvation. For two months, they subsisted off sheep's milk alone.

The last inhabitants of the island, the O'Dalys, finally moved to the Great Blasket after seeing their children leave one by one. They died in the workhouse hospital in Dingle out of the sound of the sea. Two of their grandsons had returned to live on the island in the summer, fishing and looking after the sheep. But in the end the brothers had agreed to sell their island, the most westerly inhabited island in Europe, to Haughey who knew a good bargain when he saw one. I did not ask for how much. He clearly respected them as he respected the men who built his house: 'We were lucky to buy the island. It's difficult to trace the owners of the other islands; they've either emigrated or left 999-year leases. We agreed with the two brothers that they could come and look after their sheep as long as they wanted for the rest of their lives. They were very independent and always kept themselves to themselves. They would come for three weeks every year, with their own supplies as they had always done – tea, sugar, oats, flour, butter, tobacco. They would catch fish. They refused to take any food from us but would accept a drop to drink. I would often see them sitting on the cliffs smoking their pipes for an hour or two, waiting for the tide to turn; then they would suddenly leave. They did not need a radio to listen to the weather forecast. They could read the signs in the sea and sky and knew exactly when to go. They died in their sixties. They were very craggy people, not well fed.'

We continued our walk to the narrowest part of the island. Haughey pointed out a mound which he thought was part of an old fortification. There were some stone circles and evidence of a Stone Age settlement on the island. He was clearly interested in archaeology – even though I later heard a professor declare that a site had been disturbed whilst making the rock pool. 'The Irish don't know a great deal about their past,' Haughey said. 'They need educating about it. That's why I got the TV boys to do a series called *Discovery* to give a systematic survey of the Irish race.'

And one of his lasting achievements as Taoiseach had been to resurrect the tradition of the *Aosdana* ('Ireland's Treasures'), a term referring to the Celtic travelling musicians, poets and story-tellers. Their modern equivalents need not pay tax in Ireland, a move which should inspire governments throughout the world.

We shook hands and said farewell and David and I carried on

our way down the hill. Soon the former Taoiseach became a tiny figure of white in the rolling expanse of grass bordered by the cliffs far out west in the Atlantic Ocean. He had been one of the most controversial political figures of Europe since the Second World War. But whatever his financial and political dealings, he and his family could not have been more hospitable to two strangers who happened to be sailing by on that glorious Sunday in August.

Before we left, David made off with sketch book to the western cliff-top to draw the stacks hundreds of feet below. The sun was beginning to fall towards the Inishtearaght. I joined him on the edge of the cliff and saw rabbits playing on narrow ledges and sea birds – kittiwakes, guillemots, fulmars, herring gulls – soar a hundred feet below. A kestrel hovered in the thermals, no doubt eyeing up the young rabbits. The Manx shearwaters would return soon, after their day's fishing.

Looking to the edge of the sky, I thought I caught a glimpse of the Land of the Young with its bright houses in colourful gardens and its fair women and men walking through the fields gathering flowers. But I blinked my eyes and the vision was gone. The sky was hazier now and a north easterly breeze was picking up. White horses were beginning to disturb the silver sea. I shivered in the first chill of the late afternoon. It had been a memorable day but if we wanted to reach landfall before dark, we had to be going now.

As we sailed away that evening towards the troubled waters of the Blasket Sound I looked back at Inishvickillane and its jagged outline against the golden sky. The Atlantic swell was building up and rollers which had travelled thousands of miles across the ocean crashed against its rugged shores. I thought of the two brothers sitting on the cliffs, smoking their pipes and wating for the tide to turn. The old way of life of the Blasket islanders had gone forever. We were all summer visitors now.

15

Out West

We left Inishvickillane in the late afternoon, casting off our moorings from *Celtic Mist.* The wind had picked up during the day, and the white horses were beginning to form on the disturbed sea around the islands. I was a little worried. Normally I did not drink whilst sailing but I had drunk too much good white wine during the day. We would soon have to pass through the fearful Blasket Sound and my calculations were not yet complete. Once we were clear of the island and sailing down the east side of the Great Blasket, David took over as I went down to work out our position and the best way through the submerged rocks and islands in the channel.

Celtic Gold was soon leaning hard over and I had trouble wedging myself in at the chart table. Badly stowed items began to break loose. I looked up at David through the hatch and saw an elated grin on his face. He was enjoying every minute of the hard and exhilarating sail. I asked him to reef in a little but he insisted that all was well. I was not so sure. I had the horrible feeling of hammering along to unknown danger for which I was ill-prepared. I insisted again and David reluctantly agreed to slow down. He was enjoying himself hugely but I felt we were not in a regatta or even just out for an evening sail. There were some of the most dangerous waters around Ireland ahead. It was getting late and we had another nine miles to sail through a notorious sound and around some daunting headlands with strong currents.

We had left at the right time. High tide was at 1840 and the best time to pass through the sound was an hour and a half either side. We were in 'neaps' (when high tides are lowest, low tides highest and currents at their weakest) and could expect about a two-knot north-going tide to take us through. The morning sea mist had long since lifted, but the north westerly wind was running against the tide which made for choppy conditions.

We sailed fast but safely along the steep eastern shore of the Great Blasket towards Mount Eagle on the mainland. We then altered course to pass through the overfalls between the eastern end of the Great Blasket and the submerged rocks off Dunmore Head on the mainland. I could clearly see the landing slip at Dunquin, the most westerly in Europe, below a winding path down the precipitous cliff from the village.

On the other side of the sound, on the eastern lee of the Great Blasket, was an abandoned village above a long white strand. The old patterns of the potato fields were clearly visible. The long single-storied houses stretched up the hill. No smoke had risen from the peat fires of the homesteads for forty years. I thought again of the hardy islanders who had lived such an independent and self-reliant way of life there.

'There be no restrictions in Blasket,' an old islander told R. M. Lockley before the Second World War. 'A man may cut peat anywhere, only it will be no courtesy to dig too close alongside a neighbour. A man may keep as many sheep as he likes upon the hill, only it will be no courtesy to keep too many. The wind and the weather had a wonderful way of striking the greedy ones.'

Only in the thirties, when agents landed from the Congested Districts Board of the Irish Free State, did they clearly define and fence off their vegetable plots. Before that, good will and the forces of nature were enough to regulate things.

The waters around the Blaskets were rich in marine life; indeed, the shallow continental waters of Dingle Bay had the greatest diversity in Ireland. Exposed to the full fetch of the Atlantic, the bay acted as a biological funnel concentrating warm and cold, shallow and deep, Mediterranean and Arctic species.

But the sea was dying. The islanders had a prophecy that the sea would become like a dry cow before the world's end. They lamented before the Second World War that it was already failing them and that fish were becoming scarce. Now they no longer fish the seas and trawlers with their huge nets and sonars had arrived. The sea was growing progressively drier.

By carefully keeping Cloghar Head in line with Sybil Point, I managed to steer *Celtic Gold* through the swirling overfalls of the Blasket Sound. Towards the west, there was a great deal of rough, confused water trailing streaks of foam, but a well-set sail and the north-going tide took us safely through. I thought of the two Armada ships which had foundered on the rocks here and another which had managed without a chart, and in an autumn gale, to sail through in a dazzling show of seamanship.

We passed the flat, grassy Beginish Island on our starboard side and the maze of rocks, breakers and islets beyond. As we swept by I thought of a poem of John Synge about happier times of dancing and drinking on the deserted island:

We'll have no priest or peeler in
To dance in Beg-Innish;
But we'll have a drink from M'riarty Jim
Rowed round while gannets fish,
A keg with porter to the brim,

That every lad may have his whim,
Till we up sails with M'riarty Jim
And sail from Beg-Innish

In the distance, the purple rays of the setting sun lit up the cockscomb back of Inishtookert Island. By now it was getting late, and I was worried whether we would make it before dark to Smerwick Harbour. After rounding Sybil Point, we sailed about a mile off the steep and precipitous coast, struggling against the freshening north easterly which sent a shiver down the spine after such a hot day. It was strange to get clear of the Blaskets and to be in open water. We were now totally exposed and vulnerable to thousands of miles of Atlantic swell. The ghostly apparition of a quarter moon rose above the dark cone of the highest of the Three Sisters. The coastline was sublime, with great stacks lining up, one behind the other. Then we entered the wide open bay of Smerwick and steered towards the north east corner. We anchored in about two metres at about ten o'clock. It was already dark.

We were safely at anchor in a sheltered bay. After supper, sipping our Irish whiskey in the cockpit, we were at our ease, without a trouble in the world. I looked up at the clear heavens and saw the brightly studded belt of Orion stretching out in the dark velvet and thought of the ancient Egyptians who had built the three great pyramids at Giza to mirror their position. It was almost too beautiful. I was overwhelmed by the infinite space of the Milky Way and felt irresistibly drawn towards it. I had to wrench myself away or be lost in interstellar flight from which I might never turn . . .

The night was warm and still and the water gently lapped the hull of *Celtic Gold*. The morrow promised to be another beautiful day and there would be some exciting sailing up the exposed west coast of Ireland. But I had a sense that the magical spell would not last. Before I turned over in my bunk, the words of Tómas O'Crohan echoed in my mind: 'There's many a danger lying in wait for those that follow the sea.'

We woke up next day to blue skies. David, who had kept the hatch open so that he could see the stars from his quarter berth, said he had never slept so well for years. A north easterly airflow was still sweeping across Ireland and the forecast was for Force 3 to 5. We decided to have a leisurely start and head for Fenit in Tralee Bay further up the coast for the night. We spent the morning swimming around the yacht and chatting in the warm sunshine.

For some reason, I had woken up a little apprehensive about Jenny joining me with the children for my birthday in two weeks' time. I had no idea where I would be then and it was difficult to imagine being together again in the small confines of the yacht. I was uncertain how it might work out with her since we had lived apart since the previous autumn. I thought of the irony of my life, lying in the bunk of a yacht in an unknown part of the world, without a house, with a dispersed family. Now almost fifty, it seemed that I had, as the Irish put it, preferred a hand of will to an inch of benefit. I had few possessions: a mortgaged yacht, a rebellious horse, an ancient dog, a large library, and eight published books to my name. I genuinely did not feel too attached to them. And I knew my love for my children should not be possessive: while providing them with shelter, security and love, they should be free to develop their own identities. I wanted to be like a lighthouse to them, warning of the reefs and shallows and rocks of life but letting them sail their own boats in their own way.

In many ways, I had relied too heavily on Jenny as a haven in my life. I was now seeking a new haven, not in a particular place or with another person, but within myself. It was a state of mind

I was after, not a place on earth. I wanted to be, as far as possible, self-reliant, centred and calm, not torn apart by dependence on another. And I was succeeding. Sitting under the warm sunshine in Smerwick Harbour at the foot of Mount Brandon, I no longer felt alienated, but at home. *Celtic Gold* had been my salvation and Ireland and its waters my baptism to a new life.

After an early lunch we were under sail by one o'clock. We wanted to see if we could manage without the engine. The visibility was good but the wind was the problem. It was blowing up to a Force 5 from the north east, the very direction we wanted to go. As soon as we rounded Ballydavid Head off Smerwick Harbour, we hit white horses rolling in on a high swell. We began to tack along the coast, but it was hard-going and unpleasant in the lumpy sea. The great consolation was the sparkling light and bright blue skies. We also passed along a magnificent stretch of coastline, with high cliffs rising out of the sea all the way to the summit of Mount Brandon. It was as beautiful as anything I had seen along the coasts of Cork and Kerry. Only one other yacht was about, running fast with the wind in the opposite direction, close inshore under the towering brown cliffs.

We concentrated on the sailing all afternoon, slowly tacking along the coast in the choppy sea. Around tea time, I spotted a trawler coming fast towards us. I then realised why. Just in front, about ten metres away, were the small orange corks of a drift net rising and falling in the strong swell. We only just managed to swing round in time to avoid it in the high sea. *Celtic Gold* has a separate rudder which would not have been able to glide over the net and we could have become entangled broadside on. It was a very close shave. By this time the trawler had reached us and directed us out to sea in order to go around the net. This involved sailing about two miles out at right angles to the shore; there was only one large orange buoy to mark its end. Once we had rounded the net, we came across another long one. This time we headed out to sea before the trawler patrolling the line could reach us.

I could not understand why the trawlermen had not called us up on the VHF to warn us. Only later was I told by another fisherman that they were illegal salmon nets. The season had officially ended on 23rd July, a fortnight earlier. The trawlermen did not want to be heard on the airwaves warning us. If we had hit them, we would have been in trouble. I had read that it was a good idea to have a piece of rope tied to two bricks to throw over the net to allow the yacht to pass over, but I did not have any bricks on board. I had also read in the *Sailing Directions* of the dangers of salmon drift nets on the south and west coasts of Ireland, and had tried to keep a keen look out for them, but I had dropped my guard since I had not seen any before.

By now it was mid afternoon, and the sea was even lumpier, with a strong current running against a strong north easterly. I went below to make some tea after clearing the second net only to find that the floor of the cabin was awash with water from the heads. It was a light brown colour and did not smell good. I rigorously checked the cocks every time I left port, but that morning I had inadvertently forgotten to turn them off. We had been too relaxed. The sudden movement to avoid the salmon nets had only made the spillage worse.

I set about cleaning it up. David was sailing hard and the bows of *Celtic Gold* were pounding into the waves. He looked increasingly like a pirate with his tanned face, beard and makeshift turban to protect him from the sun's fierce rays. Being below deck in such a sea is not a good idea at any time, but leaning over and mopping up water from the heads is courting trouble. I soon felt terrible waves of nausea. A large wave was the last straw and I leapt up into the cockpit and was sick over the side. I was not sick once, but many times, until I was retching up bile from a griping stomach. I had felt queasy several times before during the voyage but this was the first time that I was properly seasick. I had forgotten how horrible it could be. It is impossible to describe the sense of desolation and disorientation it engenders. But it never lasts for ever. After a while, looking at the horizon far out to sea, I felt a little better. I stretched out on the hard wooden boards in the cockpit and soon fell asleep in the hot sun. When I woke up, I immediately felt better. The sea had eased a little and the sun was going down. I went below to make some tea and check our position.

We had passed Brandon Head about three miles out at sea. I changed course towards the rocky Magharee islands at the end of the low, sandy peninsula which separates Brandon Bay and Tralee Bay. I skirted the islands in the heavy swell and then turned south east towards Fenit. It was a pleasure to get into the shelter of the bay in the lee of Kerry Head. But soon after, the wind began to drop and we were obliged to motor sail. David, like me, always hated starting the motor, but there was no option if we wanted to reach Fenit before nightfall.

The low green hills surrounding Tralee Bay were dotted with white cottages; it seemed so tame and familiar after the sublime wildness of the Blaskets and the rough cliffs and peaks of the northern coastline of the Dingle Peninsula. But with the reddish gold rays of the setting sun behind us, it was very pleasant, especially after such a hectic afternoon.

Fenit Harbour was just a rock with a long causeway from the mainland and a sheltering arm for the local fishing boats and yachts. At its entrance, there was a fine stone lighthouse called the Little Sapphire to lead us in. Cormorants stood on the seaweed-covered rocks at its base, drying their black outstretched wings. We nudged along the channel at low tide and dropped the anchor into white sand off the eastern arm of the pier. It was half past nine.

I washed out the cabin again and tied the carpet to a rope and put it overboard for the night: the sea would be the greatest cleanser. We were too tired to go ashore; besides we had to prepare for a long haul up the mighty River Shannon the following day. I had to get the tides right. They can run up to five knots in springs; with our small auxiliary engine we would never have been able to fight them.

After supper, well satisfied and safely at anchor, David entertained me with the most frightening experience of his life: 'It was during my crossing of the Atlantic. I set off with two friends and two of their girl friends after finishing at Cambridge. We were sailing through the Canary Islands at the time. There was a pleasant breeze but it wasn't rough. During the night I woke up and went on deck to have a pee. I saw a flashing light to starboard which should have been to port. I quickly realised that we had sailed down the wrong side of an island and we could have hit it head on! There was no one on deck. The skipper had been on watch but he had felt ill and had gone below for a moment and had fallen asleep – we later discovered he was suffering from hepatitis. I woke him and the crew up. He said that the chart showed rocks ahead. Looking out into the darkness, I saw white water breaking in front of us. We had new running sails up on twin jibs which we were not used to. We just managed to turn round in time in total chaos. It took us hours the next day to unravel them.'

'Didn't you have some other trouble on that voyage?'

'We certainly did. You know how tensions can build up on a yacht when you're forced to live together for weeks on end. Well, one of the girls seemed to get jealous because her boy friend, the skipper, was explaining the navigation to me. We were off the coast of Spain at the time. She suddenly picked up the navigation tables and jumped overboard with them. In the trade winds, it would have been virtually impossible for us to turn round and pick her up. As it was, the skipper sitting in the cockpit just managed to grab her hair as she was swept by. He eventually had to let go but we were towing a dinghy and she just managed to clamber into it. She sat there shivering, still clutching the navigation tables – without a life jacket!'

I knew what he meant about tensions building up. After sailing across the Atlantic with my brother and a couple of his friends, we had to go our different ways when we made landfall for the first time to give each other space.

In Fenit Harbour the next morning we got up at six o'clock to find that the weather was beginning to break. For the first time for more than a week, there were some clouds in the sky. I had decided to sail to Carrigaholt, a little harbour on the north bank of the River Shannon, the first reasonable shelter which escaped the tidal stream. It was over twenty miles away so we could count on a good seven hours' sail. High water was in mid afternoon: we would have the benefit of the flood to take us up river.

The winds proved light and variable, as forecast and we had no trouble leaving Fenit. David once again admired the solid stonework of the Little Sapphire lighthouse. All of the ones I had so far encountered were spacious, solid, and not without a simple elegance. The Little Sapphire seemed to grow out of the rock and formed a harmonious asymmetry. I was often attracted to the idea of living in a lighthouse, writing my books, the wind and the birds my companions, the wide open sky and changing sea my domain. Perhaps the reality would be very different. The solitude would not be a problem but the lack of space to move would be. And the lighthouses around Ireland had lost their souls when they had been automated. A computer is no match for a man.

We cleared the dangerous islands and rocks in Tralee Bay by sailing virtually due north, keeping the bold Kerry Head on the south bank of the Shannon in line with Loop Head on its northern extremity. The winds were light and the sea flat and calm. It grew hot and sunny during the morning, and the sun bounced off the dark-blue waters and lit up the dark green of the coastline above its low brown cliffs. We could not dawdle and miss the tide. At least when the wind did pick up a little, it was from the south east rather than the north east, so we could enjoy a broad reach across the mouth of the Shannon. We passed Kerry Head and entered the Shannon at eleven o'clock, just as the flood began. It was so calm, with little more than a cat's paw created by the puff of wind, that I was able to trim my beard which I had let grow since my departure. It had once been ginger, but now there was plenty of pepper and salt in the wayward curls.

16

The Mighty Shannon

Although it remained calm, there was a strange atmosphere on the Shannon that day in early August. Perhaps it was the hazy visibility and the mist which came and went in the hot sun. Perhaps it was the green, oily waters with their mysterious eddies, whirlpools and vortices. The buoy off Kilstiffin Bank emitted a mournful whistle, warning of hidden, unknown dangers. Great masses of water, countless millions of tons, were slowly rolling over as they were swept out of the vast estuary.

I could see why people called the Shannon mighty. Its mouth was over eight nautical miles wide. It drained a fifth of Ireland's land mass which was shaped rather like a sunken apple pie, with a wet and boggy centre. It had a system of lakes, waterways and canals which linked up the four coasts of the country. It was navigable to Waterford, to Dublin, to Enniskillen and, before the Ulster Canal was closed, to Belfast. Rising in Culgaih Mountain in County Cavan, it ran for 230 miles which makes it the longest river in Ireland and Britain, and the second longest in Europe.

The name of the river came from Sinann, the daughter of

Lodan, who in turn was the son of Lir, the great sea-god of the Tuatha Dé Danaan. According to the ancient sagas, they came to Ireland from the north and defeated the Firbolg and the Fomori, evil dwellers of the sea. Lir's other son Manannán took over his role as god of the sea and has his name preserved in the Isle of Man. It seems that the elders of the Tuatha Dé Danaan had very clear ideas about the different roles of the sexes. One day Sinann deliberately broke the traditional boundaries by going to a magical fountain called Connla's Well which was an all-male precinct.

The well was a fountain of knowledge. It had nine hazel trees growing around it which simultaneously blossomed and gave forth beautiful red nuts. These fell into the well, creating shining red bubbles which attracted the salmon. Eating the nuts produced brilliant crimson spots on the fishes' bellies and filled them with knowledge. Whoever caught them in the river afterwards and ate them would acquire the knowledge for themselves.

Now Sinann wanted to possess the masculine qualities which were only available at the well, but when she approached the hallowed spot the water rose violently and broke its banks and rushed down towards the sea. The well became dry for ever. She was drowned in the torrent which swept westwards but her name lived on in the mighty river which her boldness had created.

The Shannon provided the easiest way to penetrate the tangled woods, watery bogs and hazel scrub of the interior of Ireland. The first boats on the waterway were probably dug-outs used by Stone Age settlers. Settlements developed from around 700 BC along the banks of the lower Shannon and many gold ornaments dating from then have been found which show a very high level of craftsmanship. However, it was in the Christian era that the river bank was graced with its finest buildings, especially at Clonmacnois where a monastic community was founded in the sixth century. While the river enabled the monks to import wine from Gaul and the Middle Rhine, it also allowed the Vikings to sail up in their long boats and plunder the settlements along the river. The Normans, too, crossed the Shannon to conquer the province of Connacht in the thirteenth century, but the river continued to act as a boundary to the wilder western part of Ireland.

We continued to be blessed with calm weather that afternoon on the Shannon. The north easterly wind picked up a little and we sailed on a beam reach up river. We swept past Kilcredaun Head with its lighthouse and Napoleonic fort on a two-knot tide. I then steered towards the fifteenth-century Tower House of Carrigaholt. We dropped anchor at high tide in mid afternoon off the new quay just below the ruin. Rooks squawked and fought amongst its ivy-covered walls. There were several small fishing boats moored to the pier and one other Irish yacht at anchor. The Irish name for Carrigaholt, Carraig an Cabhailtigh, means 'Rock of the Fleet'.

We walked into town in the evening along the coastal path. It is a well-set-out town with wide roads and a spacious square surrounded by trees by the beach. Swallows and house martins swooped down after the midges which were out with a vengeance. It was a lovely summer's evening: young lovers walked hand in hand, laughing together, old men hobbled to the pubs, and children were out playing later than they should have been.

We came across the old harbour which had silted up. Large rusting bollards and heavy rings implied that it had once been a busy port, although now there were only a few day boats and some rotting hulks settling into the ooze. David remarked on the fine stonework of the harbour walls, especially a set of steps which curved down to the water: 'People just don't build like this any more. There's been a tragic loss of craftsmanship, a tragic breakdown between hand and eye . . .' he lamented.

In a pub we enjoyed some delicious fish chowder and home-made soda bread washed down by cool stout. A young local fisherman joined us at the bar and we got talking. His name was William O'Farrell. He mainly went lobster potting with the skipper of a small trawler, but in the summer, they supplemented their meagre income by taking day trippers out to see the dolphins in the lower Shannon. There was a school of up to sixty dolphins nearby, the only resident group of bottlenose dolphins on the Irish coast.

I was pleased to see that he had quite a different approach to the fishermen of Dingle who chased Fungi for all their worth. 'It's very important to respect the dolphins. You usually see six to ten together although it's sometimes twenty or thirty. The adults feel very protective of their calves and there's no need to go chasing after them; they're naturally curious and enjoy a bit of sport and will come over to the boat.'

'Why do you think they stay around?'

'Well, the estuary provides them with a breeding ground and there's a lot of fish for them. They tend to swim over to the southern shore to feed when the tide's coming in, and return north off Kilcredaun Point on the ebb. They like to swim in the fastest currents. It can be a wild place, especially in winter. Last winter, I saw a sixty-foot wave pass up the estuary. Unbelievable!' I, too, found it difficult to believe. The highest recorded wave in the North Atlantic is eighty-six feet, reported in 1972.

I noticed that he was eating a beefburger and wondered as a fisherman whether he ate fish. 'Fish?' he replied in astonishment. 'The Irish don't eat fish. It's poor man's food!' I had come across the same attitude in Cuba. Perhaps it was because in Catholic countries eating fish is always something of a penance; something you have to do for the good of your soul on a Friday.

He told us about the Spanish trawlers who fished off the

Shannon for months on end in the worst of weather. A local helicopter had gone out to take off an injured crewman in a Force 10 storm and could not believe the conditions. 'They're paid virtually nothing and have to go out in all weathers,' he remarked. 'God only knows what it's going to be like when the Spanish are allowed into the Irish Box next year.'

'You don't agree with it, then?' I asked, soaking up my soup with my bread.

'If you ask me, the EEC policy's all wrong. Foreign fishermen are invited in while the farmers are paid not to farm. Around here it could be like a garden; if anything, we should be putting up trade barriers to encourage local life and produce. Ireland's a land of farmers not fishermen.'

'Why do you work as a fisherman then?'

'Because farming doesn't pay any more!'

I woke up early feeling a little anxious. I felt I ought to be getting on. It was already mid August and I was not yet halfway around Ireland.

We weighed anchor at eleven o'clock and headed upstream with the flood on another sunny morning to Kilrush. It was still a little hazy on the river and now a south easterly breeze, about Force 3, blew on our beam. Except for a couple of coasters which overtook us in mid channel heading up to Limerick, we did not see another vessel. It was very peaceful and pleasant to be sailing in such sheltered waters. In the golden fields along the northern shore of the river, the hay had been stacked in traditional stooks. 'I'm fifty-six today,' David said, breathing in deeply the air which smelt of the sea and the earth, 'and I count my blessings!'

Our destination was Kilrush, where a new marina had recently been built. As we approached Scattery Island off its entrance, we could clearly see the ruins of the sixth-century monastery and its tall round house, a great attraction for Viking raids. The island had also been the nineteenth-century base for the Shannon pilots when the river was a busy waterway for ocean-going vessels.

Kilrush, like Limerick, had been an important port but was entirely dependent on the tides. A large new sea lock had been built to make the marina permanently at high water. The town had been, and probably will be, an important yachting centre. Since a regatta in 1832, organised by Maurice, the son of Daniel O'Connell, The Liberator, it had been the base of the Royal Western Yacht Club. Towards the end of the century, Shannon sailors made several challenges in the America's Cup. In 1925, Conor O'Brien from the island of Foynes was the first person to sail a cruising yacht – his forty-two-foot ketch *Saoirse* – round the world.

It was time for David to go back to his family in Wales. Before he caught his train for Dublin, I treated him to a birthday tea in a garden under the shade of a great tree which waved in the freshening wind. When we returned to *Celtic Gold* to collect his knapsack, we were surrounded by a gaggle of giggling girls, dressed up to the nines in summer frippery, rosy-cheeked and long-legged. They were the official 'Roses of Clare', the beauties of the county, who had been treated to a day trip to Kilrush and Scattery Island. The old berthmaster of the marina apologised for the inconvenience. 'If I had only known you were coming,' he said with a conspiratorial wink, 'I would have arranged for a couple to visit you!'

I said good-bye to David on the quayside in the hot sun. The last thing he said to me was: 'I hope you continue to exercise your wise judgment!'

I was quietly flattered by such praise and confidence from an old salt.

Kilrush, the capital of west Clare, is neatly laid out with some fine stone buildings bordering a very wide street leading from the old port to the main square. Those responsible for planning it were the Vaudeleur family, the main landlords in the area, who controlled the local economy.

Although they built the fine estate town of Kilrush at the end of the eighteenth century, the Vaudeleur family had become brutal landowners a century later. I was in Ireland whilst it was commemorating – celebrating would be the wrong word – the 150th anniversary of the Great Famine. At that time destitute families, their bones sticking through their stinking rags, flocked into Kilrush in the hope of some relief. It was not forthcoming. Indeed, where in some parts of Ireland the landlords had helped their tenants, the bailiffs of the Vaudeleur family later evicted the starving from their hovels for non payment of rent.

The initial cause of the famine was the almost complete dependence of a growing population on a single crop: the potato. In sixty years, from 1781 to 1841, the population grew from four million to over eight million. By the 1840s, Ireland was divided up into huge estates and nearly all Irish farmers rented their land; the wealthier ones sublet patches to the poor. Large communal settlements had developed on the edges of the cultivated estates which had no other staple diet than the potato. What cereals were grown had to be sold off to pay the rent. An increasing number of people were obliged to live off fewer and fewer resources. It is estimated that about two million labourers were subsisting on fifteen million tons of potatoes at the time; indeed some, like black farmers in South Africa, were only paid in the staple food. One acre of land could yield enough potatoes to feed four to six people. When the potato blight struck in August 1845, it meant total disaster.

One of the most obscene aspects of the famine was the callous disregard of the British administration. It did not offer food but public works: labourers were paid to break stones for a penny a

Seagull on Seagull in Baltimore Harbour

The ferry-boy on the way to Sherkin Island

Cape Clear Island, the most southerly of Ireland

A seal basking off Garnish Island, Glengarriff, Bantry Bay

The Italianate garden on Garnish Island

An evening sail off the Dingle Peninsula

Fungi, the dolphin of Dingle

Dunquin Harbour, the most westerly harbour in Europe

Fishing boat in the sound
between Inishvickillane and Inishabro, the Blaskets

Celtic Gold and Charles Haughey's *Celtic Mist* off Inishvickillane

The author in the ruined oratory on the summit of Mount Brandon

Fishing vessel at anchor off Inishboffin Island

Cromwell's fort on Inishboffin

Early morning off the Stags of Broadhaven

Giant's Causeway, Co. Antrim

A Red Admiral checks the chart off the Mountains of Mourne

day in the country and sixpence in the town or build roads which went nowhere – today's 'green roads'. The workhouses, normally the most hated of places, were overflowing, and the crying masses were locked outside their gates. The memories of famine live on in countless ballads and in sayings like 'A crippled beetle could look over the heap of potato skins on the table' or 'Ireland's plenty is water in a basket'.

The doctrines of Malthus, who had declared that the only checks to population are famine, war, vice and misery, were victorious. The failure of the food supply in Ireland had clearly showed that the country was overpopulated. The 'natural check' of famine would have to bring it down to the right level. Charles Trevelyan, the Permanent Head of the Treasury, argued that 'too much has been done for the people. Ireland must be left to the operation of natural causes.' Although there had been abundant harvests in England, the surplus was withheld. Maize was imported from America and held in full government grain stores in Ireland which were rigorously guarded. The *Economist* in London declared that it was no man's business to help another. The doctrine of *laissez-faire* and the free market had triumphed. The famine was not the work of man but the working out of an inevitable law of nature; it was nothing more than nature's revenge for the improvident poor. In reality, the famine was not so much about the potato but about the distribution of power, the ownership of land and the control of resources.

The catastrophe only encouraged racial stereotyping in the minds of the English. Compared to the hard-working and industrious Anglo-Saxons, the Irish in the Celtic twilight were considered thoughtless, fickle, idle and individualistic. In the west of Ireland, the poorest and hardest hit region, the peasantry were often seen as almost sub human, wild, savage and uncouth. Despite their rich Gaelic culture, full of wisdom, stories, poetry, song and music, they did not have a voice because they were illiterate and did not speak English.

It was proportionally the greatest killer famine in recorded history. It lasted for four years. Out of a population of eight million, a million went to the new world and a million to the next world. By comparison, about 50,000 died in the recent famine in Ethiopia. The experience was so horrific that hundreds of thousands more emigrated to America in the decades that followed. In Mayo, the worst affected, fifty per cent of the population left. The long-term result has been that the population of Ireland today is about three and a half million while over fifty million Americans claim Irish descent.

The famine not only wiped out millions, but changed a whole way of life. It was yet another death knoll for the Irish language. Close-knit communities with a lively Gaelic culture were broken up and dispersed. No other event in Irish history has had such a profound effect on national feeling and some have compared it to the holocaust. Although the English were not only to blame – some rich Irish farmers continued to export food – the Great Famine still casts its long shadow over relationships between Britain and Ireland. No wonder the Irish say: 'Beware of the horse's hoof, the bull's horn, and the Saxon's smile.'

I would have liked to have travelled up the Shannon from Kilrush to Clonmacnois, the monastic settlement founded by St Ciaran, and on to Limerick. There is a lovely story about the Clonmacnois monks which reflects their closeness to the air and sea as well as to heaven and earth. One day while some of them were praying in their chapel, they looked up and saw a boat sailing overhead. It was trailing its anchor which got caught in a door. A sailor then jumped out of the boat and swam down in the air as if it were water. He released the anchor but just as he was about to swim up again one of the monks grabbed him by the ankle. 'For God's sake, let me go; or else I'll drown,' he shouted. When released, he swam up to the boat with the anchor. Once on board, the boat gently sailed away. What was the meaning of this vision? Perhaps the monks had spent too much time praying on their knees, or had inadvertently eaten magic mushrooms in their potage.

I would have liked to have gone to Limerick, Ireland's fourth largest city and the birthplace of my father's mother, but it would have been a long haul up the Shannon and fifty miles back again to Loop Head. What finally decided me was the time: it was mid August, and I had to continue my journey north to the Aran islands, Galway Bay and Connemara.

There were surprisingly few yachts in the Kilrush Marina. The only other foreign yachts in the marina were owned by a French family and an elderly Dutchman on his own. He wanted to get away north like me, but the charts he had ordered from Galway had been sent to Dingle rather than Kilrush and he was forced to stay for a couple of days. I had a distinct feeling of being on my own.

The *Sailing Directions* of the Irish Cruising Club suggested that I might find difficulties victualling in the remote anchorages further north, so I filled up with water, diesel and stores. At Glynn's Mill, once a huge granary, I bought a new boathook at the chandlers for the one I had left behind on the landing quay at Inishvickillane during our hurried departure. I also bought some rope for the self-furling jib which had begun to fray.

They had built a fine marina at Kilrush and its literature assured me that there were fully-trained staff on duty twenty-four-hours a day. After pouring over the charts and working out my passage plan, I went to sleep after midnight in the confident knowledge that I would be able to pass through the lock at five o'clock in the morning in order to get the benefit of the ebb tide down the Shannon to the Aran islands.

I got up at four after having had very little sleep. I had breakfast, stowed all my gear, prepared the food and drink for the day and made ready to release the moorings. I then called up the lock on the VHF radio as I had done to announce my arrival. No answer. I tried again. No answer. I waited ten minutes. No answer. I decided to walk along the pontoons to the marina office which was, like all the facilities, in a temporary building on the quay. The light was on in the office and pop music blared from a radio, but when I knocked on the door, there was no answer. I could see through the blinds that there was no one in the office. I assumed that the nightwatchman had just popped out for a few minutes. I waited half an hour. No one turned up. I returned to *Celtic Gold* and called up the lock keeper again. It was the same old story. I kept this up, calling the lock keeper and knocking up the marina office for two hours, from five to seven. I then gave up in disgust; I had missed the best of the tide and would not be able to reach the Aran islands by nightfall.

It was very frustrating. I felt like I was locked in a cage. The great pleasure of cruising is the freedom, the ability to come and go when you feel like it, without anyone telling you what to do. Not this time. But there was more than simple frustration at work. I was about to embark solo on one of the longest and riskiest passages of my voyage and I wanted optimum conditions. I would be exposed to the full fetch of the Atlantic. There were no ports of refuge on the way, only a savage and rugged coastline which culminated in the cliffs of Moher which rose 700-feet, sheer out of sea. The forecast for that day had been ideal: good visibility, with a Force 4 to 5 southerly wind. With a bit of luck, I should have been able to cross over Galway Bay the next day from the Aran island to Kinvarra to see the 'Gathering of the Boats', the annual race of classic Irish boats, which featured the famous forty-foot Galway Hookers. But it was not to be. When the manager eventually turned up at eight thirty, I explained what had happened. 'You should have told me that you would be leaving early and I would have been up to do the locks,' he said, irritated by my complaints.

'But the leaflet your staff gave me specifically says that the marina is fully-manned twenty-four hours a day. Why leave the radio and lights on in the office if this is not the case? You know I paid for last night. The tides and time would have been perfect for me this morning, and there was a good forecast.'

'Well, there's no coverage from 3 o'clock during the week.'

'Then why don't you let visiting yachtsmen know if that's the case? What happens if a yacht comes in from the Atlantic in the middle of night?'

'We leave the gates of the lock open. There was a yacht the other night which the pilots picked up. I got out of bed to let it in.'

The manager was clearly tired and overworked and I left it at that. There was no point crying over spilt milk and no doubt I should have double-checked.

I now had to rethink my plans. I decided to sail to Carrigaholt on the ebb that evening. I did not fancy spending another night and getting locked in Kilrush again. The lock keeper was very friendly but warned me to be careful, especially as the weather was breaking. He looked worried when I told him I was on my own.

I passed through the lock at eight o'clock. It was a great relief to be clear and I had a lovely evening sail along the north shore of the Shannon on a broad reach in the warm southerly breeze. I arrived at Carrigaholt just before ten and moored alongside a blue trawler so I could make a quick getaway the following morning before dawn. The rooks squabbled among the ramparts of the old tower overlooking the pier while in the distance I could hear the tractor of a farmer trying to get the hay in before it rained. When it grew dark half an hour later, silence fell over the deserted harbour except for the gentle lapping of the water. It was very peaceful – peace, a little inner voice suggested, before the storm?

The weather forecast was not good. A cold front was moving eastwards across Ireland and Shannon was going to have the worst of it. I could expect southerly 5 to near gale 7 winds backing westerly later in the day. There would be heavy showers with moderate to poor visibility. The *Sailing Directions* pointed out that in bad visibility the only possible approach would be to make the south side of the Aran islands, as long as the visibility was good enough to identify landfall. By night it would be prudent to heave to and await daylight. They warned that with driving mist and strong to gale force winds any approach to the outer dangers would be 'foolhardy'. They added ominously that the forty-five miles of coast from Loop Head to the entrance of Galway Bay had no safe anchorages and 'being exposed to the full ocean swell is best admired from a comfortable distance'. The enforced delay in Kilrush might make all the difference between pleasant cruising and possibly dangerous conditions.

17

Snakes in the Sea

After a fitful sleep, I got up at half past five to a cloudy morning. The rooks in the castle tower of Carrigaholt were already beginning to squabble and a fisherman was making his boat ready. A fresh wind was blowing from the south east. Visibility was moderate; the barometer on the low side at 1012 millibars. So far so good.

I had decided to try and sail to Kilronan in Inishmore, the largest of the Aran islands. They were about fifty-five nautical miles away and I could expect at least fifteen hours of non-stop sailing on my own. There were no refuge ports along the rugged coastline and with a cold front passing over the country, I could count on near gale force winds and squally showers. The Shannon region was set to experience the worst weather in Ireland. It was going to be a test of my nerve and stamina as much as of my seamanship and navigation.

After stowing my gear carefully and preparing the day's food and drink, I was ready to go. I checked the sea cocks to the heads for a second time; I didn't want another spillage out in the high Atlantic swell. I called up Shannon Radio on the VHF and told them my destination was Kilronan, Inishmore, ETA 2100 hours. 'Have a good voyage, sir,' came the reply.

I cast off the moorings from the trawler just after seven o'clock, one hour after High Water Galway, just as the tide turned on my part of the Shannon. Perfect. I gave Kilcredaun Point a clear berth for I did not want to end up like the Greek steamship *Okeanos* which was shipwrecked in 1947 on the reefs below. By now the ebb tide on the river was picking up. In choppy water where the current was strongest, I was suddenly joined by half a dozen bottlenosed dolphins – part of the resident school – who had come to the northern bank to feed. They jumped right underneath the bows of *Celtic Gold*, revealing their white bellies under their shining dark-grey backs. They then dropped back and swam alongside the cockpit. They must have been between nine and twelve feet long. They swam so close that I could clearly see their small smiling eyes in their rounded heads above their short grey beaks.

It was a wonderful, uplifting experience, just what I needed at the time, a good omen to see me through the long day ahead.

I decided to pass inside the Kilstiffin Bank with its mournful whistle buoy and keep about half a mile off the northern shore. As I approached the mouth of the Shannon, *Celtic Gold* began to pitch and roll on the rising swell of the Atlantic Ocean. With the south east wind, I maintained a steady four knots on a beam reach.

I reached Loop Head about two hours after my departure. Although it was low-lying, the dark promontory was far from inviting. The sky had steadily clouded over and as I drew abeam the lighthouse, it began to rain steadily. The lighthouse was soon lost in the low cloud. I set a course for the Aran islands, turning the head of *Celtic Gold* into the high, dark-grey waves which were beginning to break. The wind was still from the south east. Having rounded Loop Head, I had passed the point of no return.

I felt very vulnerable, exposed now to the full fetch of the Atlantic. And for the next forty miles, I would find no refuge along the steep and jagged coastline.

It continued to rain all morning. I sat in my oilskins in the cockpit, the rain dripping off my nose. My body was warm inside its many layers but I did not have any gloves so my hands grew soft and white and cold. It stopped raining briefly mid morning and I could just make out some dark-grey cliffs. I estimated my position to be about five miles off the coast of Clare, but the dark cloud soon closed in again before I could take a fix.

There was a huge swell. The waves must have been about twenty feet high. *Celtic Gold* would roll as well as pitch in the running sea. She would climb up the long, curling, breaking waves, shudder, and then glide down into a deep trough when the sails would lose the wind and flap uncontrollably. I was now running with the wind, the sails spread on either side, goose-winged fashion. In the mid afternoon, the wind suddenly veered from the south east to the south west, and the mainsail gybed. As the boom swung over at high speed, it only just missed my head. I was lucky. I could have been knocked out or overboard. I thought of the man whom I had seen before my departure with blood pouring from his ear after he had been hit. I put out a preventer, taking a rope from the end of the boom round a block in the bows and then back to the cockpit to hold the mainsail out. I also poled out the jib to stop it collapsing in the troughs. It was a difficult manoeuvre in the tossing sea and I made sure my harness was clipped on to the jackstay running along the length of the deck. If I slipped overboard, there would be no one to pick me up.

Out there for hours in the wild Atlantic on my own, I reflected that I had a strange affinity with the sea. I did not feel that it was at all alien. I was conscious that as a species we had first evolved from the oceans and that our blood, which makes up ninety per cent of our body, has the same chemical composition as sea water. We also spend the first nine months of our life in the womb, breathing fluid and floating. Perhaps that oceanic feeling, the feeling of wanting to become part of the whole, is an unconscious desire to return to the watery world of the womb. If I died at sea, then I would be food for the fish; if I died on land, I would like to be cremated and my ashes scattered on the ebb tide: in both, I would dissolve in the water like a drop of wine in the infinite ocean of being.

For some the deep is a place where monsters dwell, but for me it is a space of luminous and unearthly beauty. The closest I have ever been to paradise on this planet is diving in the Maldivian archipelago in the Indian Ocean. Leaving the lagoon and swimming beyond the coral reef which drops a thousand fathoms takes your breath away, but you quickly realise that you can fly, roll, turn and drift in the warm, sunlit waters. The coral is a myriad of colours and countless species of fish live in its shelter. Dark shapes of sharks, a hundred or so feet down, glide around and giant mantra rays come in on the upwellings, but there is nothing to fear: no diver has ever been attacked because there is an abundance of marine life. When it was rough, I found it much more reassuring to be in the quiet tranquillity under water. Whatever the wild wind was doing to the surface, below it was always calm. I tried to develop the same attitude in life.

During that endless day out in the high swell and heavy rain of the Atlantic Ocean, entirely cut off from the rest of the world, my thoughts also turned to Bran, the great Celtic seafarer. I had come to realise that the early Celtic wonder voyages were very similar to the vision quests of the native Indians of North America. They involved men going into the wilderness and facing hardship in order to become clearer about their mission in life and place in the scheme of things. It increasingly dawned on me that I had been undergoing similar quests in the last few years.

I had heard an inner voice calling me to go around Africa one cold winter's evening whilst trudging in the mountains of North Wales in the pouring rain. I had felt bogged down at the time. I completed the circumnavigation and learned a great deal about myself and about what was important in my life, but it also led to the separation from my partner. I had heard the inner voice again after leaving the home I loved in the mountains where my children had grown up and where I had spent the happiest years of my life. This time it was Ireland which beckoned. This time, I hoped the voyage would heal rather than unsettle.

Vision quests and wonder voyages carry dangers as well as the possibility of enlightenment, as Bran was to find out. When he listened to the siren voice which told him to leave the comfort of his hearth and go on a journey across the sea, he gathered together a dozen strong men. They made the necessary preparations to leave on their ox hide currach. Two of his brothers insisted on joining him. They took enough food and water with them for forty days. They set sail in the spring and after many days rowing, hoisted the sails and let the wind take them wherever it would. After many days, with only the birds and the dolphins as their companions, they came across a beautiful green island. They landed in a sandy cove where an old man came down to greet them. He knew all their names: 'Welcome,' he said. 'This is the Island of Contentment. Here you will never be sad or miserable.' One of the brothers decided to stay but Bran and the others wanted to continue their voyage to see what other marvels they might encounter.

On their way, they saw a strange figure in a chariot riding the crest of a wave. He was old Manannán Mac Lir, the sea god, whose angry lips in their snowy foam would often swallow great fleets of ships. He sang:

Bran thinks this is a marvellous sea.
For me it is a flowery plain.
Speckled salmon leap from the belly of your sea;
To me they are calves and sprightly lambs.

He carried a bag made from the skin of a crane which he claimed contained the alphabet; in fact it was the skin of his wife who had tried to steal his knowledge and broadcast it to the world.

After many more days, they saw another green island in the sun. It had many bright white houses set in gardens full of flowers. On a long white strand, beautiful women in flowing white robes beckoned them to land. One came forward and said to Bran: 'This is the Island of Women. We have been waiting for you and your men. We would be pleased if you stayed with us and we will make sure that your every wish is satisfied.'

The men, who had almost forgotten their women at home, gave a mighty 'hurrah' and fell over themselves in their eagerness to scramble ashore. There Bran and his men stayed and it was true that every need and desire was satisfied. They lived like kings in great comfort and ease. During the day the women prepared the tastiest food for them and at night they taught them sensual delights which they had never imagined. The sun always seemed to shine on both sides of the hedges and the land and the sea produced food for the taking.

But it was not to last. After what seemed a year but was in fact many years, Bran's brother grew listless and dissatisfied.

'It's all very well having every desire satisfied,' he said, 'but I'm beginning to forget what my family and country look like. I'd like to see them again before I completely forget.' The other men, who had secretly felt the same thing, agreed and it was decided to set sail for home. The women seemed upset, but did not try to stop them.

On their return journey, they picked up Bran's brother from

the Isle of Contentment and after many adventures, they eventually reached their homeland. But when they approached the familiar shore, they hardly recognised it for everything had changed. There were many more houses and the pattern of fields was no longer the same. One of Bran's brothers dived from the boat and swam ashore but as soon as he reached the beach, he turned into ashes. Bran wrote down their story on a stick and threw it into the water. He turned his boat around and headed out to sea and he and his men were never seen again. The stick was washed ashore by the tide and that is how we know about the voyage of Bran.

I kept a lookout for Manannán that day sailing to the Aran islands; if I was ever going to meet him, it would be out there in the wild Atlantic. At one moment, I thought I could see his foamy lips, but no, it was a rogue wave. Strange things occur when alone out at sea.

In mid afternoon, the cloud lifted again for a brief moment, and I had my first sight of the Aran islands. They stretched out right across the grey horizon, a low dark-grey snake in the ocean. I could not see the sounds which separated the three islands. I trusted my navigation and continued my course. Cloud closed in again. The *Sailing Directions* suggested that it was unwise to approach the islands in poor visibility, high swell and fading light. I had all three. I was in two minds whether to carry on or to go out to sea and heave to for the night. I did not fancy the latter as I was feeling very weary. I had hardly slept for sixty hours and had spent a long day's hard sailing. In the end the weather decided for me. The wind was freshening; I was running in a south westerly Force 5. With the great swell, now rising to almost twenty-five feet high, spray was flying from the breaking crests of the waves.

Around tea time, the sun shone in a miraculous burst, as it had done in my approach to Glandore, and I was at last able to make out the sounds between the islands and the mainland. The great snake had divided into three. I could also see the famous cliffs of Moher, rising a sheer 700 feet out of the sea and extending for five miles along the coast.

An hour later, the visibility was good enough for me to take a fix from the western edges of Inishmore and Inishmaan, and the eastern edge of Inisheer. I was now only four miles away. The islands looked truly forbidding in the rain, forming a low, dark strip across my bow. I decided to sail through the narrow Gregory Sound between Inishmore and Inishmaan. By this time there was a two-knot tide running with me as well as a twenty-knot wind. It was growing dark and the driving rain settled in again.

Gregory Sound was only a mile wide and the sea was breaking on the craggy rocks for about two hundred yards on either side of the steep cliffs. That left me only about 500 metres leeway, 500 metres of confused and swirling waters. I tried to aim for the mid channel. But with the long, heaving swell, I felt myself being swept towards the south west headland of Inishmaan. *Celtic Gold* was corkscrewing down the waves under me.

It was too late to pull back now. I grabbed the tiller firmly and tried to steer clear. At first, nothing seemed to happen. Each wave set me closer to the boiling waters at the foot of the towering black cliffs. I thought my time had come. I could hear the roar of the pounding surf and could see the great waves crashing on the jagged foreshore, strewn with huge broken boulders, sending white spray and foam high up into the air. But I was going forwards as well as sideways, and I sensed that the waves were beginning to lose a fraction of their force. The further I went, the surer I became. *Celtic Gold*, bounced around by the waves, was at last holding her course. We would scrape by the headland of Inishmaan. Once I knew that I would make it, worry turned to exhilaration. As each wave picked me up, I surfed down its trough, working the tiller to get the best effect. Man and boat, water and wind, were in harmony again. I was soon riding the waves, walking on air!

It took me a good hour to get through the sound, the waves decreasing all the time as the island of Inishmore protected me from the full fetch of the Atlantic swell. I was now able to take in the grey barren landscape of rock-strewn fields. There was not a tree or bush in sight. After sailing around the lighthouse of Straw Island, and negotiating the narrow entrance through the bar into Killeany Bay, I tacked close-hauled against the strong south westerly wind. Yellow rays of the setting sun burst through the dark clouds. Despite the fatigue and tension of the previous two days, I thoroughly enjoyed the challenging sail. I got so carried away that I failed to notice the new red and white ferry – the *Aran Flyer* – hammering up behind me until it cut close across my bow.

When I at last dropped anchor south of the pier and near the life boat, I wrote in my log in rare capital letters: 'ARR KILRONAN, THANK GOD!' It was 1945 hours. I informed Shannon of my arrival which was two hours earlier than estimated. I was too tired to go ashore, and after an omelette, soda bread, hot tea and whiskey, I fell into my bunk, unwashed, exhausted but content.

During the night, I dreamt that I was drifting, and I woke up with a start just after dawn to find *Celtic Gold* being buffeted by wild winds and snatching at the anchor. The wind was whistling mournfully through the rigging. I went up on the deck to see a dismal overcast day. Dark clouds were scudding low over the hills from the south west, and even in the shelter of the bay there were white horses on the dark green sea. The barren fields with their few white homesteads looked bleaker than ever, and Kilronan, the biggest settlement on the Aran islands, seemed little more than a village.

I had read that in severe conditions it was unsafe to take the ground off Kilronan. I decided to put out the kedge anchor to increase the holding. I pumped up the rubber dinghy and with much difficulty screwed on the Seagull outboard; the dinghy was bobbing around like a cork. I took the kedge anchor into the dinghy with its three metres of heavy chain and fifty metres of warp, and then slowly motored upwind to lay the kedge at 90 degrees to the other anchor. I managed to do it on the first run, the warp running out smoothly with no snags. When I threw the heavy anchor and chain overboard from the little dinghy, I made sure my leg was not attached to it! Once back on board, I made myself a cup of tea and felt much more secure. To warm up I got back into my sleeping bag and fell asleep again.

When I woke up the wind had eased a little and the sun was trying to break through chinks in the dark clouds. The cold front had passed over and it was the Irish Sea, not the Shannon, which was due to experience a near gale.

Arriving in the Aran islands on 11th August, I felt that I was more than half way around Ireland. In seven weeks, I had covered over 600 nautical miles, and had experienced the delights of plain sailing as well as more exciting and challenging passages. I felt confident in the yacht and in myself, although the engine was always a worry.

It was a Saturday and I gave up all hope now of sailing across Galway Bay to Kinvarra for the weekend's 'Gathering of the Boats'. I would not have the time, either, to visit David Lea's cousin, Commander 'Bill' King, the round-the-world yachtsman, in his castle on the shores of the bay. I decided instead to spend the morning doing some maintenance. I changed the fuel filters to make sure that the diesel would be as clean and free-flowing as possible for the difficult passages ahead.

The day proved gusty with sunny periods. I went ashore in the dinghy after lunch and wandered around the narrow streets of Kilronan. I had heard so much about the people of the Aran islands and their unique way of life. They stood out in my imagination as strongly as the Blasket islanders. It was a great disappointment to find the streets covered in litter. The grander buildings had been built by the colonial administrators: barracks, courthouse, pound and coastguard station. Some have been transformed for more humane activities: the former barracks and courthouse were now pubs. Other houses were abandoned or boarded up. The village looked run-down and ill-kempt.

The only people who sauntered through the streets were foreigners: I heard the accents of German, Italian, and French but no Irish or Irish-English. I walked to the new pier and found a long line of minibuses and taxis waiting for the arrival of the next 'super fast' ferry. The few local men stood out by their red faces, big frames and large hands. In the high season, the ferries brought more than 2,000 trippers a day, travelling the thirty miles from Galway in only ninety minutes, or the twelve miles from the Connemara coast in thirty minutes. The population of the whole island of Inishmore is about 1,000 but they must have been outnumbered by three to one. Minibuses were hurtling along the narrow main road all day, forcing the cyclists to the verge in a cloud of dust. Some old men brought their horses and carts, the traditional means of transport, to offer an ethnic touch to the wealthy. Most of the visitors only stayed for a few hours. One could spend a lifetime and still not know the islanders. What could one expect to gain in a few hours?

The result of this influx of tourists was that many islanders had virtually abandoned their farming and crafts in a wild orgy of fleecing of visitors, at least for three months of the year. Every spare room was offered for hire. There was only one large store, and a bank which opened on Wednesday, but several *bureaux de change* had opened charging extortionate commission. Tourist shops and boutiques had also blossomed, selling the traditional Aran sweaters. The distinctive style of knitting had been introduced to the island in the nineteenth century and each family had created its own pattern of stitches. But now the cottage industry was over. I asked in a shop about the wool and was told that the famous 'Aran' sweaters are now imported. It would not surprise me if they are imported from the sweatshops of the Far East to be sold here in the Far West to Japanese tourists.

There were no hotels yet on the island and I went into a hostel by the harbour and asked if I could use the shower. No problem, replied a harassed receptionist, her eyes dark rims. I was directed upstairs and told that the only showers were through a women's dormitory. They did not seem to mind the invasion of this greybeard in yellow oilskins and wellies. The showers looked as if they had not been cleaned all summer. The lavatories too were filthy. I thought of the cleanliness and care I had seen in all the coastal houses I had visited in Ireland, and was saddened by the effect quick money was having on the moral fibre and traditional skills of some of the islanders.

The next day I decided to go for a walk into the surrounding hills. Abandoning the main tarmaced road (still only wide enough for one vehicle), I cut south west along a grassy and overgrown track, known as a boreen, bordered by rough stone walls. It led me up to the 'creigs', bare rocky areas on the limestone escarpment which runs from end to end of the islands. The limestone created a spectacular rock garden with sheets and crags of light-grey rock, strange shapes and hollows, all broken up by crevasses and small ravines. Rough grasses and delicate flowers gripped wherever there was scanty soil in the holes. The scarp looked towards the afternoon sun and the prevailing winds and the sheer cliffs which plunged into the surging and angry Atlantic.

From my vantage point, I could see down towards the more sheltered north east, a grey maze of stone walls, bare fields and paths on the terraces which dip gradually down to the low shore of rugged promontories, shingle banks, and sheltered, sandy coves. In the distance across the sound was the dark grey, brooding outline of the mainland.

There are said to be over 7,000 miles of stone walls on the Aran islands, thrown up over the centuries to clear the ground, to protect the scarce soil and to control the grazing. Since there was not enough wood for gates, the farmers would often build up and knock down the walls along the boreens and paths.

Nature has not been generous in the Aran islands and humans have not helped either. The limestone, as in the Burren on the mainland, was once under water and contains the shadows of millions of fossils of plants and creatures. When the first settlers arrived, the islands would have been covered in trees rooted in a thin layer of soil, but once they had been cut down, the soil was soon washed away. The exposed limestone was easily eroded by rain which seeped through the cracks to form fissures and crevasses. With the relentless effect of wind and water, the islands will eventually become a submerged reef, returning to sea from whence they came.

But while human folly first eroded the soil, human muscle temporarily replaced it. Over centuries, the islanders gradually cleared the fields by throwing the loose rocks into walls around them. They then broke down the larger stones and covered them with sand carried up from the seashore. This was mixed with seaweed to give it some fertility. Until a generation ago, women would gather the seaweed in the winter, stack it to dry, burn it in June and then carry it up in wooden baskets on their backs to the scant fields. Most of the farms were only eight to twelve hectares, but they managed to keep sheep and cattle and grow cabbages and potatoes in the few feet of soil.

As I walked along the boreens, it was tragic to see so many fields overgrown with bracken and thistles. I saw no sheep and only a few cows. The islanders had turned their backs on the work of their ancestors, men and women who had killed themselves so that their children might live. The names of thousands of places and fields, full of associations and poetry, were being forgotten. But still the intricate patterns of fields would stand for thousands of years as a monument to their labour and to the human spirit which struggled in the face of overwhelming odds, scratching a living from the bare rock.

Back in Kilronan, I met Bernie O'Toole, a young woman who was working in the Heritage Centre of the island. Both her parents spoke Irish, but she had been brought up to speak English because they thought that it would help her get on. Such an attitude spells death to the Irish language. While Irish is the first official language of the State, only five per cent of Ireland's population of three and half million used it in their everyday life. The remaining Irish-speaking areas – the Gaeltacht – were on the remote coasts and islands of the Western seaboard. If the young of the islands were dropping it, then one of the oldest Celtic languages was doomed.

There were only three schools on the island so Bernie had gone to the mainland for her secondary education and to go to university. She had come back for the summer. I asked whether she would stay: 'I doubt it. I'd like to get a job abroad, possibly working for the EEC. There's not much for young people on the island, especially in the winter . . .'

'Would you marry an islander?'

'I would if I loved him, but most girls marry outside the island.'

I thought of John Synge who had built himself a shelter of stone rocks on Inishmaan to find his speech for his plays, returning to the source of old Ireland. So many writers and scholars, inspired by Yeats and the formation of The Gaelic League, had visited his thatched cottage that it came to be known as 'The University'. One of them was the young poet Patrick Pearse who went on to proclaim the Irish Republic in the Easter Rising of 1916 in Dublin.

The women at the heritage centre were the only ones I saw wearing traditional dress. No longer did they wait on the shores or headlands for their men to return from the sea, with their crocheted shawls over their heads flying in the wind and the red of their skirts contrasting with the grey of the stone, sea and sky. Nor did the men wear the heavy Aran sweaters, brown homespun trousers, jerkins and matching caps. And their 'pampooties' – soft slippers without heels made from goatskin – were things of the past.

There were still some of the old dwellings, long, low whitewashed stone-walled dwellings with fish netting held down with stones to prevent the rye thatch from being blown away in the winter storms. But new concrete villas were springing up along the sheltered north shore and near the main road. Most of them had TV aerials and cars parked in spacious drives.

It was a far cry from the time at the beginning of the twentieth century when Synge, following Yeats' advice, had come to Aran to escape 'from the squalor of the poor and the nullity of the rich' and to discover in the life of the islanders 'the strange quality that is found in the oldest poetry and legend'. He observed that the islands and the people who lived on them had a peace and dignity 'from which we are shut out for ever'. But even in this little corner of the world they were disappearing fast. The visitors, including myself, were destroying the unique way of life they had come to see. All that would be left soon of the old Aran islands would be the great grey desert of the creigs, the incessant pounding of the waves on the cliffs, and the fading memories of the old folk.

18

Forts in the Mist

The pagans have a long and deep foothold on the Aran islands. St Enda was a pagan chief, but he was converted to Christianity. After visiting Rome in the late fourth century, he returned home to Ireland to found a monastery. Like many other Irish monks and the desert fathers, he felt closer to God in wild places, far away from the luxury and pomp of the courts in which he grew up. He chose for his base the Aran islands, a remote outpost of Europe in the savage Atlantic. Many monks followed, including St Columba. Thus grew the fame of 'Aran of the Saints' which once played a considerable role in the spread of Christianity.

On the sheltered northern side of Inishmore, I visited several ruins of churches dating from the seventh century. Overlooking a fine sandy beach near Kilmurray was a cluster called Na Seacht Teampaill, 'Seven Churches', which proved to be little more than a couple of ruined chapels, a few monastic buildings, and fragments of a high cross. They were humble places, simple and sparse, now sheltering the wren and the harebell.

Most traces of the early churches have disappeared under the drifting sands. Yet the pagan beliefs which they tried to supplant live on in the islanders' calendar. St Brigid's festival on 1st February is a veiled celebration of the older Brigid, the Celtic goddess of fertility, at the crucial time of Imbolg, mid way between the winter solstice and the spring equinox. And they continue to light bonfires on 23rd June, celebrating the summer solstice, to ensure that the sun will return to the north the following year.

The greatest ruins on the Arans were built thousands of years before the arrival of Christians. What interested me most were the so-called stone forts which are on Inishmore. The most famous and intriguing is the vast Dún Aengus complex on the southern cliffs. I approached it along a winding boreen which climbed the craggy limestone escarpment to the rocky creigs. Amongst the ancient stone walls, ivy tried to grow and at one spot the stunted growth of flowering honeysuckle had managed to take root. Grey jagged rock pillars pointed to the grey sky. Ravens circled high above in the wild wind. It was a blasted landscape on a bleak day, with nothing but a few hardy flowers to uplift the heart.

Dún Aengus, battered by centuries of storms, stands at the threshold of an older world. It dominates the landscape for miles around. It is a massive dry-stone structure, one of the finest of its kind in Europe, within four curving outer walls. The outermost wall must have enclosed about eleven acres of land. Outside the second wall, I came across a thirty-foot band of upright stones. The inner court was about 150 feet across, surrounded by walls twenty feet high and eighteen feet thick at its base. On reaching the last rampart, I was astounded to find that it was protecting a sheer cliff which fell 300 feet to the boiling surf below. It formed a hemisphere, with a massive platform looking out to sea. My first thoughts were that the building had been circular and half of it had fallen away in some great geological catastrophe.

The stones were not massive but it must have involved an

immense amount of labour to raise the walls, labour which would have required the hands of thousands. The stones were so well placed that they had withstood centuries of Atlantic storms.

The origins and function of the complex are shrouded in mystery, as dense as the sea mists which swirl around it for most of the year. Nothing is known of the people who built it. Named after the mythical hero Aonghus, folklore says that it was the handiwork of the Fir Bolg, a pre-Celtic tribe who escaped enslavement in Thrace and invaded Ireland. Modern archaeologists claim that it dates from the Celtic Iron Age, c.400 to 500, but there is a growing body of evidence to put the date back to the late Bronze Age, c.700 BC. Since it is impossible to date stone accurately, this is far from conclusive. The archaeologists are also divided on whether Dún Aengus was always semicircular or truncated by the collapse of the cliff. What is certain is that there are several other circular forts on Inishmore and its neighbouring islands and about thirty still surviving in Galway, Clare and Kerry. They are usually enclosed in massive walls and dominate the landscape.

The structure is usually called a fort but what was it protecting? What was the point of fortifying a group of barren rocks? If, as it has been argued, it was the last defence of the original inhabitants of Ireland before the conquest of the Celts, why should they want to defend the open Atlantic? If attacked, how could they sustain themselves against a siege, especially as there is no well of fresh water? While Dún Aengus might superficially appear as a fort, it makes no sense as a fort.

It seemed more likely to me that this great stone platform on the edge of the world was built for ritual purposes. Perhaps ceremonies were held here to placate the anger of the sea god, to prevent the world from sinking again below tidal waves and floods which had in myth once overtaken it. Perhaps human sacrifices were made on the platform, the priests pushing victims over the cliffs, giving life to prevent the sea god from taking more.

Lying down and leaning over the edge of the terrifying cliff, I could see that there were chiselled ledges on which guillemots, razorbills, kittiwakes and fulmars rested, buffeted but unbowed by the prevailing wind. The sight of the great Atlantic rollers hurling themselves at the rocks and sending spray high into the air filled me with fear. I imagined myself in *Celtic Gold* in such an angry expanse of water; how fragile and frail we were in the face of such an overwhelming force! I would have to dare this wilderness of sea and sky in a few days' time. I would have to head for colder and more northern climes.

An insinuating voice inside me said: 'You've gone far enough now. What more have you got to prove? You could be home in forty-eight hours . . .' It was a moment of temptation, but another, stronger voice said: 'Don't give up. You don't know what beauty and wisdom are in store for you. Continue to exercise your wise judgment and all will be well. Remember the dolphins and the birds!' The first voice said: 'You're saying that because you know that you don't have a home to return to. You've blown it away. Take it easy now, give up this crazy attempt to prove that you can live on your own and face danger on the high seas. Look at the size and strength of those great rollers out there and think of your family round a nice cosy fire. Where would you rather be?'

I felt a sudden urge to jump off the cliff. But I held back from the abyss. I still had too many accounts to put straight before I was ready to leave this earth. I looked along the cliffs and the great rolling waves which crashed into their broken base. I thought of the cliffmen of Aran who earlier this century would crawl on moonless nights along the narrow ledges of the cliffs to wring the necks of the sleeping birds. Better to go like the birds, unsuspecting, than end it all oneself.

If the origins of the forts were mysterious, an even greater mystery was that of the Aran islanders themselves. They had a different blood group from most people on the mainland. Were they descendants of Phoenicians who made their way up into these cold and misty waters from the Mediterranean over two and half thousand years ago? There were certainly connections. The Irish word for tin, *stan*, was Phoenician in origin, while the word cairn, a heap of stones usually placed over a grave, is identical with the Semitic *kern*, meaning a tumulus of sand or peak. The Irish custom of individual mourners placing a stone over a grave was mirrored in Phoenicia.

Or perhaps they were descended from the Atlanteans, survivors of the lost civilisation of Atlantis. The forts are so large and spectacular that the Irish-American senator Ignatius Donnelly argued at the end of the nineteenth century that the Aran islands might have been outposts of the outer boundary of Atlantis which disappeared under the waves. Perhaps Dún Aengus was sliced during that mighty geological catastrophe.

I had been intrigued by stories of the lost civilisation of Atlantis ever since I had read Plato's account in *Timaeus*. The island civilisation in the west was swallowed up by the sea following earthquakes and floods of extraordinary violence. He dated its sinking to 9,000 years before Solon – about 14,500 BC. In all the major civilisations of the world, there are stories about an earlier civilisation lost in a deluge. The ancient Celts of Gaul, Ireland and Wales maintained that their ancestors hailed from a lost land in the west, sometimes known as Avalon, which was swallowed up by a sea god. The North African Berbers, the Iberians, the Basques, the Norse and the Scandinavians all have similar legends of a lost civilisation to the west. This is not surprising since there had been a common Atlantic seaborne culture from North Africa to Scandinavia since Megalithic times. The great megaliths not only reflected an advanced understanding of astronomy but had common designs – spirals, circles, lozenges – which may have been maps of the night sky.

There can be no doubt that cities and whole tracts of land have disappeared beneath the waves. Trawlermen off the Dogger Bank, which is almost the size of Holland, have pulled up axe heads, moorlog (a kind of peat), bear, deer and ox bones from a depth of ninety metres in their nets. Grey waters swirl ten fathoms down where green forests of willow and birch once swayed. They were submerged at the end of the last Ice Age when the glaciers melted, over 10,000 years ago. And if global warming and melting of the ice caps continue at their present rate, low-lying lands like Holland and the Maldive islands will eventually disappear under water.

After being lost for a while on the wilder shores of speculation, I returned to Kilronan in the evening, just as it began to rain heavily. I went to shelter in the first pub I came across on the fringes of the village. The place was already packed. I sat at the only empty table. I soon realised why it was empty. A group of musicians arrived, large Aran men, chatting in Irish, with accordion, flute, guitar and Celtic drum. The flutist, a very large man with red face and silvery hair, sat down next to me and spoke to me first in Irish and then in English: 'Are you a singing man?'

''Fraid not, but I love to listen to music . . .'

I picked up my pint and made ready to go, but he insisted that I should remain. I was now sandwiched amongst the musicians. They started to play and a large group gathered around to appreciate their music and singing. I felt very incongruous in their midst. I couldn't even play the spoons.

At the break, I bought the musicians drinks. The flautist, now sweating, introduced himself as Paddy. He told me that he had seen me from the beach the other evening, sailing into the bay. He had a blue fishing boat, a thirty-five-footer, and went after mackerel and pollock. He was not a fisher-farmer, as most of the islanders of the west coast, but a fisher-flautist. I asked him whether he took his flute with him when he went fishing; perhaps like the Blasket islanders, he would ease his loneliness with his music whilst out at sea.

'No time, I'm too busy looking after the boat.'

It was his turn to enquire: 'Are you on your own?'

'For the time being . . .'

'Do you mind being on your own?'

It was a good question and I didn't have a ready answer. I couldn't go into the circumstances of my separation, the heartfelt need to come to terms with my life by going on this voyage, the challenge of being alone. Instead I replied: 'I wanted to see what it would be like. When you're travelling on your own you often meet more people than if you're with someone else.'

'Don't you find it lonely?'

'Not really, what about you?'

'It can be sometimes. But when I'm at sea, it's mainly hard work, navigating and fishing.'

I suspected that he did find it lonely, out there in his blue boat on a grey sea under a grey sky by a grey island. His music, which he said was real Aran music, was, by contrast, full of light, fire and energy.

Queuing at the bar, I commented to a middle-aged islander how busy it was. 'It's a rich harvest while it lasts,' he replied, 'but it goes up and down like a hilly road.'

'I suppose everyone's trying to get their cut from the visitors.'

'Yes. Make hay while the sun shines!' He grabbed his two pints and two whiskeys and disappeared into the throng.

It was unfortunate that money should corrode the relationship between the islanders and the visitors, but I could not really blame them for wanting to make as much money as they could. Their life had been one of unremitting struggle and for centuries they had been forgotten on their lonely outpost in the Atlantic. Their only chance of a windfall in the past had been a shipwreck. Now city dwellers were flocking to have a glimpse of a way of life and a community which was close to the earth, the sea, the sky and to each other. These things had been lost in most of Europe. Their very presence would ruin it, but at least it had given the islanders a break from their ceaseless toil. They would return to their lonely isolation in winter. The fields might be neglected but there were a few luxuries in the cupboard.

During breaks in the music, I got talking to a couple who had squeezed on to the bench in the packed pub. Sheila and Reggi came from Derry in Northern Ireland and were on holiday; her sister had married an islander. They said how much they loved it on the island; it was so quiet and restful. 'It's amazing the number of English over in the South now that the peace process has got going,' Sheila said. But they were worried by the day's news. There had been trouble that day in Northern Ireland. The Protestant Apprentice Boys had been marching again along the ramparts of the city centre in Derry which overlooked the Catholic Bogside and Craigan estates and fighting had broken out. It was the 12th July. Elsewhere in the province there had been clashes between the nationalist protesters and the Royal Ulster Constabulary. 'I hope to God the ceasefire holds,' she said. 'It would be terrible if we went back to things as they were! It's very frightening to be caught up in the riots and the bombing . . .'

It was the first mention of the Troubles; clearly I was getting closer to the border. I shared her hope but was not sure whether Ireland could escape so easily from the strait jacket of its bloody history. Sinn Fein was calling for all-party talks, but the British government was insisting on the decommissioning of arms first. I recalled the hooded eyes of Haughey on his private island in the Blaskets and his refusal to be drawn about the ceasefire.

Before she left, Sheila gave me her telephone number on the back of a cigarette packet with the message: 'May you sail on the sea of ambition and land on the shores of success.' I was trying to avoid ambition and treat success and failure with equal aplomb. But it was kind of her and I appreciated the warmth and friendliness behind the sentiments.

Around midnight, the group finished playing in the pub. Paddy told me that he was going to have a break but a ceilidh was starting at the village hall at about one o'clock. 'It usually goes on to two or three. Why don't you join us?'

As people were leaving the pub, a young fiddler who had joined the group said he could show me the way to the ceilidh. It was a beautiful moonlit night. After the rain, the clouds had cleared and the stars stood out bright and clear. We walked down a grassy boreen between dry-stone walls on the edge of the village. The moon cast a ghostly silver light on the labyrinth of small fields which stretched up the hillside. An owl hooted in the distance, from one of the few copses on the island. A cold breeze blew down the hill from the south west. My companion who only wore a shirt said he came from Cork and was living on the island. I asked him what it was like in the winter.

'Completely different,' he said. 'It rains nearly all the time, but people still entertain each other in their houses. The island returns to itself then.'

'Why are you living here?'

'For inspiration.'

The village hall was a functional, concrete building with no character, unlike the older houses built from the local limestone. Inside the great barn of a building, the bright strip lighting revealed men and women sitting stiffly on plastic chairs lined up against the walls. On the stage at one end Paddy's band was making ready to play, this time with amplifiers. Once they struck up a reel, the place was rollicking within a few minutes. The men invited the women to dance and they threw themselves on the floor with great zest. Soon everyone was flushed and smiling. I couldn't believe the amount of energy being put into it. Young lads would dash into the fray, strong and straight-backed, then return after the number, sweating and laughing. There was only coffee, milk and soft drinks for sale but everyone had been tanking up in the pubs earlier in the evening and had had more than enough to launch them on to the floor.

I could not join in because there were jigs, reels and intricate set dancing which required years of practice. As an outsider, I thought of the two aspects of the lives of these people who lived in these obstinate and brooding islands on the edge of the world. They might be lonely working under the grey sky in the fields and on the sea, but on land, in their homes, pubs and ceilidhs all was warmth and conviviality.

One young couple, a blonde girl in a long white dress and a dark-haired man in a green waistcoat and polished boots, stood out from the other dancers by their grace and dexterity. A tall, bony, red-faced islander with a dark shadow of a beard invited a short, frail Norwegian girl sitting next to me to dance. She jumped up with pleasure. Soon native Celt and Norse invader were getting on like a house on fire. I went up to get a coffee and on my return found they had taken my seat. They were welcome to it. With so many young women leaving for the mainland, I hoped that he had met a mate. Most people were under thirty and there were several groups of 16-year-old boys who were dying to get on the floor. The young had not yet been seduced by the bland uniformity of transatlantic pop; indeed for the time being the traditional music and dance of the Arans were part of their pop culture.

When I went back to the harbour at three in the morning, I found that, with the spring tides, the water had dropped about eighteen feet in five hours. I expected to find my dinghy, high and dry, hanging from its painter against the barnacles and seaweed of the harbour wall, but someone had kindly let it down. I took off my shoes in the moonlight, and dragged the unwieldy boat across the cold, wet sand to the water's edge. By the time I had rowed out to *Celtic Gold*, against the wind and waves which swept across the bay, the effects of the Guinness and whiskey had worked off. After a sandwich and tea, I fell into my bunk and slept like a log.

I met Paddy the next day on the new pier, pottering about in his blue fishing boat. He was carrying on the tradition of drift-netting for salmon in June and July, and lobster potting until the weather broke in the autumn. He was also going further up the north west coast for pollock and mackerel. Because of the bad weather, he had not gone out for a week. By an extraordinary coincidence, it turned out that my fisher-flautist was none other than the grandson of Pat Mullen who had written the *Man of Aran*, a classic account of the making of the film of the same name directed by Robert Flaherty. An old islander once said that Flaherty preferred one good picture of a currach in a breaker than all the fish that ever were in Aran. He certainly realised his ambition during a gale off the western tip of Inishmore when he persuaded some currach men to run the breakers through a deadly criss-crossing of currents among hidden fangs of rocks. It required perfect timing of eye and muscle since a currach floats like a nutshell and is doomed if caught broadside in a wave. And they had to rely on their long, thin, bladeless oars which often broke from the triangular brace set in the gunwale of the currach.

Flaherty made the centre of the film a hunt of the *liamhán mór*, the sun fish or basking shark. Some of them grow to as long as three currachs. They are still plentiful in the waters around Aran, along with killer whales.

The filming of *Man of Aran* very nearly cost the currach men their lives. But then the men of Aran were already under judgment of death once they took to the sea. By guess and by God was the only navigation they knew. The sense of doom and fear of the sea checked the spontaneous wildness, humour and passion of the women. Their lives were punctuated by the *caoineadh* or death keen for the men given up to the sea. It was a struggle which took on heroic proportions and inspired Synge's *Riders to the Sea* which was later made into an opera by Vaughan Williams.

I had noticed in my walks around the island that there were still currachs in the small sandy bays on the northern shore. They were made from tarred canvas stretched on wooden frames, not so much because of the scarcity of timber but because they were light enough to launch from the shore. Their angled bow rode the Atlantic rollers well and they could survive in seas which would probably sink a wooden boat. As in the Blaskets, it was the local custom to have a small bottle of holy water placed inside the bow. The blessing of the boats was an important task for the local priest. And the currachs are still raced, though not quite so wildly as the race described by Liam O'Flaherty, an Inishmore man, in his novel *Thy Neighbour's Wife*.

I was surprised to learn that few of the islanders could swim and most of the fishermen did not bother to wear life jackets. They did not trust the sea and did not want to provoke it; to be able to swim was considered to be a kind of challenge. It was better to appease the sea with a bottle of holy water than to try and take it on. And if a person drowned, it was simply a question of giving back to the sea a life in exchange for all the lives they had taken from it. It was difficult for the lifeboatmen to change attitudes bred by centuries of resignation and fear.

The currachs are still part of everyday life but they are no longer the lifeline of the islanders. By the end of the nineteenth century, they were unable to sustain their traditional way of life by fishing from the cliffs or from their currachs. A priest in 1886 wrote to the government saying 'send us boats or send us coffins'. Boats came and they started trawling in the rich fishing grounds warmed by the Gulf Stream. In recent years, the industry had boomed and according to Paddy Mullen had remained the mainstay of the island.

I asked him where I could get some oil and distilled water for *Celtic Gold*. 'There's no garage on the island. Ask for Adrian, the bus-driver up at the store; he may be able to help you.' There was only one store in the village but I could not find Adrian. Instead I went to the shed of the lifeboatmen at the top of the slipway by the harbour. Like most of the other islanders, they were tall, strong, dark-haired men. They were unable to help and said my only bet was to go to Galway.

In Kilronan, the greyness of the sea, sky and land, the constant whistling of the wind, the slapping of the rigging, the sense of a people losing their way eventually got me down. I felt cold inside and the damp, cold cabin of *Celtic Gold* did not help. For some strange reason, it made me feel very close to death. I was impatient to be off, but I reminded myself in my notebook of the essentials: 'NO STRUGGLE. NO DEPENDENCE. NO FEAR. NO WORRY. CELTIC GOLD IS WITHIN ME. PEACE OF MIND. BE AT ONE WITH THE WORLD. LET THE MORROW TAKE CARE OF THE MORROW.'

I had noticed that there were no other British yachts in the harbour, and only a couple of Irish ones and two intrepid Frenchmen. I knew I should be going as soon as the weather improved. I replenished my stores from the general shop and did several runs in the dinghy to fill up my tank with water from the tap on the quay, reputed to be the best along the coast. On my last run, Paddy and his son were on the pier. While his son held the painter of my bobbing dinghy his father gave me some advice: 'Peter, you shouldn't stay here any longer. It's getting too late in the season.' He looked up in the sky. Dark-grey clouds were scudding over the hills. The wind sent waves crashing against the pier. His son had his work cut out keeping my dinghy off the pier with his foot while holding the painter. 'The weather's breaking up,' he went on. 'You must be on your way. Keep an eye on the forecasts. Watch for the lows, particularly at this time of year. At least the south westerlies will take you up the coast. Better to have the wind on your quarter than pounding into it. Good luck!'

I needed it. His was the authentic voice of the Aran fisherman who had centuries of experience behind him of battling with a cruel and remorseless sea.

I was ready to go but I still needed to get some oil for the engine and some distilled water for the batteries. I decided to catch the ferry to Galway where I was also going to meet another friend and neighbour of mine from Wales, Richard Feesey. Known to his friends as 'Dicker', he had wanted to accompany me for a few days off the west coast. We had a common interest in mountains, philosophy and ecology. He had transformed an old hunting lodge on a hill, caught rain from the heavens for water, erected a windmill for energy and replaced a sterile conifer plantation with broad-leaf trees. After leaving school, he had walked and hitched for three months along the west coast of Ireland and had loved every moment of it. He liked the idea of seeing Ireland from the sea, but he could not swim properly and had never been sailing before in a yacht. He did not know what he was letting himself in for.

I decided to catch the morning ferry to Rossaveel, the nearest port on the Connemara coast, only twelve miles and thirty minutes away, and then go to Galway by bus. By Galway Hooker, the traditional means of transport, it would have taken at least four hours to reach the mainland. The Hookers were sturdy wooden boats, squat on the water, with inward sloping hulls about thirty to forty feet long. They would bring to the island peat, rye-grass sods (for thatching), poteen, and cattle and horses to graze for the winter. In return, they would export to the mainland seaweed (for iodine and medicine), osiers, salted fish, potatoes, limestone slabs for gravestones, and cattle and horses for the summer. The currachs would take out the animals, fish and goods to the waiting Hookers. It was quite different now. Fish was landed directly by the trawlers at Rossaveel on the Connemara coast. All the modern consumer goods – from televisions to toasters – came over on the fast ferries from there or Galway.

I went down to the new pier to wait for the first ferry of the day. The drivers of minibuses lounged around and spoke Irish to each other until the ferry arrived. Then they jumped up and started their patter, competing ferociously with each other for customers. 'Hi. Want to join us?'

'Hi girls, take a bus tour of the island?'

The visitors looked deathly pale and bewildered as they rolled down the gangway and took their first tentative step on solid land. There were a few Japanese amongst the Italians and Germans and French.

'They've had a rough time,' a driver grinned at me. 'They'll all be coming off sick; they'll be as sick as parrots!'

As if to confirm his judgment, a large red-faced Irishman with a thin small wife hobbled by and said: 'B' Jesus, what a crossing that was!'

19

Islands in the Sun

After sailing *Celtic Gold* out in the Atlantic for weeks, the thirty-minute passage on the ferry seemed positively calm. Many of the passengers did not think so. Ill and below decks, they missed the beautiful approach to Cashla Bay where two men in a currach were line fishing in the swell. Amongst the rocky outcrops of its shores were scattered some fine whitewashed houses. There was a cemetery by the water's edge amongst the rocks; it was strangely moving and I wondered how many seafarers it contained in its sandy soil. After the bleak greyness of windswept Aran, the greens and browns of the undulating fields were a delight.

I caught a waiting coach which travelled the coastal road to Galway. As one of the first to get on, I went to the front of the top deck, but was told by a solid 16-year-old girl that she was saving all the seats for her friends. 'We're local!' she said, blocking my way. I felt like saying that I was local too. When her friends did arrive and sprawled across the front seats, they spent the rest of the journey with their feet up and eyes closed.

It was true that the rest of the passengers with their backpacks were not local. When the driver came to collect the tickets, a couple of large middle-aged English women said they had a return ticket but had lost it. When the driver asked them what the driver of the first coach looked like, they could only come up with: 'He was a middle-aged man.' They seemed to claim special insight, though, into the racial and linguistic characteristics of the Irish. While everyone else was trying to sleep after the rough passage, they declared in loud voices: 'You see a lot of dark Irish people, don't you?'

'Dark people?'

'I mean dark-haired people.'

'Well, I've seen a lot of people with red hair and brown eyes.'

When a girl passing through the coach gave them a bilingual leaflet about Galway, the larger of the two women said: 'Is this African?'

'No, it's in Gaelic . . .'

'Oh, you mean Garlic!'

No wonder the locals tried to nod off.

The landscape along the coastal road to Galway was rocky, undulating moorland, broken up by stone-walled fields and the occasional bog. I saw no sheep but a shepherd carrying his dog. In a lay-by, there were some gypsy caravans with a few piebald horses surrounded by piles of scrap metal. Many of the fields were abandoned, invaded by bracken and thistles. A few, though, had hay stacked in round ricks with a piece of canvas like a handkerchief stretched over the top to keep off the rain and a fishing net weighted with stones to hold it all down.

As we grew closer to Galway, more new bungalows sprung up alongside the road. Their large immaculate lawns looked incongruous amongst the wildness of the rough pasture scattered with rocks and rushes. The houses soon joined together to form a suburban ribbon along the road. At least there were no billboards. We drove along the promenade of the pleasant seaside town of Salthill (complete with big dipper) before entering Galway. The road passed over the River Corrib which was clean enough to support ducks, swans and seabirds and had overhanging trees growing along its banks. After Aran, I was still not used to the green.

I got off the coach by the docks and went in search of oil. I ended up in the Commercial Dock where there was one new yacht amongst many old trawlers moored three abreast. A trawlerman pointed out an old redbrick dock building which was the offices of Stateoil. They usually sold oil by hundreds of litres, but the secretary managed to rustle me up a dusty canister of ten litres for a tenner from the back of the office. The chandlers behind the docks was one of only four chart agents in Ireland, but its selection for the north and west coasts was poor. With twenty-one per cent VAT on all goods except children's clothes and food, and the stronger punt, the charts were also almost double the price of Admiralty charts in Britain.

In the central Kenned park, I was accosted by a young woman begging with a baby in her arms. Galway had escaped the blight of poverty no more than London. But the place was mostly full of smartly dressed people, and when I went in search of stores I found great supermarkets as well as French-style cafés and well-stocked book shops.

I met my friend Dicker in the bus depot – he was instantly recognizable with his broad shoulders and round glasses – and we returned on the ferry that night to Kilronan. It must have been strange for him to row out in the dinghy under a threatening sky after a day and a night of travelling. I asked him to take off his smart walking shoes – the only ones he had with him – and I washed off the Welsh sheep dung from their soles in a bucket of sea water. He had brought some rotting cloves of garlic which I threw overboard. He must have thought that I was very fussy in my new home. Once on board, he brought out a bottle of Irish whiskey, and that eased him in.

I woke up next morning, 15th August, at six thirty. The sky was overcast, the pressure quite high and a mild south westerly was passing over Ireland. The forecast said that we could expect moderate winds and fair weather with a few showers. It should clear from the west during the day.

Ahead of us were some of the finest cruising grounds in Ireland, with a mass of small islands and inlets set against the wild mountainous coastline of Connacht. I decided to make for the remote island of Inishbofin, with Clifden as a possible refuge port.

We sailed carefully through the channel of the bar of Aran where waves were breaking in a heavy north-west swell, and headed north west towards Slyne Head on a beam reach in the fresh south-westerly wind. By the time we had cleared the Aran islands and were skirting the treacherous Skerd Rocks to the north, *Celtic Gold* had begun to roll and pitch in the choppy sea. The clouds separated for a while, turning the sea a deep blue and lighting up the white quartzite peaks of the Twelve Pins of Connemara (Benna Beola) beyond the craggy Mount Errisbeg which sparkled in the sun. It was spectacularly beautiful, but with countless submerged rocks along the deeply indented coastline, it was not a shore to be caught near in a gale.

Dicker did not feel well. It was his first time at sea and I could see that he held himself tensely against the movement of the boat. Throughout the morning I saw the tell-tale signs of sea sickness – he grew pale, listless, drawn in on himself in the corner of the cockpit. He loved the mountains of Connemara, but they could not excite him now. At lunchtime, he went down to make some soup but was violently sick. He staggered up the companionway and was sick again over the side of the cockpit until he had emptied his stomach.

'I'm not used to this,' he said, bravely trying to smile. 'I would like to go for a stroll this evening on terracotta . . .'

By tea time, Dicker felt well enough to go down below to brew up some tea. We were by now three miles off Slyne Head lighthouse which is on a low-lying island. I gave it a wide berth to avoid the dangerous race which can run up to three knots in springs; it was daunting to see the Atlantic rollers crash on its rocky shore. From now on we would be fighting the tide, but at least the moderate wind continued to blow from the west and we sailed on a beam reach towards Inishshark, a smaller neighbouring island to Inishbofin. It was still cloudy overhead, and drizzle came and went.

Inishbofin is in the middle of a large group of rocks, islands and breakers extending for eight miles. The largest to the west is Inishshark. Two white pillars in a line led us towards the harbour of low-lying Inishbofin. It was a tricky entrance as we had to avoid the submerged Bishop's Rock on our port bow and sail very close to the lighthouse on Gun Rock on the starboard side. But it was well worth the effort for we turned into a long sheltered inlet which led towards an inner haven.

We dropped anchor in white sand off a ruined fort on the rocky south shore of Port Island. A few fishing boats and a couple of buoyed currachs swung gently at anchor nearby. The rays of the setting sun burst through the clouds and cast a golden glow over the fishing boats, rocks and sandy beaches. The cries of the seabirds mingled with the song of corncrakes and corn buntings and the distant lowing of a cow. Hay was neatly stacked in ricks in the small, stone-walled fields which rose in terraces up the hillside of the island.

The name of the island comes from Bó Finne, which means 'white cow'. Legend has it that the remote island was for ever shrouded in a thick blanket of sea mist. One day some fishermen landed and lit a fire near a lake. The mist began to lift and an old woman appeared driving a white cow. She hit the cow with a stick and it turned to stone. The angry fishermen grabbed the stick and hit her and she too turned into stone. Thereafter they called the place 'White Cow Island', Inishbofin. Until recently there were two standing stones by the lake but these have now disappeared.

We pumped up the dinghy and rowed to the old quay. We made for the nearest pub by a hotel and sat for a while in a daze. It was not the kind of snug Irish pub I was used to, more like a poor imitation of a Scandinavian hall. Unlike the Aran islands and Dingle, I did not hear any Irish being spoken. Drink and food, in that order, served by a tall American girl to American pop music, slowly did their work. Dicker soon felt more human. 'I can't believe how quickly you recover from seasickness as soon as you reach land. I felt so bad and now it's as if nothing had happened!'

After dark we walked along the coastal path. It was a lovely, balmy night and the sweet smell of the earth and newly mown hay reawakened the memory of childhood summers on the Sussex Downs. On the way, two girls on one bicycle without lights shouted greetings at us, and a clapped-out car, with only one light and no exhaust, overtook us. 'The exhaust probably fell off in 1930!' Dicker observed.

The next morning we landed in our dinghy in a little sandy cove on Port Island and walked across the headland to the ruins of Cromwell's Fort. Like the Great Famine and the Rebellion of 1798, Cromwell's rule in Ireland has passed into myth. At the beginning of the Civil War in 1641, the Irish had rebelled under the leadership of Rory O'More and Sir Felim O'Neill. In yet another ironic twist of Irish history, the rebels, a blend of Gaels and Old English, were both Royalist and Catholic; *Pro Deo, pro Rege, pro Patria Hibernia unanimis* was the slogan of their confederation. The rebels did not make much headway, but the repressed anger and hatred of the peasants in Ulster led to a massacre of the Protestant settlers.

With the support of the Ulster Army, Cromwell was determined to recover Ireland for the rule of the English Commonwealth. The Irish rebels were no match in tactics or ruthlessness. A turning point was Cromwell's massacre of 3,500 people, including townsfolk and women, at Drogheda in revenge for the spilling of Protestant blood in Ulster. Cromwell charged the Roman clergy for being responsible for the war and insisted chillingly: 'I meddle not with any man's conscience, but as for liberty to exercise the mass, I must tell you that where the Parliament of England has power, that will not be allowed.' In the Act of Settlement which followed in 1642, Ireland had to pay for its own conquest and eleven years later the Irish gentry and landowners were transplanted beyond the Shannon after being given the naked choice: 'To Hell or Connacht'. Over half the acreage of Ireland was confiscated for the conquerors, although in the event many of them subsequently sold their lots and returned to England.

Before the final collapse of the rebellion, Rory O'More died on Inishbofin. It was logical to fortify the remote island against the rebels. Using forced local labour, Cromwell's officers reinforced and extended the existing castle. The job was done so well that its thick mortared walls are still in good shape four and a half centuries later.

During Cromwell's rule, the fort was used as a prison for Catholic priests. One cleric was allegedly chained to a rock at low tide where he drowned as the sea rose – the rock I had passed on my way in, now known as Bishop's Rock. When Cromwell withdrew from Ireland, the garrison on this remote island in the west was forgotten. His men apparently married local girls who must also have forgotten what the English officers had done to their priests.

I had never seen such beautifully clear water around the British

Isles. The whiteness of the sand was enhanced by the gentle swaying of the green and brown seaweeds attached to the dark rocks. I could not resist going for a swim in a cove below Cromwell's Fort. The water was cool but wonderfully refreshing. The grey shingle clinked as I walked over it. Afterwards we rowed over to the hotel by the inner haven for a bath. What a treat to lie in hot water! It was my second bath of the voyage: the last time I had one was way back in Glengarrif at the head of Bantry Bay.

The owner of the hotel told me that the population of the island was holding its own. Although it was only about three miles long and one and a half miles wide, in 1841, before the Great Famine, the island had supported 1,622 souls. For the last thirty years, it had stayed at about 200. 'The tourists are beginning to change things,' she continued. 'In the winter, the ferry from Cleggan sails three times a week. This summer, the ferry comes three times a day and there are up to 1,500 people on the island. Still, it's good for business!'

It was the same story all along the west coast. Tourism was beginning to dominate the local economy, the young were going to the mainland and rich blow-ins were buying up the houses for second homes.

Attached to the old quay in front of the hotel were a few currachs. Unlike the Aran currachs, they had a double gunwale and were boarded under the tarred canvas rather like a proper carvel-planked boat. They had two thole pins for each oar, rather than one. Their owners, a couple of fishermen, were mending their nets in the sun. Their lives as fisher-farmers had hardly changed and they still used their currachs like the monks who had come with St Colman from Lindisfarne in the seventh century. But they might well be the last generation. When the new ferry from Cleggan arrived packed with day-trippers, the visitors made their way straight into the Scandinavian pub without glancing at fort or church or hill or kittiwake or currach.

We set sail from Inishbofin in mid afternoon in a south westerly breeze for the neighbouring Clare Island, only sixteen miles away. It was a beautiful hot summer's day with deep blue skies and a few fluffy clouds. The sea was a glorious Mediterranean blue. As we said farewell to Inishbofin, I could see turf – slices of dug peat – being dried out in stacks by the lighthouse. Both would give light and warmth in the winter's darkness.

We could not have had better scenery for our leisurely cruise. We passed a series of islands in the sun: the little serpent of Davillaun, the high dome of Inishturk and low-lying Caher. The wind was light and variable, but steady enough to take us through the dangerous islets, submerged rocks and shoals. Off Davillaun, we came across surf breaking on a submerged rock and two rogue waves suddenly appeared from nowhere in the gentle swell, obliging me to steer straight into them. *Celtic Gold* rode their crests with ease, as if delighted by the sudden action.

The mountains to the east were a constant temptation to drop the tiller and pull on the boot. The Twelve Pins of Connemara gave way to the Sheefry Hills and then to the rounded summit of Croagh Patrick, the tallest and holiest mountain in Ireland. Dicker had climbed it during his earlier walking tour: 'It's almost three thousand feet but easy to climb. On St Patrick's Day more than 20,000 people walk up it, some of them barefoot. I wouldn't recommend that, though, for it's covered in broken beer bottles!'

My mind was pleasantly blank, overflowing with the beauty of the brooding mountains by the azure sea. But Dicker was thinking. 'Only the man who knows he has enough can be content,' he observed. Awakened from my reverie, I thought it was a true enough statement, but the word 'enough' was problematical.

'It depends on what you mean by enough. I'm content at the moment; I feel I have enough simply with this yacht and this magnificent view all around us. With all this, I feel very rich indeed.'

'The problem is that people don't know when to stop. I'm not against occasional excess, like killing the fatted calf for a feast, giving gifts or letting off fireworks. But most people think that consumption will bring them happiness. The more they consume, they believe, the happier they'll be. They always want more and better and are never satisfied . . .'

'Then what's needed is voluntary simplicity, a new awareness that real wealth lies in the quality of life and not in possessions . . .'

'Well maybe the market will eventually stop us from using scarce resources before it's too late by making them too expensive. Food is the only exception.'

'And food raises the issue of population . . .'

Shades of Malthus, the Great Famine, the Divine Market; it was all too much on such a gloriously hot day in such a remote and beautiful corner of the world. We let the world's problems, for a while at least, disappear in the wake behind us, opening ourselves to the deep pleasure of simply being . . .

Unlike Inishbofin, Clare Island rose high out of the sea, old potato fields climbing the saddle between its two peaks on each end of the island. As we rounded the south east edge, I could see smoke rising from a rubbish dump in a narrow cove. The open harbour of Clare was dominated by an old grey square tower perched on a hill. We dropped anchor just before nine in about four metres, in white sand north of the new pier, and went ashore immediately to get some water and to look for some food and drink.

I decided to go and look at the tower before the light faded completely. It was in fact a castle of a notorious pirate queen called Grace O'Malley, the daughter of a local chief. It must have been a perfect stronghold for her operations of trade and piracy along the deeply indented coastline. Hidden from view, she could survey from the island all the shipping coming up and down the coast – from Ulster and Scotland to the north, and Munster and Spain to the south.

I had first come across her name in a maritime museum in the main fort of Havana, Cuba. In a room devoted to pirates on the Spanish Main, there was not only a critical note on the English national hero Sir Walter Raleigh but an engraving of a wild-looking, bare-breasted woman wielding a cutlass on the poop of her ship, one 'Grace O'Malley, Pirata Irlandesa'. In Elizabethan times, the Spanish vessels on their way to Ulster often used the waters she controlled around Clew Bay, Blacksod Bay and Achill Sound as their first port of call. They never forgot the trouble she gave them, nor the earlier wrecking of many of the galleons of the Armada along the rocky coast.

Sitting on a wall by the slipway was a short, middle-aged man. He said he had seen *Celtic Gold* come in and anchor and introduced himself as Larry Butler, the son of the last lighthouse keeper of the island. It turned out that he too was a sailor and had sailed with Conor Haughey on one of his circumnavigations of Ireland. He now lived near Carlingford Lough on the east coast of Ireland. I mentioned my interest in Grace O'Malley. 'We call her Granuaile. You know, there are many stories and songs about her. On one occasion when she was sailing off the coast of Spain, she was attacked by Turkish pirates. She was forty at the time and well pregnant with child. As they were about to be overcome, she went below decks to give birth and then came up with a cutlass in her hand and slayed the Turkish captain and won the day. That's probably why she was pictured with bare breasts!'

'Did she prey on the English as well?'

'Yes, she controlled the waters all along the coast, taking harbour dues and attacking any foreign boats. In the end, the English tried to confiscate her land. She had the distinction of sailing up the Thames to Greenwich in her own boat in 1593 to see Queen Elizabeth. It must have been an amazing meeting, the pirate queen and the Queen of England, two strong ladies. They hit it off, it seems, for she was allowed to preserve her lands.'

According to the Lord Deputy, Sir Philip Sidney, she was more than 'Mrs Mate' to her husband. When she married for a second time, she insisted on a clause in the contract that the marriage could be dissolved simply by saying 'I dismiss you.' After garrisoning her men in his castles, she did precisely that, only a year later.

Despite her oath of loyalty to the English Crown – in Queen Elizabeth's words, she had agreed to 'fight our quarrel with all the world' – Granuaile was later celebrated as a great Irish patriot in many songs and poems. After the abortive 1798 rebellion, one ballad claimed:

> She had strongholds on her headlands
> And brave galleys on the sea
> And no warlike chief or Viking
> E'er had bolder heart than she.
> She unfurled her country's banner
> High o'er battlement and mast
> And 'gainst all the might of England
> Kept it flying 'til the last.

The ruins of the thirteenth-century Cistercian abbey on the island contain her remains; a stone there was inscribed with the family motto: 'invincible on land and sea'.

I particularly liked the story of the seeds she gave to her three sons. The first two planted them in soil and carefully nurtured them for a year, but when she asked her third son what he had done with his, he replied: 'I set mine in the deepest and most fertile soil of all – the ocean.'

'You are my son,' said Granuaile.

*

After a drink in the pier bar, Larry suggested going over to the Bay View Hotel on the other side of the harbour, the only one on the island. As we strolled along a sandy track that warm summer's night, he pointed out a small tent in the sand dunes. 'I'm camping there,' he said, 'to be close to the earth.' He had travelled the world for many years, visiting forty-eight countries, but after thirty-five years had decided to come back to Clare. 'I grew up here. My father was the lighthouse keeper on the north side of the island. I had to walk to school for miles without any shoes.'

'How old were you when you came here?'

'Three. My mother, being a superstitious Irish woman, wanted to move in on a Friday. It's an old Irish custom to move in on a Friday night; it's meant to bring good luck. We arrived at seven in the evening. The local boatmen got two donkeys and four baskets or creels as we call them. They put me in one and my sister in the other. It was like the flight into Egypt. We slowly made our way up the track to the lighthouse which is four miles away on the other side of the island. That's a very abiding memory with me. I could see the loom of the lighthouse through the weaves of the creel as we were going up the hill . . .'

'What's happened to the lighthouse? According to the chart, it's no longer lit.'

'I went to visit it yesterday. It's been bought by a Belgian who's made it into a beautiful guest house. There's a wedding suite now where the light used to be!'

'What was island life like when you were a boy?'

'It was beautiful on the island and I loved it. You know, island life is special. Everyone knows everything about you but it's a good thing in a way because if you're in trouble, they know it and they're there to help you and they will always help you. It's a real community, everyone depends on everyone else. It's very special. There have always been great characters on the island but like everywhere else they're dying off.'

Clare Island had not yet gone the way of Inishbofin, but it was on its way. The owner of the hotel was also the owner of the new ferry. The old one had mysteriously gone adrift and been washed on to the rocks. A substantial insurance claim was being arranged and his intention was to buy a much bigger ferry to bring the visitors in from Westport at the head of Clew Bay rather from the remote Roonagh Point.

The ferry was not the only vessel to go adrift. At the bottom of the cliffs below the hotel, I saw a demasted yacht lodged and buffeted by the sea amongst the rocks. Someone had got its engine out on to a nearby rock. Larry said that it had dragged its anchor in the previous week and had been washed on to foot of the cliffs. He told me to be careful during the rest of the voyage. 'You never know what can happen. Once we were sailing across the Irish Sea from Port St Mary in the Isle of Man to Carlingford Lough. I was on watch at night with a friend; it wasn't too rough, about a Force 5 or 6. Suddenly a huge wave came from nowhere and washed my friend overboard. He wasn't lashed on at the time. I threw him a light but he held it upside down so it didn't work! I had great diffriculty finding him in the dark. I eventually managed to pick him up. He was a simple guy and said he hadn't been worried at all: "I could see you looking for me all the time." What he didn't realise is that I couldn't see him!'

'Where do you think that freak wave came from?'

'If you ask me, it was a submarine . . .'

'Have you given up sailing now?'

'No. It's like an addiction. Once it's in your blood, it's difficult to give it up. I know an old couple from Wales who've been coming over to Carlingford Lough for years. The old man's 84 now and he's too frail to go to sea, but he and his wife spend every winter working out their passage plans. She's 72 but still sets off in the summer and does everything on her own, while he follows her progress at home.'

It was a wonderfully inspiring story, but before we said farewell, Larry added a cautionary note: 'By the way, a fisherman once told me that anyone who goes to sea for pleasure must want to go to hell for a holiday!'

20

The Ears of Achill

It was such a calm night in the harbour of Clare Island that I went to sleep confident that all was well. I should have been more cautious. I woke up at about seven to find *Celtic Gold* snatching at her anchor in a stiff easterly swell. I went up on deck and to my horror found that we had dragged the anchor during the night, narrowly missed a fishing boat and a couple of currachs, and were almost entangled with a lobster raft. Worst of all, the jagged rocks where the dismasted yacht had come to grief were not far off. I had woken up just in time.

We left Clare Island for Blacksod Bay, thirty miles away, at midday. The temperature had climbed to the high seventies. The forecast said that we could expect light to moderate winds, veering from the north east to the south east during the day.

Rounding the east coast of Clare, I spied the disused lighthouse on the rocky northern promontory. I thought of Larry Butler playing on the rocks as a boy and his father looking down from the light to see if he was all right. We soon left Clew Bay, with its myriads of rocks and islets, behind us, and steered north west towards Achill Head. The coast of Achill, which formed an inverted 'L', was grand. Beyond the mountain of Knockmore in the light blue haze rose the splendid Nephin Beg range. Granuaile's galleys would have been able to pass through Achill Sound to Blacksod Bay if the tides had been right, but a bridge to the largest island in Ireland has now blocked this short cut.

There was a steady swell. *Celtic Gold* rose and fell about ten feet as the long Atlantic waves rolled towards the broken land. The movement was mesmeric, and I found it difficult to keep awake in the warm sun. The heads of two seals suddenly popped up and they looked steadily at us with their enquiring eyes. The only setback to the balance of the afternoon was the light winds which blew from the north west and obliged us to motorsail.

By tea time we were approaching Achill Head, the most westerly point of Ireland. When its two ears lined up, we changed course. Despite the calmest of conditions, it seemed to be listening out for bad weather. Its cliffs on the northern shore, which rose to almost two thousand feet, were awesome. Even an experienced climber would have been hard pushed on such a calm day to find a way to the top if he were shipwrecked on the rocky shore. Dicker was deeply moved by the grandeur of the headland and cliffs. 'They're terrifying and beautiful,' he said. 'Sublime!'

As we headed north east for the shelter of Blacksod Bay for the night, the winds also changed direction and then dropped. The closer we approached the bay, the darker the sea became. Thick clumps of seaweed floated on the dark-brown peaty waters. I loved the name Blacksod Bay – it sounded so incongruous – but it was clear why it had been so called for the sods of turf were black indeed.

I had enjoyed my own company during the voyage, but it was great having a good friend with me at that moment. 'You know, Dicker, I very much appreciated your friendship, especially during the separation. It was a very difficult time for me last winter.'

'You always seemed very positive and cheerful.'

'Well, I didn't want to burden you with my unhappiness. I wanted to get myself sorted out.'

'You certainly didn't do that.'

'Anyway, I know you wouldn't want me to go on about my problems. You've always been a critical friend in the best sense of the word.'

'I've tried to be. The trouble with the new narcissism, all that talk about I'm OK and you're OK, about feeling good about yourself, is that there's no critical element in it. True friendship may challenge; if committed to the other person, it may even resist sometimes.'

'I agree. You don't have to accept everything your friend does, or always side with him when he's in the wrong. A friend is your fireside, a place to warm your hands. But sometimes it's good to question your friend's ideas and motives. That way you can help him to develop and grow, and he can do the same for you. You should offer your best to a friend.'

I was lucky to have half a dozen good friends in my life. Most people go through life with only acquaintances, linked by a common interest or desire. My friends were all very different and would not necessarily get on with each other but I felt that whatever situation I might find myself in, I could always count on their loving support, however critical.

But what triggers off a friendship and makes it last remains a mystery. It can happen in the most unexpected way, as my daughter Emily once observed in a poem she wrote when 10 years old:

Magical feelings
growing inside you
warm and good.
Happy and glad

you have found a friend.
Friendship can start
in little terms –
'Hello, hello' –
but soon you will find
you have happiness
for a lifetime.

*

We headed close to Blacksod Point along a low coastline. Ancient stone circles stood out of the rough pasture and cows were wandering amongst large boulders strewn along the shore. We saw two men and a young girl in a boat fishing. She was laughing with pleasure as she landed mackerel after mackerel with her rod, four at a time, their iridescent bodies flashing in the rays of the setting sun. The boat followed us in soon afterwards. It came close enough for one of the men to throw half a dozen mackerel into the cockpit of *Celtic Gold*. Seeing our red ensign, he shouted: 'Where are you from?'

'Wales.'

'Good!' They revved up and the motor boat surged away.

The mackerel were still alive. Their bodies shining with all the colours of the rainbow, they twisted and turned and flapped, splattering my clean trousers and the white cockpit with bright red blood. I killed the mackerel with a sharp knife and degutted them in a blue bucket of sea water. As I cut off their heads, I had to saw through their delicate bones and slice their smooth flesh.

For two decades I had been a strict vegetarian, although in recent years I had decided occasionally to eat fish during my sea voyages. I had not killed and gutted live fish since I was a boy. I was surprised not to feel any qualms; living on the sea, it seemed natural to live off the sea. Dicker cooked the mackerel that evening with boiled potatoes. Washed down with whiskey, they were delicious.

The strong oily smell stayed in the yacht for days afterwards, and Dicker was amused by my efforts to clean up the spots of blood on the deck and trace down the smell. I found that any unpleasant smell only made me feel queasy at sea. Dicker mused on the difference between the person like me for whom a boat was a home and the fishermen whose floating workplace would never be free of the stench of diesel and fish.

Thinking of the Ancient Mariner, I hoped the mackerel were not going to be my albatross. Having rounded Achill Head, I was now two thirds of the way around Ireland. It had taken me almost two months. With a bit of luck, I should make it back to Wales by the autumn equinox at the end of September. But I still had some of the most dangerous and exposed stretches of coastline ahead of me. It was the second most windy place in Europe and the likelihood of gales was increasing all the time.

We stayed the night off Blacksod Quay in a tranquil, open anchorage. The next morning, it was another warm, sunny day. I stayed on board to work out a passage plan while Dicker went ashore to dispose of our rubbish and to collect some water and stores. The nearby hamlet consisted only of a pub and a few whitewashed houses. After a couple of hours, Dicker came back virtually empty-handed: 'It's an amazing place. I went to the pub to get some food and water, but they've only got toothpaste and tinned meat to sell. Apparently a travelling grocer comes twice a week in a van. When I asked for some water, the landlady said that the water's limited because of the drought!'

'That must be unheard-of on the west coast!'

'She wouldn't take our rubbish either. She said there was no local refuse collection on the island, and she had to pay a man to take it away.'

'So it wasn't a very successful trip . . .'

'I've got a few slices of bread. On my way back to the quay, I knocked on someone's door and asked if I could buy some bread.

An old lady gave me all she had to spare. As I was about to offer payment, she said, "There'll be no need for puttin' your hand in your pocket, now!"'

'Coming to a place like this, you realise just how many services we take for granted: shops, rubbish collection, water, electricity. People are so used to them, that when one of the services breaks down, they're lost. It's good to be reminded occasionally of their temporary nature.'

We left Blacksod Bay at midday for Broadhaven Bay which was some thirty miles away. I skirted an easterly cardinal buoy, one of the very few on the west coast, in order to avoid some rocky shoals. Some thundery clouds were beginning to build up, but the airs were light and the sea calm, almost eerily so. I decided to pass along the inner passage between Mullet and the islands of North and South Inishkea. It involved passing through a narrow sound which could only be attempted in the kind of quiet, swell-free conditions we were enjoying. I also had to keep a constant watch to avoid the submerged rocks and to keep clear of the islands which sloped gently into the sea. Although in the lee of the islands on a very calm day, we could still hear the Atlantic rollers crashing on the western shore.

At one point, whilst Dicker was at the tiller we gybed badly because of a sudden swirl in the current.

'Are you still steering 70 degrees?' I asked abruptly. 'That's not 70 degrees. I told you to steer 70!'

I immediately regretted my outburst. I had been worried about being swept on the rocks in the sound. It was, after all, Dicker's first time steering a yacht, we were out in the Atlantic, and he was doing extremely well. I did not want to be the arrogant and demanding skipper; on the contrary, I liked the idea of sailing being a co-operative venture. I tried to make the main decisions about our destinations together, although of course I was ultimately responsible for what happened on board.

Exposed to the Atlantic storms, the Inishkeas were denuded of trees and bushes and only provided rough grazing. They had long been inhabited as there were many megaliths and the remains of some Bronze Age and early Christian settlements. Before the Great Famine there had been as many as 500 islanders who paid their rent in fish and rabbit-skins. I thought of the men who once wore black jerseys and trousers and seal-skin hats and rawhide shoes and would hunt the whales. Thousands of seals used to come to the islands in the winter. Some say a few would come disguised as beautiful women and dance their lovers off their feet or lure them into the sea. But the wild fishermen and the wily seals had gone and only the old stories lived on.

As we approached Inishgloria to the north of the string of islands, I could see some ruined cottages. St Brendan the Navigator had landed here in his ocean-going currach and founded a monastery; in the old days, passing ships would dip their sails in honour. Sparkling in the sea, the island certainly lived up to its Irish name Inis Gluaire, the Island of Brightness.

Three old men were out in a currach, laying a net across the water. I gave them a reasonable berth and they waved as I went by. They must have come from Mullet, for the islands were no longer inhabited. Like the Blacksod currachs, their oars were worked between two thole-pins so they could feather them whilst rowing. Towards the bow about a quarter of their length rode out of the water, ready to take the Atlantic rollers.

We headed out towards the isolated Eagle Island with its lighthouse. It had been as calm as a mill pond in the lee of the islands off Mullet, but as soon as we entered the open sea we felt the full impact of the Atlantic again. The brightly lit haze steadily increased. It was difficult to judge distances: features along the nearby coast seemed vast and faraway. Dicker was convinced for at least an hour that the mighty Slieve League cliffs on the other side of Donegal Bay were the modest Erris Head, thirty times closer. Near the headland, the water became confused and turbulent in an area of overfalls.

A gannet floated along close by *Celtic Gold* for a while. I said to Dicker: 'They're my friends, you know. When the seabirds are about, I never feel lonely.' Although I did not literally break bread with these companions in the original sense of the word, I felt that they acknowledged and accepted my presence as I did theirs. It was not simply the reassurance of seeing another creature in the vast expanse of the ocean but a sense of sharing a common condition, of being together. Sailors of old thought that their souls would become seabirds for a while to pay for their sins before they left for paradise. I could see why.

Towards tea time, a few heavy drops of thundery rain fell, the first rain I had seen for over a week. The wind had been variable but it now picked up enough from the south west to enable us to turn off the engine. The ensuing quiet was bliss; there is nothing to compare to the gentle splashing of a yacht on a broad reach in a gentle breeze. Dicker fully appreciated the calm sea and light winds. After being violently sick the first day, he had felt queasy the second day, but had settled down on the third. 'I dread to think what it would have been like in stronger winds,' he said.

After Erris Head, I steered *Celtic Gold* south east into Broadhaven Bay. Like Blacksod Bay, it lived up to its name. Giving the Gubacashel lighthouse a reasonable berth, we turned into the inlet which led to Benmullet. About a mile up the inlet, we anchored under sail off Inver Hamlet Bay outside the mainstream of the tide. Since we had to get up early the following day, we decided not to go ashore. Instead, we enjoyed the gentle stillness of our isolated anchorage, while a man and his son came down to fish from the shingle on the rocky shore.

As Dicker prepared the supper, I sat in the cockpit in the fading light. The sky was clouding over and there was a very light easterly breeze. I felt sad for the first time at the thought of the end of the voyage and the things I would have to do on my return. I was in a limbo world, a world of betwixt and between, sailing around Ireland, with no appointments or obligations apart from finding a safe anchorage for the night. I had not been ashore for three nights and had no wish to go. I liked the feeling of being self-sufficient and self-reliant in my little world on board. I only needed the land for water, fuel and stores. If necessary, I could even do without any stores for a while, harnessing the wind and harvesting the sea for free.

I was feeling a little anxious about meeting up with my family when they came out to meet me for my birthday in a few days' time. I was greatly looking forward to seeing Emily and Dylan; but with Jenny I suspected it would be difficult. It was almost a year since we had set up separate households and I was not sure how we would get on. It would be as familiar and close as the camping holidays we had enjoyed in the past, and yet the circumstances would be completely different. So far the voyage had helped me overcome the feelings of sadness I had experienced during the previous winter and I was coming to terms with my new single way of life.

I feared that the meeting might open half-healed scars. On the other hand, there was always the possibility that we might get back together again. Jenny had said before my departure for Ireland that she would think about things over the summer and see whether she wanted to continue to live separately or not. My last voyage around Africa had ended in our separation; perhaps this one around Ireland might end in our reunion. If that were the case, the circumnavigation would make a perfect circle.

I got up at five thirty the next morning to a still, misty day. The cries of curlews came across the quiet waters. It was going to be a long voyage: we had to sail from Broadhaven Bay all the way along the north coast of Sligo to Mullaghmore at the head of Donegal Bay, some fifty miles away. It would take at least fourteen hours and there were no decent harbours on the way. The radio warned about a floating telegraph pole, with jagged metal and concrete still attached to it, in the vicinity. So they were on the west coast as well as the east coast of Ireland!

It was still misty when we weighed anchor at six thirty after breakfast. As we headed north out of Broadhaven Bay, the sun appeared like a reddish gold orb above the cliffs in the light purple haze. A glittering band of gold fell across the dark, oily sea. It was eerie, almost surreal, peaceful and foreboding at the same time. I sailed between the steep inhospitable cliffs of the mainland and the Stags, a group of seven mighty pinnacles which loomed like shark's teeth out of the sea mist. Over 300 feet tall, they dwarfed *Celtic Gold* as she sailed by. Fulmars and gannets flew across the sun, their dark silhouettes enhancing the strange stillness of sea and sky in the morning twilight.

The sea mist slowly lifted during the morning, but it remained hazy. It was very warm, even out at sea, and we were forced to motorsail with the main up for most of the time.

By lunch time, the visibility was still poor in the haze. A slight swell was noticeable, but we were still cut off from the rest of the world. We had not seen another vessel since our departure. Only the odd fulmar flying past out to sea reminded us that there was other life on the planet. The steady thud of the engine, overheating slightly in the still heat, was the only noise. We were still in a fantastical world.

I liked the sense of isolation. After three days without touching land, I felt no desire to leave the boat. I felt complete in myself. I knew the voyage and the weather would not last, and I was not sure what storms of emotion were in store. I relaxed and enjoyed the calm while it lasted. It was a shame that such a suspended state could not go on for ever. There was enough movement to remind me that I was alive, but not enough to awaken me from my reverie. I let the half-formed thoughts and feelings come and go in the swirling mist of my mind.

But again it seemed that we both felt the need to upset the balance of the day. Dicker must have been thinking about his apple trees at home, because he suddenly said, 'I'm going to shoot the squirrels which stole my apples when I get back.'

'But can't you share some of your apples with them?' I asked.

'The squirrels eat nearly all of the apples before they're ripe. I'm fed up with putting nets over the trees which they get through anyway. I know where to get a gun and I'm going to shoot them.' Ripening apples, broken furry bodies, red blood on green grass, death in the afternoon. It seemed so incongruous on such a peaceful day.

'What effect do you think it will have on your two-year-old son seeing you take down your gun and go out and blast to smithereens small fluffy creatures which he has been brought up to cherish?' I declared, rising to the argument from my slumber.

'I shall do it discreetly. Anyway, the squirrels in question are simply vermin, Peter, vermin. It's as simple as that.'

'Not quite. What's vermin to one person is a pet to another.'

Dicker chose to change tack: 'We need to kill grey squirrels because they're a threat to biodiversity; they're taking over the habitats of the indigenous red squirrels.'

'But I still think shooting your squirrels gives the wrong message to your son and is an unnecessary evil.'

'Peter, I believe as much as you that nature is valuable in itself. But I also believe we have to manage it . . .'

We left it at that. We were both getting hot under the collar. It was too calm and soporific an afternoon to get hot under the collar about general principles.

I felt the wind pick up from the north west, and asked Dicker to turn off the motor and to unfurl the jib. We took it in turns to steer. Lying on his back in the cockpit in the sun during his break, Dicker declared: 'It's very tiring, sailing!'

After eight hours at sea, we had our first sight of land at tea time as the low-lying Lenadoon Point north east of Killala Bay loomed out of the haze. About an hour later, the island of Inishmurray appeared on the port bow whereas according to the course steered it should have been on our starboard. The tide must have been stronger than I thought. At the same time, a large white Canadian ketch crossed our track, its white ensign with a red maple leaf billowing gently in the breeze. It was the first yacht I had seen since the Aran islands, and I thought that it must have crossed the Atlantic.

We changed course and passed between Bomore Rock to the north and Inishmurray to the south. Only a mile long and half a mile wide, it had once been an early Christian settlement. I could make out the ruins of three beehive huts which were within a great circular wall, perhaps built at the same time as the 'forts' on the Arans.

As I approached Mullaghmore Head in the mist, I took great care. I did not want to end up like three ships of the Spanish Armada which had foundered on the nearby strand of Streedagh where over a thousand bodies were washed ashore. I was looking for a tower marked on the chart but out of the mist loomed a great Gothic pile on the skyline. There was no trace of it on the chart. It was soon enveloped by the mist again and if Dicker had not seen it as well I might have thought I was seeing things. Fortunately, I managed to pick up the three rocks at the end of Mullaghmore Head soon after. We dropped anchor off the entrance to Mullaghmore Harbour just around the corner, in white sand in two metres of crystal clear water. It was nine o'clock; we had been at sea for fourteen and a half hours. We celebrated after a simple supper with whiskey and peaches before turning in.

Dicker had booked a return ticket on the ferry to Wales for the following day. I walked with him for a couple of miles out of town to see him on his way. Because there was no local public transport, he decided to hitch to Sligo and then get a coach to Dublin. I asked him what he thought of his short voyage in *Celtic Gold*.

'It's been an unforgettable experience. It's an immortal first, like losing your virginity. I shan't take seasickness tablets again, though!'

'Well, it's been a pleasure to have you on board. In a few days you've become an expert at pumping up the dinghy and laying out the anchor. I always felt confident when your steady hand was on the helm!'

'There are good vibes on *Celtic Gold*. I'm very impressed by your competence and the methodical way you approach navigation.'

Flattery indeed. Before we said farewell at a fork in the road, he said: 'Perhaps I won't shoot those squirrels.'

'Perhaps they are vermin after all,' I replied.

After seeing Dicker off I walked back to Mullaghmore in the warm sun. Where hundreds of Spanish sailors had once been washed ashore families were now arriving with hampers and buckets and spades to spend the day on the long white strand of Streedagh Beach. Jack Yeats had once painted the wild horse races along the beach, but now cows ambled down to the sea through the sand dunes.

Mullaghmore was different from the other towns and villages I had visited along the west coast. It seemed much more like an English seaside resort. The food was expensive in the only shop. When I went in search of a shower, I was refused by the manager in one hotel after his receptionist had agreed, while in another, I was charged an extortionate rate for a filthy shower which had no rose. It was the first place in Ireland I had visited where the hotels did not give a warm welcome to visiting yachtsmen.

It was a popular resort for visitors from the North, especially since the ceasefire. Antrim was only three or four hours away by car. While sitting on a bench overlooking the harbour, I was joined by a young couple with two young children. They said they came from Londonderry.

'Is that the same place as Derry?'

'Yes. The Protestants call it Londonderry and the Catholics call it Derry. People are now calling it Stroke City to avoid saying "Derry-stroke-Londonderry".' He was a painter and plasterer. Both wanted the ceasefire to continue and longed for peace. 'We can't go back to the old ways. Everybody was living in fear. Now you can go out in the evening without worrying any more.'

'Do you come to the South very often?'

'Yes. We often come over the border to Mullaghmore for the weekend or for a day's outing. It's very beautiful and peaceful here. People hear all sorts of things about the South, but we've never had any problems here. When we went to Dublin for the first time, we were surprised to see how well off people were.'

Although it had a beautiful stone harbour and a magnificent beach with clear water, I would have been disappointed by Mullaghmore if it had not been for Rodney Lomax and his family. He was a boatbuilder on the edge of town who supplemented his income in the summer by taking visitors out fishing and to visit the island of Inishmurray in his boat *Celtic Dawn*. I first came across him in his boatshed where he was working on an elegant wooden steam boat. Whilst buying some diesel, we had a chat. I asked him how he got interested in the sea.

'When I was a boy I was asked to mop out a dinghy, and the owner let me use the dinghy and its engine. From then on, I never lost my love of boats and the sea. I can remember when I was nine taking girls out rowing under the bridge at the end of the harbour. I've been taking people out ever since!'

'What sort of fish do you catch here?'

'Well, a good bag should yield mackerel, pollack, cod, ling, coalfish, wrasse and dogfish, among others.'

'What about shark?' I had seen a fisherman degutting one in the harbour.

'We usually catch blue shark. Some over 100 pounds have been landed. You can sometimes land porbeagle shark too.'

I was invited to dinner that evening. After the meal, I asked Rodney about the Gothic pile I had seen on the headland in the mist but which was not on the chart.

'Oh, that's Classiebawn Castle. It was built by Lord Palmerston who also built the stone harbour. It was later acquired by Lord Mountbatten.'

'Wasn't he blown up in a yacht around here some years ago?'

'Yes, here off Mullaghmore, in 1979, along with other members of his family. He used to come every August and "rough it", as he called it, in the castle.'

'Did you know him?'

'Yes. I used to look after his boat for him. He used to go out shark-fishing – he was the first to make the sport popular here. The other fishermen thought he was crazy because he used to put them back into the sea! He often invited me up for a drink at the castle. He once showed me a flag he had found in the attic; it was from the Imperial Russian Navy. I suppose he was a bit paternalistic but he did help some local boys to go away to naval college.'

Rodney was full of yarns. He told me a cautionary one about local pilotage. 'When I was a teenager, I wanted to impress my girl friend and sail up to Salt Hill Quay at the entrance to Donegal Harbour. The local dean of the Church of Ireland told me to line up the edge of an old tram car with trees as I came in, to avoid the shoals. As I came in I just couldn't see the transit and went aground. I realised that some trees had grown to block out the tram car. The dean had seen what had happened and came out in his boat: 'What are you doing, my boy? I told you about the transit . . .'

'But trees have grown up in front of the transit!'

'Well, you shouldn't have gone aground. You should have used your initiative.'

'I couldn't "f" a dean of the Church of Ireland, but I had the pleasure of seeing him go aground the next day in the estuary!'

Clearly a little local knowledge can be a dangerous thing.

21

Up the Creek

The day before my birthday, my family caught the night ferry from Holyhead in North Wales to Dublin, and then the early morning train to Sligo. A friend of the Lomax family in Mullaghmore gave me a lift to the station to meet them. It was a lovely hot day again, and my young female driver, laughing with pleasure, declared: 'The Irish don't know how to cope with this weather! We're used to rain, not sunshine, day in and day out.'

On our way we went to Drumcliff, a village nestling below the Darty Mountains which ran down to the western sea. Yeats was buried there in a little churchyard near a high cross and round tower. The place was surrounded by tall trees in green rolling countryside.

The bare head of Ben Bulben seemed to follow me and change shape as I travelled along the coastal road to Sligo. The summit inspired a great, simple poem, the last words of which are cut on Yeats' gravestone. Nearby was Lissadell House, the ancestral home of the Gore-Booth family. Yeats was a regular visitor to this Grecian-style mansion and dedicated a poem to the sisters Constance and Eva.

Constance married the Polish Count Markiewicz, but her aristocratic connections did not prevent her from participating in the Easter Rising of 1916. She was condemned to death but her sentence was commuted to imprisonment. She became the first woman to be elected to the House of Commons although like most Irish rebels, she refused to take her seat. While still in prison she was also elected to the first Republican Dáil in 1918 and a year later became Europe's first female minister. Her sister Eva, an accomplished poet, was also a socialist and played a militant part in the women's suffrage movement in the USA and England.

Like so many young people in Ireland, my driver not only knew about Yeats but also the old Irish legends, especially the tales of Fionn Mac Cumhail or Finn Mac Cool, and had learned how he had been educated by the druid Finegas and been touched by the Salmon of Knowledge.

Not enough, it seems. The High King Cormac Mac Art had promised Fionn the hand of his beautiful and wilful daughter Gráinne. But Fionn was already old and she eloped on the eve of the wedding with the young Diarmuid. Thus began the pursuit of Diarmuid and Gráinne which lasted sixteen years. Diarmuid was eventually slain by a magic boar, his taboo animal, whilst out hunting on the slopes of Ben Bulben, thereby fulfilling a prophecy made at his birth. Fionn could have saved the life of his friend Diarmuid with cupped hands of life-giving water, but he opened his hands and let the water run through his fingers; Diarmuid was then gored to death by the boar.

I arrived early in Sligo and spent the time buying up stores, cashing some money, looking for a canister of gas, and visiting the town. Sligo had grown from a settlement around a ford at the mouth of the river Garavogue; its name comes from *sligeach*, meaning shelly river. It attained its status as a town when the

Anglo-Norman Maurice Fitzgerald built a castle to guard the crossing and later an abbey for the Dominicans. It was celebrating its 750th anniversary when I was there. In the following week there was to be a music festival which would be carrying on the tradition of Yeats' 'Fiddler of Dooney' whose music inspired folks to dance like 'a wave of the sea'.

It was lovely to see my family arrive in Sligo railway station and to hear all their news. Emily had just returned from a holiday in Italy where she had met a new German boy friend. Dylan had been spending the glorious hot summer playing amongst the sand dunes at home and swimming in the warm sea. Jenny was enjoying a break from her college teaching and soaking up the sun at every opportunity.

After taking a taxi back to Mullaghmore, we spent a relaxed afternoon on board *Celtic Gold*. Emily and Dylan jumped into the sea, swam around the yacht, and dived down to gather star fish from the pure white sand. After supper, I talked about the delights of the cruising in store for us in Donegal Bay and up the north west coast to the island of Aranmore. I read out a passage from H. J. Hanson given in the *Nautical Almanac* about the spectacular mountains rising out of the sparkling sea, the mighty cliffs reaching to nearly 2,000 feet, and the safe harbours scattered for the most part within easy reach of one another. 'Given a seaworthy vessel,' Hanson concluded,' a careful skipper of experience, provided with charts and small auxiliary power, can navigate the coast with ease and confidence.'

After two months' cruising around the coasts of Ireland in all weathers, much of it on my own, I felt that *Celtic Gold* and I could fulfil such conditions. In short, I told them that we could expect a wonderful week's yachting holiday in a spectacular corner of the world. All we needed was reasonable weather.

It was not to be. I woke up on the morning of my forty-ninth birthday, 23rd August, to mist and choppy waters. The high stone piers of the entrance to the harbour a couple of hundred yards away were only just visible. It was noticeably colder. Jenny got a birthday breakfast together – it was a pleasure not to do it myself for a change. I was just beginning to enjoy my cards and presents when an old fishing boat came up to *Celtic Gold* and disturbed our family reunion. The skipper, an old weather-beaten man, shouted across the water and asked me whether I could ferry some passengers across from the pier in my dinghy. The tide had gone out and it was now too shallow for him to go into the harbour. I reluctantly agreed, abandoned my breakfast, and got into the rubber dinghy. After much effort, I managed to start the outboard; it was temperamental at the best of times.

When I arrived at the pier I found not just a couple of fishermen but half a dozen heavy men and a young girl. It meant not one, not two, but three journeys to and from the fishing boat and pier. The men were from Northern Ireland, already impatient with the delay, and did not even thank me for my help. Each time I reached the fishing boat, though, the skipper became more concerned and apologetic. A thick drizzle had swept in and I was soon wet to the skin. The fisherman threw an old yellow oilskin into my dinghy but it stank so much of fish and diesel that I declined his kind offer. By the time I had delivered my last cargo of dour shark fishermen from the North, I was cold and soaking wet. The birthday breakfast had been ruined.

Just as I cast off from his drifting fishing boat for the last time, the skipper pushed a piece of paper into my hand. It was a twenty-punt note. Without thinking, I rolled it into a ball and threw it back into the fishing boat. He made to throw it back to me, but I told him I would not accept his money: 'You would have done the same for me!' I shouted above the sound of his engine and the wind. When I told the children about the money back on board *Celtic Gold*, they thought I was crazy. But I knew I had done the right thing. I thought of the St Christopher's medallion Dylan had given me which was around my neck: a true ferryman does not help people for money; even if they are taciturn and gruff . . .

By this time Jenny had cleared away the remains of the breakfast and I made ready to weigh anchor to sail across Donegal Bay to Killybegs, Ireland's busiest fishing port. All was prepared. I turned on the VHF radio. It did not work. I tried to find the fault but to no avail. There was no alternative but to pump up the rubber dinghy again and head off to see if I could get some help from Rodney Lomax. I was fortunate enough to catch him at home. He rang an electrician who came over an hour later. I ferried him out to the yacht; I was getting expert at it by now. The switch on the main panel proved to be the problem and the electrician by-passed the lot by taking new wires direct from the battery to the radio. It worked but the job was temporary and I had to take care that the wires did not get entangled with the fan belt. I ferried him back to the pier. More time lost, more frustration. To make matters worse, the wind was picking up all the time.

As soon as we rounded the point protecting Mullaghmore in the early afternoon, *Celtic Gold* started to rise and fall in a high swell in a stiff north westerly wind. It was the first time the family had sailed together and we could not have had a worse start or more unpleasant conditions. The morning mist had gone and visibility was good, but the wind was gusty and the steep waves breaking. Jenny was very soon sick over the side. Dylan lay down in the cockpit feeling ill. At first Emily glorified in the wild elements, but she too began to feel queasy and took to the wooden boards on the seats of the cockpit.

I was left alone, trying to console Jenny in her suffering and worrying whether we would be all right. Fortunately the crossing was only ten miles, and three hours later we passed the lighthouse of St John's Point. Once we were in the lee of Drumanoo

Head conditions improved dramatically. As we made our way up the inlet to the sheltered harbour of Killybegs, Emily and Dylan quickly recovered and began showing an interest in the sailing. Jenny was slower, having been so sea sick. I wondered whether she would ever want to come on the yacht again.

The water changed noticeably from dark-green to brown as we motored up the channel, keeping clear of the great trawlers which were constantly coming and going. But while we enjoyed the calm, another factor began to disturb us: the smell of rotting fish. I had forgotten the stench for a while. Killybegs immediately reminded me of Castletownbere where discarded fish and leaking diesel made a similar pungent brew. It was such a stark contrast from the fresh air, clear water, and pure white strand of Mullaghmore that none of us wanted to stay in the harbour. I decided to turn around and head for the neighbouring creek of Bruckless at the head of Mac Swyne Bay.

It was a tricky entrance. I skirted mussel rafts and a salmon farm where the flashing fish leapt hopelessly against the surrounding nets in a desperate drive to follow their migratory instincts. I had to leave the rocky shore of Green Island to port and the sinister Black Rock to starboard while keeping Pount Point dead astern. I anchored in mid channel just short of a stone pier. It was worth the effort. It was a beautiful place, quiet and clean, surrounded by towering green trees – a million miles away from the bustle and filth of Killybegs just around the corner. The water, though, was inky brown with peat, like Blacksod Bay, and had none of the bright sparkle of Mullaghmore.

It was six o'clock. Emily was keen to go ashore, and pumped up the dinghy and rowed to the stone jetty. While I was sorting out the yacht, a dark-haired young man talked to Emily as she sat on the jetty. An hour later, we landed alongside a pontoon which had piles of rotting mussels in one corner. The man who had been talking to Emily shook our hands in turn as we clambered on to the pier. 'Welcome to Bruckless!' he said formally, as if we had landed on a Pacific island for the first time. 'My name is Steven.' He asked whether we would like some water. I declined at first, not wanting to bother him, but he insisted and went off on his old bike.

Steve had entertained young Emily on the jetty with the subject he knew best: fish. He explained that on the salmon farm they were force-feeding them to a size of five pounds. Not long before a whale had come into the creek and smashed up the farm; they were able to escape to the open sea. There were other visiting creatures. He had seen sixty dolphins in the bay, a 100-pound blue shark had been landed in Mullaghmore, and there were many sharks – 'finnies' – to be seen off the headland.

We walked up a lane from the jetty to the main road. It had a dried-up spring and a ruined house amongst ash and hazel. The borders were overflowing with wild flowers: stands of yellow ragwort, tangles of dog rose, explosions of red and purple fuchsias, swathes of flowering grasses and sedges, and ripe, blue-black, juicy blackberries. At the end of the lane, we turned right and walked along the road to the village of Dunkineely in search of a place to celebrate my birthday. It had seven pubs, two shops but only one café. My forty-ninth-birthday feast consisted of some takeaway chips which we ate outside in the fading light. But all was not lost. We soon found a warm bar with some good stout. A group of musicians turned up, but after the hectic sail across Donegal Bay we were all too exhausted to linger long.

Back at Bruckless pier, I found a plastic container of clear water. It was delicious – cool, clean and refreshing. It was only when I collected some water later from a nearby garage that I realised that all the water in the area was brown with peat. When I asked Steve how he managed to get such clear water, he said that he had gone to a spring he knew high up in the hills above his family's farm. I was deeply moved that he should have spent several hours on his bicycle to fetch such pure spring water for us. It was difficult to imagine a more generous and meaningful gesture of welcome.

I had another fine birthday present waiting for me on the pier. As we had left earlier in the evening, I had remarked to an old man who was fishing for mackerel that he had some fine swedes in the open boot of his battered car. I now found that he had placed half a dozen in the dinghy. The fisherfolk of Bruckless were hospitable indeed.

The weather had steadily deteriorated during the evening. Waves broke against the small stone pier, throwing up spray in the air. I had a struggle to row with four in the dinghy out to *Celtic Gold* against the north west wind which came hurtling up the creek. We arrived cold and wet.

Laying in my bunk that birthday night, warm and dry at last, I counted my blessings. I was nearly fifty. I had two lovely children. I had some marvellous friends. I had travelled the world. I had published eight books. For the time being, I was out of jail and out of hospital. What more could I want? I knew exactly what I wanted – a reunited family. But I did not have it, and there seemed little likelihood of achieving it now. Jenny appeared as distant as ever, her feelings hidden. I would just have to make the best of the situation. I felt I had grown in inner strength through the suffering of the winter, and the two magical months at sea had shown me that I could enjoy life again. What the next few days would bring was anyone's guess.

I woke up many times during the night. *Celtic Gold* snatched at the anchor in the choppy sea like an angry horse on a short tether. The gusty wind in the rigging made a forlorn and wearisome whistle. I regularly checked my position with a transit between the edge of a roofless house and a tree on the shore. It would have been a disaster if we started dragging the anchor towards the stone pier or the black rocks on the other side of the creek amongst the overhanging trees. At first light, I could see dark, menacing clouds coming in from the north west. But the children did not seem to be downhearted. 'It's really strange to be on holiday with the family again,' said Emily as she slowly came to, up in the forward cabin with Jenny. 'It's good to be all together again.'

'Sailing's really fun. I can see the point now,' said Dylan from his quarter bunk in the main cabin with me.

The weather report was for a near gale for the next few days. We would have to remain in Bruckless although we were exposed to the full force of the wind. I thought of going over to Killybegs on my own in *Celtic Gold* but I knew the family would hate it there when they joined me. I decided instead to lay out the kedge anchor as a precaution and stay in the creek. I could always put the family in a local guest house if it blew up worse.

We were now literally up a creek without a decent paddle. There was very little for the children to do apart from going for walks in the pouring rain or sitting on the yacht in the wild winds so we decided to go to Donegal for the day. We caught a bus at the end of the lane. The cheery driver had put a straw St Brigid's cross over his mirror and played loud traditional Irish music on the stereo.

On the way in, we passed through a village where the church and cemetery were on one side of the street and the houses on the other. An old man with his wife behind us joked: 'This is the only place in Ireland where the neighbours don't fight. It's nice and quiet. Perhaps too quiet.' As he got off, he said: 'If life gives you a lemon, make lemonade!'

It sounded very sound advice in the circumstances.

We got off the bus in the main square of Donegal – the triangular-shaped Diamond. It was surrounded by brightly coloured shops, luring visitors in for Donegal tweeds or Irish stout or facial cream or the latest bestseller. A number of young backpackers waiting for their transport watched some New Age jugglers amongst the old men and women of the town. In the middle of the Diamond, there was a tall red granite obelisk, a memorial to the Four Annalists. I failed to interest the children in these scholar friars who salvaged the old literary remains of ancient Ireland and recorded the whole of known Gaelic history and mythology from forty years before the Flood to AD 1618.

Apart from the pubs and cafés there seemed little to do in this ninth-century market town. I went to an information centre.

'There's the O'Donnell castle but it's closed for repairs,' the girl said.

'Is there a cinema?'

'Yes, there's a cinema; it's not open.'

'What is there for a couple of teenagers on a rainy day?'

'There's a craft village not far out of town.'

The assistant gave me careful instructions. Along the shores of the River Easke we walked past an anchor from the fleet which had attempted to land with Wolfe Tone in Bantry Bay in 1798. The frigate *Romaine* had sought shelter in Donegal Bay, but on sighting English troops had cut its cable and left its anchor in the sand. We walked along a broken, narrow pavement by a winding road which climbed out of town, polluted and buffeted by countless cars and belching juggernauts. There were no signs of a craft village anywhere. We finally gave up the search, tired and frustrated.

I tried to make light of our magical mystery tour, but Emily was not amused: 'There's absolutely nothing to do in Donegal. If I lived here, I'd go mad!' She was almost in tears.

We went back to town. The children went shopping and Jenny and I went for a coffee. It was the first time that we had been alone together since their arrival. We had known each other for thirty years and had now been separated for nearly a year. It had almost been like old times with the family reunited and I had been hoping, against my better judgment, that we might indeed get back together. But Jenny said she had been thinking about things over the summer and had decided that she would like to continue her independent life for the foreseeable future: 'I thought of getting back together for the sake of the family, but now I realise I must follow my own feelings,' she said, looking into her empty coffee cup. She wanted to draw up a list of resentments, but I said for my part I did not feel any resentment or anger any more. The sea had washed them away.

It was a blow to learn the truth once and for all and the rest of our time together seemed poignant and fragile. I could not help thinking that this would be our last holiday together as a family. There was going to be no happy ending to the voyage in terms of a reunion. But I put on a brave face and tried to make it as enjoyable as possible for everyone.

That evening the wind was even fiercer and it was decided that Jenny, Emily and Dylan would spend the night in a guest house in Bruckless. The children urged me to stay the night, but I did not want to abandon ship at the very moment when I was most needed. Besides I had not slept on land for sixty-five nights since my departure and I did not want to break the rhythm. The old lady who owned the guest house said to me as I left for the creek, 'Please God that it won't be too stormy!'

I returned to *Celtic Gold* to weather out the gale at anchor. I would now have to weather out my life alone, I said to myself, without an anchor. That was going to prove a greater test than sailing around Ireland, but sailing around Ireland had prepared me for it. I would survive.

I spent most of the night up, on anchor watch, checking my position against the roofless house on the shore. The two anchors, spread out like a V, held the yacht's bows into the whistling wind and surging sea. The anchors held and just before dawn the wind abated a little. I felt wretched. I only managed to sleep for a few fitful hours, disturbed by strange and violent dreams.

22

The Relaunch

I went ashore in the dinghy and trudged cold and tired in the driving rain the two miles to Bruckless to have breakfast with the family in their guest house. They had slept well in their warm, comfortable beds. They were ready for action. We decided to explore Killybegs for the day. The son of the owner of the guest house gave us a lift in and said: 'Killybegs is a really good town. Have fun!' That sounded auspicious.

The surrounding hills ran down to the port where dozens of trawlers were moored, unloading fish, sorting out their nets, making ready for departure. The warehouses on the quay were full of boxes of fish in ice. The town was dominated by a church but the most enduring impression was the stench of fish, made worse by the presence of a fish meal factory on the edge of the town. If you don't eat fish and don't like the smell of fish, Killybegs is not for you. We retreated out of the rain to a deserted pub for lunch. Afterwards, we bought Dylan some shoes and walked up the hill to visit a carpet factory only to find that like the castle in Donegal, it was closed. Having exhausted the attractions for teenagers we caught a taxi back to the boat.

As we walked up the lane to Bruckless Creek, Emily said: 'The first day, I said to myself, I can get used to this. That lovely clear water, that lovely warm sun. But here there's absolutely nothing to do. We can't even go swimming!'

'What's the point of complaining all the time?' Dylan said.

'I'm not always complaining. But if Dad says something about craft villages or carpet factories again, I'm going!'

'Emily, you're never content,' said Jenny.

'Look, this holiday's not going to be fun, it's not going to be sunny. So let's leave it, OK!'

'I don't care what you think or feel,' said Dylan.

'I don't care if you fall off the boat!' replied Emily.

Despite everything, 13-year-old Dylan seemed to be enjoying himself, strolling along the lanes, visiting the towns, mucking about in the dinghy. Poor 17-year-old Emily! She was fresh from her holiday in Italy, missing her new boy friend, holed up in bad weather in Donegal. I had rung her from Dingle, at the height of the season, and was full of enthusiasm about all the young people of different nationalities coming over to Ireland for the music and craic. It was boiling hot and the sea was sparkling.

Killybegs could not have been more different. No night life, no international set, no sun, only grey skies, cold wind, driving rain, poor public transport, and the ever-present smell of fish. She had brought eight different skirts with her, but no pullovers, no waterproofs, no socks. Bored, cold and damp, stuck on a small boat up a remote creek with her family, it was not what she had anticipated. Even the friendly fisherman in Bruckless was ten years older and not her type.

'We're up shit creek without a sail,' was her conclusion.

At one stage, Emily and I started talking about our old house Garth-y-Foel, where we lived before the separation. 'It's weak to be upset,' she said. 'I'm probably more upset than anyone about leaving Garth-y-Foel. It was my home and now I don't have one.

I grew up in the country by a stream in the mountains. I loved the smell of the grass and the trees. I really miss it living in my friend's house in town.'

'You're right. You have to be brave. But you will always carry the experience of living at Garth-y-Foel within you. It will give you strength in times of difficulty.'

The next morning it was still very gusty but the rain had ceased and there were some patches of blue amongst the billowing white clouds. I rowed with Emily and Dylan to Green Island at the entrance to Bruckless Creek. We only just managed to reach the rocky shore without being swept out to sea by the strong ebbing tide. A couple of herons took off from a nearby copse of trees and the sound of curlews came from the mud flats at the end of the creek.

We had a lovely time exploring the rock pools on the foreshore of the island. Ever since I was a boy, I had been fascinated by them. They seemed like timeless worlds in miniature, oases of eternity. Walking across the terraces and crevasses of the exposed foreshore, we came across a magical pool under a great rock covered in barnacles and limpet shells. It was one of the most beautiful I had ever seen. Under the still water, seaweeds of all sizes and colours grew amongst the valleys, cliffs and precipices – ruby red, emerald green, amethyst blue, lichen yellow. Some of their fronds were thin and curly, others smooth and broad. The underwater rock garden was teeming with life. Once the gaze had settled, small fish, delicate shrimps, flowing tentacles of sea anemones, and tiny snails slowly emerged.

We stayed for a long time by the pool, mesmerised by its fragile, exquisite beauty. It was almost as if we needed to drink in its calm limpidity after the movement and confusion of the last few days. At a certain angle, the pool mirrored our relaxed, peering faces, and the billowing white clouds in the sky above us. I was only too aware that the stillness was temporary, and that it would be destroyed by the tempestuous push and pull of the next high tide. Mighty waves would then crash on the rocks and tons of cold water would tug at the delicate fronds.

Afterwards, we played tag on the rough pasture of the small island, releasing the pent-up energy which came from being confined on the boat or in rainy towns. We had a laughing rolling fight in which we all nearly tumbled over a low cliff on to the rocky beach below. Afterwards we sat down on the damp grass and ate chocolate and biscuits looking out across the white-horsed bay.

The conversation turned to philosophy. Emily was thinking of applying to university to study philosophy and English. I had taught philosophy once a week in an evening class for many years and thought of taking it up on my return – in the same community centre in North Wales where Dylan had his youth club. 'Dad, I don't want you to teach philosophy at the youth club this winter. It's so highbrow. No one understands what philosophy is!' I knew he would much rather have had a postman than a writer or philosopher for a father; at least you knew where you were with a postman and everyone else did.

'Philosophy is about asking questions . . .'

'I hate questions. I hate being asked questions about what I think.'

'Asking questions is really great,' Emily retorted. 'Asking questions about the meaning of life, the nature of reality, questions like Who am I? How I should act . . . ?'

'Yes, and philosophy asks fundamental questions about other subjects, so you have the philosophy of science, the philosophy of history . . .'

'The "philosophy of history"!' Dylan said with derision. 'What's that? It doesn't mean anything!'

Perhaps he was the greatest philosopher of us all.

*

On our return, there was a short friendly man with white hair waiting on Bruckless pier. He introduced himself as Kevin Donaghy. Rodney Lomax had called him from Mullaghmore to alert him of our possible arrival. A keen yachtsman himself, he had seen *Celtic Gold* come into the creek from his house on the hill. He invited us over where we met his wife Wendy. They had lived in Dublin but had decided to move to this remote area to manufacture Donegal tweeds in the traditional style. They spun and wove the material at nearby Kilcar. They admitted there was not a lot of sophistication amongst their neighbours but they did not miss city life and enjoyed the good, simple country living. 'People treat each other so well here,' Wendy said. 'A bus driver I know gives flexifares. If it's a sunny day, and he's feeling good, he might charge less. If it's an old lady who looks as if she can't afford the fare, he might adjust it a little and say "How will that do, dear?"'

I asked Wendy about the great houses with false porticos being built around Killybegs on the hills. They looked very incongruous, shining white in the wild green landscape. 'They usually belong to the owners of the trawlers, who are doing very well from the grants at the moment, or from contractors who come from the area and have made their fortune abroad. They like to impress their neighbours! There's a long tradition in Donegal of people going away to work for years and then coming back and building themselves a house. If they can, they always come back for two weeks over Christmas.'

I remarked how it was a shame to see the old long, whitewashed, thatched houses being left to rot while new, functional, characterless bungalows were springing up all over the place. 'If you'd brought up half a dozen children in a cottage which was dark, cramped, damp, and without water you'd want to move. In the fifties a cheap kind of bungalow with three bedrooms was designed and everyone who could built them in the country.

They were advertised as Bungalow Bliss. A recent book has called their spread Bungalow Blitz. They may look terrible and monotonous but they're a darn sight better to live in than the old picturesque ones!'

We were now close to the border with the North. Enniskillen was not far away and locals would often go to Derry for their special shopping. Mullaghmore was only ten miles from the border.

'Donegal used to be one of the nine provinces of Ulster,' Kevin explained. 'With the treaty of 1921 which formed the Irish Free State it was agreed that the British government would retain the six provinces of Ulster where there was a Protestant majority, but the border cuts through the traditional boundaries.'

Wendy invited us for a meal at their house, a plain, simple, beautiful house with fine views of the surrounding rolling countryside. Amongst the watercolours on the wall was a quote in fine calligraphy from Henry van Dyke:

> Be glad of life
> Because it gives you a chance to love and work
> To play and look up at the stars.

Wendy was in a unique position. She had been brought up a Quaker, and therefore felt outside the traditional Catholic and Protestant communities. At the same time her family had been strongly nationalist and supported Irish independence.

'We used to joke in the family,' she said, 'with the slogan: Up the Republic and Roast the Pope!'

She was now actively trying to heal the rift between the two communities, working part-time on behalf of the Foyle hospice in Derry which recognised no borders. She offered to introduce me to the Protestant Bishop of Derry who was also active in the campaign of reconciliation.

Although the ceasefire had made life more bearable, she was very aware of the difficulties faced by Catholics and Protestants, both north and south of the border.

'In the Republic, ninety-three per cent of the population is Catholic and seven per cent Protestant. But the Protestants were part of the land-owning class and even in the forties Trinity College in Dublin was considered to be only for Protestants; Catholics were told by their church not to go.'

'Have there been many mixed marriages?' Jenny asked.

Jenny and I had had a very mixed marriage. She was born in Martinique in the French West Indies and had grown up in France and West Africa. I was born in Sussex and had grown up in southern England. Her first language was French; mine was English. She was a Catholic; I was a Protestant. Our children were a wonderful mixture: Emily was white with blue eyes and curly light brown hair while Dylan was light brown with dark brown eyes and wavy dark brown hair. Having grown up in Wales, they both spoke English, French and Welsh. They seemed to have thrived in the rich cultural soil.

'Before, there were quite a few mixed marriages,' Wendy went on, 'but children of Protestants and Catholics had to be brought up as Catholics in the Republic. It was difficult for Protestants here because it was illegal to obtain contraception and to have an abortion. The Catholic Church and State are still very close in the Republic.'

'Have things been getting better since the ceasefire?'

'Oh yes! It's lovely to go over the border without having to worry. People are getting used to peace now and will be very upset if the ceasefire doesn't hold. But I'm afraid bigotry on both sides is still alive and strong.'

Wendy offered to take us on a tour of the region to the north of Donegal Bay. On our way we visited her family's tweed factory in Kilcar, where hand looms were still in use. The lovely subtle yellows and browns of Donegal tweed, she claimed, came from natural dyes made from heather tips, gorse and lichens. The latter, scrapped off the rocks, was called 'crothal'. The Donaghy's did the whole process from carding and spinning the wool to weaving the tweed. One of the weavers in his thirties told me that he could produce twenty-six metres of rug a day on his hand loom.

'I produce the electricity,' he joked.

He was sweating from the effort and I asked him if it was tiring work.

'I've been working at the loom for fifteen years and I'm tired now.'

After visiting the tweed works, Wendy suggested a drive to the north west headland of Donegal Bay. The coastal road passed sandy beaches, rocky promontories and stone-walled fields as it climbed towards Slieve League. Its awesome cliffs rose sheer out of the water; they reached 1,972 feet, making them almost three times higher than the cliffs of Moher, and the highest sea cliffs in Europe. We stopped at a view point and saw a wonderful shaft of light suddenly break through the grey blanket of clouds, turning the dark-grey sea into a silver pool of mercury for a moment. The constantly changing light and its magical effect on coastline and sea, was one of the most memorable delights of the west coast.

We travelled inland and after Meenavean turned off on a narrow road to Malin More. The rocky land swept down from the back of the cliffs of Slieve League to a boggy valley which was scattered with stagnant ponds of turf-coloured water. Great turfs of peat had been piled high alongside the narrow road, awaiting collection. They would warm the outlying cottages during the approaching winter.

'They're like dinosaur's droppings,' Emily accurately observed.

In Glen Malin the outlines of prehistoric field systems were still visible. The area was dotted with megaliths: dolmens, souterrains and cairns from the Bronze Age. Some of them were much earlier, built in the age of the Great Pyramids in Egypt, a thousand years before Stonehenge.

Wendy's daughter Natasha, a teacher, who worked in the Irish language and culture centre in Glencolumbkille, told me that archaeologists had discovered remnants of a people living in the valley four thousand years ago, long before the arrival of the Celts.

'It was much warmer then and they grew different crops – oats and barley – as well as keeping domestic animals. The whole area wasn't bare like today but covered in woodland. It must have been something of a golden age. They seemed to have lived in peace and plenty on the edge of the world. They built great stone megaliths but there are no signs that they had any weapons. Their way of life must have been destroyed when warrior tribes came to the area.'

We stopped and visited one of the oldest sites, a court cairn, a flat-roofed gallery fronted by a semi-circular courtyard marked out by large standing stones. Brushing away the sedges and reeds, Wendy showed us some ancient markings on a large stone, lines and circles, precursors of ogham script. Emily and Dylan hid amongst the stones which once contained the bones of the dead. It began to drizzle and soon the summit of Slieve League was lost in mist. I thought of the peaceful people who raised the stones over 5,000 years ago; they must have been far wiser than we are with our high-rise buildings which fall in a few decades and with our weapons which can destroy the world. They knew the intricate rhythms of the earth and the circular movement of the heavenly bodies.

Near Rossan Point, we saw a whole row of dolmens, three or more upright stones supporting a capstone, many of them still in place. The local farmer had them in his house field; one was even part of an outhouse. In his rich fields, he had stacked his harvest of barley and oats in corn stooks. I wondered whether he felt a strange energy coming from them like I did or whether he thought they were just rough stones in the way.

From the cliff of Rossan Point, I looked down at the angry, dark-grey sea. There was a very heavy swell coming in from the west. The great Atlantic rollers smashed against the jagged black stacks and dark-brown cliffs, their white spray flying high in the air and blending with the steady drizzle. It was an awesome sight which filled me with foreboding. The thought that I would have to pass along that coast in a few days', time when the wind abated a little was frightening. Just as on the cliffs of Inishmore in the Aran islands, I turned away, unable to contemplate for long such a bleak wilderness of water and air.

I could just make out the outline of Rathlin O'Birne Island, yet another centre for early Christians. Wendy did not cheer me up by saying that many large fishing vessels from Killybegs had been lost in the sound over the years.

We moved on to Glencolumbkille overlooking Glen Bay. Many of the whitewashed houses scattered on the hillside had rounded thatched roofs with nets thrown over them to hold them down against the Atlantic storms. Few trees could stand the winter blast, and those that did were bent and withered. The village was named after St Columcille who came here for a retreat, founded a monastery and made it a place of pilgrimage. Some of the pilgrim stations are old megalithic sites, neatly blending the Old Religion and the New. Columcille was better known in English as St Columba, another sailor saint like Brendan, who founded a monastery on Iona.

Although St Columba's English name means dove, he was not always a peaceful soul. At Cuildrevne near Drumcliff where Yeats was buried, a famous 'Battle of the Books' had taken place in the sixth century between the followers of St Finian and St Columba. Finian had lent a psalter to Columba who secretly made a copy from it. When Finian discovered this, he demanded the copy but Columba refused. They took the dispute to Diarmuid, the High King of Ireland who made the historic judgment: 'To every cow its calf, and to every book its copy.' It was a sentiment to which every author worried about his copyright would give assent.

Columba still refused to return the copy, drew up an army and went to war with Finian over the issue. In the Battle of the Book between the two saints, 3,000 men were killed in 561 at Cuildrevne. Columba went into exile. He sailed from Derry to the remote island of Iona in a currach. From Iona not only did Christianity pass into Scotland but the monks produced the fabulously illustrated *Book of Kells*. Dating from around 800 AD, it is one of the oldest and most beautiful books in the world, presently held in Trinity College in Dublin.

Although deeply homesick, Columba swore he would never walk on Irish soil again. But in 575, he returned to Ireland to attend the Convention of Druim Ceat to defend the rights of the bards; it is said that he strapped turfs from Iona to his feet, to keep his promise. Many poems are attributed to him which reflect his love of Ireland and of wild places. My favourite was 'Columba's Rock'. Its sentiments must have been felt by the monks of the Great Skellig, Inishmurray, and Inishgloria. I had experienced them myself during my voyage.

> Delightful it is to stand on the peak of a rock,
> in the bosom of an isle, gazing on the face of the sea.
> I hear the heaving waves chanting a tune to God in heaven;
> I see the glittering surf.
> I see the golden beaches, their sands sparkling;
> I hear the joyous shrieks of the swooping gulls.

I hear the waves breaking, crashing on rocks, like thunder in heaven.
I see the mighty whales.
I watch the ebb and flow of the ocean tide . . .
Delightful it is to live on a peaceful isle,
In a quiet cell, serving the King of kings.

Because of its remoteness, Western Donegal is one of the few remaining Gaeltacht areas. In the fifties, three quarters of the young emigrated but one Father Mac Dyer came from Tory Island and helped organise co-operatives and diversify the farming which dramatically reduced the rate of emigration. Even so, the young are still drifting away to the English-speaking cities, looking for jobs and education, while the urban rich are buying up picturesque second homes. The same process is at work all along the west coast, undermining the Irish language.

Natasha told me: 'There's probably now only 30,000 people left in Ireland who speak Irish every day, and about 60,000 with a reasonable comprehension. The language is certainly under threat, although a lot of young people are now trying to learn it. But they tend to come from middle-class, well-educated families. As a living language of the people, it might never recover.'

After a week, it was time for my family to return to North Wales. I decided to accompany them to Donegal Town where they could catch a coach to Sligo. Despite the weather, the distance between Jenny and I and Emily's protestations, the children seemed to have enjoyed their visit. We got up early in the morning on board *Celtic Gold* to another windy and drizzly day. As we pulled the dinghy round the stern on the painter in order to load it with luggage, one of us let it go by mistake, thinking that the other was still holding it. The wind and tide immediately took the dinghy out towards the sea.

'Marooned, a fate worse than death!' shouted Emily.

Before I could make ready to dive in, she had already stripped to her bra and pants and had dived into the cold brown water. She swam boldly to the rubber dinghy, pulled herself in and rowed it back to *Celtic Gold*. She was freezing cold but laughing. We got ashore as quickly as possible and ran up the lane with all the luggage. We only just made the nine o'clock bus. If we had missed it, Emily would have had to stay another day up Bruckless creek without a paddle . . .

I said good-bye to my family in Donegal Town. I could not hold my tears back when I saw Dylan and Emily waving to me from the back of the coach as it disappeared around a corner. I knew I would see them again on my return in the autumn, but I realised that it would probably be our last family holiday together. It was a heart-rending thought and it brought back memories of all the wonderful camping and seaside holidays we had had when the children were small. I had to harden my heart against the reawakened feelings of sadness.

It had been deeply unsettling to see Jenny and the hoped-for reconciliation had not taken place. 'That's it, then,' I said to myself. 'It can't be clearer. You've got to get on with your own life now, alone.'

I returned to *Celtic Gold*, having washed my laundry and bought additional stores, including some water for the batteries. I was sad to see my birthday cards and presents on the chart table and the remnants of their stay scattered around the cabin: Emily's socks, Dylan's sleeping bag. There was a strange silence on board without the three other bodies and souls. I got on with practical things, cleaning out the boat and making ready for my departure. I felt exhausted by the last week's events, by the disappointment with Jenny, by the effort to entertain the children, by the strain of trying to hold everything together. Perhaps I had tried too hard.

And then there had been the gale, the constant whistling of the rigging, the buffeting of the wind and waves, the worry of the yacht dragging its anchor, the sleepless nights. The wind had got inside my head. I felt tired out and longed for some peace and ease. To make matters worse, I had the unpleasant feeling of being holed up, stuck, cornered, as I had done before, waiting on weather in Kinsale and the Aran islands. Only this time, it felt worse and the situation was more serious.

It was time to pull myself together. I would have to channel my thoughts and feelings and change my attitude. I would have to go with the flow.

In the evening, I spoke to Steve who passed by in his boat going out fishing. He was not reassuring. 'Peter, you shouldn't be here now. After 25th August, the nature and the colour of the sea changes.'

'What do you mean?'

'Well, the sea goes dark and the autumn gales start blowing in. You should be on your way as soon as possible.'

Hadn't the fisherman said the same in the Aran islands? The old doubts were reawakened. Had I left too late in the season? Would I ever make it back to Wales? Would I have to abandon the yacht somewhere in Northern Ireland for the winter?

I met another fisherman who was testing an outboard motor which he had repaired. His name was John McCloskey; he was going bald on top but had jet black hair and beard with deep-blue eyes. His gaze was steady and true. He told me a story which seemed particularly apt in my situation. 'A friend of mine was on one of the trawlers from Killybegs and they were caught out in a storm. The skipper was frightened as hell. He said: "We're all going to be drowned!" My friend said: "You go down to your bunk and stay below. I'll take over." Some men were weeping and others were saying their prayers.

'"What will happen to our wives and children?" they cried.

'"This is a big statement I'm going to say," he said. "If we go down now, there's not a wife who won't be wed within a year and you'll be quickly forgotten!"

'This gave them heart. They pulled themselves together and survived the storm.'

I got up early next morning and made ready to leave. For only the second time in a week, there were patches of blue amongst the white clouds. The sun came out briefly, and with it a surge of new life and hope. I would make it around Ireland, I said to myself, whatever the local fishermen might say about the autumn gales.

When I came to weigh anchor, I had a problem. I rowed out in the dinghy and managed after much struggling to pull up the kedge from the thick dark-brown mud. The main anchor was a different matter. It was solid. I started the engine and motored over it, hoping to change the tilt and thereby release it from the mud. No such luck. As I was wondering what to do next, Steve turned up with an older man in an ancient thirty-foot clinker life boat. He took the chain on board, played it through the two wooden thole pins, and tied it tight to a thwart. He then started to rock the boat in the hope that the tugs on the chain would loosen the anchor from its bed of mud. I was concerned that the chain was grinding into the wood of his gunwale and pointed it out.

'It doesn't matter, it's only an old boat!' was his reply.

Then John McCloskey, the fisherman I had met the day before, turned up in an open day boat. 'No problem,' he said. 'I'll sort you out.' He attached a rope on the chain six feet below the surface of the water and while Steve held it taut from his boat, he motored away in his. By combining their forces and changing the angle of the chain, the anchor, after much straining, suddenly gave way. I hauled it up from the bows of *Celtic*

Gold. When it surfaced, there were great lumps of black mud still attached to it. I realised that I had been lucky to have anchored in thick mud and not in sand or else *Celtic Gold* would never have held in the gale. I was even luckier to have got to know two generous-hearted men.

Steve insisted on giving me some of the catch from the bottom of his boat: pollack, mackerel, ling, skate and wrass. I declined but he insisted. In the end, I took a handsome pollack, leaving him the rarer skate.

Before I left, he told me that only a few weeks earlier two fishermen and a boy had gone out in the old lifeboat he was using and only the boy had returned. The weather had suddenly turned bad on their way in. The two men had tried to land the boat on the rocky shore at the entrance to Bruckless. But when they jumped on the foreshore a big wave came and knocked them off their feet and the undertow dragged them back into the sea. They were both drowned. The boy landed the boat at another spot on his own.

'Can the fishermen swim around here?' I asked.

'No. They don't bother to learn. They reckon if you get into the water, you might as well get it over and done with quickly.'

'Do you ever wear life jackets?'

'No. They just get in the way.'

It was the same attitude as the Aran islanders, the same acceptance of death, the same stoic resignation. No wonder fishing was the most dangerous industry in Ireland.

It was not the first time that tragedy had struck in Bruckless. At the beginning of the nineteenth century a whole fleet of small boats had gathered there. 'The people were starving at the time,' I was told by an old man in a local pub. 'They needed mackerel to go with their potatoes but they could not wait until February when they usually come in. A report went out that a few wee herring had been seen and they came in their small boats from all over Donegal Bay, some as far away as Sligo. They cornered the herring in Bruckless Creek. It was calm in there but a storm blew up and their currachs were dashed on to the rocks. Four hundred men drowned. It was on 13th February 1813, long before the Great Famine. Whole communities got up and left the area. Ay, they were real communities in them days; they shared all they had.'

I had been caught in a gale in Bruckless Creek; I had undergone a storm of emotion, but I had survived. Unlike those fated fishermen, I was able to relaunch my boat and my life and head out to sea again.

23

To Derry and Back

After being holed up in Bruckless in a gale of wind and emotion for so long, it was a delight to get out into the open sea of Donegal Bay again. The limitless space of the sky, the gentle heaving of the sea, the great white clouds, the occasional burst of bright light, all worked their miracle. It was good, too, to concentrate on practical things, working out my position on the chart, taking fixes, trimming the sail, surveying the rocky coastline through my binoculars. A few hours at sea is the greatest tonic I know: it clears the head, steadies the nerves, and invigorates the whole being.

I had decided to sail across from Bruckless to Teelin, a harbour nestling at the end of the lavender-coloured cliffs of Slieve League. At first it was difficult to find the entrance along the coast of sandy coves and rocky promontories, but a red fishing boat which seemed to come out of some great rocks, showed me the way in. I passed into a wide estuary surrounded by the green foothills of mountains which were dotted with whitewashed cottages. Salmon making their way up the river leaped out of the clean water. I dropped anchor north east of the stone pier where a few anglers tried their luck. Totally bizarre amongst the old, lichen-covered stones of the pier was a life-size statue of the Madonna painted in garish colours inside a glass sentry box.

A woman in a rubber hat swam around *Celtic Gold* and asked where I had come from. She was a journalist, she said, who had been on an Everest expedition and had joined a yacht sailing around Ireland. While I had already taken more than two months, they had circumnavigated the island in two weeks.

I dived off *Celtic Gold* myself and rejoiced in the cool, clear water. Then I went ashore and washed myself under a hose from the harbour wall. Fresh and clean, I walked a couple of miles along the river to the nearest pub, the Rusty Mackerel, which did not seem to have changed since the Second World War. A large old man with dark eyes talked to me in Irish and then switched to English. He told me that there were still many in the area speaking the 'old language' and young people were coming in to learn it every summer. I had noticed that the fishermen in Bruckless both had Scottish names and said 'wee' and 'ay' as in Scotland. He said there had long been Scottish connections in the region.

'Bonnie Prince Charlie landed here once with his men. They taught the young lads how to fight and use the sword. Many years later when one of these lads was sixty he saw the British soldiers marching and drilling below him and he hurled a rock at them. He was arrested and challenged the captain to a duel. He was allowed to choose a weapon and he chose a sword. At first light, the two men met and swords were brought out to try. He rejected the first because it would not bend. The soldiers thought he was frightened and just playing for time. They brought more swords, this time steel rapiers. When he bent one like a hoop, he said "Ay". Before the fighting began he told the English captain: "First, I will draw blood from your nose; second, I will draw blood from your ears; and third, your end will be swift and clean!"

'They set to. The soldiers couldn't believe their eyes. The old man drew blood from the captain's nose and from his ears but just as he was about to end his life he was stopped by the soldiers. They allowed him to go free. The captain never set foot in Ireland again. Bonnie Prince Charles's men had done a good job!'

Before I left the Rusty Mackerel, the landlady told me that I could catch a bus early next morning to Letterkenny near the border with Northern Ireland and from there I could find another to Derry where I planned to meet an old friend of mine.

I got up at dawn to a grey sky, but it was calm and still. As I walked the three miles along the winding lane from Teelin Harbour to Kilcar, there was a definite feel of autumn in the air. The lane followed a river which was so low because of the drought that the salmon could not mount it to spawn. I met no car nor person on the road but as I passed the sleeping cottages dogs barked and growled on hearing my footsteps. Turfs of peat were already stacked outside the cottages for the approaching winter and lazy smoke rose from overnight fires. The red and purple fuchsias were still in blossom in the hedgerows and I picked some ripe blackberries entwined with honeysuckle from amongst the hazel and blackthorn. Twittering swallows gathered on the telephone wires, working themselves up for their autumn migration back to Africa. There was a strong smell of dew-soaked grass and the acrid, sweet fragrance of smouldering peat.

It was lovely walking out early that morning, with a rucksack on my back and a song in my heart. I walked fast and arrived in Kilcar a quarter of an hour before the departure of the bus. I sat on a bench opposite the Central Bar and watched the town slowly become alive. Crows screeched and fought on the roof tops, making an almighty din. Soon a woman arrived at the bus stop to see off her strong son who was carrying a new backpack.

Three other women turned up, two of them apparently sisters on their way to see their dying mother.

'Mummy's coming to terms with her own end,' said the first sister. 'She's so mentally alert.'

'When father died, maybe she did not grieve properly at the time,' said the second sister.

'Sometimes you grieve a long time after,' said the third old lady.

'Daddy wasn't tall, but he was tall in his head,' observed the first sister.

'Our arms are all around her,' said the second.

When she started to cough badly, the old lady advised: 'You should take some Carrigan moss. It's very good for bronchitis. They used to feed it to cattle.'

The bus turned up on time and I bought a ticket to Letterkenny. As the bus made its way through leafy lanes to Killybegs, I half listened to the news on the radio: it was 31st August 1995, the first anniversary of the IRA ceasefire, and the Irish and British governments were close to an agreement. In the Republic, there was to be a referendum on divorce since it was still not allowed. A small boat had sunk off Clifden on the west coast. There were no winners for the 1.5 million punt Loto jackpot. The Rose of Tralee (a beauty queen) had arrived in Perth, Australia. There was a high over Ireland: the winds would be light and the temperature would rise to the low twenties.

From Killybegs the bus went north to Ardara, nestling in a deep valley where the Owentocker river flows in Loughros More Bay. It then headed north east to the Glenties, a picturesque village where I changed to a smaller bus. We travelled along the shore of Lough Finn to Fintown, and from there through bleak bogland and dark conifer plantations to Letterkenny. It was the largest town in Donegal, built on a hillside on the banks of the River Swilly and dominated by the spire of a Gothic cathedral. I thought of my friend Sally who had been killed in a car accident just before my departure: her family came from the area.

I changed buses again in Letterkenny for one which crossed the border into Northern Ireland. The difference was immediately apparent: the bus was grubby and threadbare and the passengers looked pale and drawn. One fine summer was not going to wipe out years of living in fear and poverty. As we sped along the shores of Lough Swilly to the border, I saw my first political poster by the road: 'Peace through British Withdrawal'. The border itself, demarcated by barbed wire and a watch tower, was not manned but the heavy metal gates could swing shut across the road at any moment.

I got off the bus in Derry. The divisions in the city were reflected by the confusion of its names on the maps. In Bartholomew's Map of Ireland, it is given as 'Londonderry (Derry)'. On the Michelin map it is plain Londonderry. The Irish Ordnance Survey calls it Derry and it is referred to as such in all the sign posts in the Republic. It was Derry to Catholics and Republicans and Londonderry to Protestants and Loyalists. To avoid taking sides, some simply called it 'Stroke City'. I had got into the habit of calling it Derry and saw no need to change. The original Irish name was Doire, meaning 'grove of oaks' and the 'London' was added in the seventeenth century when large areas of land were granted to London livery companies.

The city is beautifully situated on hills which run down to the River Foyle. The thick walls surrounding the town reflected its military past and the continuing conflicts in the region. It had even passed into the collective subconscious of the British: the Siege of Derry, the apprentice marches, the Creggan and Bogside estates, Bloody Sunday, were all equally known and misunderstood.

Derry council had put up boards giving the bare bones of the city's history. For most people on mainland Britain, Northern Ireland was an open sore that they would rather forget about, except that the occasional bombing in English cities and the endless headlines of sectarian killings prevents the longed-for amnesia. The headlines however give little hint of the historical roots of the troubles.

The nine counties of Ulster formed an ancient kingdom and until the sixteenth century were controlled by the local Gaelic chiefs. In 1566, the first English soldiers camped at Derry on the banks of Lough Foyle. Queen Elizabeth's drive for colonisation in the New World as well as in Ireland was continued under James I. At the turn of the seventeenth century the Irish, led by O'Neill and O'Driscoll, rebelled, but after their defeat in Kinsale in 1603 and their subsequent flight abroad, the British stepped up the 'plantation' of settlers in Ulster from England and Scotland. A year later Derry was granted a charter as 'a town of war and a town of merchandise' by James. Apart from temporary lulls, it has remained so ever since.

If the name of the city is confusing, its banking system is impossible. There seemed to be three types of currency in use, the Irish punt, notes produced by the Ulster Bank and the notes of the Bank of England. Over the border in Donegal, I had been given a punt for a pound but in Derry the banks would only give me 96p to the punt as well as take away a commission. As I came out of a branch of the Bank of Ulster after changing some punt to Ulster notes, a woman with three children in tow came up to me and asked if I would exchange a twenty-punt note for a twenty-pound Ulster note. It seemed like trading currency on the black market in Africa. I explained I had just changed some.

'It's ridiculous,' she exclaimed. 'We come from the Republic and they charge me one pound to change a twenty-punt note into Ulster money. Our money is worth more than English money at the moment, but we end up with less!'

Outside the bank was a young girl calling for 'Emergency Aid for Bosnia.' She had no takers.

I strolled down to the Harbour Museum which was situated near the imposing Guild Hall. It contained a replica of the currach used by Columcille or Columba in his voyage from Derry to Iona in 563. Said to be the largest of its kind ever built, it was made from tarred canvas stretched over a light frame on the Aran model. Richard Mac Cullagh and Wallace Clark and eight others had recreated the voyage in 1963 to celebrate the 1,400 anniversary, and afterwards donated the currach to the museum. They were both men I would like to meet.

I thought of Columba's grief of leaving his homeland:

> Great is the speed of my currach, its stern turned upon
> Derry.
> Great is the grief in my heart, my face set upon Alba.
>
> My currach sings on the waves, yet my eyes are filled with
> tears.
> I know God blows me east, yet my heart still pulls me west.

While I was in the harbour museum I met Dermot Francis, the curator. He offered to take me on a tour of the city walls. We stopped on the solid stone walls to look over the Bogside and Creggan estates on the other side of the valley. A large monument at the side of a dual carriageway at the bottom of the valley declared: 'You are now entering Free Derry'. There was a crowd of people waving the Irish tricolour by a new Ford sales complex; a Republican rally.

'The recent troubles began in 1968,' Dermot explained, 'when the Catholics went on civil rights marches, demanding "one person, one vote", an end to gerrymandering in elections, an end to discrimination in housing and jobs and equal treatment by the security forces and the courts. Protestant attacks on the Bogside district culminated on 12th July celebrations and the Apprentice

Boys' March. Eventually the British Army was brought in to check the riots.'

'What's the Apprentice Boys' March all about?'

'It goes back to the siege of Derry in 1689. The gates of Derry were slammed shut by thirteen apprentice boys before the Catholic forces of the deposed British King James II. The policy of "no surrender" had begun. The Protestant citizens held out against a siege for 105 days, but by the time a relief ship arrived a quarter of the 30,000 inhabitants had died from the bombardment, disease and starvation. The walls of Derry were never breached, hence its name, the "Maiden City".'

'Why do the Orange men march on 12th July?'

'It was on 12th July 1690 that the Protestant forces under the newly crowned William of Orange finally beat King James and the Catholic forces at the Battle of the Boyne.'

'How did the Catholics react to the British Army?'

'With relief at first. They protected them against the attacks of the Protestants. They had no confidence in the RUC – the Royal Ulster Constabulary – an armed force which was ninety-six per cent Protestant. The "B" Specials were even worse.'

'"B" Specials?'

'The "B" Specials were originally a part-time paramilitary reserve and were given special powers by the Stormont government; they were little more than armed loyalists.'

I could see army watch towers overlooking the Creggan and Bogside estates. 'So why did the British Army come to be resented?'

'It was soon seen by the Catholics as an army of occupation. Bloody Sunday didn't help.'

'When was that?'

'On 30th January 1972. You see that square over there where the cars are. That's in the Bogside. It took place over there. The British Army shot into a crowd of demonstrators, killing thirteen unarmed Catholics. It was during a march in protest against the policy of internment without trial.'

We were standing at the end of Ferryquay Street within the walled city. There was a monument to the Reverend George Walker, who survived the siege, which declared that King James was 'an arbitrary and bigoted monarch'. He had an outstretched arm pointing over the Bogside. The IRA had tried unsuccessfully to blow up the plinth and his sword had been removed from his arm. Cannons, relics of the 1689 siege, still pointed out over the Bogside though. Someone had daubed 'IRA' on the one of them. Just around the corner was an Orange Lodge and the Apprentice Boys' Hall. I was at the heart of sectarian Ireland.

'I've heard the city being called Stroke City because of arguments about its name.'

'That was thought up by a journalist. It's an insult. The city's official name is now Derry in the county of Londonderry.'

'Have things changed all that much?'

'A lot. In the old days, the Unionists had a permanent majority even though they were a minority in the city. It was because of gerrymandering; all the poor Catholics lived in one area and could send only a few representatives on the council. After the civil rights movement which demanded "one person, one vote" the boundaries were redrawn and now the SDLP – the Social Democratic and Labour Party – has the majority. For the last ten years they've been power sharing and the mayor's rotated.'

'Is it still a divided city?'

'It's not as bad as Belfast. On the east side, the ratio is about sixty per cent Protestant to forty per cent Catholic. On the west side, though, its ninety to ninety-five per cent Catholic. The Catholics are in the majority; they make up about three quarters of the population. Amongst the poor, the deprivation's shared.'

After saying good-bye to the curator, I climbed the steep hill to the central square called the Diamond. There were still houses and shops which were boarded up within the city walls but many were being renovated and there was an air of prosperity. Many of the shops were painted in bold colours, as they were in the Republic. The metal gates were there ready to be slammed shut but for the time being there were no army or RUC posts.

Waiting for my friend in the Diamond, I thought of George Berkeley, Ireland's most famous philosopher, who was Dean of Derry in the early eighteenth century. Although mainly concerned with setting up a college in the West Indies and so an absentee dean, Bishop Berkeley did, in the 1730s, pose some pertinent questions about his native land: 'Whether there be any country in Christendom more capable of improvement than Ireland? Whether my countrymen are not readier at finding excuses than remedies?'

As an idealist philosopher, Bishop Berkeley had denied the independent existence of the external world beyond the human mind. In his view, something existed only if it was perceived. If I did not actually perceive the square I could not be sure that it continued to exist. I closed my eyes and the tree in the square disappeared, but I was still confident that it would be there when I opened them. And it was. Was this just a habit of perception? Did my children, my friends, my boat and my books really not exist when I did not perceive them. The good Dean got around the problem by saying that when I did not perceive an object, God always did, so that it continued to exist in my absence. Phew! So the Diamond in Derry, with its tree, was definitely there.

A limerick by Ronald Knox, with a reply, summed up Berkeley's theory of material objects:

> There was a young man who said, 'God
> Must think it exceedingly odd
> If he finds that this tree
> Continues to be
> When there's no one about in the Quad.'

Dear Sir:
Your astonishment's odd:
I am always about in the Quad.
And that's why the tree
Will continue to be,
Since observed by
Yours faithfully,
GOD.

I hoped so because it was in the Diamond that I had arranged to meet my friend Jeremy Gane. He was there with his 11-year-old son Jonathan at two o'clock, as agreed. I could rely on the existence of time and space – at least for a while.

Jeremy was my oldest friend; we had been students together in the sixties. We share a common interest in Ireland: his partner is Irish and a couple of years earlier we had been on a winter walking holiday along the west coast. He had given up historical research to become an independent artisan, but he now has a travel company as well as being a watch and clock repairer.

I was not expecting him to come with his son. He wanted to go sailing for a couple of days but I explained that I could not take him out in such wild waters off the Donegal coast; I did not want to be responsible if anything happened to his son. All the same, we decided to go back in a hired car to Teelin to see the boat. It turned out that he and his son had stayed in a hotel just a few miles from Bruckless while I was still there: we had both gone hundreds of miles to Derry just to meet up!

I told him about the unsettling experience with Jenny and my sadness at the probability that we would not be getting back together. 'Well, you old reprobate, it's time to come to life!' was his response. After a couple of tempestuous relationships, he had settled down and was devoted to his family.

Jeremy and his son stayed in a farmhouse for the night near Teelin Harbour. The owner was a fisher-farmer and his wife produced a delicious meal for us of wild salmon caught that afternoon and potatoes cooked in their jackets and soaked in butter. No one else in the family wanted to eat the salmon; they were sick to the teeth with it.

Jonathan was delighted to come on board *Celtic Gold* afterwards. When I ferried him over from the pier in the rubber dinghy, he suddenly came alive after being silent during the car journey and meal. I was sorry not to be able to take him with me, but the sight of the great white horses breaking off the cliffs of Slieve League only confirmed the wisdom of my decision.

When we said farewell that evening on the old stone pier, Jeremy said: 'Fair winds.' He was a great friend and I was sad to see him leave. We would have to wait for another occasion in another place for a sail together.

Another family friend joined me in Teelin – Emily Gwynne-Jones. She was a painter whose parents had both been painters and was herself married to an abstract painter. Brought up in the figurative tradition of her father and trained at the Royal College of Art, she had mainly painted landscapes, seascapes and portraits. I was lucky enough to have a marvellous painting by her of my daughter when she was sixteen. She had once crossed the North Sea in a sailing cargo vessel from Wells to Rotterdam. Her lack of experience in crewing was more than made up by her love of the sea and all its moods. This was matched by a great love of Ireland: she was not only partly Irish but had spent many holidays with her three children on the west coast. She had once camped on the wild and windswept cliffs of the Dingle Peninsula where her tent was swept into the sea. Although she lived in Suffolk on the east coast, her heart was in the west.

It had been a beautiful calm day when I left for Derry, but now it was changing for the worse again. 'It's ridiculous,' I said, 'The weather goes from one extreme to another!'

'It's not ridiculous,' Emily reminded me. 'That's the nature of the sea . . .'

I was anxious now to get around the north west as soon as possible. I had been in Donegal Bay for ten days waiting on the weather, and every day made the chance of autumn gales more likely. I was haunted by the Bruckless fisherman's observation that in the last week of August the colour and the nature of the sea change. Not only could I now expect a cold front to pass over Ireland which would bring strong and gusty winds but I would have to sail through a region which was reputed to be the second most windy in Europe.

We left Teelin Harbour at eight o'clock on 1st September. The eastern side of the cliffs of Slieve League were purple with flowering heather, made all the more bright by the rising sun. I had seen many marvels on my voyage, but after rounding Carrigan Head, I was still overwhelmed by the grandeur and sublimity of the cliffs themselves which rose almost sheer for two thousand feet from the sea.

The storm-shaped pinnacles and stacks along the coast at the foot of the cliffs of Slieve League were menacing. The chart also indicated that there were many uncharted rocks. I decided to go boldly through the sound between Rathlin O'Birne Island and the mainland. Once through, I felt a great sense of relief. I had overcome the self-doubt that being port-bound engenders and had proved to myself that I could still sail.

It was ten miles from Teelin to Rathlin O'Birne and another twenty-eight to Aran Road. The weather deteriorated throughout the day. Dark clouds closed in and the sea turned a sinister dark grey. The winds veered from west to north west and started gusting up to twenty knots. Oh where were the glorious blues, azures, aquamarines and sapphires of summer? By lunch time, there were squalls of cold rain sweeping in from the north west.

Dawros Head was lost in thick sea mist.

By tea time, I could just make out the dark craggy outline of Black Rock Point on the south west corner of Arranmore Island. If the weather had been more settled and the tide right, I would have taken the inner passage to Burtonport, but both were against me so I decided to sail around the top of Arranmore Island and approach the Aran Road from the north.

Arranmore Island in Donegal is not to be confused with the Aran islands in Galway. It is only four miles long and three miles wide, but the 'more' means big while 'Arran' refers to the back of a rise of land. Certainly on its exposed west coast there are menacing cliffs, 500 feet high, with the Atlantic rollers smashing at their jagged roots. I tried to keep a mile away from the cliffs but the steep waves were continuously picking me up and hurling me towards them. I came dangerously close to Arranmore lighthouse which was perched 325 feet above the boiling waters on Rinrawros Point on the north west of the island.

While I was fighting against wind and tide, the birds on the cliffs were glorying in the wild elements. Herring gulls and razorbills were circling the dark-brown cliffs, while fulmars flew over head, their short grey bodies gliding effortlessly on their blade-like wings. Guillemots lined the ledge of the cliffs, puffed up in the driving rain.

Emily seemed to be revelling in the wild elements like the birds. 'When I'm sitting safe and snug by a log fire in winter,' she said, 'I'll remember this! I'll appreciate it all the more!'

There's nothing like a hard blow, an angry sea, and spray-spewed cliffs to make one appreciate life in its quieter moments.

As I rounded the sharp headland of Torneady Point and entered Rosses Bay towards the North Sound of Aran, I had a gusty Force 5 north west wind behind me. It was a difficult entrance. I approached the white 30–foot high beacon on the Ballagh Rocks in a turbulent sea. I had to keep a steady course straight for the beacon on the rock until I could see a leading line of pillars on the eastern shore of Arranmore. I was only a few yards off when a white obelisk on the shore came in line with Moylecorragh Peak and I turned hard to starboard. I was so close that I could see the fronds of bladderwrack seaweed on the jagged rock and two large black cormorants with their wings outstretched. I managed to aim straight and dropped anchor by some fishing boats in the lee of a small island to the north, about a cable from the shore. It was not an ideal anchorage, exposed to the prevailing north westerlies, but it would do for the night.

I could see the wild heathery central plateau of the island fall away to stone-walled green fields on the eastern side. Along the shore there were fine sandy beaches between rocky promontories. Scattered homesteads clustered together in the little village of Leabgarrow. The islanders were Irish-speaking, and I would have liked to make their acquaintance, but I decided not to go ashore. I wanted to get away early next morning to Mulroy Bay, one of the many inlets on the north Donegal Coast. It was going to be a hard day's sail, for the forecast was bad, and the voyage would be long.

Emily had clearly enjoyed her first long passage in a yacht. She had not been seasick or down-spirited. Her only moment of anxiety had been when we seemed to be heading straight into the rock at the entrance to Aran Sound. While I was working out the next day's passage plan, she observed: 'I can see sailing is a terrific mixture. You've got to be careful and cautious and at the same time decisive and keep your nerve.'

'Yes. And I've learned the most important thing is to be well prepared, to have the yacht in good working order and to know where everything is. It's essential to listen to the regular weather forecasts so you can know what to expect. I also try and make as detailed a passage plan as possible, looking up all the details of the ports in the *Nautical Almanac* and *Sailing Directions*. To be forewarned is to be forearmed. But you also have to be prepared for a sudden change in circumstances, for the spontaneous and the unexpected, and be ready to throw overboard the best-laid plans and follow your judgment of the moment! You have to apply your reason in the light of the particular circumstances. And intuition helps . . .'

It must have been difficult for Emily to come on board a boat which had been my only home for over two months and which had my stamp all over it. It took her a while to find out where everything was. 'Boats are a bit like garden sheds,' she observed. 'They're very much male territory. I can see that a lot of sailors and gardeners are the same. They say they've got to go off to do some painting on the boat or to prune some raspberry canes, but what they really want is to get away from their women to a space where they can do things exactly as they wish. It's a pity it's like that, but I can see why!'

24

Rushing to Port

After a wild night tucked behind a small island in Aran Sound, I woke up at five thirty on 2nd September to another slate-grey day. But at least the sea mist had lifted and visibility was reasonable. I had stayed up late the previous night working out a passage plan which would take me from Arranmore Island past Bloody Foreland through Tory Sound to the shelter of Mulroy Bay. It was on the most exposed north west coast of Ireland, the second windiest place in Europe. If we were to make it to Mulroy Bay, it would mean a distance of thirty-five miles and about twelve hours at sea.

We weighed anchor at eight o'clock after a good breakfast of porridge, toast and tea. I headed out five miles off the low-lying Rosses coast to make sure that I cleared all the islands and skerries. I did not want to be caught on a lee shore in the north westerly wind which was blowing a Force 4 and gusting up to twenty knots. As we left, there was not a soul about: no friendly fishermen, no fellow yachtsmen, no inquisitive seals, no leaping dolphins, only a brooding grey sky bringing dark rain-bearing clouds. As we left the shelter of Arranmore and passed a group of jagged rocks called the Stags to our starboard, the sun briefly appeared. A wondrous rainbow illuminated the dark but it soon faded. Heavy squalls of rain blew in. The wind was cold and the sea was dark.

Celtic Gold crashed through the waves, sending spray sweeping across her decks. I had a very real sense that the summer was over and with it my care-free journeying. Now it would be a struggle to get back to my home port in North Wales before the winter set in.

Emily talked about her children singing in Benjamin Britten's opera *Noyes Fludde* and it seemed appropriate to sing a few lines from its opening hymn, 'For those in peril on the sea' – my favourite as a boy at boarding school which was otherwise clouded by a muscular and gloomy Christianity. Although I was not a practising Christian (my religion was inspired by elements of Taoism and Buddhism as well as Christianity), I found that I had become quite superstitious during my voyage. I would not set sail without putting around my neck the St Christopher medallion my son had given me and my daughter's ankh. Before I started my engine in the morning, I prayed that I would find a safe haven that evening.

The sun came out between the squalls although the cold gusty wind continued to come from the north west. We had to take the sea on the nose to begin with but by mid morning we altered course and were able to stop the engine and put up a reefed main and jib. There is nothing like the calm and the relief which comes with the cessation of the noise of the diesel engine.

Rounding Bloody Foreland soon after midday was another psychological barrier and physical boundary of the voyage. It had loomed darkly in my imagination but in the event it was far from frightening. Although the north west extremity of Ireland, it was a low-lying headland which would have been easy to miss.

It earned its name not from its treacherous nature but from the reddish colour of its rock.

At this stage, I switched to the *Sailing Directions* for the east and north coasts of Ireland. Whereas the directions for the south and west coasts went in a clockwise direction – the course I was taking – the new directions went in an anti-clockwise direction, which meant that I had to read the pilot backwards. It made making the passage plans more difficult.

I now had seven hours of fair tide with me, and benefited from the strong currents through Tory Sound which can run up to two knots in springs. I sailed quite close to Tory Island. It is a large rock which lies nine miles off the Donegal coast out in the Atlantic Ocean, the most isolated inhabited island on the Irish coast. It is less than a mile wide and three miles long, yet is still the home of 130 Gaelic-speaking people and a dozen or so cows.

Emily and I both wanted to visit Tory Island. It is famous for its local artists who have been inspired by the English painter Derek Hill. An islander called James Dixon had seen him working on the cliffs in 1956 and declared that he could do better himself. Hill took up the challenge and sent him brushes, paints and canvas but he preferred to make his own brushes out of donkey's tail. Dixon's neighbours then thought they could do better and the school had begun. The painters and the tourists they attracted in the summer months had helped stave off the Irish government's plan to evacuate the island.

Emily knew Derek Hill and as a painter herself had a natural interest in the extraordinary flowering of art on such a remote island. For me, it only confirmed my belief in the natural creativity of all humans, particularly those who live on the periphery of the modern world. Visiting scholars had similarly sparked off a literary renaissance on the remote Blasquet islands.

Tory was also famous in Irish myth for being the home of Balor of the Baleful Eye, the giant king of the Fomorians. He only had one eye which could kill anyone he turned his gaze on. When the Tuatha Dé Danaan invaded Ireland, the ancient Balor was carried out and his eyelid roped open in order to kill the enemy. But Lugh of the Long Arm took aim with a slingshot and killed him through the eye, thereby ending his baleful rule. Balor was probably an Irish version of Baal of the Phoenicians, a fiery deity to whom human sacrifices were made, or Beal (also known as Belinos), a solar god whose feast at the beginning of May was celebrated by the Celts throughout Britain by lighting bonfires on hilltops. The Irish word for May is Bealtaine – 'Beal's fire'.

There were no Fomorians to hurl mighty rocks at us as we sailed through Tory Sound but the dark-grey heavens lashed heavy squalls of rain at us. It is not a place to linger at that time of year and the pilot advised not approaching it except in very settled conditions. I headed east. With the northerly western wind, we sped along on a beam reach at *Celtic Gold*'s maximum speed of six knots. The rigging and I were humming with joy as we cut through the dark-green sea, with foamy waves washing the deck and cold spray splashing into my face.

The coastline of North Donegal is cut by three large inlets: Sheephaven Bay, bound by golden beaches, Mulroy Bay, a long narrow inlet enclosed by dunes and wooded hills, and Lough Swilly, one of Ireland's largest natural harbours. I decided to give the broad sweep of Sheephaven Bay a miss, and head for Mulroy Bay, the best anchorage on the north coast. It was a tricky entrance on the ebbing tide and I had to concentrate hard to pass safely between two large black rocks and the rocky shore close to the first narrows. The sand on the deserted beaches between the rocky promontories was beautifully white. I motored up the narrow inlet for four miles, pushing against the tide which was now running at a couple of knots. I should have entered with the flood, but after twelve hours' sailing I did not have any choice.

We eventually reached the broad expanse of Fanny's Bay at seven o'clock. It had been a hard slog.

We anchored by a couple of fishing vessels about two cables off the northern shore where a high hill sheltered us from the wind. A rainbow suddenly appeared as it had done when we left Arranmore early in the morning; it was tempting to take it as a sign from heaven that all was well. I had a strange sense that someone or something was looking after me. On more than one occasion during my voyage, I felt I had a guardian angel. I also had a strange intuition that I should not deliberately will any evil or else I would lose its sympathy and help. Perhaps I was becoming aware of a higher reality behind the fleeting world of everyday appearances or perhaps I had been at sea for too long on my own . . .

I would have liked to have gone to a pub and enjoy its warmth and friendliness but despite the temptation, we felt so tired after the day's sailing that we decided to spend another night without going ashore. We needed to get up early the following morning if we were going to make it to Portrush before the expected gales arrived.

It proved a stormy night. Although Fanny's Bay was well sheltered on all sides, the wind blew hard down the hill from the north. I fell asleep exhausted and slept like a log for a couple of hours but was woken up by the slapping of the halyards on the mast. I went out into the cold night to adjust them. It was a beautiful starry night and my head felt clear as a bell. I realised that in the last few days I had learned to take on the sea. I always wanted to go with the flow but I now realised the truth of what an old Greek captain had told me while I was sailing through the Red Sea during my circumnavigation of Africa: 'First you have to respect the sea. Second, do not fear the sea. Third, be prepared for its sudden changes. Fourth, know when to attack; in a storm, you must know when to go ahead!'

The forecast for Sunday, 3rd September was for north to

north east winds, Force 4 to 5, occasionally 6 at first. There was a low over northern England producing an unstable northerly air stream with showery troughs over Ireland. A gale was expected the following day. I had no option but to keep moving and to try and make it to Portrush before it broke. Wet and very windy weather was on its way. I would have to rush to port.

We woke up at five thirty to another slate-grey day. I called up Malin Head Radio Station on the radio to give our ETA at Portrush as 1800 hours. We left with the ebb tide just before eight. The wind had dropped somewhat and soft rain swept across Mulroy Bay as we headed out to sea towards Malin Head. Off Fanad Head at the entrance to Lough Swilly we were joined by half a dozen dolphins. They were not like the bottlenosed dolphins of the River Shannon and were only about four or five feet long; perhaps they were porpoises. At any rate, they played with *Celtic Gold* – which was under sail – for a long time, swimming fast along her sides and leaping out of the water near the bows, flipping their tails into the air as they dived down. They also played amongst themselves, nudging each other as they rolled and swirled.

Malin Head, the most northerly point in Ireland, was another bench mark on my voyage. It was etched in my memory as a weather report station as well as an area for the shipping forecasts. The pilot advised extreme caution in poor visibility. It was a most mysterious place with a magnetic anomaly on bearing 250° from the head for about a mile which meant that I could not rely on the compass reading in that direction. I gave it a clear berth of two miles. The setting sun sent a strip of yellow light below the towering dark clouds above, and the low headland with a rounded hill stood out into the dark sea, a lonely sentinel in the cold, windswept northern waters.

After Malin Head, I had to concentrate on my navigation. There can be a steep and dangerous sea and the tides can run up to four knots through Inishtrahull Sound. I could not count on more than four knots from *Celtic Gold* so I had to make sure that we would be going through the sound with the tide. I was fortunate that it turned in my favour at 1300 just as I approached it. I kept well clear of the coast with its rocks and the small uninhabited island of Inishtrahull four miles out to sea, but the north easterly wind was against the tide so the swell was still very steep.

We had a wonderful sail that afternoon. At around three o'clock the sun came out in the pale-blue sky and the choppy, white-capped sea turned bluish green. With a cool Force 4 north easterly on the beam and a 3.5 knot-tide running in my favour, *Celtic Gold* notched 8.6 knots across the ground, the fastest speed of the whole voyage. The rigging was humming, the boat vibrated, and the sails so well trimmed that there was no weather helm: I could steer with my little finger.

The *Sailing Directions* warned that one should not approach the entrance to Portrush in onshore winds above Force 5. As we approached the entrance, the wind was already gusting to that strength, but I did not fancy riding out the expected gale in the Skerries Road to the north of the port. I started the engine, which, thank God, did not fail me this time and took down the sails. The winds were very fluky and in the shallow water great breaking waves picked up *Celtic Gold* like a cork and threatened to hurl her on to the sandy shore ahead. But I kept a steady hand on the helm and swung her hard to port as we passed the north pier of the harbour, making sure that I avoided a submerged breakwater. The yacht lurched as the waves caught her broadside but before they could get a real hold of her, she was out of their clutches and into the sheltered waters of the harbour. I moored at the east end of the north quay below the yacht club, harbour-master's office and pub, all my immediate needs in easy reach. It had just gone six o'clock. We had had over ten hours' hard sail.

As I came alongside the pontoon, a large, red-faced man with wisps of ginger hair leaned over the pier wall and shouted down in an unmistakable accent: 'You're in the UK here! You shouldn't have that tricolour up!'

I looked up to the cross trees of the mast and sure enough there was a small Irish tricolour flapping on the port side and a small Welsh dragon on the starboard. I remembered telling myself that I ought to bring down the tricolour before arriving in Portrush but in the exhilaration and concentration of the sail it had slipped my memory.

As it was, I had a huge red ensign streaming from my backstay, but the man's eyes were on the tiny tricolour at the top of my mast. Most people would not have noticed it. He must have made a habit of checking the yachts as they came into the harbour.

I did not like the aggressive tones of the old man and replied: 'I'll look after my flags in a minute. Safety first, courtesy afterwards!'

I had arrived in Northern Ireland.

There was a lovely light over the town, the pinkish afterglow of the sunset. Children were playing on the quayside and evening strollers peered down at the yacht, no doubt wondering where we had come from. The smell of fish and chips wafted down. It was not only the first landfall for three days, but it was the first time that I had moored alongside a pontoon since Dingle in the south west, a place which now seemed to belong to the remote past. It was very strange not to ride at anchor or roll with the swell.

It also felt strange going ashore and walking on concrete. I realised that I would rather have stayed on the boat out at sea with porpoises and fulmars as company. After all my wild and remote anchorages, I was back in so-called civilisation, and it took a time to readjust.

Portrush was very much a traditional seaside town out of season. The windswept promenades were empty and 'vacancies' were up on the boarding houses which still remained open. The streets with amusement arcades and fast food outlets were deserted. I could have been in a seaside resort anywhere in England, except that there was an Orange Lodge with barbed wire on the high fence around it. Solid Presbyterian chapels, plain and grey, declared the religion of its citizens.

My first stop was for a shower in the yacht club and the second was for a meal and stout in a nearby restaurant. Returning tired and replete to the pub directly opposite the pontoon, we came across two musicians in a back room. One was a tall, thin, young man singing and playing an accordion, a postgraduate student in nearby Coleraine University. The second was a middle-aged short man playing the spoons.

He introduced himself as John Moulden and gave me two song books, one of songs of Irish emigration and the other of the Coleraine area and the Causeway coast. 'There are two things to do with a song,' he said. 'The first is to sing it, the other is to give it away.' One in the first book commemorated the Portrush Fishing Disaster of 1826 when four local fishermen were drowned in weather similar to the kind I had just experienced:

> It was not for want of courage or skill they did neglect:
> A hard squall of wind came on, their boat it did upset:
> The wind it blew tremendously and high did run the waves
> And soon the stormy ocean became their watery graves.

The other song book was full of sad laments about leaving Erin's green shore. In the eighteenth century, the emigrants had been mainly Protestants from Ulster though in the nineteenth century the seven million who left Ireland as a whole were mainly Catholics from the south and west. Both left because of hardship and poverty and in the hope of a better life in the big cities of America. Most of them, as the songs showed, left the green fields of Ireland only to find more poverty in the grey streets of the cities, as labourers or servants. One ballad written around 1825 described the sound I had just passed through:

> At twelve o'clock we came in sight of famous Malin Head,
> And Inishtrahull, far to the right, rose out of the ocean's bed;
> A grander sight now met my eyes that e'er I saw before,
> The sun going down 'twixt sea and sky far from the Shamrock Shore.

We had only just made it to Portrush in time. The following day the weather deteriorated and from the north pier next to the harbourmaster's office I looked at the wild, wanton dark-green sea. Huge breaking rollers crashed against the rocks below. An intense depression was coming in across the Atlantic and deepening off the south west of Ireland. The barometer was dropping rapidly. Every hour Securité messages were broadcast on the radio giving gale warnings. A Force 10 storm was forecast. I spoke to the harbourmaster about the best place to moor. He said I could remain on the pontoon but I could expect up to a six-foot swell coming into the harbour. He had never experienced a storm in the harbour at this time of the year when the yachts were still in the water. He expected a lot of damage to the yachts which were not adequately moored. I realised then how lucky I was to have made it to Portrush. It would not have been good to be in Bruckless, Teelin, Aran Road or even Mulroy Bay with a storm blowing in.

Throughout the day, the lifeboat moored next to me had her engines ticking over, ready for action. Following my brother's advice, whom I rang in Portpatrick in Scotland on the other side of the North Channel, I put out two anchors fore and aft on my port side which held me about three metres away from the pontoon. I could then ride the swell without being crushed against the pontoon. After my experience with the cargo ship in Wicklow Harbour, I did not want to damage my rubbing strake again. I spent the day looking for piping to protect the warps from chaffing on the fair leads.

As it turned out, the expected storm, the tail end of a severe Caribbean hurricane, did not materialise. Even so, in the gale strong winds, the sea crashed over the stone pier and surged into the harbour. The lifeboat stood by, its engine humming, but was not called out. My system with the warps, which guyed out the yacht like a tent, worked wonders. I rang up my brother who told me that the hurricane had hit the Virgin Islands in the Caribbean and his was the only yacht to remain upright and intact in the sheds where it was kept on the hard.

The only other visiting yacht in Portrush, moored alongside the pier and bouncing in the swell, was a twenty-two-footer with a large Scottish flag and a small outboard motor. On board was a middle-aged man who arrived the day after me from the island of Islay. The crossing had been bad. His 70-year-old father had been sick. On arrival, he had made straight for a comfortable hotel. He did not want to return in the small yacht in such bad weather but had to return to Scotland for an important business meeting. I suggested going by air, but they could not find a flight.

'We're just out for a jaunt, basically,' said the cheerful owner. 'We wanted to get to Donegal but the weather's gone bad on us.'

After a handsome lunch, the two of them returned from the hotel, the father carrying a great suitcase and a brief case. He just managed to squeeze his frame and suitcase into the tiny cabin. He had taken several sea sickness and sleeping pills. He was planning to knock himself out for the voyage. They set off, a tiny yacht without a radio and with a tiny outboard, in wild and treacherous seas to make the crossing back to Islay, passing by Rathlin Island off the Antrim coast where the spring tides can run up to six knots. The son, I thought, was either very foolish or very brave; from the state of his yacht, he did not seem very experienced. The old man was no doubt right to take to his bunk; I hope he survived.

Whilst waiting on weather in Portrush, I contacted Wallace Clark, who had once been the commodore of the Irish Cruising Club, had written part of the *Sailing Directions* for the east and north coasts of Ireland, and had sailed around Ireland several times. I had used his estimates for the tidal streams off the west coast in my own calculations. It was he who had skippered the currach which re-enacted the voyage of St Columba from Derry to Iona and which I had seen in the Harbour Museum in Derry. I rang him in Maghera where he lived. He was a Protestant linen manufacturer, carrying on an industry which had once been the most important in Northern Ireland.

He offered me his mooring in nearby Coleraine marina up the River Bann; he had not put his fine wooden ketch, *Wild Goose*, in the water that season because as they lifted the new wooden mast in the boatyard, it had broken.

He said he had to go to a memorial service near Portrush so we agreed to meet in the evening. He turned up in a dark suit and highly polished black Oxford toe caps, with thick wavy silver hair and a boyish grin. He hailed me from the pontoon in a pronounced English accent and stepped on board with the nimble step of an experienced sailor. I got out the Jamieson and asked him if he wanted any water.

'Jamieson's too good for water!' was his reply.

He told me that his son Miles had once been the editor of *Yachting Monthly* but had resigned to write books. After a journey to northern Russia, he had returned home with a strange illness. He got depressed and found it difficult to write and then killed himself. His father had decided to complete the book Miles had been working on from his notebooks. I thought it a wonderful thing to do but could imagine how hard it must have been to read the last words of his dead son.

He did not dwell on his son's death, but rather preferred to talk about the joys of sailing around Ireland. He had been around, in different stages, several times and had written about it. When I asked him what he most appreciated, he replied: 'The light and the craic. You get marvellous pools of light which suddenly come out of the heavens and light up the sea or the headlands. As for the craic, you can go to the remotest village, and be assured, as a visiting yachtsman, of a warm welcome. The conversation's always good when you're locked in a pub to the early hours!'

I knew exactly what he meant.

25

The North Channel

It was clear that we would have to wait in Portrush for several days until the gales blew over. It was not a bad place to be. The harbour offered good shelter and along the Antrim coast there was Dunluce Castle and the Giant's Causeway to visit. We caught a taxi to Dunluce about five miles away. It was a fine blustery day. From the light brown cliffs of the Antrim coast, I could see the surging currents and overflows off the headlands.

Dunluce Castle was perched on a rocky crag a hundred feet above the sea, with a souterrain passage to the water below it. I thought of the nomadic seafarers who had crossed over in their currachs about 7,000 BC from south west Scotland and left their flinty axes in the area. An old Irish fort on the rock had been consolidated by the Normans. I was intrigued to find the rough sketch on a stone of a vessel which looked like a Viking long ship, clearly carved by a bored soldier on duty. In the early sixteenth century, an Elizabethan mansion had been built within the walls but the kitchen had fallen into the sea – along with the cook, his wife and all the pots and pans.

We then went on to the Giant's Causeway. There was a fine

track along the coast which passed behind a headland with rounded boulders and a curving bay. I had imagined the causeway to be much larger. The flowing shapes of the smooth, lichen-covered columns stood out against the sky and the black waters of the rising sea surged amongst them. There was a strong smell of seaweed. Shaped by fire and water, it was a place between land and sea and sky, a gateway between the physical and the spiritual worlds.

In fact, the Giant's Causeway consists of some 37,000 basalt columns packed tightly together, created by red hot lava which erupted from a fissure and crystallised some sixty million years ago. Several of the columns formed natural thrones, the right size for humans to sit in and survey the sea a few yards away. The columns were mostly hexagonal, but some had four, five, seven and even eight sides. The tallest was about forty feet high. Many formed stepping stones from the foot of the cliff and disappeared under the sea.

The writer William Thackeray had written after a visit: 'When the world was moulded and fashioned out of formless chaos, this must have been a bit left over – a remnant of chaos.' Yet for me the interlocking columns gave an impression of the order and symmetry of nature. They contrasted with the high crumbling cliffs in the distance, eroded by air and sea, tide and wind.

Geologists might claim that the causeway was created by a volcanic eruption but for the ancients it was clearly giants' work, notably the work of Finn Mac Cool, the Ulster warrior. He seems to have been an early traveller: 'He lived most happy and content, /Obeyed no law and paid no rent.' Among his feats was scooping up a huge clod of earth and throwing it at a Scottish giant during a skirmish. The hole it left filled up with water and became Lough Neagh, and when it landed in the sea it became the Isle of Man. It was when he fell in love with a giantess on

Staffa, an island in the Hebrides, that he built the causeway to bring her across to Ulster.

We stayed in Portrush for five days. Gale-force north westerlies blew in day after day. I listened systematically to the weather forecasts and regularly discussed the situation with the harbourmaster: 'Don't go yet, mate,' he advised each morning. Then on 8th September the winds began to ease. The harbourmaster said that the next low tide should knock the strength out of the waves. I carefully worked out my tidal calculations for the currents through Rathlin Sound where the stream runs up to six knots at springs and causes dangerous overfalls and eddies. The chart in the area was a mass of wavy lines and spirals denoting the dangers. The harbourmaster suggested leaving Portrush two hours before local high water so that I could pass through the sound at slack water. The *Sailing Directions* also recommended that I should get to Rathlin at Low Water Dover when there would be six hours of strong fair tide to take me through the sound and down the North Channel into the Irish Sea.

We got up at four o'clock the next day to a star-studded sky. It was dark and cold. The full moon cast its ghostly light across the Skerries, a group of black jagged rocks a mile off Portrush Harbour. As soon as we left the shelter of the harbour, I realised that there was high sea running, despite the overnight drop in the wind, which set us towards the Skerries. Once we had rounded them we were able to take advantage of the moderate south easterly wind. By six o'clock we could see the first pink streaks of the sun as we sailed easterly towards the sound. We were heading for Carnlough, forty miles away in the North Channel to the Irish Sea.

Around seven o'clock I could make out the Giant's Causeway but kept two miles clear of Benbane Head to avoid the tidal race there. With the full moon, we had spring tides and I did not want to take any chances. I did not want to end up like the Armada treasure ship *Girona* which was wrecked in a storm off the coast and whose cannons I had seen at the entrance to Dunluce Castle.

As dawn broke behind Rathlin Island, sheets of golden light spread across the sky. A single dolphin joined us for a moment as if to say all would be well passing through the notorious sound. There were no boats to be seen. As we approached the sound bright golden light lit up the sky with the low dark purple masses of Rathlin and Fair Head on either side. I felt as if I was passing through a gateway to heaven.

But then it appeared, like a hound from hell, over the horizon. Against the golden light a dark shape came across the sea, straight for us. I was tacking across the sound towards the lighthouse at the bottom of Rathlin Island at the time and held my course. The dark shape came closer and closer. It was travelling very fast. I thought it might have been a naval vessel. It was almost upon us. At the last minute I tacked away and as it swept by without deviating, I could see no one on the bridge. Then an unshaven man appeared in a grey pullover with a cigarette in his mouth, climbing up the gangway. When he saw us, he looked alarmed and ran on to the bridge. As the vessel passed I could see it was a very large grey trawler from Concarneau in Brittany.

It was my closest shave with another vessel on my voyage. I thought of reporting it to the Bangor coastguard in Belfast Lough, but I had to concentrate on my sailing. I thought of the Greek captain of a container-ship who once told me that he hit yachts like flies on a windscreen.

Emily interrupted my musings with the offer of a cup of tea. This was typical of sailing. One minute one is witnessing beauty beyond belief; the next one is in danger of life; and then the most simple detail of everyday life intervenes. A piping hot cup of tea becomes transformed into an *elixir vitae* which calms a troubled world and dispels all anxiety.

By nine o'clock we had passed through the sound. We

rounded Fair Head, on the north east corner of Ireland and sailed close-hauled along the coast in the moderate south easterly. To the east I could just make out the Mull of Kintyre on the other side of the North Channel, which separated Scotland and Ireland by only twenty-one miles and which before the last ice age had been connected by a land bridge.

After the wild, rocky coasts of the west and north, we seemed to have entered another world. The sheltered bays were quiet and peaceful and the headlands no longer bold and daunting. It was sunny and bright, with isolated clouds casting their shadows across the small green fields which were divided by hedgerows rather than stone walls. I had a distinct sense of having reached shelter. No longer did I have 4,000 miles of open sea to my west; no longer did a great swell lift and lower *Celtic Gold*. I missed the excitement and savage beauty, but after so many weeks fighting the gales I was relieved to have reached calmer waters.

We sailed merrily down the west coast of the North Channel passing Red Bay and the rocky headland of Garron Point with its college nestling amongst the trees. By this time the tide had turned, and we continued slowly along the coast in a light easterly breeze to the little harbour of Carnlough.

It was made from fine stone with a dredged entrance. I was surprised to find it crowded with other yachts so late in the season but they had local owners. We moored alongside one below a pub and opposite the old tower which was now a café. I contacted Malin Head to tell them of my safe arrival.

Carnlough was a picturesque village with a curving promenade overlooking a rocky bay. Its harbour had been built to export the limestone which had been quarried nearby. A stone bridge once carried the trains from the quarry and many fine old houses were made from the white stone. It had an ivy-clad coaching inn called Londonderry Arms Hotel, built by the Marquess of Londonderry and inherited by Winston Churchill. I was told by the young girl serving in the harbour café that the village was eighty per cent Catholic. Every one was very friendly. Even the young men strolling along the promenade said 'hello' and 'good night'.

In the setting sun, the yachts were mirrored perfectly in the still clean water. Moored further into the harbour was an old wooden ketch called *Winnie*. A young man called Graham lived on board with his dog and guitar. He said that he took handicapped and mentally disturbed children out sailing; it apparently worked wonders in calming them down. 'We even take blind kids. It's amazing how soon they get used to being on the boat and know where everything is.' When we said farewell, he said: 'Fair Winds. May the Force be with you!'

We left the next day at eight o'clock to cross the North Channel to Portpatrick in south west Scotland. There were a few white clouds in the sky and the rising sun shone silvery gold across the slight sea. We sailed south towards the lighthouses on the rocks near the entrance to Larne Lough and across Beaufort's Dyke where over a million tons of munitions had been dumped since the First World War. They had been recently disturbed by the laying of a gas pipe across the northern part, and phosphorous flares had been found on the south west beaches of Scotland. Fishermen from Northern Ireland had even caught them in their nets and had seen them catch alight as they pulled them out of the sea and into the air. Chemicals had leached from the munitions and I heard dark rumours about high arsenic levels in the local fish.

We were once again in busy waters. A Dutch yacht crossed our bows and two great white ferries appeared around mid morning on our starboard quarter. They cleared us easily. Some guillemots flew over and a few large jelly fish which looked like red lungs drifted past in the beautiful, calm, silver sea. By lunch time we were in mid channel and could see clearly the coasts of

Ireland and Scotland. I could imagine the busy currach traffic in ancient times between the two countries as the local chiefs forged alliances and exchanged goods.

I heard on the radio reports of two missing divers off the Mull of Kintyre. Then quite out of the blue I heard faintly while sitting in the cockpit the radio message: 'Yacht *Celtic Gold*, yacht *Celtic Gold*. This is yacht *Sea Mate*, this is yacht *Sea Mate*. Over.' It came as a great shock. It was the first time since my contact with Stan and Betty of *Mustard Seed* that someone had called me at sea. Who on earth was *Sea Mate*? I went into the cabin and then heard the message more clearly. I could recognise the voice anywhere: it was my brother Michael and *Sea Mate* was the name of his Wayfarer. On board his dinghy were his 7-year-old daughter Julie and 15-year-old Sylvie. He handed the radio receiver to Julie and in her tiny voice she asked my ETA. '1400 hours,' I replied, playing the captain.

It was a delight to make contact with my brother. I had sailed with him many times in the past as crew on his yachts in the North Sea and the English Channel. A decade earlier we had crossed the Atlantic together to Barbados where our father lived and trained race horses. But I had not understood navigation then and had always had to rely on his judgment. Now I was sailing in my own yacht after proving myself a competent navigator and sailor in some of the most difficult of home waters. We could now meet, skipper to skipper, almost as equals, swap tales of adventure and share our knowledge of the sea!

It took longer than I had anticipated to reach the entrance to Portpatrick Harbour because of the contrary tide. But as we sailed along the rocky coastline lit up by the afternoon sun, I could see my brother and my nieces in *Sea Mate* getting steadily nearer. Eventually we met off Portpatrick, one large white yacht and one small red day dinghy coming together in a family reunion.

The white houses of Portpatrick were clustered around the small stone harbour which was sheltered from the east by an escarpment. In the nineteenth century it had been the main port from south west Scotland to Larne in Northern Ireland, before the increase in traffic made nearby Stranraer more sensible. Its lighthouse was now owned by a potter and only a couple of fishermen worked out of the fine stone inner harbour. In the summer it was busy with holidaymakers, but for the rest of the year it was a sleepy village swept by soft rain and yellow sun. There were many 'Irish-Scottish' living in the area, that is to say, Irish who had settled there.

The entrance to Portpatrick was tricky, with a three-knot cross tide running. I had to pass through a narrow channel with large rocks on either side, following a leading light which lined up on the edge of a house. On the quay were my mother Vera with my brother's partner Colette. They had been waiting for two hours and waved wildly. It was a marvellous moment. After returning their waves, I had to concentrate on going hard to starboard to enter the inner harbour. I just touched the sandy bottom and made it in time. It was five thirty. The log of *Celtic Gold* had just clocked up a thousand miles.

That evening, high on Michael's terrace garden overlooking Portpatrick Harbour, we broke open the champagne. It was a great family reunion, especially as my 79-year-old mother lived in Devon and was up for a holiday. My brother had recently returned from the Caribbean where he kept his yacht and spent two or three months every year but he was reluctant to go into details.

'The more I sail, the less I want to talk about it,' he said.

I told him how I was beginning to draw on my own experience and intuition for my navigation rather than books.

'That's the best way. First you learn it, and then you forget it . . .'

I asked him why he liked to sail. 'I do it for fun. It takes me completely out of everything and I come back revitalised.'

My mother was thrilled to see me, one of her 'boys' in his own yacht. The next day after a lunch on board I took her and my niece Julie out for a sail along the coast. 'What a wonderful boat,' she said. 'You could live in it.'

'I have been, mother, for the past two and half months . . .'

'Well, if you can't find anywhere to live, you've always got your boat to fall back on, Peter!'

After leaving the harbour under steam, I put up the sails and steered along the rocky coast towards a ruined castle on a headland. Julie, still in her school uniform, sat quietly next to her grandmother, seventy-two years difference between them.

'I'm ever so proud of you, Peter,' my mother said, relaxing back in the cockpit in the sun, her life jacket too big for her diminutive body. She seemed to enjoy every minute of her afternoon cruise along the rocky coast of Wigtownshire.

It was my turn to be proud of her when she took the helm with her small hand and steered five-and-three-quarter tons of sailing ship with the full main and genoa billowing in the gentle offshore breeze.

When we returned to the harbour in the early evening, the tide had dropped considerably and she had to climb a giddy thirty feet up an iron ladder attached to the harbour wall. She thought nothing of it. Her handbag went up first on a safety line and then I tied the line around her. There was no need. She came up as nimble as an 18-year-old.

'What would my friends say if they could see me now?' she said, laughing. 'An 80-year-old woman doing this!' She added a year to her age for good effect.

We stayed two nights in Portpatrick. I took on diesel, bought some stores and filled up with fresh Scottish water. The last words of my brother were: 'If it blows up in the Irish Sea, keep west if the wind is from the west, and east if it is from the east –

that way, you'll avoid the fetch of the sea. I'm no longer worried about you, Peter. You'll make it now!'

The sun appeared on 12th September over the edge of the fine stone harbour wall of Portpatrick at ten past seven precisely. I suddenly had a strong sense of it bringing new life and new hope every day. And as I prepared to leave, I felt a surge of joy with the thought that I was free at that moment to sail anywhere.

In the event my destination was not Cape Town or Rio da Janiero but Bangor Marina in Belfast Lough. I got out a new chart for the Irish Sea. A gentle north easterly breeze was still blowing and the visibility was good as we headed south west. Seeing my mother and brother and his family in such good humour was another stage in my healing. I rang up my mother on the VHF to say good-bye. She said I had left a notebook which she would look after. She fell into the rhythm of saying 'Over' when she had finished speaking. I thought of how it must have been for her to say good-bye to my father during the Second World War when he was a spitfire pilot and the odds were against him returning. Half a century later, things were very different.

It grew cloudy during the day and the wind backed to the west. At lunch time, I found that I was on a collision course with a large cargo ship with a black hull and high derricks called the *Rio Mar*. After my experience in the Rathlin Sound with the Breton fishing vessel, I decided to alter course, even though I was under sail, and headed behind her. As we approached the lighthouse on one of the islands at the southern entrance of Belfast Lough, we were overtaken by a great Shell tanker. We also altered course to sail around a trawler which had her nets out. It seemed strange to see all the houses and towns along the southern shore after so many weeks of wild and uninhabited coastline. I was returning to civilisation. As if in protest, as we were approaching the entrance to Bangor Marina, my log packed up for the second time.

26

Belfast Blues

The new Bangor Marina in Belfast Lough on the Ards Peninsula was swish and efficient. There seemed no one staying on the expensive yachts safely moored along the crowded pontoons. It was part of a large area with gardens and walkways which had been reclaimed from the sea. The name Bangor came from the Gaelic *beanchbor* which meant 'curved horns', referring to the curved shape of the bay. It was no more. The comely Victorian boarding houses along Princetown Road which once boasted a sea view were now isolated behind hundreds of yards of concrete. The beach which the workers of Belfast had once come to enjoy at the weekends had now disappeared. I had a long walk to the nearest pub.

The town was smart, clean and apparently prosperous. I went to a pub called Kitty O'Shea's which claimed to be the oldest in town. Live music was being played and with the rebel songs, I could only surmise that it was a Catholic pub. But so far there was no obvious sign of the troubles. The ceasefire, which had just celebrated its first anniversary on 31st August, was still holding.

That night, I slept in *Celtic Gold* in the eerie stillness of the marina, lit up by orange arc lights, and with the noise of traffic from the town. It could not have been more different from the Aran island harbour of Inishmore. The moored yachts hardly moved alongside the pontoons, brooding silently at their loss of freedom, lost in deep reverie, waiting to be released, pining for wind, yearning for the open sea.

The next morning while I was having breakfast in the cockpit in the cool watery sunlight, I kept a lookout for the rare resident black guillemots. Then a grey rubber dinghy with three men in black silently came into sight. One man was sitting at the bow with his feet dangling in the water. He carried an automatic rifle, alert like a panther. They were SAS soldiers doing the rounds of the marina. I had met my first sign of the British Army in Northern Ireland.

I said good-bye to Emily who had decided to travel from Belfast to Dublin and then catch a ferry to Holyhead. We caught a local train into Belfast, passing through pleasant leafy suburbs on the shores of Belfast Lough with names like Holywood and Carlton. Cargo ships and sailing ships plied up and down the sparkling bay. As we got closer to Belfast, I could see the giant cranes of the Harland and Wolff shipyards which had helped make Belfast the major industrial centre before the war. With half a million inhabitants, the city contained a third of the population of Northern Ireland.

Northern Ireland Rail was offering free cross-border travel to senior citizens and cheap tickets for the three-hour journey from Belfast to Dublin. At the height of the troubles, the line was not even running, as the track was regularly blown up. Other details showed the state of suspended war. I could not leave luggage anywhere on the station – for 'security reasons', said the old guard with a knowing look. Whenever a train was not coming into the station, steel gates clanged shut and prevented access to the platforms. The whole station was enclosed in narrow wire mesh topped with razor wire. Through the wire I could see some scruffy kids playing football on a vacant lot. The sign 'Mind the Gap' seemed to refer to the division between the two communities as much as to the space between the train and the platform.

I glanced through the headlines of the local papers: the *Belfast Telegraph* for 15th September shouted 'Aids Revenge: Priest Goes to Ground'. Another paper led with 'Son of Lord Mayor Jailed over Drugs'. Politics and religion, sex and drugs, the usual preoccupations of the tabloids.

I tried to get a taxi from the railway station into the city centre and was told that there weren't any. Belfast must be the only city in the world where you cannot get a taxi at its main railway station. I walked along a noisy and dusty ring road for a few hundred yards and then turned down some deserted streets which led into the city centre. There were no trees and no people but a lot of cars rushing home. It was about six o'clock.

I wandered past the City Hall in Donegall Square, a neo-classical monstrosity made from Portland stone and topped by a copper dome. Built at the turn of the century, it was clearly intended to show the wealth, power and solidity of the Protestant city fathers – a symbol of the triumph of the Protestant work ethic. A big statue of Queen Victoria was placed at its front, the inevitable emblem of empire.

All the big chains had their stores in the deserted city centre, every object a person could desire and not need was on sale there, but the place was deserted like the streets. It was only seven o'clock at night but it was like a ghost town, a town nuked by a neutron bomb which left the buildings intact but killed off all the inhabitants. It reminded me of the city centre of Cape Town before the ending of apartheid. The shopping centre to the north had been turned into a pedestrian precinct not so much for the convenience of strollers but for security reasons.

There were great steel gates on all the entrances to the centre which could swing shut. Many of the shops were boarded up for the night. Then a grey monster appeared, a grey armoured police van with slits for eyes, long steel flaps over its wheels, a confidential free telephone number for informers on its side, and its back doors ajar. My mind went straight back to the armoured cars I had seen patrolling the streets of South Africa three years earlier.

I strolled past Kelly's Cellars in a side alley, the only pub which seemed open near the shopping centre. The United Irishmen, the first republican association founded by Wolfe Tone during the French Revolution, used to meet there. By an ironic twist of history, the United Irishmen were from Belfast and virtually all Protestant.

At the beginning of the Golden Mile in Great Victoria Street there was more life. The Grand Opera House, opened in 1895 and rebuilt several times after bombings, was open for the Belfast élite to enjoy *Me and My Girl*. It was like a red cake.

Next door, a stark skyscraper, was the Europa Hotel. It was hosting an International Federation for Housing and Planning Congress, somehow appropriate for one of the most bombed hotels in the world – bombed more than twenty-nine times in the seventies and almost finished off in 1993 when the rebuilt Grand Opera House also went up. I went in and found only a couple of men drinking at the bar. In the background, the Irish folk singer Christy Moore was singing about the Irish defeat of the English football team in the World Cup of 1993. A middle-aged man turned up in a waxed coat as if he had got lost from a country pub and asked for a glass of water. It was that kind of place. I did not see any shifty journalist in a huddle with a paramilitary spokesman, only a couple of middle-aged women with their shopping.

The so-called Golden Mile was a road which stretched down to Queen's University (modelled on Magdalen College, Oxford) which had many restaurants, pubs and cinemas. It was the closest that Belfast got to a red light district. People were on the pavements but there was no sense of a vital street life, of a convivial meeting place which you find in most cities of the world. If you came at all, you came and went in your car and spent as little time as possible on your feet.

I did come across a fine pub though, the Crown Liquor Saloon, opposite the Europa Hotel in Great Victoria Street, which had a myriad of different coloured and shaped tiles on its façade. Inside, it was ornately decorated with stained and cut glass, marble and mosaics, with a large porcelain panel behind the bar advertising 'Sandeman's Wines'. Its greatest asset was the mahogany snug bars or private rooms which could be closed off. A perfect place for an illicit rendezvous, except everybody knew virtually everyone else.

The next day, I returned to Belfast to meet the brother of a friend of mine, Denis Glass, who was the Deputy Planning Officer for Northern Ireland. His office was in a new red-brick government building in the city centre. He was a deeply religious man, having gone on Protestant beach missions in the Republic during his holidays.

'I've never had trouble on the beaches spreading the gospel in the South. You don't have to get permission; they're so laid back down there.'

He admitted that in the past there had been discrimination in the civil service but that now Catholics were fairly represented, at least in the professions and in the public services. Speaking as 'a servant of government', as he put it, he acknowledged that millions had been poured into redeveloping and rebuilding the city and the rest of Northern Ireland even when there were severe cutbacks under Thatcher's government on the mainland. The British government was determined to show that terrorism did not work. But he was very hopeful about the ceasefire: 'The terrorist campaign only alienated people and entrenched them in their differences. People are beginning to get used to the peace and enjoy it. Bloody Friday in 1972, when twenty bombs went off without warning, killed off life in the city centre overnight but it is gradually coming alive again in the evenings. People socialise in their own areas, but they have started coming into the city centre to the pubs and restaurants, especially along the Golden Mile.'

He recommended visiting the Protestant Shankhill Road and the Catholic Falls on the west side of the city. I asked him whether it would be dangerous. 'Not at the moment. Since the ceasefire, it's been very quiet. Most people aren't aware that Belfast has the lowest normal crime rates for a major city. Despite the troubles, people are generally more law abiding.'

All my life I had heard of the atrocities in Northern Ireland on the news. It seemed an endless, senseless, saga of bombing and assassination, tit for tat, an eye for eye, a bloody tooth for a bloody tooth. There were the usual expressions of no surrender on either side, the same grey, lifeless tones of fanaticism and intransigence. At the same time, places like Falls Road, the Shanklin, Bogside, scenes of the worst rioting and violence, stood out in the imagination larger than life. They had taken on mythic proportions. I found the news of the conflict so utterly predictable and boring. I grew tired of hearing and reading about the violence in Northern Ireland. Like most people in Britain, I just blanked it out, mentally switched off. Why couldn't the Irish sort out their differences themselves?

I decided to walk into the Catholic Falls Road district on my own. The geography of the city reflected its political, religious and economic divides. West Belfast, which contained the traditional Catholic and Protestant working-class districts, was neatly divided by the Westlink motorway from the city centre. The border was only a few hundred yards from the centre. Armed police in Divis Street checked the traffic going in and out, despite the ceasefire. I caught up with a mother and her child in a buggy and walked through the checkpoint in Divis Street without being stopped.

It was like entering another world, a world under siege and a world breaking down. I walked past the few remaining high-rise flats which had once been the centre of fighting, a burnt-out building, and the Falls Road swimming pool, paint peeling off, windows broken, with the Irish tricolour flying from its roof. Green, white and orange, painted everywhere, was a clear sign of political allegiance. There were a few old-fashioned stores with steel shutters. The few pubs – or rather drinking clubs – had no inviting signs like in the Republic, but had steel cages over their doors to prevent bombs being thrown into them and to control the customers. Even the social security office – the dole supports the majority of the community – was protected. Litter blew in the dusty streets, rubbish collected in corners. It was drab, dilapidated and depressing.

Slogans on the walls declared the republican and nationalist demands: 'Release Political Prisoners', 'Stop Torture of Irish POWs in English Jails'. Outside the Sinn Fein headquarters, there was a mural of Bobby Sands, the IRA martyr who died in a prison hunger strike. Large boulders on the pavement protected the building from car bomb attacks. Further along the road I came across the Falls Women Centre and a cultural centre, its details announced in Irish and English, in a converted church. The only grand building was a Catholic Convent set in a spacious garden.

Opposite the Royal Victoria Hospital, which had dealt with countless gun and bomb casualties, I went into a shop to buy a sandwich. The woman behind the counter was clearly shocked by my English accent. When I asked my way a few times in the street, I got the same surprised and suspicious look. I felt like an unwanted intruder, just as I had done walking around the black district of Harlem in New York some years before.

I returned the next day, this time by taxi. I was told that I could pick one up from Castle Street in the Lower Falls, five minutes from the city centre. The republican taxi drivers operated like African buses, collecting people along the road until they were full. A large, friendly driver in his thirties offered me a tour of the republican districts for £12.00. He introduced himself as Joe. I jumped in beside him in his London-style black cab.

Republican Joe was a hale and hearty man, and very friendly. 'We're not as bad as you think,' he insisted, wanting to create a good impression. 'You people get the wrong idea over there. I know a boy who went to stay with his uncle in London and when he played football outside his home, the other kids in the street asked him "Are you sent to school in Belfast by British soldiers?"'

Joe explained that each community had its own cabs: 'There are about 300 cab drivers in Belfast, each working their own communities. We have our own areas and own roads. You get to know some of them on the other side. But I have few talks with the Shankhill drivers.'

'Do you ever go into the Shankhill? Your cab looks the same as theirs . . .'

'We've got different numbers. They would know who I am. It's very rare for me to go down the Shankhill, and then I would only go during the day. I broke down there once and one of their taxi drivers helped me. The whole world could have killed me.'

He took me first up to the Catholic Ardogne district along the motorway which divided the city. We turned off into row upon row of neat terraces, with few trees and little colour except for the odd tiny garden. He pointed out some flowers on the pavement in Rosapean Street which marked the spot where a taxi driver – one of his mates – had been shot dead. 'Disband the

RUC', shouted the slogans, 'Guilty of Torture, Murder'.

We then drove towards New Lodge along the so-called 'Peace Wall' which divided the Catholic Ardogne from Protestant Woodfield.

'In the forties and fifties,' Joe went on, 'people mixed here all right. I can remember playing with Protestants in the street when I was a boy. When the troubles began, the Protestant families started to move out. Only a few old Protestants remain now.'

Of course I knew that Belfast was a divided city, and the two communities were at each other's throats, but it was a real shock to see these working-class districts physically divided. When the troubles had begun in the early seventies, the army had thrown up makeshift walls of corrugated iron and barbed wire to keep the two communities apart, but the communities polarised behind them. The boundary had now become a permanent feature. The army had even built smart walls with coloured bricks along certain sections of Lanark Way which led up to the Fort Mone under the green western hills of Belfast.

To call the boundary which divided the warring city a 'peace line' seemed an insult to truth and humanity. They had planted trees in front of it on the way up to the barracks in the hills. The trees seemed particularly out of place, symbols of life, permanence and growth.

In the middle of the residential areas were British army barracks, protected by high walls and razor wire, bristling with antennae and cameras. They were more like forts than barracks and certainly gave the impression of an army of occupation.

We drove past Turf Lodge, and in Anderstown paused outside Connolly House (named after James Connolly, a martyr of the Easter Rising in 1916) where, according to my driver, Gerry Adams 'hangs out'. Not far away was the place where two British army corporals had been dragged out of their car and killed when they drove into an IRA funeral.

No tour of West Belfast is complete without seeing the murals. Most of the ones I saw were crude outlines glorifying different brigades of the IRA on the gable ends of the terraces, but there were a few with cultural themes which aspired to higher art. One was copied from a well-known nineteenth-century engraving of a starving woman and child during the Famine. The other celebrated the Gaelic games of hurling and traditional step-dancing accompanied by a fiddler. The captions were in Irish and English.

We ended up in the Milltown Cemetery off the Falls Road. At its entrance was another British Army Fort, its antennae and cameras permanently monitoring all who approached. 'No one goes in here without being seen,' Joe said. 'But you get used to being watched all the time. It's peaceful and quiet here and I like to come and walk the dog in the evening. We'll all end up here sometime sooner or later, however hard we try . . .'

We walked past some ornate stone memorials with Celtic crosses, and then went to the Republican burial ground, more severe and plain. This was hallowed ground for the IRA and many of its martyrs who had died in hunger strikes or shoot-outs were buried there. Below was the motorway and the high buildings of the city stretching far away. I could see the cranes of the docks in the hazy distance at the head of the bay.

As I stood in front of the grave of Bobby Sands with his photograph and fresh flowers on it, I felt the army cameras clicking away, recording my presence. That would give the intelligence wallahs something to think about. As a lifelong pacifist, the one thing I abhorred was terrorism.

'It's not so bad here as they make it out to be,' my taxi driver said. 'They're so many rumours. It's good to come and see it in real life, like you're doing.'

'How do you see the future?' I asked him.

'There should be round table talks. It's up to the British

government. We need to get the army out, get the Brits out.'

'What about the Loyalists?'

'Some's bad, some's worse, on both sides, you know. Everybody now wants to get on with their lives without the bombing. We just pray that the ceasefire holds.'

To see the other side of the peace line and for the sake of fairness, I decided to go down to North Street, as Joe recommended, and to find a cab to take me on tour of the Shankhill. The first driver I met was a thin man with prematurely grey hair. He called himself Bill. He was cheaper than Joe, but then the tour was less comprehensive and he was not so friendly. He had no doubt about his allegiances.

'We're surrounded on all sides in the Shankhill,' he declared as we entered the district. It had identical terraced housing to the Falls, except Union Jacks were flying everywhere in place of the Irish tricolour. Even the curbstones were painted in red, white and blue.

'The Greater Falls has 70,000 people; the Greater Shankhill only 25,000.'

Although Protestants formed the majority in Northern Ireland and until recently had a monopoly of political power, they clearly had a siege mentality. Not only was my Protestant taxi driver from the Shankhill surrounded by Catholics, but there were three and half million Catholic Republicans south of the border.

'I'm British,' he insisted. 'When the IRA calls for British troops out, they're telling me to get out!'

The irony is that in Northern Ireland the Catholics see themselves as Irish, the Protestants as British, but when they are in England they are all seen as Irish by the English. As I understood it, Northern Ireland is not even officially part of Great Britain. I had been brought up to believe that Great Britain consists of

England, Wales and Scotland, while the UK is the United Kingdom of Great Britain *and* Northern Ireland. I did not think that it would be diplomatic to engage in such semantics with my Loyalist taxi driver. Instead, I asked him why he hated the Republicans so much.

'The IRA, the Provos and Sinn Fein all want a green Ireland with no vestige of British presence. We'll not go because there's a million of us who want to stay. By natural and international law, we have a right to a homeland. There's two nations on this island. The Nationalists have an expansionist policy and want jurisdiction over us. We don't want jurisdiction over them.'

I could not help hearing echoes of the Afrikaaners in South Africa.

My taxi driver was an articulate man. He spoke slowly, carefully weighing up his words. He seemed very tense, on edge. He said that he had been an electrician with the Harland and Wolff shipbuilding company until he was made redundant.

We were passing through the Woodfield area of Greater Shankhill which I had seen on the other side of the 'peace line'. It had the same dreary, uniform rows of terraces, consisting of two rooms up and two down. They were placed back to back, with alleyways or 'entries' between them, which formed a rabbit warren. Until the early seventies, they had no bathrooms.

'It was a tin bath in front of the fire,' my driver informed me laconically.

He was keen to point out the sites of paramilitary killings on his patch. We stopped at one street corner where he said a member of the UVF – Brian Robinson – had been killed 'on active service' by the SAS after 'executing a Republican'. 'He was shot three times as he lay on the ground. We don't cry. We're not like the Republicans. Brian did his job. The soldier was doing his job.'

I began to suspect that my taxi driver may have had a double life as a paramilitary. When talking about them, he slipped from saying 'they' to 'we' until he realised what he was saying and quickly corrected himself. He was full of hatred. The only other places in the world where I had come across such hatred simply because of the accident of one's birth were Sri Lanka, between the Sinhalese and the Tamils, and South Africa, between white and black. In all cases there were ancient historical injustices and deep unresolved resentments at work. It was still deeply depressing to see such a visceral fear and hatred of the other and it sorely challenged my sense of the original goodness of human nature.

We stopped and got out at another street corner near some shops. 'An INLA gunman shot three men here. They were all head shots. Two were killed, but someone shouted at the third and he half turned round. The bullet went through his cheek and ended up in his top pocket instead of in the back of his head!'

'Do you think all this killing is necessary? Isn't there another way?'

'We're in a Bosnia situation now. We have to defend our own.'

I asked him to explain the bewildering initials of the different paramilitaries. On the Republican side, there were the Irish Republican Army (IRA) who had been fighting for Irish independence for more than a century; the Provisionals who split off in the sixties; and the Irish National Liberation Army (INLA), an even more uncompromising splinter. On the Loyalist side, there were the Ulster Volunteer Force (UVF), the biggest and oldest paramilitary group which dated back to 1912, the Ulster Defence Association (UDA), and the Ulster Freedom Fighters (UFF), a more militant splinter.

The proliferation of political parties was just as bewildering to an outsider. The Protestants were represented by the Ulster Unionists, the main caucus in Westminster, and the Democratic Unionist Party, a more extreme group led by Ian Paisley. Two small parties associated with the paramilitaries had recently emerged: the Ulster Democratic and Progressive Unionist

Parties. All of them were implacably opposed to a reunited Ireland. 'No Surrender' was their watchword. On the Catholic side, the Social Democratic and Labour Party (SDLP), led by John Hume, had been the voice of reasonableness in Westminster, while Sinn Fein had long held an ambivalent position, participating in elections but also having close contacts with the IRA, following the strategy of the Armalite and the ballot box. Then there was the middle-of-the-road Alliance Party which sought support from both sides but had none of the radical appeal of the United Irishmen of two hundred years ago.

In the Greater Shankhill, Gerry Adams was the devil incarnate. My taxi driver assured me that eighty-five to ninety-five per cent of the people supported the UVF. They probably did not have much choice. I was shown the murals to illustrate the point. They were neater and plainer and less imaginative than the Republican ones. Painted on the gable end of the terraces, they depicted mainly black-hooded terrorists holding automatic weapons with the name of their company and battalion underneath. Every few streets seemed to be represented by a different company. They contrasted strangely with the neat rows of houses.

'Do you think that the ceasefire will hold?' I asked.

'The Loyalist paramilitaries won't initiate the first strike. But I'm sure that the IRA and Sinn Fein will make some excuse to end it.'

He admitted that he had played with Catholics as a boy but he now had little sympathy for them. 'The Republican propaganda machine is second to none. They're always crying about being second-class citizens but if you look in the archives you'll find they were no worse off than us. Many of them have got big driveways to big houses. We Loyalists don't have them sort of houses.'

'Do you think there's any chance of your children playing with Catholics like you did?'

'Maybe my son's kids – if the ceasefire holds. If not, it would be better to have a civil war and the winner takes all. That would be better than fighting on for generations like before.'

The visible symbols of Protestant and Loyalist rule were the neo-classical parliament buildings at Stormont which stood isolated on a hill at the end of a long dipping drive. At their front was a statue of Lord Carson. He had played a leading role in the prosecution of Oscar Wilde. It was Carson who led the anti-Home Rule campaigns and raised an army of volunteers – the Ulster Volunteer Force – which had forced the British government to hold on to the North at the time of the Republic's independence. Although disused since 1972 when the British government imposed direct rule from Westminster, it was being refurbished for a possible new assembly which might even include representatives from the once outlawed Sinn Fein.

I could not help feeling that the Loyalist and Nationalist paramilitaries were like cats fighting in a sack. They were both from deprived working-class communities. They suffered from the same poor housing, same unemployment, same lack of hope. They lived in identical houses along identical streets. They were both manipulated by political and religious fanatics who did not think twice of knee capping or killing people in front of their children in their homes to ensure their rule. Unable to see their common cause, they were constantly at each other's throats, waving their flags at each other, pointing their guns across the peace line, waiting to pounce.

Everyone I met during my voyage around Ireland clearly longed for peace, but the paramilitaries had an interest in keeping the pot boiling. They wanted to keep their protection rackets going and to think of themselves as heroes whilst indulging a psychotic delight in killing and maiming. Like feuding gangsters, they needed each other to justify their rule and power and had a grudging admiration for the ruthlessness of their opponents.

The troubles in the past had only strengthened the boundaries between the communities and entrenched prejudices and bigotry, but the experience of a year's ceasefire had made the use of violence unacceptable to the vast majority. Nearly 3,000 people had been killed in the recent troubles and no one wanted them to continue. For people under thirty, it was their first sweet experience of 'peace' in the province. They had enjoyed the freedom of movement without checkpoints and army and police harassment. They knew what it was like to live a relatively normal life without constant fear of being bombed or shot.

Perhaps the greatest irony was that the people in the South who were enjoying an economic boom had now had enough of the North and its endless strife. As Larry Butler had told me on Clare Island: 'If you had a referendum now, I believe the South wouldn't want to touch the North with a barge pole. It would be too much of an economic liability!'

It was an attitude I had come across many times in the South – an emotional desire for reunification, but a revulsion for the terrorist campaigns and a fear of absorbing a million unwilling citizens. Life seemed to be getting better, so why rock the boat? In what had once been one of the most conservative and deferential societies in Europe, I had also detected a new eagerness, especially among the young, to question the authority of the Church and State and to demand that priests and politicians be accountable for their actions. There seemed a wider momentum, in both the North and South, encouraged by the ceasefire and peace process, away from the private power of paramilitaries, churchmen and politicians towards democracy, accountability, consent and trust.

It seemed obvious to me that Northern Ireland was geographically, historically and culturally part of the rest of Ireland. Yet tens of thousands of people, descendants of settlers, felt a greater allegiance to another country over the water. Their needs and aspirations would have to be accommodated but Ireland would be reunited some day, I felt sure. There was no reason why it should not flourish. The whites of Zimbabwe and of South Africa had said no surrender in a thousand years but in the course of a few years had settled down to a peaceful co-existence with their once feared and despised neighbours.

The only possible long-term solution in my view was the reorganisation of Ireland on the twin pillars of decentralisation and federation. This of course could only be achieved with the autonomy of the churches and with the consent of the people. Financial help could be given to those who wanted to settle on the British mainland or in the Republic. Then a federation could be set up between the North and the South with each side running its own affairs without feeling coerced by the other. An all-Ireland assembly could co-ordinate the economy and organise foreign affairs and defence while assembles could be set up at the district and county levels.

Mutual understanding, respect, tolerance and forbearance seem to be the key to any long-term solution. Different lifestyles and beliefs should be allowed to flourish. Just as Northern Ireland should allow the two traditions to practise their cultural activities and religions unimpeded, so the Republic should create a pluralist society which tolerates minorities within its midst, whether Protestants, homosexuals, separated and divorced people, single parents, even users of contraceptives.

Religion and politics are so intimately linked in Ireland that it often seems an almost impossible task to unravel them. But I was sailing around Ireland at a time when the ceasefire had held for a year; it was a time, as the poet Seamus Heaney put it, when hope and history rhymed. It would be tragic if the path of non-violence was lost due to the intransigence of the parties involved and their failure to negotiate a lasting settlement. The blood of Ireland has been flowing for too long.

27

Into the Loughs

Before leaving Belfast, I went down to the docks. The Port of Belfast was the largest and most modern in Ireland. The docks had been reduced to seven container berths. Once it had been a great and wealthy port as the grand neo-classical Harbour Office and Custom House showed. Much of the waterfront along the River Lagan was now being redeveloped and office blocks and apartments for the wealthy were replacing the old rough and tumble. Smooth executives with portable phones would soon be strolling where dockers once laughed and brawled. The giant cranes of the shipyards were idle. The workforce of Harland and Wolff Shipyard, which built the *Titanic*, *Britannia* and *Canberra* had been reduced thirty-fold to two thousand.

I walked past the leaning clock tower dedicated to Prince Albert, in search of the nineteenth-century Seamen's Church which had a pulpit designed to look like a ship's bow. Looking for the keeper of the keys, I went down a dirty road alongside the docks, its dust and litter raised by trundling juggernauts, past the Catholic Stellar Maris seaman's missions, and turned into the Flying Angel, the Anglican Missions to Seamen. Around the bar, middle-aged businessmen in grey suits were drinking too much; the foreign seamen, I was told, would be arriving in the evening to telephone home on the other side of the world.

The missions did excellent work, offering a warm welcome to seafarers and helping them in times of crisis or in cases of injustice. They were often the only anchor in a seaman's life of constant change, the only secure place in hostile ports in unknown lands. Seafarers not only live lonely and isolated lives away from home and family but have to cope with constant danger at sea and in port.

I had appreciated the missions myself during my voyage around Africa; they offered a bar, a shop, a telephone service and a lounge to seamen of all races and creeds. And I was aware that over ninety per cent of the world's trade is still carried by sea in nearly 80,000 ships. With two thirds of merchant seafarers coming from developing countries they were often obliged to work for poor pay in unseaworthy ships sailing under flags of convenience.

My last port of call was Green Island on the northern shores of Belfast Lough on the road to Carrickfergus. I went to see Richard Mac Cullagh who, with Wallace Clark, had designed the St Columba currach I had come across in the Derry Harbour Museum. He lived in a large new house on the edge of the lough, full of his own oil paintings. He was an artist as well as a great sailor.

During the war, he had served in an Arctic steam trawler, patrolling the coasts of the Hebrides, Orkney islands, Shetlands, Faroes and Iceland. Afterwards, he cruised from southern Scandinavia to the Baltic in his own yacht which resulted in the book *Viking's Wake*. After many years of research he had just published *The Irish Currach Folk*, a wonderful record of the way of life and the currachs of the coastal people of Ireland. It was not written from the security of his library; he had spent many years following their lonely sea trails and visiting their storm-harried islands along the west coast. His work celebrated the courage and stoicism of the currach folk and the power of a mysterious unknown world over the human spirit.

Above the fireplace in his sitting room was the drawing of an Aran islander and his wife by Sean Keating. The tired fisherman with heavy eyelids looks at the spectator while his beautiful wife in a scarf looks away into the distance. 'This drawing says it all,' Richard said. 'The man looks at you as if to say, I know the danger of the sea and what is in store for me. The wife looks into a future in which her husband is no more.'

As I got up to go, he said: 'If you stayed longer, I would have drawn you. You were born 300 years too late. You should have been with Drake!' Then, shaking my hand warmly in farewell, he warned: 'You should get back home before the autumn storms. Good sailing!'

I caught a bus back to Belfast and walked from the city centre up to the railway station. The pink sun was setting behind the green hills of west Belfast. Starlings were massing in the sky above. There was a smell of damp leaves. A cold wind blew and I felt a chill to the bone. As I walked up the hill to the railway station, I noticed in a nearby waste lot kids were burning timber and tyres on a fire. Palls of black smoke spiralled up into the darkening sky. It was my last image of Belfast. I wondered how many more sunsets and how many more fires the city would see before its sores would be finally healed and peace would return to its sleepy spires under the hills.

Back in Bangor Marina, it was blowing an easterly Force 6 which meant that the waves would be building up along the east coast of Ireland after passing over the long fetch of the Irish Sea. Holed up for another day, I decided to visit the coastguards who had their HQ in Northern Ireland over the Bangor Marina office. I talked to Bill Bennett, the district staff officer, who told me that the coastguards are responsible for search and rescue for civilians at sea and around the coasts. There are twenty-one marine rescue centres in Northern Ireland, although they manage the incidents from the operations room in Bangor. Apart from their lifeboats on permanent alert, they can call on Sea King or Wessex helicopters from the Navy or RAF.

'Do you co-operate with the coastguards from the South?'

'They have a rescue service which is separate from the radio stations. But we work together very closely. If an incident occurs in the Irish Sea, whoever is closest for resources will deal with it. Coverage in the Irish Sea is divided between Liverpool, Belfast and Dublin. The RNLI might be technically different between the UK and Ireland but no barriers are put up for search and rescue at sea. For administrative purposes, the Belfast coastguards are considered a district of Clyde in South West Scotland!'

I asked him about the EPIRB – Emergency Position Indicating Radio Beacon – which I had taken with me. Once primed, it sent out continuous signals which bounced off satellites circulating the earth.

'They're a very good idea. Depending on the position of the satellites, we would expect to pick you up within an hour. The average is about twenty minutes.'

'If you hear a Mayday, what do you do?'

'We are duty bound to investigate every Mayday. Everything else goes by the board. We hope to respond within five seconds.'

That was reassuring to hear.

'Is there a general pattern to your operations?'

'Because the sea is such a variable place, all incidents are very different. The most common cause of an engine breakdown however is dirty fuel filters. If people kept them clean, they would save us a lot of time!'

At last, on Saturday 16th September, the weather eased and I cast off my moorings from Bangor Marina on a fine sunny autumn day with a fresh north easterly breeze and good visibility. There was a complex low over Britain which was causing a north to north easterly light airflow. There was a slight swell in Belfast Lough. As I approached Donaghadee Sound, it felt great to be at sea again on my own. I sailed south east into the rising yellow sun, with blue skies above and white clouds on the horizon. I had to keep clear of a boat fishing with a net as I followed the buoys which kept me clear of Copeland Island. The tides were tricky here, eddying and changing earlier than out at sea, but I had made sure that I had a fair tide with me. It was satisfying to negotiate the hazards with confidence and ease.

Once through the sound, I sailed goose-winged down the Ards Peninsula. A light aircraft looped the loop above me, as if to weave a message of friendship in the light-blue sky. Not long after, a fast speed boat passed me, unnecessarily close, rocking *Celtic Gold* in its insolent wake. Off Ballywater, a young man on a hobbie cat, four miles out at sea, hailed me as he skimmed by, obviously enjoying the fine autumn day as much as I was.

To the west, the coastline continued flat and featureless, but I could see the Mull of Galloway in the north east and on the eastern horizon loomed the Isle of Man. I felt wonderfully relaxed sailing across the shimmering sea. I was now alone, with no yacht or boat in sight, sailing on the crest of the wave.

By tea time, I had passed South Rock lighthouse, and then steered south west towards Strangford Lough. There were dark clouds ahead further south but I could now make out the Mountains of Mourne sweeping down to the sea. As planned, I arrived at the narrow entrance to the great lough at high water. I sailed round Bar Pladdy buoy and close to the old tower on Angus Rock. The slack only lasted for fifteen minutes and the water in the narrows was choppy and swirling with many whirlpools and sudden tidal rips. Great masses of water were turning and slipping under me: 400,000 tons of water surge through the strait four times a day. I was pleased that I had not been delayed and did not have to face a tidal race which could reach up to eight knots at springs. It was still challenging, nonetheless. The *Sailing Directions* said that the narrows were to be enjoyed rather than feared. It is an attitude which applies to all cruising and one I whole heartedly endorsed.

Strangford Lough is a huge lake cut off from the sea by the long arm of the Ards Peninsula which stretches down from Belfast Lough. Sixteen miles long and about four miles wide, it is scattered with nearly four hundred islands and sand bars known locally as pladdies. As I passed through the narrows, I thought of the early sailors who bounced on the waters in their hide boats with only oars and sails to guide them. When St Patrick returned to Ireland in 432 he wanted to sail up the coast to County Antrim where he had tended flocks for six years as a young slave. But strong tidal currents – he did not have a tide table – swept his currach through the narrows into Strangford Lough and he landed at the mouth of the River Slaney. Undaunted, he set about converting the local chieftain who gave him a barn for his services. Over the next thirty years, he converted most of Ireland to Christianity. He died in 461 and was buried in Downpatrick on the shores of the lough.

I passed through the narrows without mishap. I did not even have to alter course for the ferry crossing from Portaferry and Strangford village. I decided to spend the night at Audley Roads, a pleasant backwater just after the narrows. I dropped anchor at five o'clock between a small stone pier under the ruins of Audley Castle and a pole which marked the end of a long spit. As I settled down to tea in the cockpit of *Celtic Gold*, watching the swallows gathering at dusk, I had the pleasure of watching a few returning yachts struggle with their moorings. I did not envy the crews who rowed over to the wooded bank to spend the night in their secure homes, rooted, like their lives, in the solid earth. After almost a hundred days at sea and without one night sleeping on land, I liked the idea of being a bird of passage, alighting for a brief spell in an anchorage, ready to leave at any time, carrying everything with me.

It soon grew cold after dusk but I was compensated by a beautiful starry night. Even the Milky Way was reflected in the still black water around me. The three stars of Orion's Belt stood out clear and bright in the night sky. I stayed a long time looking at them, my musings only disturbed by the gentle lap of the water and the distant call of an owl in a dark wood on the shore.

I woke up early on Sunday, 17th September, to another clear autumn day. There was a chill in the air and steam on my breath. A fresh, cool breeze blew from the north east. The weather forecast gave a high over Scotland and a low over southern England which would maintain the light north to north easterly airflow.

I weighed anchor at eight o'clock in great spirits after a good breakfast of porridge, toast and tea. All was prepared for the long day's sail to Carlingford Lough – the passage planned in detail with the tidal calculations, the food ready for lunch, everything carefully stowed away. It had become such a habit now, that I hardly thought of it. It was difficult to imagine how unsure and tentative I was when I had left Porthmadog nearly three months earlier.

Again, I enjoyed the challenge of sailing through the narrows, this time on the ebbing tide three hours after high water. The water was swishing out at several knots, and by the shallows known as the meadows it was creating ferocious whirls and eddies. Even though the wind was not against the tide, the sea was choppy and breaking on the bar. There was a clear line between the comparatively smooth fast-moving waters of the ebbing tide from Strangford Lough and the high breaking waves of the sea. I went straight into them; *Celtic Gold* rose and fell easily; after about fifteen minutes we were through. I endeavoured to get south of St Patrick's Rocks as soon as possible: despite my fascination with the currents and counter currents, it was not a place to linger.

It was another lovely sunny autumn day, with the pressure on the barometer slowly rising. I set sail south east for Carlingford Lough, some thirty-four miles away. Running goose-winged again in the northerly breeze, we averaged a steady four knots. By mid morning, I was two miles off the little village of Ardglass sailing within the Ardglass Bank. The Mountains of Mourne literally swept down the sea. Mist began to form around the distinctive peaks of Eagle Mount and Slieve Donard. I still had two clear days to go before I could complete my circumnavigation. If I did not linger in Dublin, I could still make it to Wicklow by the autumn equinox.

At lunch time, an exhausted Red Admiral butterfly landed on the prow of *Celtic Gold*. I made my way forward and gently held it in my cupped hands. It seemed so out of place at sea, so delicate and fragile in the vast expanse of the sky. I took it carefully into the cabin and released it on to the chart table, where it slowly opened and closed its beautiful red wings on the blue of the Irish Sea on my chart. I was pleased to offer it a lift, and intended to release it in Carlingford Lough where it would have a chance to land on solid ground. It slowly opened and closed its wings for a long time, but suddenly something moved it to fly and it flew straight out of the hatch and disappeared for ever into the blue haze.

As the day wore on the wind picked up and the coastline became increasingly hazy. *Celtic Gold* was humming in the choppy sea, surging through the white horses. I had no tide to worry about now for by a quirk of the tides and currents coming up the St George's Channel and down from the North Channel there was a permanent slack in this part of the Irish Sea. It was, however, a worry for those living around Dundrum Bay for it meant that radioactive waste from Sellafield in Cumbria had collected there. With the half life of uranium at 100,000 years, it was going to remain there for a long time. The Irish Sea was reputed to be the most radioactive sea in the world. Since it had a shallow seabed, with nowhere deeper than 45 metres, it was not properly sluiced out by the currents. And with ships from as far away as Japan bringing their nuclear waste to be reprocessed at Sellafield, the threat was increasing all the time.

I did not dwell on these dismal matters but kept a look out for the whistling Carlingford Buoy. It came into sight on a hazy sea. The north easterly wind had picked up to a Force 4. It was potentially a difficult entrance with its shallows and skerries but it was well-buoyed and did not have the tidal race of Strangford Lough. The thin grey tower of the lighthouse on Haubowline Rock was unmistakable. It was a beautiful late autumn afternoon as I sailed into the Lough with the Mountains of Mourne to the north standing out in the blue sky.

The only sinister note was a grey British warship anchored near the entrance: an invisible line through the beautiful and tranquil lough marked the boundary between Northern Ireland and the Republic. I had been told that the IRA were known to smuggle arms across her waters, and that mysterious night exercises were conducted by the SAS in the environs.

I headed for Carlingford Marina, on the southern shore, which was made from a sunken hulk, blocks of concrete and scrap iron. It could not have been more different from Bangor Marina. Once again, I was in the Republic but there was no interfering busybody like the old man in Portrush to check my flags. I was given a warm welcome by the berthmaster who was a young Spaniard married to an Irish girl. He worked out of a Portacabin. Despite its lack of facilities, the marina was a pleasant haven in a beautiful setting at the foot of the Cooley

Mountains only a short walk from the village of Carlingford.

The moorlands of the Cooley Peninsula are the setting for a large part of Ireland's most famous legend, 'Táin Bó Cúailinge' or 'The Cattle Raid of Cooley'. It centres around the struggle of Queen Maeve, the ruler of Connacht, and the legendary warrior Cúchulainn of Ulster.

One day Maeve became jealous of her husband Ailill's white bull. On hearing tales of the brown bull of Cooley, the strongest in Ireland, Maeve became obsessed with having it for herself. She was a passionate as well as wilful woman who took her chief warrior, Fergus, as a lover. Her husband was unable to check her, although on one occasion he stole Fergus's sword while they were amorously engaged, in order to shame him. Not content with her own husband and warriors, Maeve offered to sleep with the local chieftain Daire in exchange for the bull, as the original epic delicately put it, extending to him 'the friendship of her upper thighs'. Unfortunately for Connacht and Ulster, Daire's love of his bull was greater than his desire for the queen.

Enraged, the spurned Maeve gathered her armies together and made for Ulster. The province was virtually defenceless at the time because the men of Ulster were under a spell imposed by the goddess Macha; whenever threatened with an attack, the warriors went into mock labour. There was nothing to stop Maeve now obtaining the brown bull of Cooley except a warrior called Cúchulainn. The son of the sun god Lugh and trained in the Land of Shadows by the warrior goddess Skatha, he alone was immune to the spell.

As Maeve's soldiers attempted to cross the river at Ardee, Cúchulainn slayed many of them single-handed and brought her armies to a halt. But infiltrators managed to steal the fabulous brown bull and to take it back to Connacht. Cúchulainn was fatally wounded. He tied himself to a Pillar Stone to face his enemies, but on the third day the goddess of death perched on his shoulder and an otter drank his blood.

On Cúchulainn's death, the men of Ulster awoke from their ancient spell and routed the invaders. As for the bull, it killed Maeve's husband Ailill's white bull and then went on the rampage around Ireland. Exhausted with rage, it eventually died near Ulster at a place named Druim Tarb, 'the Ridge of the Bull'.

The moors around Carlingford were indeed wild and desolate. The road from Carlingford passed through Windy Gap, a basin surrounded by rugged peaks, where Ailill reputedly stole Fergus's sword. There was also a cairn called the Long Woman's Grave, the last resting place of a Spanish princess who was brought there by her lover, a local chieftain, with the promise of ruling over a great tract of land. When she saw the barren and windswept patch which was to be her future home, she died of shock and was buried there under its cold stones.

Carlingford itself is a medieval town, a cluster of old buildings and narrow streets huddled on the shore of the lake. I knew immediately I was back in the Republic not only by the accent, but by the number of pubs, some of which doubled up as shops, but it had a very different atmosphere from the west coast. There you could not enter a pub without someone talking to you within a few minutes. Here you could remain anonymous all evening. The locals turned away from the visitors whose talk was abstract and dry. There was none of the warm humour and friendly earthiness of the coastal communities. Their natural friendliness had been corrupted by too many visitors.

With 20 million or so oysters in the lough, Carlingford was the oyster capital of Ireland. There was not only an Oyster Tavern among the pubs and restaurants off the square but a master butcher called Des Savage, a Mourne View Guest House which did not seem at all mournful, and an Ogam Apothecary which offered reflexology, aromatherapy and Celtic Tree Oils.

The New Age had reached medieval Carlingford.

On my way back to the marina, I walked past the old Norman castle built on a rocky pinnacle. It was known as King John's Castle because the English king spent a few days there in 1210 *en route* to do battle in Ulster. The first few pages of the Magna Carta, the world's first constitutional bill of rights, were probably drafted there during his visit. It was tragic that nearly eight hundred years later the rights of some Irish people were still not fully recognised and that the IRA continued to confront the British Navy and the SAS over the waters of the tranquil lough.

28

Dublin Bound

I left Carlingford Lough on Monday, 18th September, three days before the autumn equinox. A north easterly wind was still blowing and it was strengthening all the time. Dublin Radio said that there was a ridge of high pressure over Ireland, while Belfast coastguard station said that it was to the west of the British Isles. The same place: the geography of the weather forecasting simply reflected political boundaries.

As I left Carlingford Lough, two fast rib dinghies came from the British warship with half a dozen armed men inside. They made straight for me; perhaps they wanted to question me before I left the North about my visit to Republican Milltown cemetery in Belfast. They were known to stop yachts and search them for arms. As it was, they veered off a few hundred yards away without hailing me, and sped out to sea.

Despite the high pressure, the weather was not good. The sky was a light bluish grey. The coastline was very hazy and the sea was rough, with a high fetch. White horses broke on the long waves, and as I sailed due south the wind was on the port quarter. I had the mainsail and the jib reefed a little. The cold autumn air from the north east sent a shiver through my thick clothing. I pulled my Breton cap, now salt-stained, firmly down.

By noon, the sea had picked up and *Celtic Gold* was rolling and pitching through five-foot breaking waves. At least we were going with them rather than against them. Even so, the occasional surge of waves would throw her sideways and I would have to readjust her course. My rudder had served me well in many a turbulent sound and tight harbour, but now I detected a slight looseness in its bearings. I hoped it would see me out. I only had two days' sailing now to complete my circumnavigation and a day and night to return to Porthmadog.

There were no boats or yachts about and my only companions were the guillemots and the gannets which dive bombed into the deep green sea. As I rounded Rockabill Buoy with its horn a little north of the Skerries, I heard the Holyhead coastguard in North Wales for the first time for three months. There was a large fishing vessel off my port beam which had hundreds of screaming herring gulls wheeling and diving in its wake.

By tea time, I was approaching Lambay Island in a high running sea. It had clouded over by now and the dark-grey sea crashing on the black rocks looked sinister and gloomy. Although the north easterly wind was still on my port quarter and had freshened, the tide was running against me and it was slow and heavy going. Sudden gusts of wind caught the sails. It took over two hours to sail the five miles from Lambay Island to the smaller island known as Ireland's Eye just north of Howth. As I came round it, I could see the town of Howth stretching up the small peninsula to the north of Dublin. I had returned from the wilderness to civilisation once again. It seemed strange to see the smart yachts from Howth Marina out for an evening sail; they seemed to be in a different world. The marina was built in the old harbour where many idle fishing vessels were moored three abreast along the stone jetty. By the time I had moored in the marina, it was nearly seven o'clock.

Howth Yacht Club was founded in 1895. It still boasts a fine example of the racing yacht 'Howth Seventeen' a gaff-rigged sloop which was the oldest surviving one-design keel boat in the world. It had not escaped the politics of the country. The author Erskine Childers sailed his yacht *Asgard* into Howth Harbour under the eyes of a coastguard cutter. He had on board arms for the Irish Volunteers which were used in the Easter Rising in Dublin in 1916. Childers was rewarded by being shot by his comrades during the Civil War for the illegal possession of a revolver.

Whilst waiting on weather in Howth, I also met a couple of lads who had sailed in from Strangford Lough. When they asked me what kind of boat I had and I replied a Westerly Centaur, one of them said, 'They're great. I was caught with some friends in the North Channel in a severe gale in three yachts. The coastguards had forecast a Force 4 to 5, but the wind quickly picked up to fifty knots. Two of the yachts were broached, one lost its wash boards and broke its rudder, and the other broke its anchor warps and chains. The only one that didn't get broached was the Centaur. My friend spent most of the night just motoring into the wind. I would call it St Centaur! 'What type of engine have you got?'

'An MD 2B.'

'Well, you'll be all right. It'll take anything. Good luck!'

Although I was at the end of my voyage, I still had two long journeys to do and the gales were blowing in. It was reassuring to know that I had a seaworthy and reliable yacht which could manage the high winds and heavy seas expected with the autumn gales.

Howth itself was a round peninsula, once cut off from the mainland, forming the northern shore of Dublin Bay. It was originally called Ben na Dair which may have referred to the oaks which covered its rounded dome. It was the Vikings who renamed it Hoved in the eleventh century, meaning headland, but they were soon ousted by the Normans who built the castle. The pirate queen Granuaile – Grace O'Malley – is said to have visited the place on her way back to Connacht from her audience with Queen Elizabeth. Arriving at dinner time, she knocked on the gates of the castle but was refused entry. Annoyed by the rebuff, she kidnapped the Lord of Howth's son who was playing on the beach. She only returned him when his father vowed never again to bar the gates of his castle at mealtimes and agreed to lay an extra place at his table for an unexpected guest. I was told that the custom was still honoured.

The day after my arrival in Howth was 19th September. It was the first anniversary of my separation from my wife. I wrote in my notebook:

> My voyage is coming to an end. I now look forward to returning to Wales to find myself a new home, to write a good book, to fulfil my commitments, to care for my children. I shall try and remain independent and self-reliant and look after myself as I have done during this voyage. I shall be calm, deliberate, determined, and organised. I shall not give way to any debilitating emotions, or let my mind be disturbed by anxious thoughts. My head is full of shimmering seas, bold headlands, bright stars, the flight of seabirds, and the warm lilt of the Irish tongue. Long may it last!

Since gales were forecast for the next few days, I decided to catch the DART railway into Dublin. It went along the coast of Dublin Bay. I could see large container ships making for the two tall chimneys which marked the entrance to the wharfs of the River Liffey and a white ferry boat from Holyhead in North Wales making for the little port of Dun Loaghaire a little way down the bay. A few people walked their dogs along the wet strand; the tide was going out. We paused at Black Rock, Sea Point and other suburban stops, their names given in Irish and English, with fine views of the bay.

We quickly left the suburbs for the centre of Dublin. The light-grey stone of the neo-classical law courts by the green Liffey gleamed in the sun. I passed Tara Street, named after the Hill of Tara, the ancient seat of the Celtic kings, and got out at Pearse Street, named after one of the martyrs of the Easter Rising.

I had visited Dublin a couple of times before and had always been struck by the way it had absorbed and not repulsed invaders and settlers, traders and raiders. It had recently celebrated its millennium but there were settlements along the banks of the Liffey much earlier. The city's Irish name Baile Atha Cliath meant 'The Town of the Hurdle Ford'. It was the Vikings who first settled, intermarrying with the Irish, and established a trading port in a black pool – *dubh linn* – where the River Poddle joined the Liffey, now underground. The Normans followed and also intermarried. Only the English kept their distance, refusing to adopt Irish dress, language and ways, banishing the Irish 'beyond the Pale', the physical boundary which marked the limits of polite society. But it was during the Protestant ascendancy that Dublin flourished in the eighteenth century. It became second only to London in the British Isles and raised fine stone buildings and cleared grand avenues. But with the closing of parliament and the enforced union of 1800, the gentry retreated to London.

Dublin went into decline. The efforts of Daniel O'Connell and Parnell for home rule were set back by the Famine and an intransigent British government. But there was no turning the tide at the beginning of the twentieth century. The Easter Rising of 1916 in Dublin, in which James Connolly and Patrick Pearse and other members of Sinn Fein occupied the main post office, brought matters to a head. Five years later, Dublin became the capital of the Irish Free State. The withdrawal of British troops meant the ending of 700 years of foreign occupation.

I liked Dublin. Where Belfast was tense, Dublin was relaxed and convivial. It has a soul. It is a city on a human scale, a city to explore on foot, a city which is not in a mad rush. Yet it does not have a provincial air; indeed, I was impressed by how cosmopolitan and dynamic it seemed. It might be one of the smallest cities in Europe, but it vies with Paris, Barcelona and Rome for atmosphere, colour and flair. The people seem relaxed and friendly, pleased to see rather than fleece the visitors. The pubs, restaurants and clubs are overflowing: Ireland has the youngest population in Europe and every third one is a Dubliner.

The northern suburbs may have been run down, and much of the old architecture cleared, but it has wide open streets like O'Connell Street, pedestrian ways like Grafton Street, and fine Georgian terraces and buildings like the Four Courts, Leinster House (Ireland's Dáil or parliament) and the Custom House. And then there is the thin finger of the Liffey running through it all, with lazy grey mullet in its green opaque waters, spanned by fourteen bridges including the spidery Ha'penny pedestrian bridge built in 1816.

I went to visit Trinity College. It is opposite the fine stone rotunda, now part of the Bank of Ireland, which housed the Irish parliament before it voted itself out of existence in the Act of Union of 1800. Founded by Queen Elizabeth on land confiscated from a monastery, she hoped that the students of the university would not be 'infected by popery'. The Catholic Church continued to forbid its faithful to attend until 1970 although the majority of the students are now Catholic. Crossing its spacious quad, I made for the Old Library to see the Book of Kells. It consists of the Four Gospels which are marvellously illustrated with intricate designs, sweeping spirals and serpentine forms. Probably produced in Columcille's monastery on Iona during the late eighth century, it is one of the oldest and most beautiful books in the world. The book is housed in a magnificent eighteenth-century library known as the Long Room, a triumph of the Enlightenment in its space and order and clarity, with busts of Socrates, Swift and Burke. It also has a rare copy of the Proclamation of the Irish Republic which was read out by Patrick Pearse at the beginning of the Easter Rising.

I spent an afternoon in the Berkeley Library (named after the bishop/philosopher). Despite Ireland's independence, as a copyright library it is entitled to a free copy of every book published in the UK. I had spent years researching in the Reading Room of the British Museum and felt the familiar stillness and womb-like security. It was very seductive. Outside in the quad the trees were swaying in the gusty, gale force wind but inside all was quiet and calm. The books on their shelves stayed in the same place for years, the motes which danced in the sun slowly accumulating on their backs like invisible snow. I could not imagine a place more different from being out at sea on the west coast of Ireland, with its fierce rollers breaking on desolate and savage shores. I turned my back on the dusty stack and went out into the wild autumn wind.

In the Georgian street opposite St Stephen's Green I found the Kildare Club, where I was due to meet Wallace Clark, the yachtsman I had met in Portrush. It was a solid ivy-clad building, the oldest club in Ireland. Round the corner was Kildare Street. It took its name from the Earl of Kildare who, in 1492, became involved in a furious dispute with the Earl of Ormonde in St Patrick's Cathedral in Dublin. A peace was patched up but the two men could not bear to face each other, and a hole had to be hacked through a heavy door so they could shake hands on the agreement. Hence the phrase 'chancing one's arm'.

I thought I would do the same in the club named after him. Wallace Clark was expecting me and greeted me warmly. As I could not enter without a jacket and tie, the doorman gave me a tweed jacket which was too big and some sort of regimental tie. I found a fiver in its pocket and gave it to the doorman.

Wallace introduced me to his wife. She excused herself discreetly by saying that she had some shopping to do. Wallace and I went upstairs to a lounge with elegant leather chairs, but the noise was too loud from the street outside for a recorded interview so we went up to the next floor which had rooms for members from the country to stay overnight. It was still too noisy. We ended up in a bathroom with an adjoining lavatory at the back of the building. During our conversation, an elderly member passed through the bathroom to the lavatory without batting an eyelid. Who was he to question the tastes of other members?

I mentioned to Wallace my surprise in discovering that the fishermen on the west coast did not wear life jackets and apparently could not swim. 'Yes, it's a real problem. We've tried with the RNLI to encourage them to wear life jackets but they say they get in the way. When an islander dies, they accept it stoically. They say the sea shall take her own; the sea shall have her way.'

'It strikes me that it is a kind of primitive sacrifice to the sea which goes back to the earliest times when men set off in their currachs to brave the waves.'

'You might have something there.'

I asked him again what he got from sailing. 'I love it because it takes you right out of your everyday worries and away from it all. You concentrate on practical things. And when you come back you're weary in body but fresh in spirit.' Amen.

Wherever you go in Dublin, it is difficult to escape the literary associations; there is even a Dublin's Writers' Museum. I came across several plaques on pubs celebrating the fact that they had appeared in *Ulysses*. There was even a literary pub crawl on offer. Enjoying the friendliness and sardonic wit of the pubs, I could see why Joyce had used them so much for the setting of his masterpiece. The act of drinking is one of the most essential acts of human communication, like the breaking of bread or making love.

Looking at the bust of the eighteenth-century playwright Oliver Goldsmith outside Trinity College reminded me of a literary evening I had spent on St Patrick's Day in the previous spring, in a huge Victorian chapel in Islington, London. The proceeds of the evening were for a noble cause – to help the immigrant Irish youth. It was an extraordinary scene. There must have been more than a thousand people present and pints of beer and glasses of wine stood where prayer and hymn books once were. This was the new religion: cultural nationalism. The only pews available were on the right side of the dias at the front. Having sat down with my pint, I suddenly realised that I was sitting with the literati who were waiting to read their works. The poet Seamus Heaney sprawled uncomfortably in the pew, urbane, dapper, his large body constrained in his suit, white hair low on his furrowed brow, heavy eyelids over oriental eyes which suddenly sparkled with passion. The novelist Edna O'Brien sat erect, with a slight smile on her thin red lips, in a rich black velvet gown. With her chin held high and her delicate nose in the air, she had a slightly theatrical look. Her famous green eyes had faded a little with age and experience.

Seamus Heaney was announced as the greatest living poet in the English language and the grand old man of Irish letters. He ambled up to the dias where he referred to himself, with a sparkle in his eye, as 'the queen mother of poetry readings'. He exuded good humour and bonhomie, the patron saint of the young Irish immigrants in London.

Heaney recited one of my favourite poems, 'Digging', in which he watches his father digging a drill of potatoes and is reminded of his grandfather cutting turf. The poem is redolent of the fertility of the earth, of the despair of famine, of the closeness of the blood tie.

Heaney ended with what he called a 'bit of rhymed verse', a political poem for the times, a plea for the peace process. History says don't hope on this side of the grave, but at the end of the poem he suggested that now 'hope and history rhyme'. The audience clapped enthusiastically: they knew what horrors lay dormant in the bloody tale of their history.

Edna O'Brien took to the dias. In a vibrant, strong and slightly sibilant voice, she declared: 'Ireland is a house. We may love her or we may hate her. She's a female . . . We are from her and I'm very glad we are.'

Ireland honours its writers and artists, and even allows them to live tax free, yet so many have gone into exile. Its strict laws of censorship have not helped and its stifling religious and political atmosphere have hardly been conducive. Heaney and O'Brien have spent much of their lives commuting between Ireland, Britain and America. But the old Gaelic tradition of telling tales and reciting poetry is still alive throughout the land and continues to inspire countless would-be writers.

Whilst the gales blew over Howth, I came back to Dublin every day for a week. I visited the National Museum, admiring the eighth-century Tara Brooch which showed Celtic art at its best. In the National Gallery, I was drawn to the paintings of Jack Yeats and Paul Henry. I wandered about Merrion Square, the centre of Georgian Dublin where Oscar Wilde was born and Daniel O'Connell ('The Liberator'), W. B. Yeats (Jack's brother), George (A.E.) Russell (poet, mystic, and painter), and the Austrian physicist Erwin Schrodinger all lived. I avoided Dublin

Castle, first built in 1204 by King John, which had been the pivot of British power and the official residence of the viceroys of Ireland. And I strolled past the fine Georgian Leinster House where the modern Dáil meets and Charles Haughey, the chieftain of Inishvickillane, once held court.

I did spend some time in the pubs of Dublin, especially the ones in Temple Bar, a maze of narrow lanes and alleys down by the Liffey, one of the old parts of Dublin not yet destroyed by the planners. The music and craic were particularly good at one Sunday session, the wan sun illuminating the spiralling smoke in the dim interior. The middle-aged men and women were animated and laughing as they tossed back stout and whiskey and gin, but their faces were pale and tired. The struggle to survive in the city, the round of dole queue, factory and office had taken their toll.

I had the same melancholy feeling that I often had in great cities. Civilisation is said to have developed in the city first, but most city dwellers seem to have lost their way. It is as if all the artificial sounds and lights cloud their vision; they no longer hear the song of the earth and sea and sky. The people I had met during my voyage who lived in the remote islands and peninsulas seemed more at the centre of things, in touch with what was essential, natural and important. On the other hand, those in the towns, caught up with consumerism, materialism and fashion, appeared more on the periphery of what really mattered.

While I was holed up in Howth, I saw two friends in Dublin whom I had met at a ceilidh in Dingle some years before. Anne was a teacher and single-parent, and Terri was a reflexologist, divorced from an Englishman. They were representative of the new breed of educated Irish women who were not content to sit at home or play second string to their men. Anne told me: 'Irish men have a selfish streak in them. They want their women to do everything for them, cook, iron, wash . . .'

'Are there any new men,' I asked, 'ready to help with the domestic chores?'

'Maybe, but they're yuppie types and they don't have kids.'

They appreciated New Age spirituality, occasionally attended church, but did not like the way the priests tried to interfere with the private lives of their hearts and bodies. They liked the excitement and elegance of the new restaurants and hotels but enjoyed a pint with their mates in the old pubs.

My strolls through the city took me down O'Connell Street which led from the Liffey to north Dublin, the widest street in the city. I found it ironic that in a country which still did not allow divorce, the three great monuments raised in the street – O'Connell at the bottom, Parnell at the top and Nelson in the middle – were all notorious adulterers. Nelson had stood at the top a Doric column, built thirty-two years before the one in Trafalgar Square until it was blown up in 1966 during an unofficial fiftieth celebration of the 1916 Easter Uprising.

I often found myself ending up in Grafton Street which led from Trinity College to St Stephen's Park. Now a walkway, it was a lively street where the buskers were not moved on: jazz, folk, country and western, and punk vied with each other in a glorious cacophony. On one occasion, a group of young lads, hardly more than thirteen, had set up their electrical equipment and belted out wonderful renditions of Beatles classics, gathering around them a large audience of middle-aged and well-heeled shoppers and office workers. With such talent, I could see why Ireland had produced so many successful bands and musicians.

My place of refuge was Bewley's Oriental Café. It had a dim interior illuminated by the glow of large stained-glass windows and coal fires. It reminded me of the old Lyons Tea Houses of my youth in London, while the names of the teas on offer evoked the mysterious richness of the East: Java and Keemun, Assam and Darjeeling. A blend of the last two produced some strong Irish Afternoon Tea. It was the sort of place where you could shelter over a tea for an hour and where single women and old men could linger without being harassed. It even provided newspapers to read.

While I was glancing through the *Irish Times*, there was a sudden crash behind me. I just saw a tray go flying and a small round man collapse on the floor where he lay. There was a shocked silence for a second, newspapers were lowered, and then everyone began talking. Red-faced waiters peered anxiously at the commotion. But rather than go to his assistance, people simply moved away with their coffees and teas. A couple of women continued their animated conversation right next to the collapsed man as if he did not exist. I got up to help but was beaten to the scene by a couple of men who tried to resuscitate him with the kiss of life. Chaos had disturbed the ordered flow of the afternoon. Death had appeared in a tea cup.

The chatter of the large room resumed. Solitary men returned to their newspapers. Parents with trays quickly guided their children away as soon as they caught a glimpse of the man sprawled on the floor. Eventually two ambulance men arrived with a stretcher and carried him away.

'Tea is reviving,' said my elderly neighbour, and he raised his cup with a twinkle in his eye.

While waiting on weather in Howth, I was invited to dinner at the National Yacht Club in Dun Laoghaire on the other side of Dublin Bay by Michael Laughnane, the charterer I had met in Kinsale. A solid stone building built in 1863, it overlooked the harbour where fast ferries from Holyhead made the yachts tug at their moorings. Inside, its wood panelled interior exuded ease and comfort. It was celebrating the triumph of two of its members who had just won the world Fireball championships.

Chatting in the bar, I asked why the other yacht clubs in Dun Laoghaire – the Royal Irish and the Royal St George – had retained the 'royal' in the staunch republic. A man next to me turned and said: 'I'm a member of the Royal Institute of Architects. By Jesus, if we got rid of the royal, we'd have nothing left!' Certainly architects and planners had not done Dublin well in recent times.

I was introduced to a stocky young man in a blazer and tie with large gold cuff links and was told he had sailed around the world and raced round Ireland ten times. When I told him that I had spent three months sailing that summer, he declared: 'You must have the record for the slowest circumnavigation of Ireland!'

I took this as a great compliment and was quietly pleased.

In the afternoon, I strolled along the promenade at Dun Laoghaire above the rocky shore to visit the Martello tower where James Joyce had once lived and which was the setting for the opening of his novel *Ulysses*. It is now a little museum, opened in 1962 by Sylvia Beach, the Paris-based publisher who first dared to put the novel in print. I was intrigued by two death masks of the novelist on display, the nose so distinctive, yet strange without the glasses.

There were some fine views from the top of the tower. Below in the Forty Foot Pool, men dived off the rocks as Buck Mulligan had done in *Ulysses* although now women were allowed there and togs had to be worn after nine o'clock. Across Dublin Bay, I could see Howth Head with its lighthouse to the north and Dalkey Island with its signal tower to the south east. Although it was sunny, the sea was rough and there were many white horses. I would be passing down that way as soon as the wind abated a little.

29

Ancient Mysteries

Every dark cloud has a silver lining and the gales enabled me to realise my last great purpose in Ireland. I used the opportunity to visit one of the greatest sites of the ancient world in the Boyne Valley and to watch the sun set on the autumn equinox from the hill of Tara, the spiritual centre of the early Celts and the place of the last stand of their kings and druids.

I prepared myself by going to the National Museum in Dublin to investigate the pre-history of Ireland. I came across a beautiful flint hand axe which had been found in Dún Aengus on Inishmore, and dated from 4,000 BC, from the Paleaonthic Age. Another great discovery was a boat over forty-five feet long – the Lurgan longboat. Hollowed out of a great oak, about four and a half thousand years ago, it had been preserved in a bog in Galway. I had a great urge to touch it, to make contact with those ancient mariners who had sailed it up the rivers and lakes, and who knew the movement of the tides and the stars. There was also a beautiful little currach made from gold with tiny oars, which was probably a child's toy. Dating from the first century BC and found in County Derry, it showed that currachs had been around Ireland for at least 2,000 years.

The Boyne Valley was an hour and half's drive north of Dublin. Since I could not sail up the river like the currach sailors and Vikings of old, I caught a coach from central Dublin. We passed by the old canal and out into open country. It was good to smell the sweet, damp earth once again. After months at sea, my senses had developed, and I was acutely aware of the odour of diesel, the smoke of car fumes, and the clogging of dust. It was a lovely autumn day with great white clouds scudding across the sky. A strong wind was blowing the yellowing leaves off the trees, and playing with and bending the brown tops of the long grass.

In a dramatic loop of the River Boyne, I came across three huge green mounds. Built some 6,000 years ago, (3,500–2,700 BC during the Neolithic Age), these wonders of the ancient world were older than Stonehenge, Mycenae and even the pyramids of Egypt. The most famous was at Newgrange. It stood out on a low ridge in the soft, green rolling farmland. It looked like a huge green flying saucer, with a white front which gleamed and sparkled in the autumn sun. As I approached it, I realised that the white façade was made from countless pieces of white quartz, interspersed with oval granite boulders. The whole mound must have been 250 feet in diameter and about fifty feet high, covering an area of almost an acre. There were other such Megalithic sites in Europe, but none so fine as the one at Newgrange.

There was an incomplete circle of huge standing stones about thirty-six feet away from the mound, encircling an area of about two acres. Both the stone ring and the mound itself were slightly heart-shaped. I walked slowly around the mound, pausing to investigate the ninety-seven colossal kerb stones. Eleven were decorated with elaborately carved designs: spirals, lozenges, chevrons, circles, horseshoes, parallel lines, and radials as well as other more enigmatic shapes.

At the entrance, there were three vast stones, the largest of which, in the middle, was twelve feet long and about four feet high, with beautiful double spiral designs. It was the apogee of Megalithic art. One marvellous motif had three spirals which looked like maps of labyrinths all interconnected in the middle.

Entering the mound, I walked up a slight incline along a narrow passageway bordered by large standing stones. Sixty feet inside, about a third of the way to its centre, the passage opened up into three adjoining recesses: the whole formed a cross with a very elongated staff. In each recess there was a large chiselled stone basin. They once contained cremated human bones. All the great stones were dressed and many had been delicately decorated with spirals, lozenges, triangles and squares, similar to the ones I had seen on the outer kerb stones. The most beautiful was a three-spiral figure, a wonderful example of ancient geometry.

After nearly 6,000 years, it was as dry as a bone inside the inner chamber. It had a magnificent corbelled vault, the finest of its kind in Europe. Edges of large stone slabs overlapped each other until the roof was closed in with a capstone. Even more impressive were the grooves in the large roof slabs which were skilfully arranged to carry off the rainwater. Exceptional care had been taken in the design, engineering and orientation of the whole monument.

The slight incline in the passageway into the inner sanctum and the placing of the huge stones were not accidental. Where Stonehenge is orientated towards the midsummer sunrise, Newgrange faces south east in the direction of the midwinter sunrise.

Above the entrance, a rectangular roof box has been discovered. At dawn on the winter solstice, from 0958 the sun appears above the local horizon and shines through the narrow gap directly down the passageway to light up the basin stone in the end-chamber in the heart of the monument. After a few minutes the thin beam of light widens dramatically to illuminate the side- and end- chambers as well as the corbelled roof. At 1004 it begins to contract again and by 1015 the inner chamber returns to complete darkness. The entering and withdrawal of the sun lasts for a total of seventeen minutes. Direct sunlight penetrates the mound for about a week before and a week after the winter solstice but it reaches its greatest intensity on the shortest day of the year.

During those dark days of winter, when the seventy-foot sunbeam illuminated the inner chamber with golden light on the winter solstice, the word would no doubt have been relayed by the keepers of the monument to those gathered outside. The news would have sparked off a great celebration. The sun had returned after the longest night and would surely gradually return to the north, bringing the promise of warmth and light and a new harvest. Life, at its lowest ebb, would rise and blossom again. All would be well.

Most mainstream archaeologists describe Newgrange and its sisters as passage graves. Yet the mound was clearly a celestial observatory as well as a powerful centre of ritual and celebration. The cremated bones found in the stone basins in the inner chamber were too few to suggest that it was merely a burial chamber; they were probably there to sanctify the meaning of the monument. The combination of sunrise with the winter solstice suggests that rebirth follows death. The penetration of the dark chamber by a shaft of light implies a cosmic union between father sun and mother earth; it no doubt celebrated the celestial rhythm that organises life and brings energy to the world.

The carvings on the outer kerb stones of Newgrange were probably complex sun and moon dials, designed to be used in conjunction with shadows thrown by sticks of certain lengths. The design on the entrance stone could well have been a chart of the ancient night sky, a map of the stars. What is certain is that the abstract designs had profound religious symbolism.

I immediately wanted to return to Newgrange on the winter solstice to see the real rays of the sun touch lightly on the stones of the inner chamber but on further enquiries I was told that the event was fully booked until 2007. They were taking no more bookings. Was this significant? Would the world, fulfilling some ancient prophecies, have come to an end by then?

Newgrange is the most famous and impressive of the mounds in the Boyne Valley, but nearby are two others of similar size, Knowth and Dowth, half a mile up and downstream respectively. Dowth is in a poor state, having been plundered and eroded over the centuries. On the other hand, Knowth, which is being excavated, is even more complex than Newgrange with two passages and surrounded by seventeen satellite tombs. Its builders understood the moon's approximate nineteen-year cycle and orientated two passages towards the sun and the moon so that each could shine down into the mound, mingling the silver feminine lunar light with the golden masculine light of the sun.

All three mounds are visible from the summits of each other. They are part of a Megalithic civilisation which developed throughout Western Europe, and similar structures have been discovered in Spain, Portugal, Brittany and Britain, but nowhere did they reach such perfection as in the Boyne Valley. The great stone circles of Avebury and Stonehenge in Wessex, the stone rows in Brittany and the great chamber tomb at Maes Howe in the Orkneys show that the builders at Boyne were an advanced branch of a great civilisation which spread down the western seaboard of Europe.

The builders of the Boyne may well have been part of a migration which came by boat from the Mediterranean. Certainly the early myths of Ireland talk of a people from Greece led by Partholon who settled but were wiped out by a plague. These were followed by the warrior race of the Fir Bolg, possibly from the Black Sea area, who were then ousted by the Tuatha Dé Danaan, an advanced and civilised people. I thought the last of these legendary figures were the most likely to have built the monuments in the Boyne Valley.

Were they the survivors of a lost civilisation, overcome by a catastrophe, who set off in their boats to settle in the north of Europe while their fellows went to the Americas and the Middle East to trigger off civilisations there? My old friend Graham Hancock, author of *Fingerprints of the Gods*, who had wanted to join me at Newgrange but who got married instead, certainly thought so. The mounds of the Boyne Valley had many features in common with the great Megalithic structures of the Middle East, with the pyramids of Egypt and the ziggurats of Mesopotamia, which were raised at roughly the same time.

I found an intriguing reference in Geoffrey of Monmouth's *History of the Kings of Britain*, written in the twelfth century, which supports the link between Megalithic builders in the Mediterranean and in Britain and Ireland. He records that Merlin suggested to King Aurelius that he raise a lasting monument to heroes – Stonehenge – and to send for the Giant's Ring on Mount Killarus in Ireland. He adds 'many years ago the Giants transported them from the remotest confines of Africa and set them up in Ireland at a time when they inhabited that country'. In the myths of many countries, it is common to find references to giants who raised the great monuments of old.

There are many legends associated with Newgrange, which was long known as Brú na Bóinne, the 'Palace of the Boyne'. The stories of ancient Ireland were handed down orally from generation to generation, but King Cormac Mac Art had the chronicles written down in the third century AD. In the seventh century St Patrick also insisted that the legends and myths be written down lest they be lost. The Bardic colleges outside the monastic schools produced *ollamhs* and *files* (scholars and poets) who kept the tradition alive. All the chroniclers whose works have survived claim to have used much earlier sources.

One legend claims that Newgrange was built by the Great God, And Dagda Mór, for himself and his three sons Aonghus, Aodh and Cermaid. The builders were endowed by later story-tellers with wondrous skills, reflected in their names – Nuada of the Silver Hand, Lughaidh Lamhfhada, the great craftsman, Dagda Mór, the embodiment of power and wisdom.

Another legend associates Newgrange with Aonghus, the chief of the Tuatha Dé Danaan. They were defeated by the invading Milesians who originated in Egypt and reached Ireland via Spain (around 1700 BC). The Tuatha Dé Danaan, then retreated to a subterranean kingdom beneath their raths and dolmens, becoming transformed into Fairy Folk, sometimes aiding later heroes or working mischief with their magic lore. Mil, the leader of the Milesians, named the new homeland Scotia in honour of his wife who was considered to be the daughter of an Egyptian pharaoh. The country was then divided between two chieftains but when one died, Eremon became the first High King of Ireland and ruled from Tara.

After Newgrange, I visited the nearby Hill of Tara which is about twelve miles south in the Boyne Valley. At first sight, it appears little more than a green hill with mounds and hollows. But it has been hallowed ground for millennia. One of the mounds was a Megalithic passage grave dating from 2,500 BC. I had seen in the National Museum in Dublin a fine gold torc worn around the waist which had been found at Tara and which dated from the Middle Bronze Age (1,500–1,000 BC). The Hill of Tara was the seat of the Celtic kings after their arrival from Central Europe between 600 and 400 BC. Tara remained the capital of the country until the sixth century AD. To the Irish people, Tara is a great spiritual centre. It derives its power from the association with the goddess Maeve and the mythical powers of the druid-kings who ruled from there. It is a place of ancient splendours and legendary deeds, of wonders and miracles.

Walking up towards the hill through a churchyard, I came across a nondescript weather-beaten standing stone – the Lia Fáil, the 'Stone of Destiny'. The Tuatha Dé Danaan were supposed to have brought it to Ireland from the mystical city of Falais and set it up at Tara. Some say it represents the union of the gods of the earth and those of the heavens. Others claim that it was the pillow on which Jacob rested his head and dreamt of an angel descending on a ladder from heaven. It was used by the early Celts at the coronation of their kings; if touched by the true king, it would give out three roars. I touched it and needless to say it remained silent.

Although there were kings of Tara, they ruled with the consent of the chieftains. They would meet every three years for the Feis at Samhantide (the beginning of November around Halloween) when they would meet with the scholars to settle disputes and resolve matters of common interest. It was a great occasion for merry making. They revelled in plunder and battle, but they also appreciated fine arguments and craftsmanship, good music and poetry.

I wandered around the ruins of the old banqueting hall, stretching north and south on the slope of the hill, imagining the chieftains and their henchmen on their couches, drinking from their horns and chewing hunks of dripping meat. They would have been entertained by storytellers, buffoons, *files* (poets) and harpers, until the lights flickered low. As long as the Feis lasted, they pledged to do no violence to each other or else they would immediately forfeit their lives. But they were a warrior people and disputes split the country. From the first century AD, the ruthless King Tuathal enlarged his lands of Meath and extorted tribute from Leinster which sowed the seeds of strife between the two provinces for the reigns of forty kings until the seventh century.

Death was very much part of life for these Celtic chiefs. They were pastoralists who lived and died with their cattle. They were bloodthirsty warriors who would tie the heads of their enemies to their horses by their hair or place their skulls over their thresholds. In the National Museum I came across a strangled corpse found in a bog which had ground mistletoe seeds in its stomach and its throat cut, implying that the man had been the victim of a ritual sacrifice. After Cúchailainn failed in his defence of Ulster against Queen Maeve, a friend of his came to Tara to find two men playing football with his head. He killed them and returned to Cúchailainn's grieving wife with her husband's head and a large bunch of enemy heads strung cheek to cheek on a withy wand. He then recited her a poem called 'The Lay of the Heads' about each of their original owners. Few chieftains died in bed with their heads intact. Their leaf-shaped swords and elaborate rapiers were not only carefully wrought but often used.

It was Christianity which put an end to their pagan ways, although many of their beliefs and customs lived on in a disguised form. It is said that on the eve of Easter in AD 433, King Laoghaire and his court were about to light a mighty fire on the Hill of Tara when they saw a light appear upon the nearby Hill of Slane. It was in direct contravention of a royal decree that no fire should be lit in sight of Tara. The incensed Laoghaire was restrained by the advice of his druids who warned that the man who had kindled the fire would surpass kings and princes.

Who was this insolent intruder? It was none other than St Patrick who had travelled from the North with his gospel of love and forgiveness. The next day he was summoned to Tara and on his way composed his famous prayer: 'At Temair today may the strength of God pilot me, may the power of God preserve me, may the wisdom of God instruct me . . . may the Host of God guard me against the snares of demons, the temptations of vices, the inclination of the mind, against every man who meditates evil to me, far, near, alone, or in company.'

The king proposed that a trial be made between his chief druid and the newcomer. His first suggestion was that their books be plunged into water and those which emerged unblemished would be accepted. The druid refused as he had heard that Patrick worshipped the element of water, baptising men in the name of his God. Then the king suggested throwing their books into a fire, but again the druid declined, saying that he worshipped now water, now fire. Patrick replied that he adored no element, but that he worshipped the Creator of all the elements.

In the end the dispute was not solved by argument but by miracle. A house was built, one half made of green wood and the other of dry wood. A boy wrapped in the druid's coat was placed in the dry part of the building and the druid clothed in Patrick's garment in the green part. It was then set alight. The druid was consumed to ashes with the green part of the building but the dry part of the house, the boy, and Patrick's garment remained intact.

It was on the Hill of Tara that St Patrick is said to have first used the three-leaved shamrock (an Arab word for a trefoiled leaf) to illustrate the idea of the Holy Trinity – Father, Son and Holy Ghost – separate and yet one. The symbolic encounter between the pagan druid and the Christian saint marked a turning point in Irish history. The king's attendant Earc, who had greeted Patrick scornfully, was converted. But King Laoghaire himself did not change his ways. His father and his forebears had taught him to hate his enemies and exact a head for a head and he could not accept the new philosophy of love and forgiveness. He died a pagan in 458 whilst on his way to exact tribute from

Leinster, continuing to worship celestial deities and nature spirits and to hold trees sacred. His body was brought back to Tara and he was buried in the old way in the rampart of his rath, standing up, with his shield and sword in his hands and his head facing south towards his old enemies.

The early Christians, for all their gospel of love, became warriors themselves, not only fighting with great armies like St Columcille and St Finnian over the ownership of a book, but also against King Diarmaid, one of the last High Kings of Tara. When Diarmaid came into conflict with St Ruadhan, he came with other saints to fast upon the King at Tara in order to shame their opponent. The king in turn fasted on them, passing every other night without food. The contest dragged on for years, neither giving way, until eventually the saints cursed the king and the place. They prayed to God that no king or queen would ever after dwell on Tara and that it would become waste for ever. And so it came to pass. Today it is a windswept hill of grassy mounds, hollows and ghosts.

But the Hill of Tara remained hallowed ground for the Irish nation. In 1843 Daniel O'Connell the 'Liberator' drew on its ancient associations when he addressed the greatest crowd ever gathered in Ireland in one place. The independence of Ireland and the emancipation of the Catholics were his themes. More than 750,000 people turned up. The passions aroused were so great that they could easily have led to armed rebellion. Fearful of the bloodshed which might result, O'Connell thereafter refused to hold mass meetings in the open air.

Tara continued to cast its mysterious spell and in the 1890s a group of British Israelites dug into the rath on the hill in search of the Ark of the Covenant. Their leader claimed to have seen a mysterious pillar although in the badly excavated site it never came to light.

*

On that autumn equinox, I sat down and meditated by a standing stone on the edge of the Hill of Tara. A pale yellow light spread across the hazy horizon beyond the darkening blue plains of Meath. I felt the burden and the release of history. For thousands of years before me the people of Ireland had watched the sun go down from this vantage point on the equinoxes, marking the short rhythm of their lives by the annual waxing and waning of the sun. I was alone and yet not alone. The spirits of the past were all around me. The great battles and feastings which had taken place, the historic confrontation between the high druid and St Patrick, the great oration of Daniel O'Connell to thousands, all put my own preoccupations into perspective. I had now been away for three months. My vision quest was nearly over. It was definitely time to leave Ireland and its waters, time to return home to Wales and my family and friends again.

As I meditated in the afterglow of the sun, I lost my sense of being as a separate self. I journeyed through the spirals of the mind and the circles of the heavens which had been carved on the ancient stones of Newgrange. I roamed through the realm of betwixt and between, between sand and foam, night and day, winter and summer, death and life. A cool easterly breeze brought me back to my senses. I got up stiffly. I turned my back on the yellow haze in the west and walked towards the darkening east. I would have to sail that way soon, the direction of illumination and new life. I had passed through the dark night of the soul and was looking forward to a new dawn.

30

Over the Irish Sea

I had hoped to complete my circumnavigation of Ireland on 23rd September, the autumn equinox, three months after my departure from Wales on the summer solstice. I was only five hours' sailing time and twenty nautical miles short of achieving my end on a voyage of over twelve hundred miles. But the equinoctial gales blew in, one after another, and I had no choice but to wait on weather, bouncing at my moorings in Howth. One night I was even woken up in the early hours by claps of thunder and hail hammering on the deck of *Celtic Gold*.

After more than a week of gales, the strong unstable north westerlies at last veered westerly to a gusty Force 5 or 6. I decided to leave for Wicklow. Now was the time for my Westerly Centaur and I to see what we had learned during the last three months.

On my last night in Howth, I shaved off my beard which had grown during the voyage; there seemed more salt than pepper in it now. I had no mirror on board *Celtic Gold* but when I finally looked into one I saw a man I hardly recognised: head like a brown berry, clear blue eyes, and a slight smile playing on his lips. It was very different from the tired, pallid and slightly haunted look of the man I had seen in the mirror in the barber's in Wicklow over three months before.

After carefully working out the tides, I left Howth at noon. It was a great delight and relief to pass through the harbour piers and then swing south around Howth Peninsula. I sailed under the Baily lighthouse on a promontory on the south east side. Visible up to twenty-six miles on a clear night in the Irish Sea, it was usually the first land sighting for mariners approaching Dublin.

In Dublin Bay the offshore wind was very gusty and the sea lumpy and uncomfortable. Water from rogue waves slurped into the cockpit. Great white clouds passed quickly overhead in the light-blue sky. By lunch time the tide had turned and I sailed on the south-going ebb which, since it was springs, gave me an extra couple of knots over the ground.

I kept clear of the banks down the east coast because in rough weather they could be very dangerous. I passed inside the Burford Bank in Dublin Bay and after passing close to the Muggins lighthouse off Dalkey Island I gave the Frazer Bank a wide berth. The wind was gusting up to twenty-five knots off the cliffs. After passing the Breaches Shoal, the westerly offshore wind began to ease a little. I let out the reefs in the main and jib and steered on a fine broad reach for Wicklow Harbour a little west of Wicklow Head.

I arrived at 1700 on 28th September. I had completed my circumnavigation of Ireland. *Celtic Gold* and I had sailed 1,050 miles, excluding the passage from Wales. The harbour was very different from when I had arrived on the 21st June. Then it was packed with yachts, a band was playing, and families and lovers were strolling along the jetty in the setting sun. Now it was cold and grey and empty. Thickening black clouds rolled in from the west. There was not a soul about on the piers, only a few screaming herring gulls rising and falling in the wind. It was not a place to linger.

I moored alongside the wooden pylons on the east pier where there had been a raft of four yachts in the summer and I had had my rubbing strake damaged by the stern wave of the rogue coaster. It was almost low tide and the sea wrack on the wall glistened. I listened to the BBC shipping forecast just before six. There was another low deepening in the Atlantic heading for Ireland. The wind would increase to a 6 or 7 and occasionally Gale Force 8 the following afternoon, but overnight it would be a fresh westerly 4 or 5. This meant that I had a narrow gap in the weather to cross the Irish Sea. I calculated the tides for the Bardsey Sound at the end of the Lleyn Peninsula in North Wales. By a stroke of luck, it worked out that if I could reach the sound by eight o'clock in the morning, I would get through before the six-knot tide began to run against me.

I had not slept well the last few nights with the noise of the whistling rigging and slapping halyards in Howth and felt tired after a hard day's sail on my own down the east coast to Wicklow. But I was determined to go. I prepared some bread, soup and fruit for the crossing which would take me at least sixteen hours overnight. I called up Wicklow Radio and gave my ETA in Porthmadog as 1300.

It was already getting dark at eight o'clock and I switched on the navigation lights. The tricolour of red, green and white at the top of the mast failed to come on. I then tried the steaming lights, but although the white stern light and the red port and green starboard lights worked the light half way up the mast remained in darkness. I could not believe it. I had checked them in Howth and they had been fine. I spent an hour trying to trace the fault without success. I decided to set sail all the same without the mast light. I knew it was potentially dangerous but I would lash a torch to the mast whenever I saw a passing ship.

This was the first time during my voyage that I would sail alone during the night, and I tried to recall the rules of the road and the lights which I had learned during the previous winter. It seemed so long ago. At night, it would be difficult to tell the course of another, if it weren't for lights: red on the port side of a vessel and green on the starboard. I had learned like generations of seamen before me the 'port to port rule' by memorising Thomas Gray's verses:

When you see three lights ahead,
Starboard wheel and show your Red.
Green to Green, Red to Red,
Perfect safety, go ahead.

I eventually left Irish soil at 2100 hours on Friday, 29th September, three months and a week after my arrival. It had been a wonderful summer but now I felt the bitter lash of winter and knew it was time to be going. It was not a sad farewell; I knew I would return to Ireland; I had begun a friendship which would last for the rest of my life.

This time there was no one to see me off as I slipped out of the harbour and headed east into the dark horizon. The visibility was good and although there was no moon the stars were bright. I could even see the Milky Way meandering like a river in the night sky.

The westerly wind was right behind me and I spread out my sails in a goose-winged fashion, poling out the genoa on the starboard side and the main on the port. I attached a preventer to stop the boom swinging over violently in a gybe.

Under the stars, running with the wind in a dark and boisterous sea was magical. I still had a rush of adrenalin after completing my circumnavigation. I felt confident and I knew I could rely on *Celtic Gold* to see me through. The lack of a mast light was worrying though. I knew I would become tired during the night after sailing virtually non-stop for a day already on my own.

Running with the cold autumn wind into a steadily mounting sea, I thought of Pope's lines: 'On life's vast ocean diversely we sail, Reason the card, but Passion the gale.' I could see what he was getting at. Reason was my compass and passion the wind in my sails. But I also felt that it was good to feel at ease tossing and drifting in mid ocean without a compass, to open my soul to what was there and then, to go with the flow wherever it may lead me.

The key to navigation is to know where you are on your voyage, or at least to know where you are not. It is good to know where you are in life. If you stay the course, you will arrive at your goal. At a deeper level, in both life and navigation perhaps it is better to appreciate the process rather than to be goal-orientated, to enjoy the journey rather than long for the arrival.

After much study and three months' practical experience, I had at last discarded my navigation text books. I was now sailing by my own experience and knowledge of the ways of the sea, the wind and the yacht, bringing the three into harmony, making them hum together. I did not consciously think about doing it, I just did it. I felt confident in what I was doing, so I could act spontaneously and move instinctively to meet any sudden change or challenge. I was prepared for the unexpected.

My mind was now focused and my body relaxed. Moving, I was like water. I did not notice where I put my feet, or how I ducked my head. My centre of gravity was in my belly and my body balanced itself on the pitching boat with ease. I did not know whether the wind was riding me or whether I was riding the wind.

Sailing around Ireland had confirmed for me the truth that the wise person uses no force but leaves nothing undone. He is spontaneous. He works without effort. He follows the line of least resistance. Without rigid rules, he acts in the light of the circumstances. He is ready to change his course according to the changing conditions, shifting with the times, now a dolphin, now a fulmar, now a flying fish. He rolls with experiences as they come and go, up and down, like a boat in a swell. He understands the flow of nature and goes with it. He lives in the streaming now and the now streaming. Like the early Celtic monks, he lets himself drift with the winds and the currents, trusting in the goodness of the creation, confident that he will reach a shore.

As I sat at the helm that night in the middle of the Irish Sea, it occurred to me again that sailing was like a happening, a spontaneous creation. It was something beautiful in itself but which was completely temporary, something which was magical and short-lived, like a ripple of wind on a still pond, or a shooting star in the night sky. It also seemed to be a perfect parable for ecological living, for living harmoniously on earth. By observing and understanding the way of the heavens and the sea, we had learned to channel their energy for our own ends, but without causing any harm or hindrance. Sailing across the sea, we left nothing behind us in our wake. Having been slightly disturbed, wind and water immediately return to their own course. If we could live lightly on the land like that, then life on earth would be more sustainable and fulfilling for all.

During the last three months, I had become intimate with the moods of the sea, its anger and stillness, its indifference and love. It had revealed itself to me as a symbol for many things: a symbol of the unconscious, for it has unknown beings living in its undelved deep; a symbol of death, for we will all be absorbed into the ocean of being like a river is absorbed into the sea; a symbol of the infinite, for it will for ever escape our reason and imagination. But above all, it is a symbol of eternity, constantly changing but always the same, forever coming and going, breathing in and breathing out, dancing and being still.

*

Despite my new found harmony and musings, the voyage that night across the Irish Sea was not without mishap. Running goose-winged in a fresh westerly wind, *Celtic Gold* rolled sickeningly from side to side. Passing through the overfalls off the Codling Bank at two o'clock in the morning, I suddenly felt ill. I had just gone up forward on deck to lash a powerful torchlight to the mast so that a passing cargo ship should see me in the dark night. I was clearly at my lowest ebb: I had sailed virtually non-stop in rough weather since the previous morning. I was very cold, despite six layers of clothes, and I was very tired having to keep alert during the Dead Man's Watch from midnight to four.

After going down below to work out my estimated position on the chart at about three o'clock, all of a sudden I felt an irresistible urge to be sick. I clambered out into the cockpit and emptied the paltry contents of my stomach into the pitch black sea – several times. I huddled up in the cockpit, concentrating on my steering and keeping a keen lookout as I was now in the middle of the main shipping lane in the Irish Sea. I felt very cold and tired and sick and realised that I would have to watch myself. I set an alarm clock to ring every half hour in order to stop me falling asleep and to make sure that I completed the log on the hour every hour. I carefully worked out my course each time I halved the difference between Ireland and Wales. As *Celtic Gold* continued to roll sickeningly, I steadied myself by looking at the star-studded belt of Orion as it moved through the dark night sky. After a few hours it began to grow less dark and my seasickness gradually abated.

Just before five o'clock in the morning, I began to see the lighthouse on Bardsey Island off the Lleyn Peninsula of North Wales. It flashed five times every fifteen seconds. It was beautiful and reassuring: I knew I was on course and all would be well. My only worry was whether I could reach Bardsey before the tide turned.

I was not prepared for the dawn. The word glorious is close but does not describe its splendour. The bright red sun began to show above the dark mountains of the Harlech Dome, made from some of the oldest rock in Europe. Then, without warning, bright rays of reddish gold suddenly shone through the great billowing clouds, sending shafts of light to the heavens which fell like liquid gold on to the surging sea. *Celtic Gold* was sailing into a truly Celtic golden dawn. Having been cold, sick and exhausted, I felt a huge surge of energy. With the rising of the sun came new life, new confidence and new hope. I had passed through the dark night of the soul. I had survived.

I sailed safely by Bardsey Island, the island of the saints, the most westerly point of Wales, just before eight o'clock. I steered across Tremadog Bay for Moel-y-Gest and the Moelwyns, the mountains which had cradled my life during the last fifteen years. I made a good breakfast of tea and toast and marmalade and ate it on the foredeck under the billowing genoa. The sun grew warmer by the minute and my body thawed in its caress.

My voyage had proved a wonderful healing experience. I felt strong and fit, especially my arms and shoulders which had carried so much over the summer and had pulled on anchors, warps, halyards and sheets. When I bent over to pick something up, I was surprised to find that I could easily touch my toes. The constant movement of the boat and my unconscious adjustments to its rhythm must have made my body supple and keen.

I felt transformed, washed clean like a pebble on a remote shore. Having left in such a rush and in such difficulty, I was returning home relaxed, centred and whole. I had learned that I could keep a steady hand and head in a crisis. I had found unknown reserves of strength deep within me. I had developed a new sense of self-reliance and independence and felt content with my own company in wild and remote places. I had feared the sea from the shore, but once underway, I felt little fear.

I looked down at my old grey deck-shoes, splitting at the seams, encrusted with salt, down at heel. They had served me well. I had worn them during my 18,000-mile circumnavigation of Africa three years before and now they had taken me over 1,200 miles around Ireland. I did not intend to hang them up for a long time; I had plenty more voyages to undertake. I knew I could go to the four corners of the world in *Celtic Gold*.

Celtic Gold had looked after me; she had been a wave which had lifted me up to a new life and understanding. I knew her from top to bottom, her darkest corners in the bilges to her brightest point at her mast head. I knew her moods, her caprices and her ecstasies, her wildness and her stillness. I had bumped my head so many times clambering through the low entrance to the heads and the forecabin that I moved through it instinctively. I had squeezed myself into the stern locker to repair her exhaust pipe and been for hours upside down grappling with the fuel tank. I had learned that there is a Lotus Flower in the piston of the diesel engine and barnacles living in the outlet from the heads.

Although determined not to be goal-orientated, I could not help feeling that I had made the greatest and happiest achievement of my life. I had shown that a novice skipper with a reasonable grasp of navigation in a reliable yacht could sail around Ireland and face the full range of weather and sea conditions. I now knew how to navigate, how to sail, how to maintain a diesel engine, how to look after myself, how to cope with constant change, how to see the world in a drop of water, how to hold eternity in an hour, how to ride the wind. In solitude, I did not feel alone and in the wilderness, I was at home. I had faith in the goodness of creation like a grain of mustard seed.

During the last three months, I had had more than my fair share of Celtic gold. I would never forget the bold headlands, the sheltered bays, the shimmering water, and the infinite space of sea and sky. I had experienced the African heat of the east coast of Ireland, the gentle breezes in the south west, the dark-grey days of wind and rain off the Aran islands, the gales of Donegal Bay, the near-storm of Portrush and the hail of Howth. I had encountered flat calms and angry twenty-five-foot waves, sparkling light and thick sea mist. I had gone from spring to autumn, from the tropics to the tundra and had enjoyed nearly every minute of it.

Every day I had been exposed to the wondrous forces of nature. The rising and the setting of the sun, the waxing and waning of the moon, the coming and going of the tide, and the movement of the stars in the firmament had marked the daily rhythm of my life. I would never forget the clarity of the water, the purity of the sand, the dance of the seaweed, the roll of the wave, the fulmar's flight, the seal's eye, the dolphin's leap. They were heart and soul for me.

I would never forget the hospitality and warmth of the people I had met on the way, who spontaneously shared their music and poetry, their wit and their wisdom with me.

Above all, I had discovered a seam of real Celtic gold deep within my being. A mysterious alchemical process had taken place without me knowing it. After such a leaden beginning, the dross in my soul had imperceptibly turned to gold, gradually shining forth through the nimbus clouds like a glorious Celtic dawn. I had discovered the gold of the Philosopher's Stone which the alchemists of old knew frees and protects you from sadness and trouble and leads you from darkness to light, from the desert to home.

High tide in Porthmadog was at eleven thirty. The *Nautical Almanac* recommended arriving one and a half hours before or after high tide in order to pass safely over the bar at the entrance of the estuary. It was a race against tide and time. I did not reach the fairway buoy until one thirty and it was touch and go whether I would make it. I just scraped over the bar with a few inches to spare. I glanced at the buoy by the bar where I had left my coat of gloom in the early morning mist over three months earlier. I hoped that it had been swept away into the Irish Sea and out into the Atlantic where it had been absorbed like a drop of wine in water.

The spring tide must have been running at five knots at Garreg Goch – the Red Rock – where the channels of the Glaslyn and Dwyfor rivers meet. My sturdy and well-maintained engine just made headway against it and saw me through. I looked up to see the Croesor valley nestling between the mountains of Cnicht and the Moelwyns and knew I was coming home. Everything looked so familiar, yet I felt completely different.

I arrived in Porthmadog at 1400 hours unannounced and without a welcome. I quietly took up a mooring in front of the Porthmadog and Trawsfynydd Sailing Club. I had left Howth in Ireland at 1000 hours the day before. Apart from one hour moored in Wicklow working out my tidal calculations, I had undertaken a thirty-hour sail on my own through the day and night in difficult conditions. After many exciting sails in the past three months – around Carnsore Point, the Old Head of Kinsale, Fastnet, through Dingle Sound, the Shannon, the Aran islands, Malin Head, and Rathlin Sound – it had been the most challenging. I had made it. I had left in mist and disarray, and had returned in order and in sunshine.

I called up the Holyhead coastguard and asked him to relay news of my safe arrival to Wicklow Radio. My log told me that I had sailed 1,217.6 nautical miles. My moorings secure, I put away my compass and folded up my chart for the last time. Then I fell into my bunk and slept.

Index

Achill 262–77
Achill Head 262, 263, 266
Achill Sound 262, 263
Adam Island 106, 110, 120
Adams, Gerry 358
Africa 21, 27, 31, 76, 78, 221
d'Aguila, Don Juan 89
Algiers 124
Anglo-Irish Treaty (1921) 40
Antrim, County 335, 367
Aonghus 234
Apprentice Boys' March 313
Aran Islands 166, 213, 214, 216, 217, 218, 223, 226, 227, 229, 231, 232, 233, 236, 241, 242, 243, 247, 249, 252, 273, 241, 242, 243, 247, 249, 254, 238, 302, 304, 409,410
Inisheer 224
Inishmaan 224
Inishmore 224, 225, 227, 298
Kilronan 217, 218, 225–6, 227, 230, 237, 244, 249
Straw Island 225
Aran Road 318, 331
Arctic Circle 60
Ardnakinne Point 139, 143
Ardglass 369
Ards Peninsula 345, 366, 367
Arklow 47, 49, 50, 53, 56, 78
Arklow Bank 33, 48
Arranmore Island (Aran Island) 319, 320, 322, 326, 364
North Sound of Aran 319, 320, 322
Atlantic Ocean 6, 11, 13, 17, 25, 55, 62, 66, 68, 77, 79, 98, 118, 125, 127, 130, 136, 138, 154, 157, 160, 162, 168, 195, 196, 202, 214, 215, 217–220, 225, 225, 228, 234, 239, 247, 263, 268, 273, 247, 298, 322, 324, 402, 410
Atlantis 236
Audley Castle 367
Australia 4
Avoca, River 50
Avondale House 40

Baginburn 63
Ballagh Rocks 320
Ballycotton 75, 77, 84
Ballydavid Head
Ballyhack 64
Baltimore 118–125, 127, 130, 134, 138
Bandon, River 86, 98, 103
Bann, River 333
Bantry Bay 139, 254, 287
Barbados 4
Barclay, John 116
Bardsey Island 406
Bardsey Sound (Ynys Enlli) 26, 29, 402
Barri 12
Barrow, River 65
Barry, Peter 88
Beach, Sylvia 387
Beara Peninsula 151
Bearhaven 138, 140, 149
Beaufort, Admiral Francis 58
Beaufort's Dyke 340
Beaufort Scale, the 58
Beginish Island 154
Behan, Brendan 99–100
Belfast 90, 204, 314, 344, 345–62, 374,

379
Belfast Lough 338, 344, 345, 346, 363, 366, 367
Belfast Telegraph, 347
Queen's University 348
Benbane Head 337
Ben Bulben 278
Benmullet 269
Bennett, Bill 365
Bere Island 139, 140, 148, 149, 150
Berkeley, George 315
Big Sovereign Islands 85
Black Rock Point 319
Blacksod Bay 257, 262, 263, 267, 268, 269
Blacksod Point 265
Blacksod Quay 266
Blasket Islands 166–8, 173, 175, 176–7, 183, 184, 187, 189, 191, 193–6, 200, 227, 238, 243, 238, 324
Bishop's Rock, 251, 253
Clifden 250
Great Blasket 30, 168, 175, 177, 183, 184, 189, 193, 194
Inishabro 176
Inishshark 251
Inishbofin 65, 93, 112, 176, 177, 250, 251, 256
Inishvickillane 173, 176, 178, 182, 184, 189, 191, 193, 384
Blind Man's Cove 153
Bloody Foreland 322, 323
Bloody Sunday 313
Boa Esperanza 79
Bognor Regis 5
Bolus Head 152
Bomore Rock 273
Bonnie Prince Charlie 307–8
Books, Battle of the 298–9
Borth-y-Gest 2, 8, 9, 15, 23, 24, 27
Boyne, Battle of the 90, 313
Boyne, River 389
Boyne Valley 388, 389, 393, 394
Bran 220–3
Brandon Bay 200
Brandon Head 200
Bray Head 154
Brazen Head 77
Breaches Shoal, the 401
St Brendan 94, 95, 96, 268, 298
Brightness, Island of (Inis Gluaire) 268
St Brigid 233
Bristol Channel 12, 67
British Isles , meteorology of 57–8
Brittany 114
Broadhaven Bay 267, 269, 271
Bruckless 283–286, 289, 290, 291, 301, 304–6, 316, 318, 331
Bryce, Annan 146
Bull, the 151
Bull, George 5
Bush, George 125
Butler, Larry 257, 262
Byrne, Seamus 45

Caher Island 93, 255
Cahirciveen 154
Calf, the 151
Canary Islands 201
Cape Clear Island 83, 118, 127, 130, 131, 135, 138, 186
Cape Clear Stone 133
Capel island 78
Cardiff 12
Cardigan Bay 29
Carew, Sir George 150
Caribbean 21, 25, 114, 332
Carlingford 372–3
Carlingford Lough 257, 260, 368, 369, 374
Carnlough 337, 339
Carnsore Point 53, 54, 55, 410
Carrickfergus 363
Carrigaholt 202, 215
Tower House of 206, 217
Carrigan Head 318
Carson, Lord 359
Cashla Bay 247
Castletown Bearhaven (Castletownbere) 138, 139, 140, 141, 142, 283
Castletownshend 120
Catholic Church 41, 295
Cavan, County 204
Celts 4, 7, 145, 234, 297, 325, 388, 396
Celtic Christianity 4, 29, 44, 45, 232
Celtic languages 230
Celtic Dawn 275
Celtic Gold 1, 15, 17, 19, 20, 23, 24, 28, 45, 46, 47, 48, 50, 51, 52, 59, 60, 87, 88, 92, 98, 102, 103, 104, 107, 110, 121, 129, 135, 136, 138, 141, 144, 146, 147, 155, 158, 174, 177, 193, 195, 196, 199, 209, 214, 218, 219, 224, 225, 235, 242, 244, 247, 257, 263, 265, 269, 271, 274, 242, 244, 247, 280, 281, 285, 286, 288, 293, 300, 301, 302–3, 308, 317, 323, 325, 327, 339, 341, 346, 366, 368, 369, 375, 400, 401, 404, 406, 408
Design 198
Specifications 49, 328
Celtic Mist 92, 93, 138, 173, 177, 178, 184, 193
Charles II, King 91
Cheek Point 64, 67
Cheng Ho, Admiral 31
Childers, Erskine 376
Chuang Tzu 15
Churchill, Sir Winston 140, 339
St Ciaran 212

Clare, County 91, 219, 234, 259
Clare Island 255, 256, 260, 262, 360
Clark, Wallace 312, 333, 363, 380, 381
Classiebawn Castle 276
Cleggan 254
Clew Bay 257, 260
Cloghar Head 195
Clonmacnois 205, 212
Cnicht 3, 24, 410
Cobh 78
Codling Racon Buoy 33
Coleraine 333
  University 330
Collins, Michael 40, 180
St Colman 254
St Colman's Cathedral 78
St Columba 232, 298–9, 312, 333, 363, 380, 398
Connacht, County 91, 206, 250
Connemara 213, 227, 246, 245, 246
  Twelve Pins of (Benna Beola) 250, 255
Connla's Well 205
Connolly, James 378
Copeland Island 366
Cook, Captain James 30
Cork 73, 75, 80, 111, 145, 158, 198, 240, 240
  Accent 105
  Blarney 82
  Castle 78, 79, 82
  deforestation in 145
  Harbour 77, 78, 79, 84, 85
  history of 82
  Royal Cork Yacht Club 78, 83
  St Ann's, Shandon 81–2
Cornwall 136
Corrib, River 249
Courtmacsherry 94, 103
Cow, the 151
Criccieth 27
Croaghmartin 175
Croagh Patrick 255
Croesnor valley 410
Cromwell, Oliver 62, 91, 252–3
Crooke 62
Crookhaven 136, 137
Crosshaven 78, 79, 83
Cuildrevne 298, 299
Culgaih Mountain 204
Cullen, Charlie 5
Cumail, Fionn Mac 100

Dalkey Island 387, 401
Danes 4
Danger Rock 26, 410
Dar-es-Salaam 164
Dark Ages 4
Darty Mountains 278
Darwin, Charles 41
Daunt Rock 85
Davillaun 255
Davis, Thomas 124
Dawros Head 319
Deakin, Lynn 129
Decca navigation system 2, 16, 28
Derry 239, 275, 294, 299, 308, 310–12, 313, 316, 317, 333
  County Derry 388
Devil's Ridge 29
Diarmuid, King 299, 398
'Dicker' (see Richard Feesey)
Dingle 123, 155, 156, 160–74, 182, 207, 213, 252, 290, 329, 384, 410
  Bay 30, 155
  Harbour 155, 158, 160
  Peninsula 155, 174, 185, 317
  Races 184
Dixon, James 324
Dogger Bank 237
Donaghy, Kevin 293, 294, 296
Donaghy, Wendy 293, 294, 296, 297
Donegal, County 286, 287, 289, 290, 293, 294, 300, 301, 309, 316, 320, 325
  Bay 269, 271, 276, 282, 284, 295, 296, 305, 306, 318, 324, 332, 409
  Fanny's Bay 325, 326
  Mulroy Bay 322, 325, 327, 331
  Sheephaven Bay 325
Donaghadee Sound 366
Donnelloy, Ignatius 236
Downpatrick 367
Dowth 392
Drake, Sir Francis 85
  Drake's Pool 85
Drogheda 253
Dromberg Stone Circle 107–10
Druim Ceat, Convention of 299
Drumcliff 278, 298
Drumgaroff 41
Dublin 4, 40, 204, 231, 274, 278, 293, 369, 375, 377–89, 401
  Berkeley library 380
  Dublin Bay 35, 376, 386, 387, 401
  Easter Rising, the 231, 376, 378, 380, 385
  National Gallery 383
  National Museum 383, 388, 394, 396
  Radio 374
  Temple Bar 384
  Trinity College 295, 299, 379, 382, 385
Dun Aonghasa 233, 234, 236, 388
Dun Loaghaire 377, 387
  National Yacht Club 386
Dun na Long ('Fort of the Ships') 127
Dunboy Castle 150
Dunboy Bay 149
Dunboy House 149, 150
Duncannon Fort 64, 71

Dundrum House 370
Dungarven 75, 125
Dunkerque 6
Dunkineely 284
Dunluce Castle 335, 337
Dunmore East 53, 62, 63, 72, 73, 75, 78
Dunquin 175
Dwyer, Michael 41
Dwyryd, River 26, 27

Eagle Mount 369
Easke, River 287
Eagle, Mount 194
Eastwood, David 15
EC (European Community), 208, 230
Elizabeth I, Queen 232, 311, 377, 379
St Enda 232
English Channel 6, 341
Enniskillen 204, 294
EPIRB (Emergency Position Indicating
Radio Beacon) 1, 17, 365
Erris Head 269
Errol, Lough 133
Eve Island 106, 110, 120

Fair Head 338, 339
Famine, Great, the 102, 210, 254, 256,
305
Fanad Head 327
Faroe Islands 163, 363
Fastnet, the 135, 136, 158, 410
Fastnet Race 113, 114
Feesey, Richard ('Dicker') 245, 249–252,
255, 263, 265–9, 272, 274
Fenit 197, 200, 202
Fianna Fail 179, 180
Le Figaro Yacht Race 89
St Finian 299, 398
Finn, Lough 309
Fintown 309
Firbolg, the 205
First World War 92, 340
Flaherty, Robert 242
Flower, Robert 185
Fomori, the 205
Foyle, Lough 171, 311
Francis, Dermot 312
'Fungi' 157, 173, 174, 207

Gabriel, Mount 135
Gaelic culture 211–2
Gaelic League, the 231
Gaeltacht 132, 230, 300
Gaia, theory of 65
Galan Stones 133
Gallarus Oratory 169
Galloway, Mull of 366
Galway 213, 218, 227, 234, 244–249, 388
Bay 213, 214, 216, 226, 226
Hookers 214, 245, 246

da Gama, Vasco 25
Gane, Jeremy 316–17
Gane, Jonathan 316
Garavogue, River 279
Garnish Island 144, 146
Garreg Goch
Garron Point 339
Garth-y-Foel 3, 4, 290, 291
Gascanane Rock 131
Geographical Club 30
St George's Channel 52, 53, 54, 369
Giant's Causeway 335, 336, 337
Giza 196
Gladstone, William Ewart 39
Glandore 103–7, 110, 112, 113, 114–5,
118, 121, 122, 224
Glass, Denis 349
Glaslyn, River 26, 27
Glencolumbkille 297, 298
Glendalough 37, 39
Glengariff 143–4, 147, 148, 254
Woods 145
Glen Malin 297
GPS (Global Positioning System)
17, 28
Goldsmith, Oliver 382
Gore-Booth family 256, 279
Lissadell House 278
Granny Island 138
Gray, Thomas 403
Great Circle Route 32
Green Island 78, 291, 363
Greenland 31
Greenwich, Royal Observatory 31
Gregory Sound 224
Le Gros, Raymond 63, 67
Gulf Stream 55, 244
Gun Rock 251
Gwynedd Marine Boatyard 14
Gwynne-Jones, Emily 317

Hancock, Graham 393
Hanson, H. J. 280
Harland & Wolff Shipyards 346, 356,
362
Harlech 27
Harrison, John 31
Hart, John 12
Hatchett, John 68
Hatchett, Pat 68
Haubowline Rock 370
Haughey, Charles 178–85, 188–92, 384
Haughey, Conor 138, 177, 179, 181,
183, 186, 188
Haughey, Emer 179
Haughey, Maureen 179, 184
Heaney, Seamus 361, 382–3
Heather, William 30
Hebrides, the 363
Hell's Mouth (Porth Neigel) 28

Hill, Derek 324
Hill, Rear Admiral 30
Holyhead 28, 33, 34, 278, 375, 377, 386, 410
Hook 62
Hook Head 62, 63, 72
Howth 375–7, 383, 384, 386, 400, 401, 402, 409
  Howth Head 387
Hume, John 358
Hutchinson, Eddie 161
Hyne, Lough 121

Imray 18
Indian Ocean 6, 22, 32, 134, 156
Indian Royal Navy 32
Inishgloria Island 299
Inishkea, North and South Islands 267, 268
Inishmurray Island 273, 299
Inishtookert Island 196
Inishtrahull Sound 328
Inver Hamlet Bay 269
Iona 298–9, 333
Ireland 1, 3, 11, 13, 21, 24, 25, 30, 39, 52, 53, 54, 76, 84, 121, 158, 199
  Character of the Irish 117
  Conversion to Christianity 232
  Economy 117
  Flora and Fauna 55, 63, 154, 160, 200
  History 38, 63, 69, 335
  Language 300, 308
  Legends 279, 324–5, 336, 392–5
  Music 70
Ireland's Eye 375
Irish Cruising Club, the 24, 54, 67, 153, 213, 333
Irish Free State 294
Irish Republican Army, the (IRA) 314, 353, 354, 370, 373
Irish Sea 1, 3, 23, 26, 28, 29, 32, 49, 55, 56, 59, 269, 337, 343, 344, 365, 69, 370 401, 406

James I, King 311
James II, King 90, 313
James, Naomi 94, 97–8
John, King 373, 384
Joyce, James 382, 387
  Ulysses 387

Kay, Lough 155
Keating, Sean 364
Kells, Book of 299, 379–80
Kennedy, Edward 184
Kerry, County 158, 198, 234
Kerry Head 202, 203
Kerry, Ring of 187
St Kevin 42
  Kevin's Cell 42
St Kieran 130, 132
Kilcar 293, 295, 308
Kilcredaun Head 206
Kilcredaun Point 207, 218
Kildare, Earl of 380
Killala Bay 273
Killeany Bay 225
Killybegs 282, 286, 289, 290, 293, 298, 309
Kilmakedar Church 161
Kilrush 208, 209, 210, 212, 213, 215, 216
Kilstiffin Bank 218
King, Commander 'Bill' 225
Kinsale 86, 87, 88–94, 98–101, 102, 103, 106, 302
  Old Head of 85, 103, 105, 410
  St Multose Church 91
Kintyre, Mull of 339
Kinvarra 214, 226
Knockadoon Head 77
Knockmore 263
Knowth 392
Knox, Ronald 315
Kowloon Bridge 120

Lagan, River 362
Lambay Island 375
Land of the Young 191
Lao Tzu 15
Laoghaire, King 396–8
Larne 342
  Larne, Lough 340
Laughnane, Michael 92, 386
Lea, David 15, 226
Lee, River 80
Lemas, Sean 179
Lemon Rock 154
Lenadoon Point 273
Letterkenny 22, 308, 309, 310
Liffey, River 384, 385
Limerick 4, 209, 212, 213
Lindisfarne 254
Little Island 67
Lleyn Peninsula 26, 27, 29, 402, 404
Lockley, R. M. 194
Lomax family 278, 282
Lomax, Rodney 293
London Boat Show 13
Londonderry (*see* Derry)
Londonderry, Marquess of 339
Loop Head 203, 213, 216, 218
Loughnane, Michael 92, 99
Loughros More Bay 309
Lurgan 388
Lusitania 92

Mac Art, Cormac 393
Mac Cool, Finn 336
McCloskey, John 302–3

Mac Cullagh, Richard 312, 363
MacDyer, Father 300
MacMurrough, Dermot 63
Mac Swyne Bay 283
Mafia Island 6
Maghera 333
Magna Carta 373
Maldives 32, 156, 220, 237
Malin Head 327, 331, 339, 410
Malin More 296
Malthus, Thomas 211, 256
Man, Isle of 336, 366
Manannan 205, 223
Margharee Islands 200
Marshall, Dylan 2, 7, 20, 270, 280, 282, 286–8, 291, 292, 295, 297, 301
Marshall, Emily 2, 7, 21, 264, 270, 280, 282, 284, 286, 287, 288, 291, 292, 295, 296, 297, 300, 301, 320, 324
Marshall, Michael 21
Marshall, Peter
  thoughts on completing circumnavigation of Ireland 404, 407–8
  affection for *Celtic Gold* 408
Martinique 295
Maryport 13, 14
St Mary's Port 260
du Maurier, Daphne 150
Mayo, County 212
Mediterranean 60, 69
Meenavean 296
Merchant Navy, the 123
St Michael 151
St Michael's Mount 151
Milford Haven 68
Millard, Sally 22
Miller, Betty and Stan 68, 121–123, 171, 172, 341
Milmurray 232
Min-y-Mor 8
Mine Head 77
Minihane, Con 130
Miskish Mountains 143
Mitterand, Francois 188
Mizen Head 92, 133, 136, 138
Mizen Peak 138
Moel-y-Gest 3, 407
Moher, cliffs of 214, 224, 29
Molewyn Mountains 407, 410
Monmouth, Geoffrey of 393
Mont-St-Michel 151
More, Christy 348
Moulden, John 330
Mountbatten, Lord 276
Mountjoy, Lord 90
Mourne, Mountains of 366, 369, 370
Moylecorragh Peak 320
Mozambique 6
Mullaghmore 271, 274, 275, 276, 278, 280, 283, 284, 293, 294
  harbour 273
Mullaghmore Head 273
Mullen, Pat 242
Mullet 268
Munster 257
Mustard Seed 67, 68, 99, 106, 118, 121–123, 158, 171, 172, 341

Na Seacht Teampaill 232
Nautical Almanac, the 53
Neagh, Lough 336
Nelson, Admiral Lord 385
Nephin Beg mountains 263
Newfoundland 68, 161
Newgrange 389–94, 399
  Astrological significance 392
  comparison with other ancient sites 393
New Ross 65
Nicki 19, 20, 26, 48, 49, 50, 51, 60, 66, 72, 87
Normans 4, 206, 377, 378
North Sea 6, 341
Northern Ireland (*see* Ulster)

O'Brien, Conor Cruise 130, 209
O'Brien, Edna 382–3
O'Connell, Daniel 209, 378, 383, 385, 398, 399
O'Connell, Maurice 209
O'Crohan, Tomas 167, 168, 186
O'Donnell, Hugh 89, 90, 150
O'Driscoll clan 124
O'Driscoll, Sir Fineen 124
O'Flaherty, Liam 243
Okeanos 218
O'Malley, Grace 256, 257, 377
O'More, Rory 252, 253
O'Neill, Sir Felim 252
O'Neill, Hugh 89, 90, 150
Orange Order, the 90, 313, 314, 330
Orkney Islands 363
Ormonde, Earl of 380
O'Shea, Kitty 39, 345
O'Sullivan, Maggie 147
O'Sullivan, Maurice 166, 167, 178
O'Toole, Bernie 230
Owenboy, River 78, 80, 84
Owentocker, River 309
Oyster Haven 85

P&O Shipping Company 6
Paisley, Ian 91, 180, 357
Palmerston, Lord 276
Panama Canal 68
Parnell, Charles Stewart 39, 385
St Patrick 151, 185, 192, 255, 367, 393, 396–7, 399
St Patrick's Cathedral 380
St Patrick's Causeway (Sarn Padrig) 28

St Patrick's Rocks 369
Pearse, Padraic 231, 378, 380
Peto, Harold 146
Piper Sound 149
Plas Menai (National Watersport Centre) 11
Pilcher, John 16
Polo, Marco 95
Pope, Alexander 404
Porloch Weir 12
Portaferry 367
Port Island 252
Porthmadog 1, 8, 14, 15, 25, 26, 27, 56, 159, 368, 402, 409, 410
Porthmeirion 6, 30
Portpatrick 21, 22, 331, 340, 341–4
Portrush 326, 327, 328, 329–35, 337, 370, 409
Promise, Island of 162
Ptolemy 54
Puffin Island 154
Pugin, Edward 79
Puxley Castle 150
Pwllheli 14

Queenstown (Cobh) 78, 79
Quiberon Bay, Battle of 30

Rabbit Island 106
Raleigh, Sir Walter 257
Ram Head 77
Rathdrum 40
Rathlin O'Birne Island 298, 318, 332, 338
Rathlin Sound 337, 344, 410
Red Bay 339
Reenadolaun Point 154
Rinrawros Point 319
Rio Mar 344
Roche's Point 77, 78
Rock Island 136
Romaine 287
Roonagh Point 260
Rossan Point 297, 298
Rossaveel 246
Rosslare 53
Round Ireland Race 35
Roundstone 45
Royal Geographical Society 30, 95
Royal Navy 30, 56
Royal Ulster Constabulary 239, 313, 315, 353
Royal Western Yacht Club 209
Royal Yachting Association 11, 13, 27
Rupert, Prince 91
Russell, George William (A. E.) 147, 383

Salt Hill Quay 276
Saltee Islands 53, 55
Sands, Bobby 354
Sayers, Peig 166, 167, 177
Scattery Island 208, 209
Sea Mate 341
Second World War 182, 183, 191, 194
Sellafield 370
Servants of Love, the 44, 45, 47
Settlement, Act of 91
Seven Heads 104, 105
Severin, Tim 93–8, 168
Seymour, John 64
Shannon 216, 217
Shannon Radio 217
Shannon, River 201, 203, 204, 205, 206, 208, 209, 212, 213, 215, 218, 226, 327, 410
derivation of name 204–5
Shaw, George Bernard 144, 147
St Joan 146
Sherkin Island 118, 125, 130, 131
Shetland Islands 363
Shipping Forecast, the 59
Sidney, Sir Philip 258
Silver Stand 126
Sirius 78
Skellig Islands 151, 152, 154, 158
Great Skellig 151, 299; Little Skellig 153; Skellig Michael 151, 152, 153, 154, 187
Skerries, the 337, 375
Skerries Road 328
Skibbereen 128–9
Slaney, River 52, 367
Slieve Donard 369
Slieve League cliffs 268, 296, 297, 306, 317, 318
Sligo 271, 274, 278
Smerwick harbour 169, 188, 198
Smith, Nigel 172
Snowdonia 3, 28
Solent, the 30
South Georgia 60
Sovereign Islands 85
Spanish Armada 273, 337
Spanish Island 131
Staffa Island 337
Stags, the 120, 121
Stranraer 342
Strangford 367
Strangford Lough 366, 367, 368, 370, 376
Streedagh 273, 274
Suir, River 53, 62, 63
Swift, Jonathan 115
Swilly, Lough 310, 327
Swilly, River 309
Sybil Point 196
Synge, John 144, 195, 231

Tall Ships Race 79
Tan-y-Bryn 8

Taoism 15, 60
Tara, Hill of 388, 394–5, 396–9
Teelin 306, 308, 316–17, 318, 331
Thackeray, William Makepeace 144, 336
Thatcher, Margaret 181, 182, 349
Thompson, William 113
Three Castle Head 138
Tipperary 137
Titanic 78
Toe Head 120
Tone, Theobold Wolfe 143, 287, 348
Torneady Point 319
Tory Island 300, 324,
Tory Sound 325
Tralee Bay 200, 202
Tremadog Bay 6, 27, 407
Trevelyan, Charles 211
Troubles, the 239, 310, 312, 356
St Tudwal's Island 28
Tuskar Rock 53,54
Twyn Cilan Point 28

Ulster 180, 239, 257, 302, 308, 310–12, 329, 330, 337, 342, 346, 350, 355–6, 360–1, 365, 370
Canal 204
Union Hall 118
United Irishmen, the 348

Valentia Island 150, 154, 182; radio station 154
van Dyke, Henry 294
de Valera, Eamon 40, 180
Vancouver 68
Vaudeleur family 210
Vaughan Williams, Ralph 243
Ventry Harbour 174
Ventry Bay 175, 176
Verne, Jules 86
Victoria, Queen 144
Vikings 42, 52, 63, 70, 107, 208, 335, 377, 378

Wales 52, 53, 111, 170, 292
Walker, Governor George 314
Washerwoman Rock 152
Waterford 52, 52, 63, 64, 66, 67, 68, 69, 70, 71, 78, 124, 204
Wave of Life 8
Westport 260
Wexford 53
Whiddy Island 144
Wicklow 25, 28, 33, 35, 36, 45, 47, 50, 123, 158, 369, 400, 401; Mountains 41, 42; Radio 34, 48, 402, 410; Yacht Club 25
Wicklow Head 33, 38, 48
Wigtownshire 343
Wild Goose 334
Wilde, Oscar 359, 383
Williams-Ellis, Clough 30
William of Orange (King William lll) 90, 313
Wright, Frank Lloyd 169

Yeats, Jack 274
Yeats, W. B. 144, 278, 279, 298, 383
Youghal 75

Zanzibar 134
Zenobia 71
Zobel, Jenny 20, 280–2, 285, 286, 287, 288, 295, 300, 301